The Bohemian

and

The Abolitionist

by
Ann Prehn

Cover design by Ann Prehn
using 1860s public domain paintings.

ACKNOWLEDGEMENTS

To all my friends at Harbin Hot Springs
who have taught me so much over our years together;
To friends and fellow writers – Rebecca Rees,
Carol Thompson, Edward Miller, and Bonnie Olsen –
for reading this book early and offering edits and advice;
To my daughter, Lacy Lackey, my cousins, and my parents
the Dr.'s Prehn, who read it early and liked it;
To all of you who have read it, the few who have raved –
especially Jim Conlin, Diane Tegtmeier and Quentin Wood –
you gave me faith in the book when I really needed it;
To Ray Gaspard for taking me to see Edwin Booth's room;
To Walt Crowley, deceased, for your strange visitation;
To the geniuses behind Lehigh.edu, Wikipedia, Etymology
Online, and those who share old books and articles on the web;
To the many scholars and researchers before me
who made my job easier,

Thank you!

DISCLAIMER
This is a novel. Historical characters
have been necessarily, if unintentionally,
fictionalized and should not be taken
to accurately depict any person living or dead.

CONTENTS

Prologue

In the spring of 1859, at a private home in the abolitionist stronghold of Concord, Massachusetts, a clandestine meeting was taking place. Some twenty men and women were there, waiting with bated breath for the guest of honor. Most were idealists of white Puritan stock who were willing to put up their money to bring a swift end to slavery. Others were Negroes, active on the Underground Railroad, who had come to offer their help to a man who was legendary and had a price on his head. When John 'Osawatomie' Brown strode into the parlor, newly disguised in a flowing white beard that embodied him as a Biblical Prophet, there were sighs and even tears.

Only weeks earlier, he had completed a daring rescue, liberating eleven slaves in a midnight raid across the Kansas border into Missouri. It had taken him and his eighteen men eighty-two days, with relentless pursuit and a battle won against overwhelming odds, to deliver the slaves safe to Canada. Along the way, he'd mocked his pursuers in the press. Already infamous for the Osawatomie Massacre that led to "Bleeding Kansas," John Brown garnered top attention from both the authorities and the public. At the mission's completion, he'd auctioned off his horses at celebrity prices.

Now John Brown wanted to grow his small band and strike into the South, liberating the slaves plantation by plantation and state by state. It was a thrilling idea, and no one who heard him doubted that he could do it. All he needed was money.

One by one, they opened their purses to him, pledging a few dollars and a few hundreds of dollars. He had ongoing patrons who pledged continuing support of a few thousands, to hole up in the mountains with a growing army of escaped slaves. But to start the ball rolling, he still needed thousands more in immediate funds.

John Brown did not like begging for money, so he stated his additional need and stood silently, gazing with dignified grace from face to face, waiting for someone to speak. The room was quiet as his audience each calculated how much more to give, and how much risk to take on in a criminal conspiracy. For a moment, it seemed the entire venture would be abandoned or delayed.

Then, from the back of the room, a young white woman spoke. "I can get you $5,000," she said with some uncertainty. The room stirred, breathing easier. Someone was stepping forward, someone they'd known since her childhood – Lily Ann O'Leary Ferguson would see that Osawatomie Brown had enough. He bestowed a radiant smile on her like a personal blessing from God Himself.

Her sleeve was tugged by a young colored lady beside her. "But Lillian," Ruby whispered, "how are you going to get so much money?" Indeed, Lillian's allowance was committed well ahead to her two passions – Ruby's school on the Underground Railroad and Laura Keene's theater. But she had another passion to which her husband trusted her with his own money – the buying and selling of American art. While her husband was in Europe, she had grown his vast collection in value. She was sure he wouldn't notice if she sold some of the more expensive pieces and replaced them with other, cheaper works.

She looked at Ruby with urgent eyes and squeezed her hand. "I can do this," she whispered back.

"And when could I expect these funds, my dear?" John Brown's voice sounded intimate despite the distance across the room.

"Summer's end," she said softly. He inclined an ear towards her as the whole room strained to hear. Lillian cleared her throat and spoke up, "Summer's end." Once again, he beamed a holy smile of beatification that made her sure, though she wasn't particularly religious, that the angels would support her endeavor.

Then John Brown spoke of Gideon's war with the Midianites, how they hid their lamps in pitchers and snuck up by night on the Midian camp. As he recited the Bible by heart, it seemed to his listeners that he was describing the adventure ahead:

"When I blow with a trumpet, I and all that are with me, then blow ye the trumpets also on every side of all the camp, and say, The sword of the Lord, and of Gideon.

So Gideon, and the hundred men that were with him, came unto the outside of the camp in the beginning of the middle watch; and they had but newly set the watch: and they blew the trumpets, and brake the pitchers that were in their hands.

And held the lamps in their left hands, and the trumpets in their right hands to blow withal: and they cried, The sword of the Lord, and of Gideon.

And they stood every man in his place round about the camp; and all the host of Midian ran, and cried, and fled."

BOOK 1

The Last Limner

A man should live
In a garret aloof,
And have few friends,
And go poorly clad,
With an old hat stopping
The chink in the roof
To keep the Goddess
Constant and glad.

~ Tom Aldrich
Excerpted from "The Garret"

Chapter 1

Spring, 1859

The horn of the *S.S. City of Manchester* blasted with more exuberance than 4th of July fireworks. Along the ship's rails, immigrants pushed and shoved, vying for a look at their new homeland. In the center of the deck away from the mayhem, a young American artist sat sketching a child. The artist had dark tresses fluttering into his face, and a short beard which an unfortunate lurch of the ship during the act of cutting had rendered uneven. His brown eyes regarded his subject and, seeing she could no longer contain herself, Wendell Harte Parry rolled up the sketch. "It appears we've arrived."

The child gripped her prize as she leapt from her seat and shouted in a thick Irish brogue, "Hoorah! We're here! We're here in America!" then bobbed a curtsy and dashed across the deck. He stood to see her go, stood to see her little hand slip safely into her mother's, to see her father take charge of the sketch. With final waves goodbye, the newcomers boarded barges and headed for the round red edifice looming ahead – Castle Garden, New York's immigrant terminal. Their excitement infected him and he hugged his frock coat as he silently wished them well.

"America – 'tis a good time to be coming home," he told himself. He had spent three years in the art capitals of Europe, and now collectors were beginning to buy American art. Perhaps in America, he could sell his art without bowing and scraping to royalty and aristocrats. Besides, Europe was imminently at war.

With the steamship again underway, Wendell sketched the harbor. Around the point, poking against scattered clouds, the skylines of Brooklyn and Manhattan rose on either side of the East River, with taller buildings than he remembered. Salt mist and seagulls obscured a blue sky smudged by the smoke of steamers, and draped with the dazzling white sails of schooners and clipper ships. *'Cobalt violet, lapis, smalt, red ochre,'* he scribbled in the margin.

He managed several rough sketches before the tugs pulled alongside and guided the enormous screwship into Manhattan's South Harbor. On the wharf below, swarthy men – tattooed Islanders, Africans, and men baked brown by the sun – hawked their wares, labored as dockers, or skulked about in rags. Among them, pale gentlemen in black, some beside a cloaked lady, warily sought conveyance. *'Egyptian brown, umber, ivory black'* Wendell noted before stowing his sketches and scanning the dock for familiar faces.

He heard a "Harte, old chap!" and connected a waving hand to Fitzhugh Ludlow, jumping up and down beside a grinning Sam Stockard. Wendell's heart swelled and he made his way down the gangplank to meet his two old college mates with hugs and handshakes.

"Your arrival has been noted in all the papers," Fitzhugh informed him. "Not just the *Crayon* and the *Saturday Press*, mind you, but the *New York Times* and even the *Tribune*!"

"I assume you're writing for those papers," responded Wendell drolly, noting the tweedy attire and red whiskers appropriate to Fitzhugh's new literary status.

Fitzhugh laughed, "Not for all of them! I simply noted in *Vanity Fair* how atwitter the ladies are that the famous artist, Wendell Harte Parry, will be living amongst us. They're lining up to pose for you!"

"Fitzhugh, no!" Fitzhugh's confirming grin earned him a playful shove.

As they waited for Wendell's trunk, Sam, too, teased him, "I see you had a rough voyage, Parry. Ha, ha. You have cut your beard uneven." Sam Stockard was himself clean-shaven, tall and blond, with an honest look that would serve him well should he succeed in becoming a lawyer.

The friends soon commandeered a cab and after stopping at the moneychangers, were on their way up Broadway, moving with the flow of traffic at the end of the day in the financial district. Carriages, omni-buses, horse-cars, buggies, and pedestrians coursed uptown with unruly cacophony, while coal smoke and horse dung assailed their nostrils. Showy signs advertised expensive European goods behind vegetable stalls and vending carts which lined the crowded sidewalks.

Along the way, the friends congratulated one another for their successes. "Your painting, *Sands of Morocco*, is a triumph!" said Fitzhugh. "A pity you weren't here for the showing."

"'Tis a pity the money is spent," the artist opined. "Financial success seems more elusive even than fame."

As Fitzhugh nodded his agreement, Sam bragged of Fitzhugh's book, *The Hasheesh Eater*. "The recounting of Fitzhugh's pharmaceutical adventures has raised a fair bit of interest."

"And more than one eyebrow!" Wendell laughed, "Even in Europe I could not escape it!" He clapped Fitzhugh on the back. "Who knew your disreputable college experiments would reward you so handsomely!"

"I, too, have spent most of the money," rued Fitzhugh. "My situation is so dire, my new bride and I have moved into a socialist household. Not unlike the one you will be living in, Parry."

Abruptly, the horses reared and the carriage braked. The driver raised his whip and lashed out at the cause of their mishap, a thin girl in rags. She bore a limp babe in her arms and stubbornly held out her hand, not letting them pass.

"Hold!" yelled Sam to the driver who was about to strike at her again. "She's a child!"

The girl, who looked not more than fourteen, grabbed the carriage window and beseeched the passengers with an Irish lilt, "Pray, sirs, a penny for the babe?" They found a coin to bribe her, which brought no smile but did grant them passage. Wendell thought of the little Irish girl on the ship and wondered with a pang what would become of her – America seemed suddenly not so welcoming. As their carriage continued, he watched the young mother almost get hit again.

The incident was soon forgotten in the hubbub of the city and the excitement of their reunion. Fitzhugh described, rather floridly, his Florida honeymoon, while Sam had also married and bought a townhouse near New York University where he studied law.

"Now we must find a wife for Wendell!" cried Fitzhugh.

"And we shall," said Sam. "There'll be a soirée at my house tomorrow night and many eligible young ladies are invited."

"Come come, Sammy-boy," Fitzhugh teased, "once again you mis-lead the court. The 'eligible young ladies' who will be at your soirée are all confirmed bachelors. Ha ha. They would rather be artists and writers than housewives."

"I'd hoped," ventured Wendell, who could not afford a wife, "to continue the free-spirited bohemian ways I enjoyed in Paris."

Sam winked. "Ah, but you haven't met Margaret, my sister-in-law – she comes with a dowry!" At this, they all laughed merrily, and broke into the song Fitzhugh had written for their dear Alma Mater:

> *"Then here's to thee,*
> *The brave and free,*
> *Old Union smiling o'er us;*
> *And for many a day,*
> *As thy walls grow gray,*
> *May they ring with*
> *Thy children's chorus."*

They were still singing when the carriage reached the quiet outskirts of the city and turned off Broadway onto 10th Street in Greenwich Village. The driver reined the horses in front of a handsome building made of brick and sandstone with small wrought iron balconies. Opened the previous year, the Tenth Street Studio Building, with its twenty-three studios and central exhibition space, was already the envy of artists worldwide. Wendell's artist friends had inveigled a space for him ahead of the waiting list.

Sam and Fitzhugh made their goodbyes and Wendell took up one end of the steamer trunk while the concierge took the other. By the time they reached the third floor landing, a large number of artists were in tow, eager to greet the newcomer. Being assured that there would be an opportunity at supper to meet everyone, Wendell begged to rest and found himself alone in his new home.

After the cramped ship, the sudden spaciousness of his atelier was intoxicating. He looked around to see a small bed made up in one corner, presumably left by the previous tenant, along with other handy furnishings including a paint mixing bench and cabinets. Whiffs of linseed oil still clung tenaciously, though a thin coat of dust said the room had been unoccupied for some weeks. Beyond the arched windows were the grassy backyards of tenements where women gathered their wash from clotheslines – a peaceful picture in a haven of spacious quiet.

Wendell ran his hand along the smooth woodwork that surrounded the window casements and wainscoting, and imagined which pictures he would hang on the many nails which protruded from higher on the walls. Above a large wardrobe, he saw a small balcony where visitors might view the artist at work. High overhead, light streamed in through a generous skylight with a luster perfectly suited to painting. Even in the approaching dusk, this was a brighter workspace than he had ever had.

Wendell locked the door. He opened his carpetbag and withdrew a strange oval mirror formed of layered convex lenses. The designs on its gold-leaf frame placed it from the Orient, but revealed nothing further. This magic mirror was his muse, and as the sun set into deepening gloom, he propped it on the bed and lit a candle. The secret ritual he then performed, once sinister and superstitious, was now as necessary to his art as wielding brush and paint.

Late next morning, Wendell Harte Parry woke feeling as though the ship still pitched and yawed beneath him. The screech-scrunch of shovels scraping horse dung from nearby 6th Avenue gave him a visceral lurch. He groaned and tried to sit up. Supper in Thomas's atelier had been quite merry, with much drink and excellent food provided by Mrs. Winter, whose breakfast in the basement mess-hall he had surely missed. Today his canvases would arrive, and tonight was the soirée at Sam's. It was all too much; he lay back and pulled the cover over his head.

There was a knock. Before Wendell could reply, Thomas Buchanan Read popped in followed by Cat, the resident tabby. He carried coffee and a covered plate which he placed on the small table, then sat at the edge of Wendell's bed, looking down on him with humored sympathy. "'Tis the Indian in you," he teased, "you can't contain your drink."

Wendell's eyes tried to focus on the friend he had lived with in Florence, wondering at how the thirty-seven year-old's soft features could belie the harsh loss of his wife and children to cholera. It was a sorrow which Thomas tried to assuage with affable sociability as he stroked his goatee and tipped his beret to one side. "Hmmm," Thomas said, "a hair of the dog that bit you might be in order."

"Or that coffee," said Wendell, beginning to feel better. "I thank you, Thomas."

"Oh, that was Mrs. Winter. She wondered where you were this morning." Thomas handed him the mug. "Mrs. Winter says you paid $1.30 for a week of breakfasts, and she's intent on keeping her part. I just came to tell you that a reporter from the *Crayon* is brown hair and a white blouse tucked into a brown hooped skirt. As she unlocked the door to an atelier, she smiled. "That's a lovely *djellaba,*" she said boldly. "Men ought to dress that way all the time."

Wendell stood with his mouth open, caught quite off guard.

"Forgive me," she continued. "You must be the new tenant. I'm Anna Mary Freeman."

He made a small bow. "Pleased to meet you, Miss Freeman. I'm Wendell Parry." Then, betraying his incredulity at the presence of a lady, "Do you live here?"

"Sometimes I do, but right now it's just my studio space. I paint miniatures and write poetry."

They were attracted to the commotion of yet another lady running unseemly down the hall. "Anna Mary," she called, "I'm sorry to be late!"

She was breathless when she reached them, and Anna Mary said, "No matter. I've only just arrived."

The newcomer was of average height, long of neck and round of bottom, with a high sweet bust and soft shoulders – the perfect proportions, Wendell noted, for nude portraiture. She was dressed in plain green linen, the skirt reefed with ribbons, revealing trim ankles in short black boots. In the bohemian mode, she wore no hoops or petticoats. An errant strand of dark hair fell from a precarious pile into large verdant eyes above a full mouth and well-shaped chin. Wendell was fascinated. She looked at him, and gave him a smile that made him feel, foolishly, that he was falling. He took a step back, trying to steady himself.

"Ah yes," said Anna Mary. "Miss Lillian Flax, may I introduce Mr. Wendell Parry."

On announcement of his name, Miss Flax's smile was replaced by a most charmed and astonished look. She gasped, "Wendell *Harte* Parry?" She seemed to struggle with her thoughts, then blurted, "Many a dream I've had of meeting you on the sands of

Morocco. And here you are, dressed the part!"

"You know my work?" He was staring back at her, into viridian eyes that seemed startlingly familiar. There was something of destiny in them that took his breath.

"Aye," she said reverently, "your painting has a thrill of freedom in it."

"Is freedom important to you, Miss Flax?"

"Freedom is everything."

Anna Mary looked annoyed and pulled her friend into her atelier. "Good day to you, Mr. Parry," she said, and closed the door.

Chapter 2

"Many a dream I've had of meeting you on the sands of Morocco," she had said. As Wendell proceeded down the hall, almost skipping, he was filled with wonder. *Sands of Morocco* had been exhibited and engravings widely distributed. Still, he was impressed and delighted that she knew the painting, and – she had dreamed of him.

He was still thinking about the encounter when he poked his head inside the grand entry of the exhibition hall, and was amazed to see an immense landscape, fifty square feet at least, in a mahogany frame being lifted by pulleys into place. The celebrated artist, Frederic Edwin Church, directed the placement of *Heart of the Andes* and turned to see Wendell watching. "Hey Parry," he shouted across the gallery's expanse, "What do you think?"

"Staggering, Mr. Church!" Wendell was on his way in when a tap on his shoulder turned him round. It was George, the concierge.

"Your canvases are arrived, sir." Wendell followed the pinched little man to find a great many large crates and trunks blocking the entrance.

"I'm afraid the porters have left. My apologies, sir."

"It's not your fault, George." Wendell put his fisted hands on his hips and looked around. "But what am I to do about it?"

Just then Fred Church came out of the gallery, flushed with accomplishment. "By Jove, Wendell, we got it in place. 'Staggering' is exactly the right word for it." He paused, stroking one of his sizable mutton chops, and looked at the blocked hallway. "It appears that it would be to my advantage to help you." The good man spun on his heel and disappeared, returning seconds later with Wendell's friend Thomas, artists Sanford Gifford and Jervis McEntee, and yet another woman – Gertrude McEntee lived with her husband in his atelier and came along to add her feminine concern for the safety of the packages.

"All right then, Gentlemen," Church said, taking command, "Hoist away!" Within minutes, all the canvases and trunks had been carted up the two broad staircases and deposited in Wendell's room.

More artists crowded in, milling expectantly as Wendell opened a steamer trunk. He pulled out a variety of valuable pigment powders and brushes, rare or expensive or simply novel. Soon, the word had spread and almost all the tenants packed into the atelier for the traditional swap. Especially prized were jars of Egyptian brown said to be ground from real mummies, ivory black from charred tusks and teeth, and vibrant blue jars of lapis lazuli from the mines of Afghanistan, more valuable than gold. Too, there were the yellow and blue cobalts from Bohemia, and the highly prized new green called viridian. Wendell delivered to Thomas the Venetian red that he had asked for, and others traded stretched and sized canvases in gilded frames and the more mundane tools of their profession, including white flake lead, beeswax, and cured linseed oil. A sable fur brush from a Siberian marten garnered not only admiring gasps, but a twenty foot roll of the best hemp canvas.

After the trading was complete, Fred Church, still in an exuberant mood, commandeered the other artists down to his studio on the second floor, to celebrate his coming exhibit of *Heart of the Andes*. Wendell stayed behind to ready himself for Sam's soirée.

He sighed happily. It had been a scintillating day and he hadn't even gotten out of his nightshirt. He took his time dressing, wanting his appearance to be impeccable.

Through an open window, he heard a newsboy call from Sixth Avenue, "*Tribune*, *Tribune*, get your *Tribune* here! Free Negro kidnapped into slavery! Get your *Tribune* here!" Wendell had heard of such kidnappings. Still, he was startled at the nearness of it – slavery was something that had always seemed far away, in the

South, or in the past – his grandfather had been a slave, an impressed seaman in the Royal Navy.

He closed the window, then got out his magic mirror. Cat sat on the bed and watched, a deep purr coming from his belly. "Cat, you are the only one who has ever witnessed this," said Wendell. He lit the candle and gazed into the glass.

Sam and Elizabeth Stockard's Washington Square brick house, graced at night by the lovely glow of gas lamps, was only a few blocks from the Tenth Street Studio Building. As Wendell approached on foot, carriages arrived filled with well-attired guests. Veritable valentines floated in voluminous romantic dresses complete with ornate shawls and carefully-coiffed hair, while solicitous gentlemen looked dapper in black overcoats and top hats. Wendell himself was coatless but quite turned out, in top hat, tails, and well-shined shoes.

Fitzhugh hailed him on the sidewalk, and ushered forth a visionary creature for Wendell to meet. "Harte, my man, allow me to introduce my wife, Mrs. Rosalie Ludlow." Fitzhugh was beaming over his prize. "This, my darling, is one of my dearest friends in all the world, Mr. Wendell Harte Parry."

Wendell doffed his hat. He took the proffered hand, tiny and gloved, and inclined himself in a deep bow. She was indeed beautiful, eighteen years old, with sweet mischief in her eyes and flowers in her brown hair. "I'm delighted," he said.

Inside, a gentleman helping out as butler took his hat, while modest chandeliers illumined the handsome milling crowd. Couples danced as a string quartet played chamber music near the staircase. Sam's wife, Elizabeth, took Wendell's arm and escorted him to meet the guests. He was happy to see artists he knew from the Tenth Street Studio Building, including Thomas.

Elizabeth left Wendell by the punch bowl where he filled a glass and surveyed his options. An actress, exotically dark and exquisite with boyish short hair and pouty lips, caught his eye and raised an alluring eyebrow. As he was about to approach her, the most famous man in the world, heavyweight boxing contender John "Benicia Boy" Heenan, came up behind her and, with a warning glance at Wendell, handed her a drink.

Wendell sighed and looked around at the other ladies. Laura Keene, actress and owner of the Laura Keene Theater, was flirting with his friend, Thomas Read. And Margaret, Sam's "sister-in-law with a dowry," was quite occupied with a handsome actor, Edwin Booth. Meanwhile, Fitzhugh swayed above them, clinging precariously to the staircase banister, while Rosalie Ludlow danced close with a baby-faced poet named Tom Aldrich. "No, Fitzhugh! Not now!" thought Wendell. His good friend was clearly floating in a hasheesh haze through paradise or perdition while his new wife flirted with the besotted Mr. Aldrich.

Wendell filled his glass again and looked across the table. And then he saw her – the loveliest of ladies was looking back at him, with soft verdant eyes. His heart fluttered and he lowered his drink.

She was wearing green taffeta, and the small white gardenias in her dark upswept hair matched the larger one pinned to her slender waist. Her décolletage, well off the shoulders, revealed an expanse of creamy white skin and the half-orbs of sweetly swelling breasts. Silken arms were exposed to the wrists, where small green kid gloves were each bounded by the most delicately jeweled bracelets. He did not believe his excitement had ever been thus aroused at the mere sight of a lady. He knew he was staring but there she was, unabashedly staring back.

"Miss Lillian Flax," he stammered.

She smiled and once again he felt himself falling. "Wendell Harte Parry."

Their host came by and nodded. "Ah, I see you two have met," Sam said. "That's good. I was just coming to introduce you."

Without reply, Wendell and Lillian were on the dance floor,

drawn into each other's arms as if by magnets. He rested his cheek against her hair, smelling her gardenias, and she drew closer.

"Do gardenias grow in the sands of Morocco?" she whispered.

"Abundantly," he breathed.

Through the layers of silk, crinolines and hoops, Wendell felt her pressing against him. His excitement was as exquisite as her beauty, as her scent, as her feel – as her name, "Lillian." Despite the rules of etiquette which mandate changing partners, they stayed like this for three songs – nay, forever – pressed against each other, hardly daring to breathe, aware of every movement in each other's gracefully swaying body.

The music stopped, and Sam invited everyone to join him in the drawing room.

She took his arm and Wendell easily led her through the parlor doors. It felt so natural, her arm in his, as if they had always been together thus. Nothing could break the spell, and as they took chairs next to each other, he was aware of her presence as if they were still dancing. Not all the intoxicants that Fitzhugh took could be anything like the intoxication Wendell felt with Lillian.

It was to be a salon of poetry. Sam introduced Walt Whitman as the first poet, who sat on a well-lit dais before his rapt audience.

> *"Passing stranger," Whitman began softly,*
> *"You do not know how longingly I look upon you,*
> *You must be he I was seeking,*
> *or she I was seeking,*
> *(It comes to me, as of a dream,)*
> *I have somewhere surely lived*
> *a life of joy with you.*
> *All is recall'd as we flit by each other,*
> *fluid, affectionate, chaste, matured,*
> *You grew up with me, were a boy with me,*
> *or a girl with me,*

> *I ate with you, and slept with you –*
> *your body has become not yours only,*
> *nor left my body mine only."*

Not daring to breathe, Wendell watched Lillian out the corner of his eye, the slight movement of her bodice as she, too, seemed to hold her breath. She looked down at her lap and casually laid her gloved hand against his thigh, sending an involuntary shiver – nay, an electric shock – up his leg to his heart.

Gently, Wendell picked up the gloved hand and undid the button on the inside wrist. He slid his fingers inside, massaging her palm, until the glove fell free. Then he tenderly pressed her upturned wrist to his lips. Ah, how sweet, how sweet! She was breathing now, deep breaths that alternately collapsed and swelled the boning of her gown, and the ecstasy within him came nigh to making him moan. Indeed, he had to remind himself where they were.

The baby-faced poet, Tom Aldrich, had taken the dais and was reciting,

> *"Spirit of verse, which still eludes my art,*
> *You shapes of loveliness that still do haunt me,*
> *O never, never rest upon my heart,*
> *If when I have thee I shall little want thee!*
> *Still flit away in moonlight, rain, and dew,*
> *Will-o'-the-wisp, that I may still Pursue."*

Wendell's hand embraced Lillian's athwart his thigh, and he thrilled to see how strong it was. Not the hand of a pampered lady, but a hand that nurtured, strove, cared – a gentle hand, a worthy hand, a hand to trust and rely on. Deeply he sighed as time eluded him. He could think only of Lillian. The poets read stirring verses of idealism and transcendence, but Wendell could not hear. As the audience clapped and cheered, Wendell's eyes sought out his love's, and this time they drank each other in. Her eyes were deep and trusting, her face flushed. A trembling smile spread across her glowing features. How miraculous that between them so few words had been spoken, yet he was certain he knew her and she him. Perhaps some other life, some magic plane; he squeezed her hand and was content.

Now Thomas Read was reading,

> *"Bring me the juice of the honeyed fruit,*
> *The large translucent, amber-hued,*
> *Rare grapes of Southern isles, to suit*
> *The luxury that fills my mood."*

Lillian's hand in his lap returned his squeeze, and Wendell's bliss grew exquisitely beneath it.

> *"For I would wake that string for thee*
> *Which hath too long in silence hung,*
> *And sweeter than all else should be*
> *The song which in thy praise is sung."*

Wendell did not join the applause though he loved the verse – their handclasp could not be undone. He looked at her to see if they might leave. No, her eyes answered back, a trace of fear in them. Ah, she would not be rude, could not be rude – that, too, he liked in her.

Wendell was so caught up in his new love that he didn't realize Anna Mary Freeman was holding forth from the dais, and that curious eyes now turned with amusement upon him and Lillian:

> *"But the lovers could not hear,*
> *For he was nibbling at her ear,*

> *And when he squeezed her dainty hand,*
> *Their minds soared forth to fairyland.*
>
> *Be ye poets not dismayed –*
> *Poems are not for lovers made!*
> *But serve love's sweetest memory,*
> *When what was love hath fade."*

Embarrassed, he released her hand and they both clapped, laughing self-consciously.

Too soon, the event was ended. Lillian put her glove back on and composed herself as Wendell helped her up. She smiled sweetly. "Thank you," she said, suddenly formal. "It's been a lovely evening." They moved among the crowd, shaking hands, bowing, making goodbyes. Wendell retrieved his hat at the door and helped Lillian with her wrap. He turned to find Sam and gripped his hand, beaming across at Elizabeth.

"Thank you so much!" he enthused. "A thoroughly delightful evening! I have never attended a better salon."

Sam wore a polite but concerned expression as he and Elizabeth said goodbye to Lillian and thanked her for coming. As Wendell turned to follow Lillian out, Sam caught him aside by the arm. "Come back when you've seen her off," he said.

Wendell hurried after his love, and took her hand. He smiled, and then sensing her shyness, bowed low and formally. "I do believe this has been the most wonderful evening of my life, Miss Flax. May I see you again?"

She laughed. "Mr. Parry, I would like to commission you to paint my portrait." He stood erect and looked at her, not knowing what to say. Her cab pulled up and was waiting.

"Uh, the pleasure would be mine," he stammered. "How shall we make arrangements?"

"I'll find you. I know where you live!" She turned and climbed into the carriage. With a wave and a clatter of hooves, she was gone. Wendell stood a moment, hopeful and helpless, looking after her down the gas-lit street. Then he brushed past the other guests to keep his appointment with Sam.

Sam and Elizabeth were waiting by the door. They grabbed his arm and pulled him close. Quietly, Sam said, "You do know that Lillian is married, don't you?"

"What? Marr…," he could not say the word. "What?" She had just been in his arms! She had just been his! "No, you're quite mistaken. That's not possible!"

"We're so sorry, Wendell." Now it was Elizabeth who spoke. "Her husband is the shipping magnate, Henry Ferguson. We thought you knew."

Wendell's stomach was queasy and his knees felt weak. His hand went to his forehead as if to keep himself from falling. "What?" he said again. Having a name gave more truth to it – Ferguson. No! Henry Ferguson bought *Sands of Morocco*! "But you wanted me to meet her!" He looked at Sam, almost shouting in his pain, "Why did you want me to meet her?"

"She's a patroness of art," said Sam. "A very rich one." He paused, letting it sink in, and put his hand on Wendell's shoulder. "That's why I wanted you to meet her. Not for love. Lillian is a patroness of art."

Chapter 3

Cat woke him next morning in time for breakfast. Not that Wendell had slept; but after excruciating ecstasies of love, hell and humiliation, he at last decided that nothing untoward had happened. He had been momentarily attracted to a lady he did not know, had danced with her and held hands – that was all. His honor was intact, as was hers; there would be no angry husband, no duel, no scandal and, alas, no love.

To the delight of the other artists, he went to breakfast in his djellaba, and was glad to see Mrs. Winter feeding Cat. The basement mess-hall was abuzz with excitement. He sat down with his friends, Thomas Read and Sanford Gifford, a plate of potato pancakes and coffee. Great interest was being lavished on Fred Church's *Heart of the Andes*, which exhibition opened an hour hence in the gallery and would run all week. "Twelve thousand tickets are sold," marveled Sanford. "I have concerns whether we tenants will be able to get in and out of our own building."

"It surprises me that folks would come this far north of the city to see a painting," said Thomas.

"Perhaps it's the excellence of the work that brings them," Wendell suggested.

Sanford laughed. "'Tis the size! Not to take away from it – it's an astounding piece. But Americans do love things big. I venture to say that's our national weakness."

"Do you include yourself in that?" asked Thomas.

"Yes, indeed," said Sanford. "Like most Americans, I am drawn to what is triumphal and grand." Sanford Gifford leaned back in his chair, and twirled the end of a lightly waxed mustache. He had always looked to Wendell as a man who could handle a bear as well as a brush. "It was a fine salon last night," Sanford went on, then teased Thomas Read with a smile. "Are you keen on

Miss Keene?"

"It's my understanding that Laura Keene is betrothed," said Thomas.

"Alas, Miss Flax is married!" Wendell cried.

Sanford scoffed, "I believe 'tis her husband's money she's wed to."

"We are all wed to her husband's money," laughed Thomas. "Lillian's patronage has proved most generous."

Sanford looked at Wendell and added, "Yet, there is hope. I believe she espouses 'free love.' Still, be careful. I have met Henry Ferguson and would not want to cross him."

Back in his studio, Wendell took a hammer to the crates. Over the next few hours, he carefully disentombed his beloved canvases and gave them a proper resurrection on the walls. Except for a few carefully copied Old Masters, the landscapes were original. There were luminous studies of European castles nestled in verdant hills, many Moroccan deserts and villages, and older paintings of Upstate New York and the Hudson River Valley. Then came the portraits. Some were copies of famous people, painted from daguerreotypes: *Mona Lisa,* George Washington, Colonel Andrew Jackson – these never sold for much but they always sold. Finally there were his original genre pieces: artists in their studios, street scenes from Paris, London, Venice, Fez. He liked their casualness, their sense of a fleeting moment captured by a brushstroke.

Last was the unfinished commission – a portrait of his former patroness, the Comtesse de Clairmont. Her patronage had been both blessing and curse, as he never knew whether to credit his art or his gifts in bed. Truth be told, she was part of the reason he'd left Paris.

As he pulled the Comtesse away from the boards of her packing crate, he yearned for the day when he would no longer have to do portraiture and could earn his living entirely from landscapes. It was not that he was ever bored with a face, but the features that attracted him – the too close eyes, perhaps, or the weathered skin, the asymmetry that suggested a struggle in the soul – these were the very features that his subjects demanded he obscure. This particular portrait was a false study in perfection. Worse, the Comtesse had been excited to be exposed before his flattering eye, and hence his time had not been spent painting. Now it was the devil to pay, for it should have been done well before he left Europe. Particularly troubling was that the long expanse of her back - seated naked on the posing bench with a drapery demurely clutched - was wrong, did not quite balance the sensuous curve of her neck and the softly molded face that peered coyly over her shoulder. *"Merde à l'enfer!"* he swore under his breath, still not sure how to fix this. It had to do with her belated vain insistence on a teasing tit being shyly revealed. Now, he did not have even a model to rely on, only an impatient Comte and the added cost of shipping the thing back to France.

Wendell felt quite distracted and helpless as he stared at the unfinished portrait. But, though the bronze nameplate attached to the gilded frame clearly said *Comtesse de Clairmont*, the face that looked back at him was not the comtesse's – Wendell admitted that he was still thinking of Lillian Flax and had been all day. He knew the comtesse had what she called a *"mariage de l'amour libre,"* a marriage of free love. Was it possible that Lillian, too, had such a marriage?

There was a knock, and he opened the door to George, the concierge. "A gentleman to see you, sir."

"A highly dubious supposition," proclaimed Fitzhugh Ludlow from the corridor.

"Fitzhugh, come in! Welcome to my chummery. I've only just unpacked."

George had bowed and taken his leave, while Fitzhugh extolled the extra effort the concierge had made to accommodate him through the crowds. "My dear Harte, have you looked out? It defies belief! I am sorry the man left – we may need his help if I am to steal you away to Pfaff's."

"I would certainly quit this place for a meal," Wendell admitted.

"Allow me first to survey your new habitat. It has a romantic air, and big enough to swing a cat."

"Mayhap a tigress," grinned Wendell.

Fitzhugh's gaze fell on the unfinished portrait. "That must be the comtesse – she of the Narcissus nipple."

"Indeed."

"Mmmm, she's fetching." Then, "I noticed a balcony off the front staircase which oversees the street. We can assess the crowds better from there."

Wendell felt no need to lock. He grabbed his sketching satchel, and they made their way down the corridor to the stairwell and unbolted the small door on the landing. It opened onto an outside balcony, just large enough for the two of them to stand and lean over the ornate iron railing. Below was 10th Street, where an orderly line of excited art fanciers stretched to the east down the sidewalk and around out of sight on 5th Avenue, waiting patiently to see *Heart of the Andes*; another stream of humanity exited to the west. Carriages and buggies added congestion, while the Metropolitan Police patrolled the ruly crowd with a large presence.

"I believe Mr. Church has made history today," said Wendell admiringly.

They made their way down the west side staircase and paused on the last landing to overview the throng. Just outside the gallery entrance, a young writer had set up a table and was attempting to sell his book, *Companion to the Heart of the Andes*. "When it comes to commerce, there is no stone unturned!" laughed Fitzhugh above the din. "Let's see if Ted's ready for a break."

"Mr. Winthrop!" Fitzhugh greeted him. "Would you care to

waste a bit of your life with us? We're on our way to Pfaff's."

Ted Winthrop was a well-built young man, albeit somewhat short and whiskery, with the pale skin and brown hair typical of New Englanders. "It would seem that a fair bit of every life must be wasted," he responded philosophically, "and better to waste it at Pfaff's than here."

The three men pushed through the crowd and soon passed New York University on Washington Square. "There I lived," Ted pointed to one of the university's mullioned windows. "It's not a jail, as one might suppose from its grimmish aspect. Not an asylum. No lunatics that I know of. Well, Anna Mary Freeman lived there, not quite a lunatic. It tries to look medieval and thus learned, but it smells of new paint as does the rest of America. Still, it is a formidable setting for the queer novel I'm writing."

"Your work must be quite gothic," Wendell suggested, enjoying the writer's comedic charm.

Ted smiled. "Indeed, I would hope it has something of Poe."

"Do you live there now?"

"Why I am your neighbor! I live at the Tenth Street Studios. They have deigned to let a writer have the windowless basement room."

On the corner of Bleecker and Broadway, Wendell, Ted, and Fitzhugh descended paved steps into a steep portal that plunged into darkness beneath the busy Broadway sidewalk. Fitzhugh opened the heavy door at the bottom and they entered a high vault that extended back towards an imposing wood bar. Tobacco and cooking smoke assaulted Wendell's nose – it hung in huge clouds around the ceiling lamps, and mingled with the more delicate odors of alcohol and coffee. Slowly, his ears adjusted to the cacophony of boisterous patrons, mostly bearded and dressed in frock coats, who surrounded the small tables and tipped back in flimsy chairs, some falling over onto the dirt floor. There was an air of devil-may-care and excitement which seemed to Wendell a combination of the rathskellers of Hamburg and the coffee shops of Paris.

Wendell heard calls of "Hey Ludlow!" and "Winthrop!" coming through the mists as he followed them to the bar where they ordered each a beer. As they made their ways toward the alcove in the front, Wendell passed the table of Walt Whitman. The poet was sitting with a newspaper, a cup of coffee and a scribble pad, seeming content to contemplate those around him. "Hello, Mr. Whitman," said Wendell politely. "I just want to remark how much I enjoyed your poetry last night." (In truth, he much preferred that verses should rhyme.)

Walt Whitman looked up at the young man with kindly amusement. "If you say so. It appeared to me that you didn't hear a word I said, you being elsewise occupied."

Wendell flushed. "Perhaps I was distracted. I didn't know the lady was married." Why he said this, he did not know except that the hoary, bushy-bearded Whitman seemed a comforting figure.

"I wouldn't worry much about that. I don't think it carries much import with Lillian."

Wendell smiled uncertainly as Fitzhugh hailed him with a seat at a long table in the farthest alcove. He crowded into it, enjoying a vague conspiratorial feeling as he imagined feet hurrying unaware on the Broadway sidewalk above him. Some at the table he recognized: Rosalie Ludlow sat next to her husband, blowing soap bubbles from a clay bubble pipe, while the besotted baby-faced poet, Tom Aldrich, sat on her other side and tried not to look at her. The actress who had been dancing with the prizefighter John Heenan at Sam's soirée beckoned with smoldering eyes from beneath a rakish gaucho hat, not dissimilar to Wendell's own, which he raised politely. Adah Isaacs Menken winked and blew smoke at him from her cigarette.

Directly across from him was a pretty blonde woman with a young boy beside her. Like Adah Menken, she wore her curly hair short and parted on the side like a boy. She hoisted a beer mug, licked her lips enticingly, and waited patiently to be introduced. Fitzhugh did the honors, introducing her as Ada Clare, the "Queen of the Bohemians," at which moniker she preened in jest and batted her eyelashes. "*Miss* Ada Clare!" she said with a soft southern accent, "and my son, Aubrey." Wendell nodded cordially, taking note of this rather shocking emphasis on her unmarried status.

Lastly, Fitzhugh introduced him to the thin, bearded man in his late thirties with a black pipe and imposing grey eyes whose reputation had preceded him: Henry Clapp, editor of the *Saturday Press* and the "King of the Bohemians." It was a title brought back from Paris where Bohemia was thought to be the origin of a gypsy people, famed for their freedom from the constraints of society.

"Henry has just moved into the Unitary Household next door to me," added Fitzhugh.

"I'm afraid I don't know what a Unitary Household is," said Wendell.

"'Tis a communist den," Clapp declared, "rife with the iniquities of 'free love.' Or so says the *New York Times*."

"And what say you?"

"Far be it from me to dispute the *Times!*" His grey eyes twinkled. He took a puff on his pipe and considered. "Not free love – cheap love, perhaps. By sharing maid, cook and parlor, we live in affordable camaraderie – an arrangement not unlike your Tenth Street Studio Building."

"So Mr. Parry," asked Miss Ada Clare, the Queen of the Bohemians, "what did you gain from going to Europe?"

Wendell felt the influence of the dark beer and was enjoying himself. "I believe I left a provincial, and came back a disreputable bohemian." This was greeted with cheers.

"You went native then," said Henry Clapp wistfully. "'Tis the bane of every government that its citizens should not merely travel, but go native."

"Mr. Parry," Tom Aldrich challenged him, "What is your definition of bohemian?"

Ada Clare was suddenly intent. "Yes, how do you define bohemian?"

Wendell's grin dimpled his cheek. "A bohemian is one who refuses to be bound by definition." His cleverness was rewarded with a gratifying explosion of laughter and mugs drumming the table. "And what do you say that it is, Miss Clare?"

Her hand reached across the table and picked up the latest edition of the *Saturday Press*. "I expressed it rather well in this issue," she smiled, and twisted a strand of her short hair as she read. "*The bohemian is by nature, if not by habit, a cosmopolite, with a general sympathy for the fine arts, and for all things above and beyond convention. The bohemian is not, like the creature of society, a victim of rules and customs; he steps over them with an easy, graceful, joyous unconsciousness, guided by the principles of good taste and feeling. Above all others, essentially, the bohemian must not be narrow minded; if he be, he is degraded back to the position of mere worldling.*"

There were expressions of approval and mugs pounded. "Your turn, Henry," she said.

He puffed thoughtfully on his pipe. "I believe the bohemian is most successful when the world thinks him least so," the King of the Bohemians responded, "for the world counts by numbers, and does not see that the fixed point may be the center of a circle whose circumference is infinity."

There was a moment of bemused silence before the beer mugs drummed.

Henry Clapp then turned to Fitzhugh. "Mr. Ludlow!" he demanded, "Might I suggest that you consume more opium, so Britain will have less need of forcing it on China!"

"Hear, Hear!"

Fitzhugh groaned at this reference to the second Opium War,

and Wendell wondered if his friend now imbibed opium as well as hasheesh. "I confess," said Fitzhugh, "I have not done my part of late. But better the Chinese than me."

"'Tis the advantage of Empire," noted Miss Clare with a giggle, "that the Brits should insist on paying for their Chinese tea habit with opium grown in India."

"Mr. Parry!" the actress Adah Isaacs Menken pouted, "Will France and Austria go to war?"

"Imminently, I'm sure we shall hear of it by the next ship."

"I wish the imperials would stay out of Italy's business," said Ted Winthrop. "I love Italy and would like to see her whole. I must say, I am impatient for faster news of her."

"Aye," agreed Tom Aldrich, "how could the telegraph have worked so well for a week, then failed so utterly?"

"The telegraph rested on a mistaken notion of water," explained Fitzhugh. "Water does not compact at depth as was thought. So rather than landing on compacted water, the wire sank all the way to the Atlantic's floor, where it was prey to rocks and crevasses. I'm afraid 'twill take some time before investors will risk another go."

"I'm glad I didn't invest my money in it!" exclaimed the always broke Henry Clapp, evoking a chorus of laughter.

Wendell was amazed at this new information about the nature of water. In college, he had studied the mathematical formulae for just how far the telegraph wire would sink.

Tom Aldrich perched on his chair, an animated mop of unruly curls bouncing above his boyish face, as he commanded the power of having the *New York Tribune*. Wendell began to sketch him.

"Karl Marx's column is, as usual, fascinating," Tom said. "It seems that Britain, in addition to its abominable balance of payments with China, has utterly failed to pay for the Crimean War, much less the recent uprising in India. The Empire is by now running a large deficit, fueling fears of insolvency. The deficit for the Indian occupation alone is accumulating at 12,000,000 pounds per year."

As Wendell concentrated on the sketch, everyone seemed to be talking at once.

"Astounding! 12,000,000 pounds for India alone?!"

"But what then of the Irish poor? Is there no money for them?"

"I think the policy is to rid Ireland of all its poor."

"Capitalist bastards! We should begin a wager pool, when Britain's empire will expire of its own greed and overreach."

"Hear, hear!"

"It gives the lie to Darwin's theories that man is descended from anything so smart as monkeys."

"Nay, descent from monkeys is apt. Darwin's mistake is in not calling it 'devolution,' ha ha."

"An upward spike in cotton prices would be yet another dagger to pierce the Brits' armor. A war here would likely finish them."

"Or bring Britain in on the side of the South."

Wendell's ears pricked up. "But surely, war here is not imminent!"

Henry Clapp's grey eyes darkened. "'Tis a country founded on cheap labor. If the factory worker ever made common cause with the African slave, Marx would get his proletariat uprising. Rather, the bourgeois will pit them against each other. Divide and conquer. War is the great distraction for the masses."

"And mark this, Parry," said Ted. "Powers right here in Gotham want New York City to secede, to continue the cotton trade as a nation on its own."

Wendell was genuinely baffled. "Is this a joke? Is this cause for laughter?"

"Everything is cause for laughter in bohemia!" declared Fitzhugh. "Come, let's order up some food."

As they ate, two women brushed through the tables towards

them with skirts held high, greeting those they passed: Anna Mary Freeman and Lillian Flax, the latter carrying a guitar. Wendell felt his breath suck in as he and several men stood in formal acknowledgement of the ladies' presence and rounded up chairs. Lillian flashed a flirtatious smile and slid in beside him. She looked expectantly into his eyes.

Chapter 4

Wendell shifted uneasily under Lillian's gaze. "You must forgive me," he confessed, "I did not know last night that you're married."

Her smile faded. "I'm so sorry, I thought everyone knew." Sensing a drama, the others at the table had gone quiet and turned rapt attention on the pair. There was silence.

"Is your relationship," asked Wendell, throwing caution away, "a *mariage de l'amour libre?*"

Lillian blinked. "I don't think so. Perhaps more an *arrangement de commerce coercitif?*"

The rowdies at the table found this amusing, but were hushed by the actress, Adah Menken, "Come, can't you see that Wendell is distressed? Lillian, explain yourself, there is clearly passional attraction between the two of you. Doesn't the young man have a right to know how you can ignore your wedding vows?"

"Fie!" Ada Clare admonished, "You sound like Mrs. Grundy!"

"Even I have not heard the story," Anna Mary pressed, "but have always just assumed your innocence."

Lillian heaved a sigh and looked down at her clasped hands on the table. "I am brought to trial then," she said. "No matter. It is easily defended." She looked up at everyone, then turned her gaze to Wendell, who was watching her with adoring eyes, already having acquitted her as he recognized with some excitement that she might be free to be with him.

"Were I a son," Lillian's story began, "I would have been heir to my father's shipping company. But I am a daughter and my father, not wishing to disinherit me, arranged for me to marry Mr. Henry Ferguson of Ferguson Shipping, the only consideration of my happiness being that I receive a sizable allowance – so long as I remain married. As Mr. Ferguson has no interest in my person other than to secure my father's business, I am free to dally. And, as he lives with his mistress in Europe, I am content for now with the arrangement. Should I ever divorce, I shall be quite penniless."

"A fine kettle!" exclaimed Anna Mary. "You are completely exonerated. The unfairness is infuriating. It is the fate of all unmarried women to face a penniless future…"

"Marriage for a woman is akin to slavery," muttered Ada Clare.

"Are you free," asked Adah Menken, amazed, "to buy whatever you wish, without your husband's signature?"

"I am free, in most cases, to sign his name – his instructions to the bank were explicit." The women sighed in envious chorus. "So you see, everything I buy is in his name. I own nothing." Now the women hissed in sympathy.

"Then it was you, not Henry Ferguson, that bought *Sands of Morocco*?" Wendell's mind was reeling with the revelations.

Lillian regarded him worshipfully, "Yes, *Sands of Morocco* is my most treasured piece, more so now that I've met its creator."

"But what if your husband comes home?" asked Menken.

"He'll kill you, surely," said Anna Mary. "Your abolitionist leanings are bad enough. He ships cotton! And you dare to add a dalliance?"

Lillian winced. "Fie! I disparage marriage! Let us speak of more pleasant matters."

It was Fitzhugh who mentioned the guitar, prompting everyone at table to beg for a tune. Lillian picked it up and they all joined in, Aubrey the loudest, as Lillian led them in singing a popular abolitionist song:

> *"Ho! The Car Emancipation*
> *Rides majestic thro' our nation*
> *Bearing on its train the story,*
> *Liberty! A Nation's Glory.*
> *Roll it along, Roll it along,*
> *Roll it along, thro' the nation*
> *Freedom's Car Emancipation."*

Lillian had a good voice and played with competence and style, her strong hands fingering the frets and her back resilient. Almost everyone at Pfaff's joined in.

"See the people run to meet us,
At the depots thousands greet us;
All take seats with exultation,
In the Car Emancipation
Huzza Huzza Huzza, Huzza huzza huzza
Huzza huzza huzza, Emancipation
Soon will bless our happy nation."

"Huzza huzza huzza," sang Wendell. Written in 1844, this song had been a favorite since childhood. He was supremely happy. Lillian's husband was in Europe, she was free to dally! How quickly he had met her, how quickly he had friends, what a delight New York City was turning out to be. He felt, in this dingy hole called Pfaff's and in his new living situation among his fellow artists, he had found something akin to paradise.

Ada Clare announced that it was time to get her son home, and all the ladies stood to accompany her. Wendell rose and took Lillian's proffered hand. "I hope I haven't been too presumptuous," he said. "I do want to see you again."

Lillian's smile had a tantalizing tease in it. "Alas, I am entangled for the next several weeks." She leaned her fists against his chest, and swooned ever so slightly towards him. "Because of that, I had hoped you would be more presumptuous."

Wendell moved closer and took her shoulders in his hands. Her eyes held his for an indelible moment of "Yes" and then, irresistibly, his mouth found hers.

Wendell felt her body surrender into softness as their arms went around each other and she clung to him, swaying gently, their lips exploring. Time slipped away and they stood kissing forever, hearing the sounds of an orchestral crescendo soaring in the background.

Their audience broke into applause, and with some embarrassment they pulled apart. "Our first kiss," she whispered, smiling.

"I shan't forget it," he breathed.

Anna Mary yanked Lillian's dress and handed her the guitar. "You shall hear from me," Lillian called gaily, and all the ladies pushed out the heavy door.

The several weeks dragged by with unbearable slowness. On May Day, Wendell heard a knock and, upon opening the door, giggles and a departing patter of hurried feet. A May basket was hung on his doorknob, and in it white gardenias. Wendell's heart raced, and he took off after the footsteps, only to see Anna Mary running a flight ahead of him down the stairs. But surely, he thought, Lillian put her up to it.

Back in his studio, he admired the flowers. The last time he'd received a May basket, he had been a child in Ithaca. His sister, by then his only mother, had been gathering flowers to go a-Maying, and she'd given him a May basket and told him that in his life, he would receive many May baskets from admiring girls. But from that day to this, he had not received another.

A sudden nostalgia overtook him, and he sat down to write his father and sister that he would soon visit them in Ithaca.

Finally, inspired, he took out his paints and placed an early study of blowing Moroccan sands on his easel. To this he added white gardenias, growing out of the desert, and bare footprints leading away across the dunes where they were filled in by soft drifts. Toward the horizon, an elusive figure vanished into a sand storm, her green dress billowing. And then, emerging towards her, he painted himself in his djellaba. Overhead, a cold orange sun poked through the sand sky, and, for a reason he could not discern, buzzards circled in the distance.

Wendell had become quite lost in the painting when George, the concierge, knocked at his door and handed him a visit card announcing a Mr. and Mrs. Robinson. It was attached to a sealed envelope – from Lillian! Wendell opened it with excitement and found three crisp one hundred dollar bank notes, drawn on Merchants Bank New York, more than his rent for a year. There was also a card saying she was commissioning a portrait from him of the Robinsons as an anniversary present. Wendell was stunned. She was commissioning a sitting but not of herself? And too, there was something not quite right about taking her money, though the commission was not out of line with his prices. With some confusion, he responded to the concierge, "Please, show them up," upon which George flushed, and looked at the floor embarrassed. "What is it, George?" Wendell asked.

"They are colored, sir," said George.

It took Wendell a moment to recover from his surprise. "That's fine," he said gently. "Show them up." And then, overcome with self-consciousness, an uncertainty how to act, he placed the screen in front of his bed and threw a spread over the painting of the Comtesse. Hastily, he looked in the mirror and combed his hair. He had met Africans in Paris and Morocco, had even been given his muse mirror by an American Negro named Dr. Paschal Beverly Randolph. But in this country, because of slavery, he expected to feel awkward in their presence.

They entered, shyer than he, peering at the studio with wide eyes. Then Wendell shook Mr. Robinson's hand and kissed Mrs. Robinson's, and everyone relaxed. After finding chairs, Wendell made them coffee and conversed as he set up his paints and easel. "I am told this is an anniversary present. Have you been married long?"

Mrs. Robinson giggled. She was petite with large fringed eyes and deep dimples in both her round cheeks. She wore a bright indigo day dress with a fine white lace collar and petticoats, her hair in tight curls closely framing her pretty face. "This is our tenth anniversary," she said proudly, "I was fourteen when we married."

Tuck Robinson explained further, in a deep musical baritone, "We ain't been together but a bit of that. Ruby born free, but I done hafta wait for the mastah to die afore I get my freedom." He was a rugged tall man in his late twenties with a handsome wooly beard, navy blue frock coat and well-shined shoes. Ruby Robinson elbowed him playfully. "But I had to wait for the master to die," he corrected himself. He looked abashed and explained, "Talkin' southern can make folks 'round here take you for a runaway." Wendell nodded, aware that the Fugitive Slave Law made it a crime to be a runaway, even in the North.

He had donned his red silk painting smock and now instructed them in a pose. The luminous quality that Wendell sought required grinding the pigments into the utmost fineness. Because of the paint's toxicity, he worked with great cleanliness and care, taking notes on the right mix of pigments for the skin tones, and a background color to complement. He underpainted the first coat in darker tones than usual so that the Negroes' skin could be light against the background.

"How did you meet, then?" he asked.

"Well sir," said Mrs. Robinson, "I was hired as a writer's assistant, and in the summer of my fourteenth year, she took me to Baltimore with her. I was home by myself and sitting on the porch swing when the handsomest man in Maryland came riding by on a big black stallion. He stopped by the fence and tipped his hat, so I offered him some of my fresh baked cookies." She giggled shyly, and added, "After that, he came by 'most every day."

Tuck Robinson continued, "We got to marrying, and soon had us a son name of Wilberforce. So Ruby and the baby come down there to Baltimore pretty regular after that. Then the master gets wind of it, and sells me down to South Carolina." They both went silent, their portrait smiles changing to a look of agony. They paused for a response from Wendell, but he was speechless.

Mr. Robinson went on. "I trained horses real good for the new master and he took a likin' to me, so I told him about Ruby and why I been sold and he promised to free me when he die." He grinned. "Good thing he so old!" he said wickedly.

Wendell was fascinated with their story. "So how long have you been here?"

"Well sir," said Mr. Robinson, examining his hat for lint. "I'd say a little more'n a week."

"You've only just received your freedom?" cried Wendell, astounded.

"I hadn't seen him for almost four years," Ruby continued. "But our son never did forget him. He saw him on the stairs and before he even knocked on the door, Willy said, 'Mama, it's my Daddy. He's come home!' He was so excited!" Here she became choked with emotion. "I don't ever want to forget this time, and our tenth anniversary coming."

A heavy silence filled the room. "'Tis a shame and a travesty what you've been through," said Wendell finally.

"Lillian's present is overwhelming to us." Tuck said.

"Could I ask how you met her?"

Ruby sounded apologetic. "I'm afraid you'll have to ask her."

"Not meaning any disrespect, sir," said Tuck.

Wendell did not want to make them sit longer than necessary, and had enough to complete the portrait. They stood to go, thanking him and giving him their address in the Five Points for delivery.

They were startled by a strong knock. The door flew open to reveal George the concierge, and two dusty men wearing pistols. "Two gentlemen to…" but the men knocked George out of the way mid-sentence and strode into the room, their hands menacing their side-arms. One grabbed Tuck Robinson's shoulder.

"You Ben Tucker?" he demanded as Ruby grabbed Tuck's other arm.

"No," said Tuck firmly. "My name is Robinson."

"This is my home. You've no call," Wendell said indignant, trying to break the man's grip.

The second man shoved papers in Wendell's face. "This here states our claim to a Ben Tucker, absconded property of a Virginia plantation owner."

"I'm not he," Tuck protested in the best northern English.

"These people are known to me as free persons," lied Wendell.

"It's against the law to harbor a fugitive," he was warned.

"I'm not a fugitive," insisted Tuck. Ruby pulled papers out of her handbag and pressed them forward.

"Forgeries," hissed the first man. He took out his gun and pointed it at Mr. Robinson. "Ain't no such thing as a free nigger."

"No!" Ruby screamed, pushing the papers forward again. "That's not him. He's a freedman. He's free!" even as cuffs were placed on her husband.

The other one grabbed her and now everyone was struggling. He let her go and shot the gun into the ceiling. Plaster fell. There was a sudden hush, and the gun was pointed at Wendell. His anger turned to fear – he had never had a gun pointed at him.

Ruby grasped Tuck's sleeve and they all descended the stairs, passing a host of artists who gathered to stare at the scene. As they pushed by George, standing open-mouthed at the bottom, Wendell heard one of the captors say, "Thank ye for the tip."

Wendell grabbed George by the collar. "You will never do that again!" he hissed.

George whimpered and grew small. "Begging pardon, sir."

Wendell hurried after the kidnappers – for that was surely what they were – who had vanished with Mr. Robinson out the main door. He saw them heading up the sidewalk towards 6th Avenue. Tuck was walking calmly, head up. Ruby had disappeared.

Meanwhile an angry crowd of both coloreds and whites chased after them, shouting curses, and would have overtaken the hostage had not one of Tuck's captors turned frequently and menaced them with his gun.

They crossed 6th Avenue and threaded their way through the market stalls, attracting even more hostility, and entered the building beneath the city's 100 foot lookout tower where the court rooms were. At the court room door, the crowd was halted by Metropolitan police, and Tuck Robinson disappeared inside with his captors. The door slammed behind them.

As the crowd dispersed Wendell lingered, his eyes searching anxiously for Ruby Robinson. He felt a wave of nausea. He didn't care whether Tuck Robinson was a fugitive or not, he only knew he had let Lillian down. She had sent her friends to him as an anniversary present, and this had happened.

Hours passed. He leaned against the building and watched the crowds thin and the market stalls close for the night. The guards changed and he tried again to get in and was again rebuffed.

Then he saw Ruby and Lillian at the far corner of the building get into a carriage. They had Tuck with them. Wendell ran after them, calling their names, but the carriage sped up and turned out of sight down Greenwich Avenue.

Chapter 5

The following week Lillian had still not gotten in touch, nor had anyone at Pfaff's heard from her. After what he had seen, Wendell found this deeply disquieting.

It was a Sunday, and Wendell and Thomas were invited to share Sam's parents' pew at the Plymouth Congregational Church in nearby Brooklyn. Wendell had not seen the elder Stockards for awhile, and had been quite fond of them.

"It's so quiet here, with *Heart of the Andes* finished," observed Sam as Wendell and Thomas climbed into the waiting carriage. A soft rain was falling, glistening on the sidewalks and muddying the streets. "Is another exhibit scheduled?"

As the carriage got underway, Wendell beamed. "The next one includes yours truly, in concert with the other artists."

"Aye," said Thomas, "we'll be hosting the public in our studios."

"Oh, how exquisite!" squealed Elizabeth. "I have wanted to see where the artists work. It has the delicious air of something forbidden to ladies."

"This event has always been particularly enticing to the gentler sex," laughed Thomas.

They exited the carriage downtown at the ferry terminal and soon were racing across the East River, the giant side paddle wheel scooping water while the smokestack belched overhead. The horn blasted for the many wind-driven sloops and schooners to get out of the way, as a new era left the old behind in its wake.

At the wharf in Brooklyn, they hired another carriage and were off to Brooklyn Heights, where a glance to the west afforded a splendid view of Manhattan across the river. On the carriage's east side, brick and brownstone buildings nestled along pleasant tree-lined sidewalks, beyond which a nostalgia of fields and farms in the full bloom of spring stretched away toward the forested horizon, a far-off thunder cloud flashing above it.

The need for prior seating arrangements became apparent as they drew near to Plymouth Church. Sweeping into the grand brick and granite edifice was a massive gathering of elegant parishioners, who quickly occupied the 2800 pews that faced pulpit and pipe organ in the two-tiered rotunda.

Wendell, Thomas, Sam, and Sam's wife, Elizabeth, squeezed in next to Sam's parents with appropriate greetings and awed reverence. While a Negro boy pumped the bellows of the pipe organ, the music soared and crescendo'd, uplifting the spirit and inviting the soul to God. The congregation stood and in walked the Reverend Henry Ward Beecher. Everyone opened his hymnal.

> *"Not to us alone,*
> *But be Thy mercies known*
> *From shore to shore:*
> *Lord, make the nation see*
> *That men should brothers be,*
> *And form one family*
> *The wild world o'er."*

"And form one family, the wild world o'er," repeated the Reverend Beecher as his parishioners sat down. The famed abolitionist's large head had the jowls of a hound dog beneath a wolf pup's eyes, and his adamant message would switch in an instant from compassionate to furious.

"I have been asked if it is just to disobey an unjust law," he was saying. "Every citizen must obey a law which inflicts injury upon his person, estate and civil privilege, until legally redressed; but no citizen is bound to obey a law which commands him to inflict injury upon another. We must endure but never commit wrong. I refuse to obey the Fugitive Slave Law which says I must turn in the runaway slave – it is a sin against God and man to obey it."

Wendell sucked in his breath.

The reverend Beecher continued, "If we would benefit the African in the South we must begin at home. No one can fail to see the inconsistency between our treatment of those amongst us who are in the lower walks of life, and our professing of sympathy for the Southern slave. You ought to set your face against and discountenance anything like an insurrectionary spirit."

He then quoted from his sister Harriett's book, *Uncle Tom's Cabin*, which everyone had read – Wendell had even seen the play three times: " *'Not by combining together, to protect injustice and cruelty, and making a common capital of sin, is this Union to be saved, but by repentance, justice and mercy.'*

Let us pray…"

The organ was playing as they left the building, so deep in their own thoughts that no one noticed the sun had come out. Wendell helped Sam's mother into the carriage, and climbed in behind her. As they drove off, they were silent for a long moment.

Finally Sam's mother spoke, "Well, Mr. Read, what did you think of the sermon?"

"I must confess, I am confused by it," said Thomas. "I am sympathetic with any peaceful solution and with leaving the matter to God if one can. But did not the Reverend Henry Ward Beecher smuggle muskets to Bleeding Kansas? Is he not a supporter of John Brown's militia?"

"Aye, muskets cleverly labeled Beecher's Bibles," said Sam. "He was adamant that slavery not expand into the territories."

"But if he's willing to countenance violence in the territories, why not in the Southern states? That is surely where John Brown will strike next."

Sam's father spoke up, "Sending muskets to the Kansas Territory was to keep the Missouri slavers out, so that Kansas could vote itself in as a free state. If more free states enter the Union, there will be enough votes in Congress to outlaw slavery."

"Father," said Sam with surprising force, "Congress is too evenly divided to vote in more states, free or otherwise. War is coming. Nothing Reverend Beecher does can stop it. When it comes, the best course is to be ready."

"There have been a lot of wars, and not one was worth the fighting," his father responded wearily. "Generally, folks will do the right thing far quicker if you just leave them be."

Mrs. Stockard's voice choked as she spoke up. "Sam, it was unbearable for me when your father was gone to the Mexican War. When he returned, it was a long time before he was right again."

"What say you, Wendell?" asked Mr. Stockard, deflecting his wife's recollections.

Wendell shook his head. The whole conversation seemed unreal. "I'm afraid I have been gone too long to know what to think. I fervently believe the slaves should be freed, but I hope there isn't a war!"

They were stopping at an imposing building with an inscription, The Brooklyn Armory. "Well, I intend to be prepared," said Sam, sliding out of the carriage. "I beg your indulgence – I will return momentarily."

As they watched him disappear into the brick fortress, the elder Mrs. Stockard tried for some cheer. "Elizabeth," she said, "your husband is looking quite fit."

Elizabeth flushed profusely. "I think he looks rather dashing," she confided, as if sharing a secret. This caused both women to titter behind their gloved fingers and the gentlemen to smile.

As promised, Sam returned shortly carrying a packet. He was excited as he settled into the seat and the carriage proceeded. Out of the packet he pulled daguerreotypes of himself in a military uniform, standing with a regiment in one picture and posed wearing sword and sidearm in another.

Wendell gasped. "Sam, old fellow, you have quite surprised me! Does Fitzhugh know?"

"He does. I have been training with the 14th Brooklyn since last summer." He smiled with pleasure at his wife. "I believe Elizabeth is quite proud of me." She nodded happily and wrapped herself around his arm. He went on, "It's an abolitionist social club for the most part, but we practice enough to acquit ourselves proudly if it should come to that."

"I admire a man who follows his convictions," said Wendell with such obvious uncertainty that everyone laughed.

Thomas teased, "You should, however, get some better uniforms – something with more dash. You gentlemen look like you've already lost!"

"Mmmm," considered Wendell, "something more *Zouave*." The Algerian Zouave look of the French elite regiments, with red ballooning pants and fez hat, was much admired. They all laughingly agreed and went to the older Stockards' house for a delightful dinner.

The next weeks were hectic. The coming studio open house had all the artists preparing. Despite his busy schedule, Wendell found time to stop in at Pfaff's, at Fitzhugh's Unitary Household, and even at Ada Clare's Sunday salon – all with vain hopes that Lillian would be there. After the Robinsons affair, he worried for her incessantly.

In the remaining days before the open house, there were furious bouts of painting, framing, and rearranging. Even the artists who did not live at their studios were staying late, and hosted raucous dinners for the others catered by Mrs. Winter. Everyone wanted to see all the displays in every atelier, and the evening parties moved from room to room till the wee hours.

Wendell hung some Moroccan pieces in the main gallery and in his atelier, covered the Comtesse with a lovely silk and propped up easels with genre paintings and portraits in front of her. He locked his toxic pigments and oils in the cupboards. The mise-en-scène was largely French, Italian, and Moroccan, items that he'd brought back, as well as many that he'd bought on Broadway or found in the basement. His small bed (with Cat on it) was hidden behind the screen, his walls covered with paintings of Upstate New York, Europe and Morocco. He placed chairs, small tables with vases of flowers, cups for tea and plates for cookies. Strolling minstrels would provide music.

On Friday the thirteenth, everything was in readiness for the next day, and an eerie quiet fell over the Tenth Street Studios. The artists were tired and going to bed early. Wendell took out his magic mirror – his muse – lowered the gaslight, and lit his candle. After the ritual, he fervently prayed Lillian would come to the open house. It had been much too long since he'd seen her – since he'd kissed her.

He put the mirror away and let his trouser braces fall. He was taking off his shirt when a light rapping was heard at the door. He opened it, and there, gently lit by what remained of the candle, was Lillian Flax.

Chapter 6

Lillian's neck and shoulders were bare above gathered gauze tucked into a smooth blue skirt, her décolletage trimmed with a delicate lace. The scent of gardenias pinned to her waist wafted into the room and mixed with linseed oil and candle wax.

Wendell dropped his shirt from his hand and looked at her, noting how her eyes flickered across his chest curls. Neither said a word. He reached out and took her wrist, and gently pulled her into the room, closing the door behind her.

Her arms went around his neck as he pulled her to him and bent to kiss her mouth. The warmth of her lips, the feel of her breasts pressing through the gauze against his bare skin, was an unendurable delight. He wanted so much to take her slowly, to savor every moment. Gently, he pushed her away, trying not to gasp. She too was lightly panting as she stepped back and took the measure of him.

Undaunted, Lillian kicked off her shoes and released her dark flowing hair from beneath a small white satin bonnet, then unpinned the gardenias and laid them on the table. She turned her back to him, revealing a line of small buttons down the length of her blouse, which she proffered, bending her head. As he stepped forward and undid each one, he rewarded her trembling back with tiny kisses. Slowly, he lifted her camisole over her head and, nuzzling her neck, reached to feel the ripeness of her breasts. Finally, he undid the buttons of her skirt and slipped his hands inside so that it fell to the floor. She wore no corsets or petticoats, but only pantaloons that gapped and teased in the center, and knee high stockings held up by lace garters. When the pantaloons, too, were on the floor, Wendell pushed the screen aside and spun her around onto the bed. Lillian's face flushed as she fell back against the pillow and watched him undo the buttons of his trousers. She had the soft smell of honeyed lemon, a concoction with which many knowledgeable young women sought to prevent pregnancy.

"Do I need a *capote?*" he whispered.

"No," she breathed. "Pull out."

With that, he was on top of her, kissing her and stroking the silky skin of her thigh. Their excitement grew, and at her insistence, he thrust himself into her. She caught his rhythm and moved with him, gasps and moans escaping from some primal place.

Wendell had never felt anything like this before, this willingness, this oneness. Wishing the experience to last, he kept his control, until she let him know that it was blissfully time for him to lose it. He jerked himself out of her with exquisite and searing regret, just as the white stuff came pumping out of him, tearing from his groin with fierce urgency over her trembling belly.

Wendell groaned and put his arm around Lillian's shoulders, pulling her close. Tears dampened her cheeks. They lay like this for a moment, not wanting their feelings of intimacy to dissipate so soon. Finally, he got up and wet a cloth in the bedside stand. He washed her off, feeling tenderness – and love.

As he wiped himself, she rose and found her handbag, then put on his djellaba and went to the washroom to attend the honeyed-lemon.

When she returned, he had lit a new candle. Lillian took off his nightshirt and slipped under the covers beside him. But they didn't talk. Instead, they made love again – slowly. In the wee hours of the morning, entwined and breathing softly on the small bed, Wendell Harte Parry and Lillian Flax finally drifted together into deep and contented dreams.

They were awakened by an insistent knock on the door. Wendell opened his eyes and snuggled the sleeping Lillian contentedly as the morning light streamed in across the coverlet. He willed the intruder to go away. The knock came again and then Thomas Buchanan Read's voice, "All rise! It's show time!"

"Maintenez vos chevaux," responded Wendell as he reluctantly dragged on his trousers. He cracked the door, smoothing his tousled hair.

"We have less than an hour before the open house," said Thomas. Then he called beyond Wendell into the room, "Good morning, Miss Flax! Mrs. Winter says you're welcome to accompany Mr. Parry to breakfast in the mess-hall."

Wendell flushed as Lillian called back unseen from the bed, "Thank you, Mr. Read." Thomas was enjoying his friend's embarrassment as Wendell frowned and shoved the door closed in his face.

"Anna Mary?" he guessed.

"No," laughed Lillian, luxuriating under the covers. "She wasn't here last night. I was seen, I'm afraid, on my several honeyed-lemon trips to the washroom. You'll not be able to keep many secrets at Tenth Street."

He kissed her warmly and stood to finish dressing. Then she, too, was up, her beautiful limbs in motion as she found her somewhat rumpled clothes and hastily put them on.

Soon they were eating in the basement mess as the hour pressed upon them. He expected her to bring up the Robinsons, but instead she said, "You are going to have a great many visitors today."

"Why so?" asked Wendell.

"Because you have a famous painting hanging in the gallery."

Wendell's eyes grew wide with surprise and pleasure. "You brought *Sands of Morocco?*"

"Of course." Her smile was teasing. "What else would I have been doing here last night?" That produced a droll dimple on Wendell's cheek. "'Tis true!" she protested, laughing. "Had you not been standing by candlelight in the doorway with no shirt, I assure you, sir, nothing would have happened."

"Then, *mademoiselle*, I bless the candlelight."

"If I may," she added, "I have a suggestion about marketing." Wendell nodded, convinced of her expertise. "I think that when your guests arrive, they should find you painting my portrait."

"Ah oui," came a response from the next table. It was the Creole, Louis Remy Mignot. There were but a few artists at breakfast this morning, and all were listening with rapt attention to the conversation at Wendell's table. "It will attract a great attention."

Wendell's leisureliness shifted and he rose with some haste. "I'd best tidy the room," he said. Lillian left the remainder of her breakfast likewise uneaten, and they both sprinted up the stairs to his atelier. As they passed the lobby, they saw that already the front door had been thrown open by George, the concierge, and a queue was formed outside.

On reaching the third floor apartment, Wendell flew at spreading the bed and moving the screen to hide it. Lillian looked on respectfully. "May I?" she asked. Wendell nodded, stepping aside, and busied himself preparing easel and paints for the portrait sitting as Lillian pushed the small bed against the wall. She threw pillows on it from the surrounding chairs, creating a new day bed for seating space, and put the screen across the back to hide the workbench. Next she spread the easels and pulled the silk off the Comtesse.

Wendell glanced at her uneasily as she stopped moving and gazed critically at the crooked portrait of his erstwhile paramour. Finally she said, "Please, could you paint out that annoying tit?" Wendell grabbed his brush and mahlstick and hastened to do her bidding, relieved that this was what he would send to the Comte – and damn the demands for a nipple where one did not belong! "There," said Lillian with satisfaction. "She's lovely and will also draw a crowd."

Mrs. Winter showed up then with cookies for the empty plates, and the sounds of strolling violins began wafting through the halls.

In a more leisurely mood, Lillian surveyed the other portraits, her approving gaze falling on the Robinsons. "Oh, it's beautiful," she said with sincere appreciation. "They will very much like it. When can I take it to them?"

Wendell felt a twinge of mortification. "I apologize that I could not prevent Mr. Robinson's arrest."

"We are in your debt, Wendell. Had you not persisted in following them to the courthouse, no doubt they would have skipped the legalities and abducted Tuck straight away to the South."

Something in the way she said it gave him pause. Tuck was a fugitive, Wendell was sure of it. And Lillian wasn't going to tell him. "They have given me their address. My plan is to take it as soon as the open house is over."

There was fear in her green eyes. "The Five Points is ruled by wicked gangs. I see Ruby frequently, I'll take it to her."

"I am curious to see the Five Points, and I will take the utmost care." Wendell was firm – he wanted to know from Tuck Robinson just what had happened that day and he was determined to keep her out of it.

Lillian relented. "Pray, do not venture far from the travelled roads – even the police will not go into the interior of the Sixth Ward."

Then her eyes fell upon the fanciful desert storm with blooming gardenias and haunting buzzards circling in the distance. She gazed at it a long time. "I want to buy this one," she said.

Wendell shook his head. "Never." He took her in his arms. "I would not have it be the property of Mr. Henry Ferguson – it is not for sale. Nor is your portrait." As they were melting into a kiss, they were pulled apart by the sounds of approaching guests. Lillian took a seat on the posing bench and Wendell put on his red silk painting smock and began building an underpainting upon which to rough out her likeness. It was not long before a crowd had gathered, watching the artist with fascination, as if each stroke were an impossible feat of magic.

By mid-afternoon, when Wendell chased everyone out to other ateliers so he and Lillian could find food in the basement, he had garnered three portrait commissions and sold several genre paintings. He had also sketched the beginnings of a beautiful portrait of Lillian.

Back in the room, they made love by twilight, then he lit a candle and poured her a glass of wine while they sat on the bed and talked. They were both excited from the day's successes and eager to get to know each other. Lillian had read Wendell's interview in the *Crayon*, and now he wanted to know everything about her. She laughed, enjoying the wine and the few remaining cookies. "Alas," she rued, "I am getting crumbs in your bed."

"If I am kept awake tonight, I promise 'twill not be because of crumbs. Speak, please, before I kiss you, and once again your story eludes me."

She gave him a coy look over the rim of her wine glass, then seeing he was sincere, she began to talk. "I grew up in Massachusetts," she began, "an only child. I'm twenty-five if you want to know." Wendell had wanted to know – she was a year older than he. She went on, "My mother was second cousin to my father, and my guess is that I was early conceived and prompted a hasty wedding." She paused here and smiled. "Or," she continued, "I am a medical miracle in premature births! My mother did not like being married, and in fairness to my father, would probably have disliked being married to anyone. I was only five or six when she left him, and, taking me with her, went to live in the Transcendentalist community, Brook Farm."

"You lived at Brook Farm? I have heard much about it!" Perhaps growing up in the Transcendentalist community explained her boldness of speech, her ease with making love. "Did you know Hawthorne there?" The writer's presence at Brook Farm had contributed to its fame.

"Brook Farm has its reputation," she confessed. "To this day I call Nathaniel Hawthorne 'Uncle.'" Wendell watched her with fascination and sipped his wine attentively. "I believe my mother was truly happy there," she went on. "She was free and equal, earning equal pay to the men and doing whatever work suited her. She read endlessly, and indulged herself in crafts and theatricals. There was a progressive and international school where I took all the same lessons as boys. I excelled at my studies, and even at base ball! At Brook Farm, I had the blessing to grow up not realizing that women are deemed inferior."

"You must have been only thirteen or fourteen when Brook Farm failed," observed Wendell.

She nodded. "'Twas a sad day. As mother could not now support me, my father claimed me, and for my sake, my mother lived again as a married woman. But my father could not forgive her, and she was treated like a servant, with no discernible love between them. Finally, she left." Lillian's voice had begun to quaver and drift.

"Pray, do not go on if it upsets you," cried Wendell in dismay. He could see there were tears in her beautiful eyes.

"Ah," she rallied, "but I'm just getting to the good part. My mother went to the Northwest and became a saloon dancer in Chicago." She clearly liked the idea of her mother as a dancer, but then her smile broke and she heaved a sigh that was more akin to a sob. "But she died," was all she choked out.

Now she was crying, and Wendell took her into his arms. She clung like a child as he kissed away her tears. Soon, they were making love again, the depth of her emotions leading to yet deeper passion. When they finished, Wendell knew he was irretrievably in love.

For a moment, as he listened to her quiet, even breaths in the dark, he felt frightened and vulnerable. "Have you been with many men?" he blurted. From the shadows, he heard her answer.

"Would you want me to ask that of you? Who besides that countess you've sported with?"

"No," he admitted. Was the Comtesse so obvious?

Lillian squeezed his hand. "I'll tell you this, Wendell Harte Parry, and this is all you need know. I have never made love with anyone else, least that I would now call 'making love.' In that sense, I was virgin till you."

"Forgive me," Wendell begged, "the question was unworthy. It's just I…" She placed her finger against his lips.

"I know," she said, "you're a man." And she climbed on top of him.

Next morning, she was up early and pulling on her rumpled clothes as Wendell's eyes cracked open. "You're leaving," he said.

"Even I," she laughed, "would be embarrassed to be caught here yet another morning. And dressed in such dishevel!" He rose then himself, searching for his trousers.

"But the morning is so young."

"I have a luncheon engagement with Laura Keene and Edwin Booth. I may invest in their new play, with a possible role for Adah Menken. The public is clamoring to see the lady who makes weak the mighty prize-fighter, John Heenan!" Wendell laughed, then picked her up and swung her merrily around.

"Lillian Flax, you make me strong!" he cried. "I feel I could whip a thousand John Heenans!" She was smiling broadly when he set her down. "Were I to kiss you now," he said, kissing her, "you would miss your luncheon date. Perhaps we should save our kisses for the sidewalk, where we would be better constrained."

"Ah," she said regretfully, "there is too much gallantry in you." She stepped away from him and affixed her bonnet. "I will return for *Sands of Morocco* if you would like to keep it for the continuing open house – the painting attracts favorable attention."

"Perhaps I can deliver it to you," he offered as he finished dressing.

Lillian hesitated. "I'll retrieve it later," she said. "It would not be appropriate for you to deliver it to Mr. Ferguson's mansion – or safe." Besottedly, he kissed her again, pushing aside the small alarm her words set off in him.

As they went together to the sidewalk on 10th Street, they congratulated each other on the success of the opening, and she agreed to meet him at an inn on the Hudson River where he would be going soon with Sanford Gifford and Ted Winthrop before heading to Ithaca to see his family.

A carriage pulled up to the curb and Wendell helped her in. He held onto her hand and bowed low over it. With great formality, he said, "Miss Flax, the pleasure has been mine. I await the honor of seeing you again."

"Thank you, Mr. Parry," she said. And the carriage departed, down the paved street toward Fifth Avenue and the pink lining of an impending day.

Chapter 7

Monday morning found the artists in a celebratory mood. As they gathered in the Studio Building mess for breakfast, all cheered the success of the weekend and their added wealth. Wendell was especially singled out for toasts and torment.

Louis Mignot stood with his coffee cup aloft and cried out to the room, "I would like to drink to our great fortune! And to think, we did it all without help from our erstwhile benefactress, *la belle Madamoiselle Flax!*" His audience howled.

"Sir, are you jealous?" called Wendell from his seat, not sure if he should take offense.

"Certainement!" laughed the Creole. "You have accomplished what the rest of us could not, and are the better man for it!" Everyone cheered and toasted him with their coffee. Wendell sensed good will beneath the teasing.

"I confess," said Wendell flushed, "I am in love with her!" This brought another round of cheers, along with back-slapping and glad-handing.

Wendell's plan was to deliver the painting of the Robinsons to the Five Points. He would deliver the painting, then perhaps have a beer with Tuck at Almack's where he had heard of a new dance called tap or juba jig. The prospect of an adventure pleased him, the idea of finding himself someplace foreign.

Wendell had retrieved *Sands of Morocco* from the Gallery and placed it safe in his room next to the easel that held *The Robinsons*. Now *The Robinsons* in its gilded frame was carefully wrapped and placed in a heavy leather satchel, made for the purpose. He slipped in some sketching paper and *les crayons*: waxes, charcoals, chalks, and pencils. The weather had grown warm enough to wear only a simple vest and not his good one – he did not want thugs thinking him wealthy. He put his flat-brimmed hat on his head and a few coins in his pocket. Before he left, he thanked Cat for not holding a grudge about Lillian, put the tabby into the hall, then closed the unlocked door and set off for Broadway. There Wendell hailed a cab, but within a few blocks decided to jump off and consult his fellows at Pfaff's about his journey.

Henry Clapp waved him over to the alcove under the sidewalk. Pfaff's on a Monday morning was empty save for the little group of bohemians – Tom Aldrich, Henry Clapp, Walt Whitman, Ada Clare, and an inebriated young man they called "Macaroni" – who were having a *Saturday Press* meeting. Papers were strewn about, pencils were working, discussions taking place. Charles Pfaff appeared from the kitchen with a good German lager which he placed in front of Wendell. "*Bitte setzen*, und have a bier," urged the jovial host. Wendell thanked him and sat down to linger.

"Getting this paper out is a big job," remarked Tom Aldrich in a self-congratulatory manner.

"Aye," said Macaroni drunkenly. "Let no effort be spared to extol the idle virtues of bohemia."

"Extol them we will!" laughed Ada Clare. "I believe that's the point of it."

To Wendell, the task did indeed seem daunting, to write, collect, and lay out six columns times four pages backwards in a tray every week. Yet the paper was often quoted in the far corners of the country and even in Europe. "You should be rich by now, Henry, with so many acclamations."

"I am rich in spirit," Clapp asserted, his grey eyes glinting as he paused to light his pipe. "But as I take no payment for flattering reviews, I starve while other papers prosper."

Tom Aldrich pointed to an article on the table. "I see here you have dared to challenge some of *The New American Cyclopedia*'s entries with your own scholarly arguments. Are you trying to destroy them?"

A slow and satisfied look spread across Henry Clapp's features. "Perhaps there is power in a bohemian's willingness to starve."

"So Mr. Parry," said Walt Whitman, "what inspires you to come here this time of day?"

Wendell indicated the satchel and proclaimed his mission to deliver the portrait to the Five Points. "As I have not yet been there, I thought I might seek your advice."

Mr. Whitman's eyes glittered with amusement. "I see," he said, stroking his beard. "Perhaps you were wondering if you should sequester a pistol beneath your vest."

Wendell smiled. "Indeed."

"I love the Bowery myself," Whitman continued. "In just a few blocks you will run into more color and variety of humankind than you thought possible, and all shoved off the sidewalks with the same rude indignity, be they nobility or riff-raff. And you'll be safe enough on the railroad, which will stop conveniently right at Walker and Centre. Below that, don't go with a satchel – they'll take it. Or, if you must, be ever prepared to make a sketch of any menacing tough and say it's for the papers – the gangs thrive on publicity."

"That, and Tammany Hall's largesse," said Aldrich.

Clapp added, "The gangs rioted two years back, during the depression of '57. The state's militia was called in, and the governor replaced the mayor's corrupt Municipal Police with the state's Metropolitan Police. The Muni's wouldn't have it, and the two police forces fought each other near to death in front of City Hall. When the Mets prevailed, the mayor was arrested. They didn't keep him, of course, and he's running again. Now he uses immigrant gangs as his police force and the Mets stay out of the Five Points."

"Aye," agreed Mr. Whitman. "Come November, the Irish gangs will make it very unpleasant for anyone voting against Mayor Wood, while the other choice is the anti-immigrant 'Know-Nothing

Party.'"

"A good reason not to vote," said Clapp. "Too bad the Republicans have not fielded a candidate."

Wendell found the story both amusing and alarming. "So the gangs just bash each other for criminal territory and otherwise do Tammany Hall's bidding?"

"Not quite," said Whitman. "They'll take out your liver if they don't like the look of you – and the mayor will look the other way."

An hour later, full of talk and beer, Wendell took his precious satchel east a few blocks on Bleecker to Bowery and boarded the horse-drawn Harlem Railroad headed for the Five Points. The morning rush being past, he found a window seat and eagerly began to sketch a sad-looking character that squinted through a hairy face beneath a much-abused hat. At the next block, the brakes squealed metal on metal against the rails, bringing the patient horses up with a lurch, and the subject departed. Theater girls began to enter, with shabby wraps thrown over extravagant costumes. They too ignored the artist, but left him time for only a quick sketch before climbing off. Wendell marveled that they would choose to pay for a ride rather than walk the few blocks, but seeing the sidewalks crowded with swells, hawkers, and pick-pockets, he felt their pennies well spent. After an interesting strumpet in red exited before her likeness could be completed, Wendell determined to just watch the scenery – the seedy grandeur of The Bowery that grew in gaudiness and crowding as the railcar rolled downtown.

Presently, the horses followed the rails away from Bowery and skirted the northern edge of the notorious Sixth Ward, only blocks from the heart of the Five Points. The scenery changed to sagging wooden tenements with few windows, and reeking garbage-strewn sidewalks where pigs rooted freely. Here colored and white folks lingered and talked, going nowhere.

As the rails turned again onto Centre, Wendell signaled his stop, and got off where Canal, Walker, and Centre all converge. A heavy odor-filled dampness assailed him, hovering about the street as if the buildings themselves sweated. He found the Walker Street address on a decent brick building above a greengrocer's, and climbed the stairs to the fifth floor and number 5C. Wendell knocked and heard Tuck Robinson call out "Who that?" followed by the sounds of several bolts being thrown before Tuck cracked the door open. "Could y'all wait a few moments?" Before he could close the door, Wendell clearly saw a young lad seated at the table oiling a gun. Mr. Robinson hesitated, then threw the door wide. "Never mind. Y'all come on in."

The tiny apartment was pleasant, clean with lace-covered windows and a small sturdy table where sat young Wilberforce Robinson, oiling the pistol. It was not specifically illegal for the black race to bear arms in New York, but the recent Dred Scott decision had declared Negroes to be non-citizens, which certainly made their Constitutional rights doubtful.

Tuck regarded Wendell uneasily and apologized. "Ruby say she done been here a long time without guns and she don't like 'em neither." Wendell took the proffered seat across from the boy.

"Doesn't like them," Willy muttered without looking up. His father's English seemed an embarrassment, particularly, Wendell surmised, in the presence of a white man.

"Coffee?" asked Tuck and, without waiting an answer, went to the coal-fired brazier in the tiny kitchen corner to get it. Beyond the kitchen was a door that Wendell guessed led to the one bedroom, while young Wilberforce's straw mattress was evident beneath the front windows. On the wall next to the hallway door were colorful rustic oil portraits of Ruby's family, along with several framed daguerreotypes. Wendell saw now why Lillian's gift was so appropriate.

"I want to thank you for sticking up for me," Tuck said in a confiding manner when he'd returned. He placed the steaming coffee in front of Wendell and sat down.

Wendell breathed a sigh. "How did you get out?"

"I cain't talk about that. I weren't cheap!" He grew uneasy. "Mind, I be speakin' out of school, but you do yourself a favor stayin' away from Lillian. When her husband get home, he be wantin' a better accountin' of all them pictures she buy and sell with his money. Still, I thank you. And that's plenty 'nough said."

Wendell's disquiet was growing by the moment. He changed the subject, "It's a lovely place. Did Mrs. Robinson grow up here?"

"Yessir," said Tuck, relieved. "She been here all her life. But the neighborhood ain't nice like it used to be. Used to be all coloreds live round here, respectable families, but now guns is necessary. There's a shame to it, but a man's got to protect his family." Tuck stirred his coffee. "Just yesterday," he continued, "Ruby got run off from the out-house by some low-life Irish jezebel and her jehu. It ain't safe round here." He was gathering momentum, evidently enjoying having someone with whom to vent. "Ruby done gone to a colored school, a good one, right in this here neighborhood. Used to be colored churches, too, and playhouses. Ain't none now since them Irish riff-raff gangs burned 'em down and chased the coloreds out. Willy here, he have to do his book-learning at home from Ruby."

Willy piped up, "And gives you a chance to do your book-learning as well." Clearly Ruby was bringing up the priggish Will to believe in the power of education.

"Had you expected better?" asked Wendell.

"Ah," Tuck relaxed back into his chair. "That's an interesting query. I ain't sure what I expect. Don't know as I expect nothin'. I just wanna get out from where I was! So I ain't regretting – just observing. I be free here to live with my family and protect 'em. And that's something grand. I thank the Lord for that, every blessed day. I got me a lot, there's thems 'at got far worse! Some of them Irish live three or four families in a place this size. But I ain't got no vote, and the Irish do. Ruby and Lillian say they ain't got no vote neither cause they be women, but here I am a man, and it's more a shame to me. And I ain't got a job, the Irish done come and took all the jobs."

Wendell wasn't sure how to respond, not wanting his sympathy to sound condescending. He sipped his coffee and wondered again about the relationship to Lillian. "What about at Almack's?" he said finally. "Do you get on with the Irish there?"

A small smile poked at the corners of Tuck's mouth. "Now Almack's is altogether different. Seem when folks is into they art, such as dancing and playing music – or like you yourself – they bond up with they fellow artists, and it don't make no nevermind what race they from. Myself, I play the fiddle." Young Wilberforce was rolling his eyes again at his father's English, and Wendell quietly hoped he and Ruby wouldn't have too much success correcting it – he liked listening to the soft poetic cadence in Tuck's rich baritone. "That art studio of your'n," Tuck continued, "that where y'all live?"

Wendell nodded.

"How that? Living under one roof with all them other artists there – kinda peculiar, if you don't mind my saying."

"Yes, it is peculiar," laughed Wendell. "I quite like it. In truth, I've never been happier."

Tuck nodded. "I can see where it could be a right good life. Artists is good people. And," said Tuck, "you brought us our anniversary gift and I thank you for that! I been eager to set my eyes on it." They both rose to unveil the prize from where it sat on the floor in its satchel.

They were interrupted by a rhythmic tap on the door, like a code. Tuck picked up the cleaned pistol and cracked the door open, raising the hairs on Wendell's neck. The pistol was handed to someone on the other side amidst whispers, of which Wendell caught, "Lie low a stretch." Willy looked tense as Tuck pushed the door closed and bolted it, then came back to the satchel with nonchalance. He offered no explanation, just, "So let's have us a peek at this here work of art."

As Wendell drew the picture out of its wrappings, his ears were acutely tuned to the outside hallway from which he half expected to hear a gunshot. The cloth fell away, and Tuck whistled under his breath. "My my," he said admiringly. "I knowed Ruby was that pretty, but I never knowed I was!" Wilberforce had risen as well, and came over to see what was surely the most expensive item his family ever owned. His fingers touched the gilded frame reverently, prompting Tuck to admonish his son to wipe his hands.

"Where are you going to hang it?" asked Wendell. He didn't want to appear anxious to leave, though by now he surely was.

"Oh, we got us a place," said Tuck happily. He went over to the wall beside the door and took down a wooden cross that hung there. "This here is going in the bedroom," he said referring to the cross, and in its place he hung the portrait next to the other pictures. It made the small room suddenly into a grand affair. The enraptured Tuck and Willy stood together with father's arm around son's shoulders, admiring it for a long while. Tuck turned to Wendell and began pumping his hand. "I just can't thank you enough, nor Miss Lillian neither. Whewee! I can't wait till Ruby lay her eyes on it!"

Wendell smiled, almost forgetting the threat from the hallway. "I wish all my subjects were so pleased!" he laughed. He put the satchel back together and hastened to make his goodbyes. "I had best be off. I thank you for your hospitality. I thoroughly enjoyed my visit."

"Next time, maybe we go to Almack's," said Tuck.

"Yes," said Wendell, "I'll look forward to it."

As Wendell started down the stairs in the hallway, he heard

hushed whispers below and froze, listening. Even in their quiet, he recognized the cadence of the voices as Southern. The hairs again bristled on Wendell's neck, for he suspected they must be fugitives and that Tuck was involved in something very dangerous — harboring runaway slaves was a serious offense, and having a gun could get a black man hanged.

He waited till he was sure they had departed, then went on down. Outside the greengrocer's he saw them, a small cluster of frightened men, women, and children in ill-fitting city clothes, waiting for him to leave so they could go on up. Wendell was certain that Lillian was involved. With that disturbing insight, he decided he'd seen enough of the Five Points for one day, and hastened to catch the railcar home.

Later that week, he returned from Pfaff's to find *Sands of Morocco* gone and a note from Lillian saying simply that she'd taken it and so sorry she'd missed him. As he pondered this bit of sad news, there was a knock and Thomas Read came in, looking jovial. "It seems we are both in need of company this evening, and as I have two tickets to *Our American Cousin* at Laura Keene's Theater, I hoped you might join me."

"'Birds of a feather gather no moss,'" laughed Wendell, quoting from the popular play. They had a nice supper at a French restaurant nearby and then enjoyed the light comedy, which starred Laura Keene herself.

Afterward, Wendell's mind was again on the week's revelation that Lillian was involved in harboring fugitives – armed fugitives – risking prison for herself and worse. Much as he wanted to join Thomas for an after-theater drink, Wendell's fear it would loosen his tongue prompted him to plead fatigue and retire to his room. He wasn't good with secrets. His dreams of late were full of furtiveness and danger. He wanted to be with Lillian, to protect her, to ply her with questions. If only he could go to her! But he didn't even know where she was.

Chapter 8

The rising sun shone along the shiny cobbles as the carriage bearing Sanford Gifford, Ted Winthrop, and Wendell Parry rolled downtown on West Street, toward a windy rainbow-shrouded wharf at Chambers. The hustle and bustle increased, but not of the sort found on the East side. The men who plied their trade along the Hudson were not bankers, swells, or dandies, but stevedores, laborers, and longshoremen. As the carriage clattered across the railroad tracks to the busy docks, trains blew traffic out of their way, their smokestacks belching black, their brakes squealing against the momentum of massive burdens. All about, cargoes of every description were being loaded and unloaded from railcars, steamers, schooners, and barges, employing lines of sweating men from the world's far corners and impressive looming cranes.

Sanford had gone out onto the dock and was talking to Captain John Collyer of *Rival*, returning with four of the sloop's seamen who heaved their trunks aloft and onto the pretty ship. Boyish excitement gripped the artists as they hurried up the gangplank and took side by side seats on the bench, well beneath an enormous boom and facing bucolic Hoboken.

As the crew cast the lines and made fast the giant sail, Captain Collyer addressed his guests. "We've got the flood tide with us, but the wind is blustering, so we won't carry topsail or jib. I'm afraid, Gentlemen, that the voyage may take longer than planned. Should the heavens open, I've warmed the galley where hot tea is available. I hope any delay will not prove too uncomfortable or inconvenient."

"Not at all, John," said Sanford, who at thirty-seven had spent many years exploring the Hudson River Valley and knew the Captain well. "We want an adventure, or we'd have taken the train."

"Quite," agreed Ted. "I myself am hoping for pirates." The

good skipper laughed and excused himself to attend the tiller – navigating the traffic to gain the open river required all of his attention.

Sanford Gifford rolled a cigarette and, passing the smoke around, the three fell into a pleasant camaraderie. The sail luffed, then came round while the stays creaked overhead. The boat heeled and picked up speed, heading toward open waters.

"Are you a reader, Parry?" asked Ted.

"Aye," said Wendell.

"And what are you reading?"

"Margaret Fuller's *Woman in the Nineteenth Century*." Wendell flushed, not sure a man should be reading Margaret Fuller.

Sanford laughed, "Did Lillian give it to you?"

"She suggested it."

"Ha ha. The ladies seem ever ready to recommend Margaret Fuller to their gentlemen friends," Sanford said. "Though I confess, I have not read her myself. Do you like it?"

"It has given another way of understanding the gentler sex."

"I met Miss Fuller," said Sanford, "and would not describe her as the 'gentler sex.' Back when she was reporting for the *New York Tribune,* she had rather a scandal opposing Mr. Poe."

"Did you know him, too?" asked Wendell, impressed.

"Indeed, yes. When I arrived in Greenwich Village in 1846, he was the true king of the bohemians. His ghost hovers over Henry Clapp to this day, and speaks with him often."

The winds had steadied and the boat was on a good run, angling lightly past the massive cragging cliffs of the Palisades.

"How quickly is the city left behind!" cried Wendell.

"And what, Mr. Winthrop, are you reading?" asked Sanford.

It was Ted's turn to blush. Half standing and leaning into the salt spray of the heeling boat, he put his hand over his heart and quoted a voce falsetto, "*'If all else perished, and he remained, I should still continue to be; and if all else remained, and he were annihilated, the universe would turn to a mighty stranger: I should not seem a part of it.'"*

The others laughed heartily at his presentation. "Winthrop, no!" exclaimed Wendell, "*Wuthering Heights*?!"

"I am a romantic," confessed the chagrined Ted, "'tis my fourth read of it."

From the tiller, Captain Collyer asked, "Have you read Melville's *Moby Dick*?" They confessed they had not. Captain Collyer rued of the great writer's latest and failed work, "No one has interest anymore in whaling, with coal gas now replacing whale oil. It is seen as antiquated."

Sanford said, "Ned Booth tells me his brother Wilkes has invested in petroleum, which may replace even coal gas."

"Ah, the actor," said Collyer. "He shall doubtless triumph. It seems the new always replaces the old, even before it is old."

The ship made good time past the Palisades and into the green rolling countryside where white clouds, trees and mountains reflected brightly on the water's rippling surface. On Wendell's sketch pad, he noted the pigments he would use to paint it, '*viridian, lapis, ochre, cobalt yellow.*' *Rival*'s merry crew feigned racing a train that chugged along the water's edge, as the sloop passed steamers towing impossibly long barges, and gained the dock at Irvington shortly after ten on the clock.

Asher Durand was waiting for them and amidst greetings and introductions, climbed aboard. The sixty-year-old was well-known to Wendell as patriarch of the Hudson River artists, and meeting him in so casual a setting confirmed Wendell's own status – he felt almost giddy with success.

By now the wind was fair, the weather never better for sailing. Durand sat down with his old friend, the skipper, who offered Asher condolences on the recent loss of his wife. He handed him the tiller with instructions to 'keep her steady.'

"Seeing Washington Irving has put me in a nostalgic frame,"

said Asher. He had a fringe of chin-beard on a weathered angular face and blowing white hair that made him look quite the old salt. "Though he is still vigorous, I fear he will not be with us much longer."

"Why so?" asked Sanford.

"He doesn't care to live long enough to see his young country torn apart, which he now feels a certainty."

There was silence – no one wished to discuss the possibility of civil war.

Captain Collyer lit his pipe and began to reminisce. "I miss the packet ship days," he said. "Ferrying you artists was good fun."

"Is there no market for that now?" asked Durand wistfully.

"Not for passengers – they go by steamer or by rail – always in such a hurry." Collyer took a puff, and looked almost confiding when he said, "This sloop will be out of business in a year or two – all the sailboats will be. The number of barges that the steamers tow has gotten too many to tack against. Hundreds of yards long they are, and more of them every year. You just can't beat across 'em."

"It's much as the artists' situation," said Durand at the tiller. "The Hudson River is yesterday's vanity. Now it's the Rockies, the Andes, places well beyond an old man's reach. And photographers will take over realism. They've already taken over the limners' business. To differentiate, art will become vague impressions."

Wendell, who had been watching a wind-blown spider spin his web in the rigging, protested. "But a photograph is no kin to a painting. It hasn't the luminosity or the spirit."

"For many people, a painting is just a way to see a place they haven't been," said Ted.

"I don't much like vague impressions as paintings," Wendell pouted, "they seem crude and heavy-handed."

The Captain laughed, "By Jove, it's good to hear not all young people embrace everything new! There're folks would replace the soul with a machine if they could!"

"An artist seeks to celebrate God," said Sanford, "but a machine seeks to replace Him."

"I must confess," said Wendell, "I am fascinated by cameras."

"Machines are enthralling," admitted the skipper, "like a fine opiate. You did the better part, young man, by choosing to follow Nature, for whom the machine is ever a mortal enemy."

By now, all the artists had sketch pads in hand and were rendering impressions of the Hudson River Valley with its nestled boroughs – all except Wendell, whose excitement at soon joining Lillian had him sketching her as Lilith, the wild and wonderful first woman, and himself as the angel Gabriel who alone could tame her.

As evening fell, the sloop *Rival* passed West Point and came in sight of the dock at Newburgh, a bustling river port of brick buildings and small manufacturing plants. Soon, the able crew made fast and the artists bid their farewells to the good captain.

The Weigand Tavern and Inn on Liberty Street was a sorry wooden affair with few windows, and a boozy boisterousness that leaked from it onto the busy sidewalk. Inside was dense with smoke and beer, but not a lady in sight and no sign of Lillian. Wendell asked the barkeep, apparently also the innkeep, if Lillian had checked in. "We don't cater to ladies traveling alone," replied the disagreeable man. "I sent her to do her business elsewhere." Wendell felt a rush of panic, and found himself gripping the innkeep's shirtfront.

"*Merde à l'enfer!* You sent her alone into the streets?" His companions were pulling him back, trying to constrain him.

"God rot your impudent hide!" shouted the innkeeper. "Choose your weapon! Pistols? I'll gladly shoot ye." It took the three others to hold Wendell's arms as he struggled to get at the man again.

"You will apologize to the lady first!" Wendell yelled as they hustled him out of the bar.

"Lady? No woman traveling alone is a lady," shouted the vile man after him. "She is a siren and a temptress, and an abomination before God!"

An older man followed them out anxiously, shouting for attention over their commotion. "Did you say you were looking for Miss Flax? Sirs, I beg you! She left a note."

Wendell forgot the barkeep as the worried artists huddled around the letter, which informed them that Lillian had gone on to the Eagle Hotel at Fishkill Landing and would try to check in there as Mrs. Wendell Parry.

"Please accept my contrition, Wendell," offered Asher Durand. "This tavern was recommended by a fellow artist with thought to save money and no thought of having a lady along. But all is not lost. I believe the ferry is still running to Fishkill Landing and the Eagle Hotel."

Wendell suddenly desired to part ways. "If your thought is to save money," said he, "why not stay here tonight and I will go alone to meet Miss Flax."

"We can't stay with that scurrilous cur!" protested Ted.

"No matter," Wendell persisted. "Had she checked in as Mrs. Wendell Parry here, she'd have been better treated." The companions agreed, and that they would meet at the Eagle Hotel's restaurant in the morning.

Wendell had a bit of a wait at the dock, until finally the graceful paddle wheeler pulled up and its gangplank lowered. As a full moon rose and sparkled over Newburgh Bay, Wendell began to relax and very much look forward to seeing Lillian.

The Eagle Hotel, in contrast to the Weigand Tavern and Inn, was alive with stylishness and laughter and surrounded by elegant grounds, gas lamps and carriages. The concierge assured him that his wife awaited him in the lobby. Wendell tipped him to take the trunk to his room, then saw her from behind, seated with an older gentleman at a round table, engaged in animated conversation. The curve of her neck beneath her upswept hair excited him, and his stride lengthened. "Lillian," he called as he approached. She turned and disarmed him with her smile.

"Come Wendell," she gestured, "and meet my friend." The gentleman stood and reached out his hand. "This is Mr. Gerrit Smith," Lillian continued. "And this is the awaited artist, Mr. Wendell Harte Parry." Wendell shook the hand of the well-known abolitionist and land reformer who had run for President and been a congressman with the Free-Soil Party. He wondered while he did so what deeper abolitionist mischief Lillian might be into.

"Miss Flax tells me you are shortly on your way to Ithaca," said Mr. Smith as Wendell sat down and partook of the victuals set before him. The 62-year old Smith, with piercing eyes and an unruly white beard, looked as radical as his reputation suggested. "Could I interest you in a commission?"

"I am always interested in a commission," Wendell admitted.

"I am dabbling in Ithaca real estate and have become quite entranced with the beauty of the place. There is a magnificent gorge and a falls called Buttermilk. Do you know them?"

"Very well," said Wendell. His smile deepened as his hand squeezed Lillian's under the table.

"I would be interested in four pieces altogether," continued Mr. Smith. "One of the gorge, one of the falls, one of Cayuga Lake and one of farmland and pastoral scenery. Would $1000 for the four be sufficient?"

"I'm sure it will," said Wendell, trying to remain calm – $1000 was enough for three years rent. "I will be returning to the city come September, and will have sketches then for your approval."

"You'll be gone till September?" gasped Lillian. "It seems so long."

"I could return sooner, and could be available to help in your endeavors," said Wendell, and, hoping to impress Lillian, added, "with which I concur wholeheartedly."

"Thank you, my boy. That's nice." Gerrit Smith pondered a moment, seeming to size Wendell Parry up as he did so. "My intention is that parcels of land be sold to members of the Negro race, to give them a franchise. As you may know, unlike the white race, coloreds must still own land in order to vote in this state. From what you know of Ithaca, will they be accepted there?"

Wendell considered his answer carefully. "I think with time, they will. I followed your experiment at North Elba, and feel perhaps that the Afric community needed to grow at a slower pace. Rural people do not wish to be suddenly inundated with outsiders, colored or no."

"Yes, I see what you mean. Ironically, the Afric community insists on the safety of large numbers. Yet a greater reason that North Elba failed was the poor quality of its mountain soil for farming. On that score, I anticipate more success at Ithaca." They exchanged visit cards and Mr. Smith rose to go. "I must depart at dawn's first light. I am delighted to meet you, and look forward to your sketches." Wendell stood as well and bowed over the hand that shook his. Then Mr. Smith bowed low over Lillian's hand and kissed it. "And thank you, my dear Lily Ann. A pleasure, as always."

As the good man walked away, Wendell was bursting with questions for Lillian, and struggled to be discreet. He sat back down and took her hands across the table, leaning in towards her. "How deeply involved are you, Lillian, if I may ask?" He spoke quietly, so that no one save her could hear. She looked startled and somewhat frightened.

"How deeply involved am I – with you?"

Wendell was amused. "No, that's not what I meant, but it is perhaps the more interesting question."

She smiled, evidently relieved at his good humor. "Whatever you meant, I'm sure I cannot answer. It all shifts from moment to moment, sometimes quite like a dream."

Now Wendell looked serious. "I want to be both real and in your dreams, *Mon Coeur*. I want to be part of your life. I have very much struggled with not knowing where to reach you or when I would see you again, and all the while afraid you were in danger."

Her eyes filled with gratitude, and she squeezed his hands. "If ever I am in danger, I will truly come to you," she said. She looked at him with such adoration, Wendell hardly felt the sting of her rebuff. 'It will come in time,' he thought, 'the relationship is yet young.'

"Well Mrs. Parry," he said playfully, "shall we call it a night? I am most eager to see what elegant accommodations await us."

"I assure you they are adequate, Mr. Parry." She laughed as they stood and she took his arm. They strolled toward the staircase, he admiring her smart mauve travel dress, and apologizing for the trouble she had encountered at the inn in Newburgh. "I forget where I am sometimes," she sighed. "It's my fault for attempting to register as an unmarried woman."

As soon as they rounded the corner in the stairs and out of sight of the lobby, Wendell grabbed her hand and ran, dragging her laughing up the stairs. "This floor?" he said, and when she shook her head, yanked her up another flight. They were breathless and giggling when the room was reached, and she shoved the key in the lock. Without hesitating, he picked her up and carried her across the threshold.

He laid her on the bed and kissed her, then began to undo the topmost tiny button of the scores of tiny buttons running down the front of her gown. She pushed him away. "Please," she said, "I must insert a honeyed lemon." She rose and drew a small pouch out of her carpet bag. "I will return," she promised, and disappeared down the hallway toward the washroom.

Wendell took the opportunity of her absence to light a candle and bring forth his muse mirror for a rather hasty ritual. She returned just as he was concluding. She stood respectfully quiet while he wrapped the mirror and put it away with a whispered closing. "I've interrupted something," she said, enthralled. Wendell flushed.

"We both have our secrets," he murmured and, standing before her, began again to undo her buttons. A mesmeric aura enveloped them in the candlelight as Wendell worked his way down slowly, reverencing the outlines of her body. Finally, he dropped to one knee to undo the last buttons, and looked up at her curves swelling beneath the exposed camisole, crowned by an angelic face. "You are so beautiful," he breathed.

"And if I weren't, Wendell, what then?" and he saw her look of fear. He stood, searching her eyes. "Would you still want me if I weren't beautiful?" she asked again. Her question touched him.

Suddenly he grinned, picturing her quite differently. "You mean if a wart grew on your nose?"

A smile crept through her melancholy, "Aye," she said, "if a wart grew on my nose."

"It would be a true work of art," he declared, "your beauty set off by a wart – and you, unlike my other subjects, would not ask me to paint it out." Wendell raised her chin and said earnestly, *"Mon Coeur,* I'll still love you when we are both wrinkled and sagging, with no hair and no teeth. I will love you always, I am sure of it. Even should you reject me, I will love you." She regarded him, her mood shifting. "Right now, Lillian, we are young and beautiful. And I would celebrate that with you."

When they had satisfied their passion, they lay in each other's arms in the flickering candlelight. "I am truly at home with you," said Lillian, "as it were where I am meant to be." She kissed his ear, a soft caress of her hand trailing across his naked belly.

Wendell murmured, "I have been wont to ask, though it may seem not my concern…"

"What is it, sweet Harte?"

"Since visiting the Robinsons, I have worried for your safety." She froze, and he heard her slow and measured breaths in the darkness. "I'm sorry," he said quickly, "I have overstepped my bounds."

"No," she said, "you have overstepped nothing. I was but thinking how to answer." She was quiet again, avoiding his eyes in the candle light. "Tuck told me what transpired that day. There is nothing to concern yourself about. It's only a small school behind the market, where coloreds are taught by Ruby to read and write. Except for financial support, I am not involved."

As she spoke, her discomfort betrayed her. Wendell had seen the fugitives there and Lillian was risking prison by sheltering them. He was about to speak to it, then felt the warning pressure of her hand. Finally Wendell said, "You know they have guns."

"As does everyone in the Five Points." She resumed kissing his ear. "Pray, don't mention it again. I am in no danger." And though he did not find her pronouncement assuring, he did find her charms alluring, and roused himself again to be with her.

Chapter 9

Next morning, the buckboard got an early start from Newburgh, and paid two cents toll to travel the south plank road westward through the countryside. Metal wheels slipped noisily along the dew-wet wood behind the hollow-sounding footfalls of the horses. Miss Josephine Walters had joined them, and sat between Lillian and Asher Durand, who controlled the reins keeping the horses at a leisurely pace to match the other artists on foot. A tall and pretty girl, just Lillian's age, Josephine had a hearty laugh and flame red hair beneath a diminutive hat. She was dressed in fashionable plaid taffeta with moderate hoops and tiny shoes not well-suited to hiking. Lillian, as was her wont, eschewed the corset and hoop for a comfortable moss green day dress, the skirt reefed and tied almost to the knees and high soft leather boots.

As Wendell walked behind with Gifford and Winthrop, he breathed deep of the moist air and felt the familiar boyhood thrill of being in the woods. An oak canopy stretched overhead into cloud-dappled sunshine, shading giant white and lavender flower clusters of rhododendron in full bloom. Here and there were magnificent chestnuts and stands of sugar maple, white ash, and yellow birch, each species with its own distinctive shades of bark and leaves. All around, honeybees buzzed in the flowers of black raspberry brambles, while robins and red cardinals sang as they feasted on purple chuckleberries, and turkeys gobbled in the underbrush.

The artists continued on in reverence, each seeing finished paintings in the luminous dappling of the woodland. Finally, the small band came to a clearing where appeared a pretty lake called Orange beside a rolling verdant hillside covered with yellow stands of naturalized tansy and a grazing herd of white tail deer. In the distance was a small red barn with black and white dairy cows.

Durand pulled up on the reins and, with a whinny from the horses, the wheels squealed to a halt. "While I very much wish to sketch," he said, "I wish to eat even more." They found a sandy bank beneath a tree to lay their cloth, and brought forth red wine, bread, and cheese *à la Française.*

Attention riveted on the new girl as the men sought to ascertain her story. Ted tried to talk but was surprisingly tongue-tied, and ended up closely examining his fingernails. Sanford Gifford spoke, "You are the student of Asher Durand, an artist known to not take students. Pray tell, how was this miracle accomplished?" At this, the girl flushed as red as her hair and, ungifted in articulation, fell to laughing wildly. But for the laughter, she was as tongue-tied as Ted and since she towered over him in height, they made a comical pair. Her laugh quickly infected the others, who lifted their wine glasses in salute to her.

Durand came to her aid. "Believe me," he said jovially, "this girl gives the lie to Emerson that every artist was once an amateur. I discovered her enrolled in an art class at Cooper Union, and immediately invited her to apprentice with me."

"It is no small thing to be a student of Asher," said Sanford. "I do believe you are the only one." Then he added, teasing, "He will, of course, teach you to paint as he does – close woodland scenes in vertical format."

Asher laughed. "She already paints like that, which may be what draws me to her! I prefer the intimacy of close woodland spaces, where trees and rocks can be felt as hosts in their own home."

Wendell was lying on his back, gazing at a circling flock of buzzards, to whose awareness he'd nudged Lillian. Now his attention was drawn to the group with a question from Sanford, "And why, Parry, is your preference for the horizontal?"

Wendell considered a moment. "I like to portray the land as the Indians saw it, free and expansive, without borders between private owners. One can only observe Nature's unity if one steps back from it." He had heard this concept as a boy, perhaps from reading Emerson, and it had always stuck with him. Indeed, it evoked a knot in his throat, some innate memory of his grandmother's people.

"Ah," said Durand, "and I have always been drawn to the fences and hedges of the settlements and grazing cattle. I like to see Nature as home to man, where man and God commune. Perhaps 'tis a generational difference, the wild untouched landscape of youthful imagination being currently whelmed with overuse."

"Or perhaps," said Ted, finding his tongue at last, "'tis a matter of age itself. When you are young, you look forward to adventure in the wild; when you are old, you look back on accomplishment."

"Nay," objected Wendell. "Artists seek timelessness, a transcendence of the temporal. 'Tis the transcendent spirit that is important, not the scene."

"Agreed. And I," said Gifford grandly, looking intimately into Josephine's brown eyes, "seek for something luminous and biblical in my landscapes. My mountains, like Sinai, are shrouded in mystery and touch a majestic sky." To Sanford's chagrin, the intensity of his gaze provoked another wild outburst of laughter from the girl. He quickly turned to Lillian to distract his embarrassment. "Lillian, surely you must paint?"

"I have tried, of course," said Lillian. "I love art – and artists – above all else. But I have no gift for it."

"Do you have a preference, one style for another?" asked Asher.

"I do," she said, "but as a patroness, I would not want my preference to unfairly influence your painting." The arch in Sanford's eyebrow as he shot a glance at Wendell prompted her to coyly add, "And lest you think that my preference can be unfairly influenced in turn, let me say that Mr. Parry has refused to sell me any of his art." This set off another round of laughter.

The picnic packed, sketch pads were brought out. Asher and Josephine headed to the edge of the wooded area to find a stream that fed the lake, while Wendell, Sanford, Ted and Lillian climbed the grassy bank.

Upon the bluff, Ted and Lillian were quietly writing while the artists made their sketches. After much of the afternoon had elapsed, Wendell inquired what Lillian was writing.

"I am writing a speech," Lillian said delighted, "which I am to take on the lyceum circuit. I have been accepted in six cities thus far, the first next week in Owego."

Wendell was stunned and proud. "How did you come to be invited?"

"'Twas Frederic Douglass recommended me." Her audience looked at her curiously, that she would know Frederic Douglass, the escaped slave who spoke so eloquently on abolition's behalf. Lillian flushed and went quiet – it was another of her secrets.

"Perhaps you will read it for us after supper," invited Wendell.

"It's not ready yet," she said.

As evening approached, Lillian let down her hair and crowned herself with a golden circlet of camphor-smelling tansies to ward off mosquitoes. Lightning bugs danced and played at the water's edge while she and Wendell picked handfuls of the pretty flowers to take back to camp. The twilight of the sun set cobalt purple clouds ablaze with linings of crimson and gold. Wendell thought she'd never looked more glorious and told her so with kisses.

They found their way back to their comrades, seated on logs around a campfire enjoying rations of beef jerky and beer. Beyond the firelight stood three conical tents of oil cloth, each containing carefully arranged sleeping comforts, while from deeper shadows, the horses whinnied in quiet conversation with each other.

"Whilst you were at the Weigand," Wendell asked the three men, "did you see the ghost that is said to haunt it?"

"I wish we had," said Asher, "'twould be a good time for a ghost story."

"Perhaps they had brought in a medium to exorcise it," speculated Sanford. "It seems unkind to let a soul wander about lost, just for the amusement of tourists." He looked over at the ladies. "Do you believe in ghosts, Miss Flax?"

"Perhaps – though I would think they were more commonly seen."

"They are commonly seen," said Wendell earnestly, his eyes lit with the flickering fire, "by those with sight to see them."

"And do you commonly see ghosts, Wendell?" asked Lillian.

"My sister is a practicing medium," he revealed, "I have been to séances with purpose to talk to my grandmother, and have been amply convinced of her presence."

Josephine Walters now surprised everyone by speaking up. "Calling forth the dead is dangerous," she said, her eyes large with remembered fear. "'Tis addictive, and consuming."

"Do you know this of your own experience?" asked Sanford.

"Yes," she said tremulously, then inexplicably the wild laugh. Was she teasing them, or insane? Sanford was first to join the laughter, then all save Lillian obliged – better to think it a joke and let the matter rest.

Lillian, however, was intent on finding out more. "What does it consume?" she asked.

The girl flushed and looked down at her hands. "The soul," she whispered. This time she stifled her guffaw.

"Poor dear," said Lillian tenderly, "you have had a shock, haven't you – are you now recovered?"

The girl shook her head. "It's not me, it's my mother. My whole childhood and 'til now, she speaks to ghosts – many ghosts – obsessively." There was another loud snort which, on effort to stifle, turned to sobs. Lillian put her arms around the poor girl and pulled her close. The men sat with quiet concern, poking occasionally at the fire. At last the girl took a deep breath and sat up, blinking and wiping her eyes as if waking from a dream.

"I'm glad 'twas your mother and not you," said Lillian, attempting cheer, "since I am to share my tent with you. I don't much like ghosts." Lillian picked up her guitar, and waited with concern as Josephine rose and headed for the tent. "Shall I go after her?" whispered Lillian to the men. But straight away, Josephine emerged carrying a fiddle.

"I hope we know some of the same tunes," she said to Lillian as she sat again on the log.

They began to play, the fiddler surprising everyone with a polished performance and perfect harmony.

"...Silk and Satin flounces and Hoops of all dimensions
Had this dame of New York City fair
Soon the fashion changing, her wardrobe disarranging
She'd cry I declare I have nothing to wear."

The singing continued into the evening, everyone joining in on the favorites, until at last they all retired happily to bed.

Idyllic summer days passed quickly with playful romps and everyone becoming more comfortable with one another, till even the bashful Josephine and the more bashful Ted Winthrop were peeling off their clothes to swim. The three suitors made a friendly truce since each knew the others were as besotted as he.

Too soon, it was the last night. Around the campfire, Wendell asked if Lillian's speech was ready. "A much shortened version, perhaps," she said shyly, "with much sympathy from the audience for my amateur efforts." Being assured that she was among friends, she stepped forth with guitar in hand and gave a curtsy.

"I bid you good evening," Lillian began her speech, *"and thank you for your kind welcome. But I doubt 'twill be a good evening, for I speak not of this lovely night, but of the eve of war. I may be*

only a young woman, but I know that war is never good, not a good evening, nor a good morning, nor a good day. In my opinion – and we ladies do have opinions!" – here she waited for the laughter, then continued gravely, *"there has never been a good war, save perhaps our own dear Revolution. But even all the sacrifices of that hallowed memory will have been for naught if brother takes up arms against brother and tears this union apart.*

"I know you say, 'But what of slavery? How can such a vile institution be endured?' And I say with you, 'It cannot.' But were we honest and not hypocrites, we of the North would also end the slavery in our own house."

As Wendell watched her, full of love, he found her words prompted a deeper passion for the subject, and he listened attentively.

"Perhaps you say, 'But we have not slavery here!' True, the African slave does not toil in our fields for bed and board, nor clean our houses. No! Workers in the North receive a pittance for their hard work, not sufficient for bed and board, but are blessedly free to leave their employ. In that, we are far superior to our Southern comrades. But I speak to you of Northern slavery none-the-less.

"Primarily, I speak to you of persons without property. Ownership of the land or business for which one devotes his labors is the only path to freedom. No other has yet been devised since that noble red man was wont to own all things in common with his neighbors. For a person without property, life is slavery. Consider again the Northern poor, who often survive in conditions less healthful than the African slave must endure in the field. And not to own one's home means subjecting oneself to the whims of the landlord, often capricious and cruel as many slave owners."

Here, Lillian boldly began to play a song of her creation to a tune similar to *Turkey in the Straw*, whilst Josephine, the men, and especially Wendell, foot-tapped in rapt admiration.

"Oh, the factory shut its gate
And the landlord raised his rate,
The almshouse is full and woe begotten.
I could go to Alabama
And live there with my Gramma,
But you don't get paid for pickin' cotton.

Oh there's thievin' in the street
And I don't have what to eat,
The church gives me food that's almost rotten.
I could go to Alabama
And live there with my Gramma,
But you don't get paid for pickin' cotton."

Everybody joined in the chorus, clapping and tapping their feet.

"Oh, you don't get paid,
Oh you don't get paid,
You don't get paid for pickin' cotton
I could go to Alabama
And live there with my Gramma,
But you don't get paid for pickin' cotton."

"My friends, my most wonderful audience," Lillian continued passionately, following the spate of applause, *"you of the elite and privileged classes – the answer for the poor, and including the Negro slave, lies in the right of workers to become shareholders in the enterprises for which they labor. Above all, workers of the North must make common cause with their enslaved brothers of the South – a common uprising! – and together form a union against unjust conditions. It is a workers' cause and must be seen as a*

workers' cause.

"With war, not only would the soldier and the family suffer, but the freed slaves would flood into the North, competing for jobs and tenements with the poor already here, driving wages further down and rents further up, pitting freedman against worker, causing riots and hardship. But with a socialist model, wherein all men – and women! – have ownership of their means, why would war be necessary, as the cotton-picker will own his share of the plantation and finally be content to work the fields, as the factory worker will own his share of the factory and move to have conditions there made decent? God did not fashion men – or women – to be bereft of hope and destitute, and this great nation should not either.

"I thank you kind souls for your attention, and once again on this beautiful night, I bid you good evening, and pray that it is not the eve of war."

Here she curtsied, and sat back down by the fire to thunderous applause. "Bravo!" was heard, as well as "Hear, hear!" and "Well said."

Wendell slid his arm around her waist and was surprised to feel the brave girl tremble. His ardent kiss upon her cheek landed on wet tears. "Forgive me," she sniffled, "I am so gratified at your reception. It means so much to me that I should finally be able to earn my own money." Her breath caught. "I know you had planned to go to Ithaca, but..."

"I would love to," Wendell finished for her. "I had hoped you'd ask." She sighed and snuggled gratefully against him.

Chapter 10

The church spires of the Village of Owego caught the evening light across the Susquehanna River. Wendell sat at the hotel window with his sketch pad and added formulas in the margins for the colors he was seeing – he was eager to master the many shades of green made possible by the new viridian pigment he had brought back from Paris. Behind him at the secretary, Lillian sighed over the final wording of her speech.

"You are overly concerned, *Mon Coeur*," said Wendell. "Your speech is wonderful."

"You don't think it too strident? The lyceum wants its lectures to be informational, not inflammatory."

Wendell put down his *crayons* and gave her his attention. "What part do you think inflammatory?"

She snorted derisively. "All of it. They think my speech will be about the right of women to speak publicly. Indeed, there is no other subject about which women may speak publicly."

"But since it is Frederic Douglass recommended you, it must be assumed you will speak of slavery."

Lillian looked at him lovingly, as at a child. "My dear Harte, are you so naive?" She rose and came over to him, then sat on his lap and put her arms around his neck, teasing. "Of course you are – you're a man."

Wendell grinned. "Not without charms, surely."

"Aye," she surrendered, "not without charms."

The seats were filled but not overflowed at the modestly-sized Methodist Episcopal Church on Main Street. Wendell sat in the back noticing that he was one of the few men there. Whatever Lillian had to say, the women were eager to hear her.

A man introduced her, saying not much about her save that she was new to the lyceum circuit. Lillian stepped to the pulpit, arranged her bonnet, strapped on her guitar and cleared her throat. *"Ladies and Gentlemen of the lyceum, I bid you Good Evening..."*

The ladies put aside their fans and leaned forward with expressions of astonishment and pleasure as they discerned that the topic was slavery. Lillian was emboldened by their interest. When she at last had them singing along with her, *"You don't get paid..."* Wendell knew the speech was a triumph. His heart swelled with pride in her.

Other thoughts surprised him: Had she an income of her own, might she divorce and marry him? But wasn't he a bohemian, a free-lover? Wendell had to admit what his heart had already told him – that he wished to marry her with his every breath.

Back at the hotel and exceptionally pleased with herself, Lillian was giddy with desire for him. Their lovemaking went on till the wee hours, and when she fell happily asleep in his arms, Wendell thought he had at last found the key to her: "When she is happy with herself, she is happy with me." It was not something over which he had much control, yet he rose early and found breakfast to bring her, along with the morning paper which, he was sure, would contain a glowing review of her speech.

Lillian declared herself a queen in his care as she imbibed the potatoes and searched the paper for the review. Alas, it was too soon. The review would not come until the following day. In the meantime, the picturesque Village of Owego provided ice cream and a bowling alley, shops, and parks on the river.

They strolled arm in arm, the very picture of young lovers. There was no doubt now that Wendell would accompany Lillian to the remaining five lyceum lectures – he happily wired his family in Ithaca that his visit was delayed.

The next morning, Wendell awoke to the sound of crying. Lillian was sitting on the bed, fully dressed, having already retrieved the morning paper.

"What is it?" asked Wendell alarmed. Wracked with sobs, she handed him the review:

"A socialist screed was delivered at this week's lyceum by a woman – we cannot call her a lady – for whom it seems Everything is Slavery. *As she rails against slavery in the South, she rails equally against 'slavery' in the North, decrying as 'wage-slavery' even honest employment.*

"Further Miss Lillian Flax, by which name she introduced herself, was accompanied to Owego by a man. Since they registered at the hotel under the name of 'Mr. and Mrs. Smith,' it can be assumed they are not married. As most socialists, Miss Flax is doubtless a 'free-lover' and deems marriage, along with everything else, to be 'slavery.' It is a scandal that Owego would give such a woman a podium from which to insult our own ladies and incite them with dangerous and un-ladylike rhetoric."

Wendell felt his stomach knot. "What does this mean?"

She stood, gasping, flailing her arms. Her face was filled with agony.

"It's nothing," Wendell pleaded. "One review. One man's review. The audience loved you. Surely you will continue the tour."

"Yes, of course I'll finish the tour," then added ruefully, "and this review will precede me at every stop."

"Will your husband hear of it?"

She looked at him, sniffling. "I pray not. Flax is my mother's name. Mr. Ferguson knows my maiden name as Lily Ann O'Leary. Still, it is but a matter of time. And then there're the others..."

The unspoken conclusion hung until Wendell voiced it. "So you will continue without me."

Lillian nodded. When she came into his arms, her body trembled. That night, she spurned his advances and fell into a clinging, fitful sleep.

The wide-gauged steam train lumbered noisily through rolling farmland and dense forest, depositing in its wake a grimy layer of coal-black soot. Soon it reached wooded giant palisades where shallow and endless switchbacks assisted its ascent. Its pace crawled to almost halting, and it seemed frequently in danger of rolling back down. Wendell had been sketching the sleeping passengers, mostly merchants in waistcoats and bowler hats, but now he turned to the dramatic view through the gritty windows. This was the scenery for which Upstate New York was famous, with picturesque and solitary trees clinging precariously to each craggy outcropping, and huge gashes through the cliffs where fell magnificent waterfalls. He had sketched views like this many times and never tired of it.

As the train finally reached level ground and rolled into Ithaca Station, Wendell was relieved that, despite his time away, everything looked familiar – including his 29-year-old sister, Catherine Cayuga Parry, who sat in a buckboard by the tracks. She wore a patient chiseled face above quiet gingham and a single braid of thick dark hair. Soon they were embracing and loading his trunk. Catherine let her younger brother drive the team, wending their way through pretty farms and woodlands on carefully maintained dirt roads.

After pleasantries, Wendell ventured into more personal matters. "Are you not tired of living with Father? It seems by now you would have married or otherwise left home."

"Ah," she sighed, "it's a question I frequently ask myself. I wish to marry for love, and have been recently left heart-broken. Father needs someone to help him, which my beau was willing enough to do had father made himself more affable. And here I have resentment of you, dear Brother, as you have ever been free to go where you will, whilst I have been left to keep the home-fires burning."

"I had not thought of Father as needy," spoke Wendell in

dismay. "Surely he is able, and the neighbors still help each other with planting and harvest."

"I wrote to you of his foot injury," claimed the surprised Catherine. "Did you not know he has difficulty walking?"

"No, I didn't know, not a thimble full." Wendell was shocked. He reined the horses to a stop, and turned to look at her. "You wrote me last year of an injury, which I assumed to be of passing inconvenience. Is it the injury that makes him ill-tempered? Can he walk?"

"It's not the injury so much," agonized his sister, "as his fear that I should marry and leave him alone. He is still affable enough, except to my suitors."

Wendell put his arm around her shoulders and hugged her. "I'm sorry," he said, "I did not know. Has Father no money with which to hire help?"

Catherine's response was muffled as she hid her face in her hands, looking destitute. "Nay. We have only such as I can bring in from eggs and séances, and the small crops he can still manage." She looked up, clear-eyed where he thought she had been crying. "The neighbors offer help, but as he is of no help to them, they are not indebted – their obligations must first be elsewhere."

Wendell felt a moment of panic. "Does he, like you, begrudge me my freedom?"

"Assuredly he does," she said flatly. She straightened and he turned back to driving, going slower now, less eager to reach their destination. But by the time he turned into the familiar drive, scattering the chickens, he was anxious to see his father and make amends.

Harte Jefferson Parry was standing on the porch of the aging farmhouse, leaning on a cane as his children approached. Still an attractive man at not-quite-fifty, he was considerably blonder than they, clean-shaven with somber blue eyes and the same strong chin as his son. To Wendell's relief, he wore a welcoming smile.

Wendell leapt from the seat and strode to his father, leaving Catherine in casual family custom to climb down on her own. As Wendell held out his hand, the elder Harte gripped it with both of his, letting his cane clatter to the ground. He pulled his son close, and to Wendell's surprise, hugged him tightly. "My boy," he said, laughing and patting Wendell's back, "my boy."

Wendell followed him inside and was pleased to revisit the old family portraits – accurate likenesses in crude but compelling strokes, that still hung on the flowered wallpaper; he had always been charmed by his father's paintings. Soon they were gathered round the little square kitchen table, upon which his sister had set bowls of chicken soup alongside plates of salad and biscuits. Catherine took Wendell's one hand while her father took his other, and, with all holding hands in a circle, she closed her eyes. As she began her blessing, Wendell glanced questioningly at his father who shrugged indulgently at this ritual that had apparently become a family fixture.

> *"Thanks be to Mother Earth for food.*
> *Thanks be to Father Sun for fire.*
> *Thanks be to the rivers for water.*
> *Thanks be to the wind for breath.*
> *Thanks be to Hyenwatha for his wisdom.*
> *Thanks be to the Great Peacemaker for the Law of Peace.*
> *Thanks be to Creator God for all life.*
> *Dogehs. "*

"Amen," said father Parry, somewhat incongruously. Catherine opened her eyes and smiled radiantly.

"Beautiful. This is new since I was last here," commented Wendell, moved and curious as to what prompted such honoring of forsaken roots.

"It was taught me by my spirit guide," responded his sister.

"When I go into mediumistic trance, Hyenwatha himself speaks through me." Wendell looked at his father questioningly, prompting a subtle upward roll of the older man's eyeballs. Catherine caught the impertinence and stood abruptly, throwing down her napkin.

"I do not expect you to understand, Father, as you are not Indian!" With that, she stomped to the door, tied on her hooded cape, and stormed out. Wendell rose to go after her, but the elder Harte put out a hand to stop him.

"Let her go," he murmured. "This scene recurs almost daily. She refuses to say a Christian grace."

Wendell was sitting back down when there was a loud grunt from the yard, and the sound of his steamer trunk hitting the dirt; then a "Heeyah!" and the buckboard departed, leaving a cloud of dust billowing in through the open window.

"What the devil?"

His father sighed. "Of late, your sister has become the very bane of my existence."

"Perhaps she would prefer to live elsewhere," Wendell ventured cautiously, remembering the conversation in the buckboard. His father's response surprised him.

"In truth, I wish she would." He looked at Wendell defensively, "You seem alarmed at that. She is, after all, almost thirty."

"You misunderstand my look," said Wendell. "It is not alarm, but surprise! I had only just asked her why she was not married and moved out."

"And what did she say?"

Wendell felt he was on dangerous ground but, wishing for clarity, persisted. "She said there was a beau of late, who left her broken-hearted for not wanting to live here with you – that it was your need of her that precluded her going with him."

Harte Jefferson Parry shook his head sadly, his bright blue eyes growing dull. "I have concern for your sister's sanity," he said wearily. "There was no beau. There was a hired hand, whom she herself chased away with her constant ghostly communications. Beyond that, she has a cupboard full of intoxicating patent medicines and will tell me nothing of their purpose."

At this information, Wendell felt a cold chill shudder through his body. His sister had been his security as a child and any instability in her psyche would find an echo in his own. 'Calling forth the dead is dangerous,' Josephine had said, 'it is addictive, and consuming.'

His father continued, "She has a group that convenes regularly, to receive communications from this Hyenwatha. As the group is open only to 'those with blood of the red race,' it is closed to me. Whilst you are here, I would appreciate it if you would go and report to me what happens there."

"I will go should I be invited," said Wendell, "and I will take your concerns with me. But I will not spy on her. Catherine's prayer was beautiful, and I'm certain it doesn't stem from evil. But tell me, Father, would you be able to live on your own without Catherine? After all, the work is hard and your foot remains tender."

"Alas, I am still able enough if she would not chase off my hired hands. I am not yet an old man, I could easily replace her cooking with remarriage. A few missing toes affects my balance, that's all. But my home is falling on bad repute – room and board no longer suffice as payment to work here."

They finished the meal without relish, then Wendell rose and begged to retrieve the steamer trunk from the yard. Harte Parry followed him out, and together they wrestled it inside and up the stairs to the small dormer room which had recently belonged to the hireling and historically belonged to Wendell. Wendell bid his father sit on the high familiar bed whilst he opened his trunk and drew out the three one-hundred dollar banknotes, still untouched, that Lillian had paid him for the Robinsons. "Here, Father. I wish to do my share if I can."

His father looked doubtful as he took the tender. "This is quite a sum. Can you afford this, Son?"

Still squatting beside his open trunk, Wendell smiled up at his sire. "I am actually doing quite well," he said with attempted modesty. But his dad was grinning fully.

"Yes, my son is a successful painter," he bragged. "I have clipped all the notices from the papers. As an artist, you have done what I could not, and made me most proud." With this, he bent and kissed the top of his son's head, then left him to unpack and get settled.

Alone in the familiar room, Wendell Harte Parry sat on the bed. Behind the modest headboard, his grandmother's portrait gazed at him with disturbing nostalgia. Suddenly, he felt small and helpless; his sister's outburst had shaken him. Indeed, he could not remember such a display of anger from the gentler sex, save on the more unsavory sidewalks of city slums – never from a gentlewoman. He began to go over the day's events in his mind, trying to make sense of them. His father seemed not at all to begrudge him his freedom, but rather to celebrate it. Had there ever been an indication growing up that Catherine could go crazy? She had been to him a pillar of sanity, his rock, caring for him after his grandmother died.

But now as he closed his eyes, he saw her. Twice as a child, she'd had outbursts that had frightened him so deeply, he'd been prevented from breathing. She had been angry at having to assume their grandmother's duties at so young an age, and his childish mind was sure that she blamed him for their mother's death and that she too would leave him. And now, here she was twenty years later and the same bitterness remaining. As Wendell thought about it, he felt an old fear of abandonment gnaw at his core.

Lost in thought, he sat quite still until the sun's rays began to lengthen through the little dormer window, then he finally unpacked and went downstairs, where he found Catherine in the kitchen making supper as though nothing had happened. As they sat down to the meal, Catherine offered her strange grace, then stayed on the safe topic of Wendell's trip to Europe and new abode in Manhattan. Afterward, Wendell and his father retired to the front porch for a smoke, leaving Catherine to wash the dishes.

Purple sky deepened in the west behind dark silhouettes of oaks and maples. Past the pungent wisps and glowing embers of father's pipe and son's home-rolled cigarette, the men enjoyed a sparkle show from dancing lightning bugs, orchestrated by cooing doves and vibrating crickets. Evening primroses popped out gay yellow blossoms in visual percussion to the whimsical tune.

"How does it feel to be home, Son?" his father asked with great satisfaction.

"Strange, a bit," confessed Wendell, "being no longer a child. Yet I've missed this peaceful scene and am grateful for it. While I'm here, I would like to help with whatever needs doing."

"Hmmm," his father considered, "I appreciate that. It's much the same as when you were a boy – stalls need cleaning, fences need mending, there's some patching on the roof. You needn't worry about the rest of it – Catherine generally slops the hogs and biddies, tends the crops and puts 'em up, does the milking and churning and marketing."

"So what would you do without her?" Wendell was startled at the list, knowing that she also cooked and cleaned and mended. "How could you find all that, even in a wife? It seems you would have to hire someone, or even two, to take her place."

"I don't believe Catherine's going anywhere – any offer of marriage she's had, she's given the mitten, and she's had no offer lately that I know of." The older man puffed his pipe and his eyes went steely in its glow. A strange quiet enveloped them as the topic again became dangerous of discussion. Just then, Catherine's presence was discerned gliding onto the porch in the darkening gloom.

"I'm sorry, I won't join you gentlemen tonight – I'm very tired and am going to bed." And with a soft bang of the door, she departed.

Over the next weeks, Wendell helped his father with chores, hunted rabbits, and sketched scenes for Mr. Gerrit Smith. And while Catherine did not repeat her outburst, she yet seemed quiet and withdrawn to him. Indeed, her mood bordered on morose, except on Tuesdays and Fridays when she would leave supper on the stove for the menfolk and take the buckboard to her mysterious gathering. Unable to stand this silence from his closest family member, Wendell finally broached the subject of his attending the gathering with her. She was hanging out the wash when he approached her.

"Dear Sister," he said, "I've very much wanted to hear Hyenwatha speak, and wondered if I might accompany you some evening."

"Wendell," she responded forthrightly, "if you come for the purpose of spying, of judging me alienated, and of reporting back to Father that I am possessed of the Devil, then no, I do not welcome your company."

"It appears to me," considered Wendell softly, "that far from being alienated, this gathering is the only healthful thing you do for yourself." She looked at him curiously, then finally nodded assent.

That evening, as he sat on his bed, Wendell actually heard Catherine Cayuga humming below while she did the dishes. With a sigh of relief, he lit his candle and drew out his mirror. Gazing into the muse, he became aware of his tension, that now perhaps would lift. Deep into his ritual, he was unaware that the door had been quietly pushed open until Catherine gasped with surprise. He looked up at her and saw she was smiling with delighted amazement. "Excuse me," she said softly, and departed.

Chapter 11

The next day, Catherine Cayuga Parry strangely seemed even more wary of Wendell, hardly looking at him as she went about her chores. As the shadows of late afternoon lengthened in the yard, he climbed up beside her on the buckboard and she urged the horses to a gentle trot. "So, Brother," she ventured, glancing at him, "what did you with your day? Mend a fence?" He nodded, uncertain as to her intention. "It is so good of you," she continued, "to help Father with his labors." Again, Wendell remained silent. Finally she spoke again. "Has it never dawned on you to help me with mine? Of the two, I have the more daunting role. Or is women's work beneath you?"

Her attack startled him into chagrin. For all his supposed concurrence with the philosophy of women's equality, it had never occurred to him to help his sister. He said nothing, and as they drove along in silence, he made a commitment to himself to make amends.

With the rising sounds of evening, they came upon horses and other wagons converging on a woodsy log cabin. Now at last, she began to brighten. Friends and followers hastened to greet Catherine Cayuga and assist the celebrated medium down from her carriage. As they went in, Catherine introduced her brother to several of the curious, then was helped to an ornate chair on a riser facing the rough benches of her audience.

The throng quieted. A mesmerizing drumbeat commenced and myriad candles were lit as Catherine closed her eyes, sinking deeply into mediumistic trance. Wendell watched with fascination, suspending his disbelief, as her features changed utterly and a deep male voice issued from her unconscious lips. Wendell had been to other mediumistic possessions, popular throughout New England, but none that invoked an Indian saint and a transformation of gender.

"Where is my love?" asked the voice of Hyenwatha. So convincing was it as a man's that chills went up Wendell's spine. An older woman stood, dressed in Indian buckskins and dark plaited hair.

"I am here," said the woman, and stepped up on the riser, kneeling before Hyenwatha. A bowl was handed her, and slowly, ritually, she removed Catherine's shoes and began lovingly to bathe her feet. The drumbeat became more insistent as the woman finished her ablutions, then stood and kissed Catherine warmly and fully on the mouth. A satisfied sigh and gasp came from the audience, as this display of love further heightened the sensation of Catherine being now a man – Hyenwatha, patron saint of the Haudenosaunee nations. Then the older woman resumed her seat again on the rickety benches.

"Where are my moccasins?" boomed the voice of Hyenwatha above intense drumming. Now a man stood and brought forth high moccasins and tied them lovingly onto Hyenwatha's feet.

"Where is my robe?" asked Hyenwatha, whereupon an Iroquois blanket of many colors was wrapped about his shoulders. Then finally, "Where is my headdress?" and yet another adherent placed the Seneca feathers upon the Haudenosaunee saint's head, and smeared ochre paint across his cheekbones, completing the transformation.

The drumming crescendoed and the audience held its breath as Hyenwatha rose from the chair before them. Spirit lights of indefinite form flew about him, lit against pungent white smoke which curled up from a painted Indian vessel. Then all stood. Abruptly the spirits departed and the drumming stopped. "I greet you from the spirit realm," said the saint, and the audience said as one, "We greet you, Hyenwatha, and seek for guidance from the spirit realm."

"Ask me what you seek," said Hyenwatha, sitting again as the throng before him sat. Then each petitioner in turn knelt before Hyenwatha and asked for news of loved ones passed, seeming deeply affected and satisfied with his answers. Finally, Wendell stepped up and kneeled before the saint.

"Ask me what you seek," said Hyenwatha.

And Wendell said, "I wish to speak to my grandmother, whose name in Cayuga is Gohnégageh Oyęgwa, and in English, Jane Whitesmoke."

"She is here," intoned Hyenwatha.

"Peace be with you, Grandmother," said Wendell, moved as he sensed her presence. He watched his sister's strange and entranced countenance, "I wish to know how I may win back my sister's love."

The face did not stir except for the moving lips which said in Hyenwatha's voice, "You must give her your right hand."

"I'm not sure that I know how," said Wendell, confused. "Is there no more to the message?"

And now the voice that issued forth from his sister's body was neither that of his sister nor that of Hyenwatha, but the long-ago remembered voice of his grandmother. As he heard it, every hair on Wendell's body bristled to attention. "You must pay your debt, Little Deer," she said in her wise and gentle tones. "Your sister has sacrificed greatly for your sake, Mrs. Ferguson has not." At this, his head reeled and two parishioners rushed forward and grabbed his arms to keep him from falling backwards off the dais. As they reseated him on the rough bench, he heard Hyenwatha's voice again, asking the next person what was sought. But Wendell had told no one about Lillian, much less "Mrs. Ferguson" – of that he was certain, he had paid particular care not to. Had he now to choose between Lillian and his sister?

The element of time seemed meaningless and even imaginary, in the stuffy log cabin with its myriad candles flickering eerily upon the walls. The Indian saint stood, and all stood with him. His costume was removed in the order it had been placed upon him – lastly his lover kissed him goodbye and all sat down, as Catherine's shoes were placed again upon his feet. Hyenwatha's voice spoke one last time, "The veil descends and I depart to the spirit world, until we meet again – *Dogehs!*" Then he led them in a prayer quite like the one Catherine spoke at supper.

Finally the parishioners with one voice said, "Farewell, Oh Hyenwatha, depart with our gratitude to the spirit world, until we meet again. *Dogehs!*" Wendell watched, still mesmerized, as Catherine's lids began to flutter and her face softened into its familiar features. For a moment, she seemed not to know where she was, then two parishioners lifted her up and slowly walked her down from the dais, holding on till she recovered, while well-wishers crowded around to thank her.

Another crowd was gathered in the back by a table, where offerings were placed in a basket. Catherine made her way there and collected the coins, then turned to the table's opposite end where a dark woman and a child sat behind a display of patent medicines for sale. The woman and child were thin almost to starving, and looked grateful as they did a brisk business. Catherine bought two bottles, then turned to find Wendell and urged him to do the same. He gave the poor woman her due, and read the label by candlelight – the ingredients were hasheesh and absinthe wormwood.

Back in the buckboard, Wendell took the reins and Catherine sagged against him, hanging onto his arm, as they wearily made their way home.

"Do you remember nothing?" he asked her.

"During trance, I am as one dead. Did you speak to Grandmother?"

"Yes. And even more, she spoke to me – with her own voice." Catherine looked at him. "She even," he went on, still reeling with the mystery, "mentioned the name of a lady friend that you could not have known."

"Oh? Do you have a lady friend? Who is she?" She perked up in her seat, hungry for the gossip, but Wendell evaded her with his own question.

"Have other voices come through you before?"

"I have been told so, yes. And even I sometimes harbor disbelief that it is real, thinking it some dramatic gift of unconscious imagination. But then when spirits know things I don't, it gives the lie to that."

This time he helped his sister down from the wagon. As she took the hand that was offered her, he heard again the words, "You must give her your right hand," and felt a warm, protective glow.

For the next weeks, Wendell helped wash the dishes and spent much more time in his sketches, thinking that he would give the whole thousand dollars from Gerrit Smith to his sister. Several times, he took her with him to Buttermilk Falls, where the wide waterway cascaded merrily down a long and shallow descend, looking like dancing white lace or buttermilk over the rocks. They swam in the deep and picturesque pools below the falls, where water running over smooth boulders in the grotto presented a magical setting suited for nymphs and fairies.

One evening, Wendell had helped with supper and dishes so they could both join their father on the porch to watch the lightning bugs. Harte drew on his pipe and sighed contentedly – he and Catherine had been getting along better. "Do you have a commission for those sketches you're doing, Son?" he asked.

Wendell nodded proudly. "Mr. Gerrit Smith, the millionaire, has offered me a nice sum for four canvases." Suddenly, his father's mood darkened.

"I don't like Mr. Gerrit Smith," he said roughly. "Of course, it's no fault of yours and I don't begrudge you the commissions. But I wouldn't trust him – the man is thieving scrum."

"How so?" Wendell was incredulous.

"He is selling all his land in these parts, every stick of it, to coloreds induced by his largesse to vote his way. Temperance will soon be the law in Tompkins County."

True enough, thought Wendell, Gerrit Smith's zeal against drinking was almost better known than his anti-slavery zeal.

"I approve his temperance," began his sister, with a passionate edge to her voice, "but he swindles the people who buy his land, then starves them."

Wendell was genuinely distressed at the vehemence in his sister's voice – Gerrit Smith was an abolitionist hero and Lillian's friend. "How can this be true? He is generally well thought of."

Catherine turned to look at him, her eyes penetrating and earnest in the deepening twilight. "Do you recall the woman at the gathering selling patent medicines?" He nodded. "Her name is Mary Jane Randolph – she is the wife of the man who I believe sold you your magic mirror, Dr. Paschal Beverly Randolph?" Again Wendell nodded, this time in stunned disbelief that his sister would know the maker of a mirror given him in the Orient. His sister continued angrily, "That same Gerrit Smith starved her! He starved her! And he starved her other child to death!"

"Tell me what happened," urged Wendell gently.

"Dr. Paschal Randolph is of African bloodline, a requirement to buy land from Gerrit Smith, which he was eager to do. But while you were abroad, in '57, the country fell on hard times and Dr. Randolph sought to sell his land in turn. Only then did he learn that the land was indentured, and all his personal effects as well. He could sell nothing, not even his watch! Mr. Gerrit Smith claimed title to everything! Since Randolph had signed an agreement to sell, he now faced a crippling lawsuit if he didn't. All of the doctor's pleas fell on deaf ears until at last the Randolphs were forced to abandon their property, and shortly after, their little girl Winnie died from starvation." Here, Catherine's voice caught and tears sprang to her eyes.

It was hard for Wendell to believe that Paschal Randolph had not badly mismanaged his affairs or otherwise brought this upon himself. But the charges were too dire to dismiss. "And what now of the poor destitutes?" he asked.

"Mary Jane stays with my parishioners by turn, she and her remaining child, while her husband sends patent medicines from abroad."

"And you do your part in buying them?"

"Yes," she said, "I have a cupboard full." Wendell caught his father's relieved sigh at this explanation, and once more their attention turned to the lightning bug show, though each was consumed with private thoughts.

Eventually, the elder Parry spoke again. "So Wendell," he cleared his throat as he relit his pipe, "your sister tells me you have a lady friend. Can we expect that you will be marrying soon?" Wendell flushed deeply and was grateful for the dark.

"She is but a casual acquaintance," Wendell said.

"Balderdash!" protested Catherine. "Why then would Grandmother's spirit have mentioned her?"

Ashamed of himself for lying when spies from the spirit world lurked so convincingly, he tempered his phrasing. "I am most smitten with her," he admitted, "but she has not even given me how to reach her." He said it with such genuine sorrow that the others had to accept the truth of it, and indeed, it was true and much on his mind of late.

"Well, I hope that changes," declared his sister earnestly. "It would solve all our problems for you to take a wife and live here with us – wouldn't it, Father?"

His father came to his rescue. "Surely Wendell's business affairs keep him in the city. That would not change were he to marry." His sister sighed and once again, they each disappeared into their own small reveries. But this was not to be the end of their discussion about Wendell's lady friend.

Later that week, a letter arrived bearing the return address: Miss Lillian Flax, Unitary Household Building One, 106 East 14th Street, Manhattan, New York. Wendell returned to the house from sketching, only to find both Catherine and Harte waiting anxiously for him, the letter sitting on the kitchen table between them. Wendell grabbed it and hurried up the stairs to his room in the dormer.

"My Dearest Wendell," he read, *"Great news! I have taken rooms just below Fitzhugh and Rosalie. As you have been here many times, you know the place. I am delighted that many of our mutual friends frequent here, even without invitation from me. A ball, to raise funds for the* Saturday Press, *is planned in the fall, so when are you returning???*

"Adah Menken has finally opened in The French Spy *at Laura Keene's Theater – her notoriety naturally attracts adoring crowds and bad reviews. (I think she is intent on becoming more prone to scandal than Lola Montez!) If all goes well (Can I say that of it?), she will marry John Heenan in September.*

"At last, my darling, you have a place to write me, so write!!! And let me know that you will be home soon. I will not schedule the lyceum tour until I hear from you. (Yes! I have made the rounds and am invited back!) I miss you. My loving arms await your return, Lillian"

Wendell was in great fettle when he went whistling down the stairs to supper. His mood, however, was not matched by his fellow diners. Catherine looked sad and said, "You're leaving soon, aren't you?"

"Yes," he admitted, "I will be leaving almost immediately. It's time for me to start painting my larger canvases. When they're done, I will send you what I can by way of support."

"You have already given so much," said his father, humbled. He stopped his thoughts as Catherine took his and Wendell's hands for the blessing.

After the food was passed around, Wendell continued, "I would like you to use what I gave you to hire help for Catherine. It won't last long, but I'll endeavor to send more."

"That's a big commitment, Son. I'm grateful for the offer. But it seems to me you had better keep your money for your wife – you will want to support her in some kind of style."

"Father, I'm not getting married," insisted Wendell.

Now he saw his father's face flush and knew that some unpleasantness was coming. "This Miss Lillian Flax has her own apartments in a Unitary Household? Such a place is notorious for 'Free Love.' Son, if you are having relations with her, I'd far rather you made an honest woman of her and not give me bastard grandchildren. She may say she has no wish to marry, but she is doubtless either under the influence of wanton communists or is not worthy of your affections – perhaps even both."

Wendell looked to Catherine for help, but she had reddened and was staring down at her hands folded carefully in her lap. There was silence, until she finally looked up at her brother and heaved a sigh. "If you love her, Brother, you will marry her."

Wendell surrendered – he did not wish to fight on the eve of his departure. "I do love her," he confessed, "and will see if she will have me." At this, the family brightened, certain now there would be a wedding.

"Whiskey!" demanded Harte Jefferson Parry. "We must drink a toast to my future daughter-in-law!" And over Catherine's vehement objections, he found a bottle and together father and son toasted everything on into the night, to the extent that Wendell had to wait yet another day to depart. But he posted a letter to Lillian, wondering whether he or it would get there first.

Chapter 12

Wendell arrived by carriage back at the Studio Building well after dark, and was deposited with his steamer trunk onto the sidewalk. The front door of the building was ajar, and just inside Thomas Buchanan Read was wrestling with several large crates. Wendell offered him good cheer as he dragged his own trunk in through the door and locked up behind him. "Have you just returned as well?" Wendell asked, knowing his friend had also been upstate.

"Yes, and to an empty building – few of our fellows are back from their summer haunts. Come, your assistance would be appreciated, then I'll give you a hand with your trunk." Together, they hoisted the crates to Thomas' atelier, and then up the little staircase to the balcony over his loft.

"What have you brought back?" asked Wendell, intrigued. "These have the feel of paint boards."

"It's a secret," said Thomas, coloring, "but not an unprofitable one. Come, keep it to yourself and I'll show you." Wendell watched as Thomas drew a panel out of the crate. On it was a beautifully crafted near life-sized half-portrait, but altogether lacked a face, being bare where the head should be.

"What is this?" asked Wendell with astonishment.

"You are looking," laughed Thomas, "at the work of Incognito, the great Italian artist."

"I fail to follow your drift," smiled Wendell.

Thomas continued, "As you are aware, my portraits command a handsome sum…"

"Quite," agreed the bemused young artist, "but have they not usually a face?"

"Wendell, I am on the horns of a dilemma. Generally, when I receive a commission, I spend it almost immediately, and then have to find how to survive till the next one. But when I am in need of a quick sale, I can't lower my price, or my reputation will be similarly lowered, and hence also is lowered my ability to command a high price – a vicious circle! And so, under guise of sketching landscapes, I return to my limner life, traveling off the beaten path in anonymous fashion, making easy but elegant portraits by having the bodies pre-painted."

"Brilliant!" exclaimed Wendell. "Most ingenious! Ha ha. And as customers have no patience anymore for sitting, you have solved that problem as well!"

Thomas had a self-satisfied smile, seeming to enjoy the accolades over something that would normally embarrass him. He continued enthusiastically, "And you know how fusty folks can be about their persons, what they should wear, and how they don't like this or that background. Those annoyances also dissolve themselves by having them choose a handsome body ready-made and clothed."

Wendell picked through the thin but sturdy and nicely finished boards, amazed at the variety of the torsos and excellence of the work. "How much did you garner, if I may be so bold?"

"Even in the backwoods, a high price commands respect, and it is the small town business owners and professionals who can afford my work. But once you sell the first, the whole town queues up, so at fifty dollars each, it is quite lucrative. I have brought back two thousand dollars profit from just three small villages!"

"Two thousand dollars?! An astounding sum! And I had been pleased with my paltry commissions!" Wendell looked incredulously at the faceless portraits and broke into laughter so contagious that Thomas joined him. What a fine joke! Between guffaws, Wendell managed, "Do you suppose everyone at Tenth Street Studios is doing the same?" which rekindled the hilarity to new heights.

After they had delivered Wendell's trunk to the third floor, the two friends returned to Thomas' room and opened a bottle of wine. Ted Winthrop, having been almost alone in the building most of the summer, came in to join them. He was followed by Cat, who seemed likewise grateful for company. "So how are you coming with your book, *Cecil Dreeme?*" asked Thomas, as young Winthrop lit up a sweet-scented bowlful. "Will we get to read it soon?"

"It has taken a whole new tack," said Mr. Winthrop, "after seeing Adah Menken's play. A pity you can't see it, it closed last night."

Wendell stroked Cat, who had deposited himself on his lap, and marveled at the writer's enthusiasm. *"The French Spy?* What about the play inspired you?"

Ted puffed his pipe with excitement. "Adah plays a woman playing a man, an attractive man, who is admired as a man by other women. There is something most sensually arousing when she dons the uniform of a soldier and wields her sword. I was quite captivated. Indeed, she had charms to captivate both male and female in her audience. In consequence, I am rewriting my novel to disguise the heroine in men's clothing."

Thomas laughed. "It seems you are quite besotted, Ted, old chap."

Ted smiled ruefully. "I would be, but for Mr. Heenan. I would not want the Benicia Boy's bare knuckles on my mug." He sighed. "If you had seen the play, you would be in love with her, too."

Wendell was grateful for the company that continued into the night, and felt as he returned to his room that the spying aspect of his grandmother's ghost had departed – he had not realized how on edge he had been. Ah, bohemia – freedom at last – sanity, art, culture, and Greenwich Village! He took a deep breath and looked forward to wending his way to East 14th Street in the morning, to see what other social adventures might await him.

But tossing about in his bed that night, he realized he was

wrong – his grandmother had not departed. "You must give her your right hand," she said in his dream and, taking his hand from him, handed it to Catherine. "Your sister has sacrificed greatly for your sake, Mrs. Ferguson has not."

At daybreak, the sun rose slowly with sickly pallor, casting its beams through dirty windows and detailing the drifting dust and spider webs that had accumulated during his absence. Wendell donned his djellaba and made his way to the empty breakfast mess where he tried to shake off his dreams with potato cakes and coffee. Lonely Mrs. Winter greeted him like a lost friend, and fervently hoped that other artists would soon return. She was glad to hear that Thomas was back, but had seen not hide nor hair this morning.

Wendell dressed and made his way to Broadway, where he bought a beautiful potted tea rose at a flower stall. Then he crossed against the heavy morning traffic of fancy carriages headed for the financial district, and finally crossed Bowery to a quiet row of townhouses opposite the elegant Academy of Music. As he had been here before to see Fitzhugh and Rosalie, the maid answering the door assumed those two to be his hosts and, before he could announce himself, called to them in the dining room. Fitzhugh came to the door, delighted to see him and admiring the plant. "I imagine this is for our new tenant," he laughed, "who is perhaps more deserving of a present than we are." Wendell doffed his hat as he stepped inside.

"Is she about?" he asked, somewhat awkwardly.

"So you have not come to see me at all, your old friend? Ah, you do have a fickle heart. Fortunately, she sits with Rosalie in the dining hall where she is eating breakfast, so you may join her and us as well." His smile faded, "Unless you are intent on disappearing immediately to her private chambers."

"I would think that were up to the lady, hey?" Wendell followed Fitzhugh around the corner to where Lillian was seated with Rosalie and several other tenants at a large communal dining table.

Lillian saw Wendell and rose, smiling broadly, then accepted the potted plant into the crook of her arm as she lifted her mouth for a kiss. Without a word to him, she addressed the breakfasters, "I hope you will excuse me – I beg to retire to my apartments." She placed the back of her hand dramatically against her forehead, "I feel faint and need to lie down."

"As the papers say," mourned Fitzhugh, "'tis a veritable den of Free Love."

"Nay, not free," protested Lillian, "it has cost Wendell the price of this lovely tea rose." Wendell grinned and bowed low to the diners as Lillian yanked him playfully with her free hand toward the staircase. Down the hallway on the second floor, she turned a knob and ushered him with a curtsy into a sunny sitting room. Behind a velvet love seat, *Sands of Morocco* graced the wall with an endless sea of dunes. Wendell had loved and caressed every grain of sand, every eddy, and had been sorry when he finally called it complete and the painting ended.

He examined the rest of the room. Through large open double doors was an airy bedroom and high four-poster bed covered with white Egyptian cotton, while sheers billowed about a French door that led onto a small balcony. Lillian placed the little rose bush on the balcony and tipped her head up expectantly as Wendell swept her into his arms. As he kissed her, pressing against her yielding warmth, he knew for certain he was home, and that despite whatever dreams and forebodings he may have had, all was well.

It was more than a few days later that Wendell saw the other artists in the Studio Building mess. "Hurrah! You are back!" he cried at seeing Sanford Gifford, then cheered that Mignot and even Fred Church had returned with *Heart of the Andes*, which was to go on exhibition again in the gallery.

"In fact, we've been back awhile," said Sanford, "and have

been conversing as to your whereabouts. We guessed you'd come upon nicer accommodations."

"Now you make me feel disloyal. I'm delighted to see all of you and to eat Mrs. Winter's fine potato pancakes." In truth, he would not have been at breakfast but for an early scheduled meeting with Mr. Gerrit Smith to view his sketches. But the delightful camaraderie of the artists as they shared their summer adventures gave him resolve to attend breakfast with them more often.

Shortly after, Gerrit Smith arrived at Wendell's atelier. He expressed rapturous approval of the proffered sketches, now rendered in oils to resemble their finished appearance. As they talked, Wendell studied Mr. Smith carefully. Above all, with no vanity of wealth in his demeanor, the man exuded intense honesty. It seemed quite impossible that he could have cheated his Negro clients in any way, or done anything to bring harm to them. Indeed, it was untenable for Wendell to conclude anything other than that the whole affair with Dr. Randolph was based on unfortunate circumstances beyond Mr. Smith's control. The meeting ended well, with Mr. Smith having no inkling of the doubts that had lurked in Wendell's mind. The young artist once again offered his services in any way he could, to end the whole business of slavery. "And have you any new insights as to how our venture will be received in Ithaca?" the good man asked.

Wendell flushed, laughing, "They have fears that your new voters will install the laws of temperance in the county."

Gerrit Smith nodded. "Yes, I hope they will, my lad. I hope they will."

Finally, wishing to draw his benefactor out, Wendell said, "And living in Ithaca is a Mrs. Mary Jane Randolph, with whom the locals say you have had unfortunate connections."

Gerrit Smith winced. "Hmmm, that wretched dealer in hasheesh and misery," he opined, stroking his beard. "I thank you for alerting me – she could make trouble." Then he left.

That afternoon, Wendell dressed in his evening finery for the *Saturday Press* benefit "Free Love Ball." Then with Sanford, Thomas and Ted, he hailed a carriage and was soon joining other guests arriving at the entrance of Unitary Household Building Two. Lucy, the maid, dressed as one of the guests, held out a hat for their contributions.

Inside, the guests were dancing to classical chords played by a pianist introduced as Anna Mary Freeman's betrothed. Sanford immediately spied Josephine Walters and squired her onto the dance floor while Thomas approached Laura Keene who was regaling admirers with her adventures. Wendell searched out his hosts, the principals of the *Saturday Press*, and found them seated in the dining room, laughing drunkenly and rather rudely blocking access to the food. Wendell greeted them and asked where Lillian might be.

Fitzhugh was seated next to Rosalie, who wafted bubbles across the table from a clay pipe. The young writer dubbed Macaroni, who sported three moustaches, the third in the tiny cleft below his bottom lip, said drunkenly, "She's next door."

Rosalie added, "She's waiting for you to escort her, and is doubtless in a froth."

"Honestly, Parry," Clapp agreed, "in bohemia, you must be mindful of the rules that govern 'no-rules', which, it seems, are many." The party convulsed with laughter.

Wendell feigned alarm. "Will I have to pay again at the door?" he joked.

Macaroni, slouching dangerously, dismissed this with a wave of his hand. "Nay, Lillian will pay it for you."

Wendell bristled quietly to himself. He did not like the frequent teasing about Lillian's greater wealth. But when he turned to go, he saw Lillian smiling at him from the front door, already having made her own way over. She was dressed in Spanish black voile and lace over a bright copper satin, and took his breath away.

Wendell took her black-gloved hand formally and bowed, bringing it to his lips. "Please forgive me," he said. "I did not mean to leave you waiting."

"Have you danced with anyone yet?" she asked.

"I have only just arrived."

"Then I shall be inclined to forgive you, sir, if you will have your first dance with me." Wendell took her in his arms and pressed against her. He was quickly caught up in her aura, an aura of satin and romance set to the music of Chopin's *Nocturne*. Wendell slid his fingers inside her glove, and elicited a deeply satisfying sigh.

Eventually, they joined the discussion in the dining room. Beside Fitzhugh, Rosalie, and Henry Clapp were Macaroni and Tom Aldrich, while Ada Clare, Adah Menken, and the besotted Ted Winthrop sat opposite Edwin Booth and his most intimate and refined friend, Adam Badeau. Lillian wondered aloud that John Heenan, Adah Menken's betrothed, was not present.

"As prize fighting is illegal, he keeps his whereabouts secret," Adah lamented. "Alas, I am not to be called 'betrothed.' His trainers welcome his match with the English champion Tommy Sayers, but somehow find threatening his match with me."

"No!" cried Ted Winthrop, trying hard to look upset. "The wedding is off?"

Her eyes grew big at the thought. "Oh no," she said, "Johnny and I love each other too much. There is definitely to be a wedding. It's just that news of it should not appear in the papers."

"You forget with whom you are sitting," Clapp teased.

Ada Clare could stand it no longer. "Balderdash and bunkum! Are we to believe that a wedding to you is too scandalous for the refined followers of boxing?"

"Alas," said Adah Menken, asserting her right to infamy, "it's not my first marriage."

With many a gentlemen laughing openly, Lillian stepped in lest the evening descend into rudeness. "I applaud you, Menken, that you are yet the romantic, having had your heart broken so many times."

Ada Clare interjected, looking crestfallen. "Is everyone to desert me, then? Even Anna Mary is planning to wed."

"I'm afraid, Ada, that I, too, am betrothed," Edwin Booth announced to everyone's amazement, especially as they thought his intimacy with Adam Badeau would preclude such a thing. This brought a chorus of astonishment and wonder at who the mystery lady might be. "I am to wed the actress, Mary Devlin," he said proudly. "I played Romeo to her Juliet, and am in love for it." Everyone cheered – toasts to the nuptials of Edwin, Adah, and Anna Mary were offered all 'round.

"So Ned," said Adah Menken, "why didn't you bring Miss Devlin here for us to meet?"

"Miss Devlin is sixteen years old. At Adam's suggestion, she has taken a year in seclusion and spiritual cleansing, with her parents in Brooklyn."

"Have you no need for a spiritual cleanse, Menken?" asked Macaroni aside for which he received a punch to the shoulder. "Ouch!" he winced, "Your fiancé has taught you a thing or two!"

"Miss Devlin is studying French and the classics," Adam Badeau clarified, "and will no longer be gracing the stage."

"Is that her wish to quit the stage?" Ada Clare demanded of Ned. "The stage is the only venue in this straight-jacketed world where a woman may express her authentic soul."

"It is her wish," responded Ned. "Indeed, I have no wish to suppress her authentic soul, but only to know it – intimately."

This was followed by silence until Josephine Walters appeared and gave a loud guffaw. Everyone laughed and toasted, as they wished Ned well in surviving the year. Wendell watched Lillian's face, flushed with the romance of it all, and remembered the awkward pledge to his family to propose marriage.

Adam Badeau broached the purpose of their gathering. "So Henry, in how bad shape is the *Saturday Press?*" he asked.

"Tonight will keep the venture afloat, for which I can't thank you enough, as I believe the *Saturday Press* to have some importance," said Clapp. "It is artists who fashion the culture and from that culture arise politicians and governments. The true revolution of our time, ladies and gentlemen, is not the form of government, but the widespread dissemination of literacy and culture. Just look at the power of a book or an image to shape the common bond of society. Indeed, that is why democracy needs its art and why artists are so feared by governments."

"Ah, 'tis true," said Aldrich. "Note how Harriet Beecher Stowe has shaped the common bond of abolition with *Uncle Tom's Cabin.*"

"Abolition will come through culture," declared Adah Menken, "not through war."

"But the culture of the South is quite different," Wendell mused aloud.

"Not so!" scoffed Aldrich. "The South relies on New York and Boston for its culture, same as the rest of us. It was those New England Puritans who, to counter the Pope's lone power to interpret the Bible, insisted on spreading literacy. If the Southern states secede and the mail's cut off, they will not go two months without their *New York Traveller, Vanity Fair*, or *Harper's*. Even the hated *New York Tribune* would be missed in short order."

There was a moment of silence as everyone reflected on the possibility of secession. Finally Henry concluded, "For all its flaws, Gentlemen... and Ladies, America has a more benign government than the world is used to. And 'tis the freedom of its artists has made it so."

Bubbles wafted across the table from the clay pipe of Rosalie Ludlow. "...for a white man," she mumbled.

They were feeling the effects of the wine, and now Wendell looked over at Fitzhugh, who had been altogether too quiet. His pupils looked unfocused and he was swaying dangerously in his seat.

"Merde à l'enfer!" said Wendell, "Fitzhugh looks quite poorly." Wendell ran to him just as Fitzhugh's head began to sag forward into his food, and pushed him sideways instead, onto Rosalie's lap. Rosalie looked helplessly at her prostrate husband. "What is it he consumed?" demanded Wendell.

"He had been smoking opium," sighed Rosalie.

"What? The Devil! You can't mix wine and opium! He needs air." Several of the men had risen and helped pull Fitzhugh to his feet. Fitzhugh regained some of his conscious faculties, and struggled weakly to free himself as they bore him by his arms through the front door and sat him down on the stoop. "Fitzhugh, old boy, will you recover?" asked Wendell. Fitzhugh nodded, drawing huge breaths and mumbling an apology.

Wendell's attention, however, was attracted to a commotion across the street. Folks in front of the Academy of Music were pointing with excitement in the deepening twilight toward the northern sky behind the Unitary Households. Wendell looked up and gasped. He yelled in astonishment, "What is it? Come see this, what is it?" Streaks and flashes of dancing fairy lights, some white, some red, were begging to be viewed from a better angle. Rosalie stayed with Fitzhugh while the rest of the company ran across to the opposite sidewalk to watch from the opera house steps.

As the sky darkened, the fairy nymphs intensified in brightness and number. Soon they surrounded the city entirely. The sidewalks were filling up, traffic stopped and people appeared on rooftops to watch the awesome sight. Some fell to their knees, sobbing in wonder – that indeed, they were witnessing the return of Our Lord – while the sky became brighter than daylight, and turned red as if the whole city burst into flame, sparks shooting to the zenith.

Through it all, stars dazzled and meteors shot across the firmament as if the end of the world were indeed at hand. Lucy passed out dessert, and a string quartet emerged from the building and began to play.

Wendell sat on the opera house steps, his arms around Lillian, their faces lit by the rapturous glow. "The Northern Lights," she breathed, "the Aurora Borealis." The air crackled with electricity as heavenly sounds of Beethoven wafted aloft in celestial sympathy.

After an hour or so of deepening intensity, Wendell whispered, "Can we not watch from the balcony of your room?" So they said their good-nights and crossed over to Unitary Household #1. They pulled Lillian's feather bed off its bedstead and placed it on the balcony next to the tea rose. There they made love in front of God and man as all eyes were distracted to the spheres above.

Chapter 13

The sun rose with strange normality, waking them early to the sounds of the morning rush. Lillian was leaving for her Redpath Lyceum tour and had her bags packed. She assured Wendell that James Redpath, a prominent Boston abolitionist, was a good friend and that she was in good hands with him as her contractor. After a quick breakfast and a fond farewell, she was off, leaving Wendell to linger with uncertain malaise at the dining table.

He was about to return to the Studio Building when he heard shouting coming from the apartments above. It was Rosalie. "If you love her so much, marry her instead!" and the door slammed.

Fitzhugh shuffled down the steps in his nightshirt and launched sideways onto the sofa. He groaned and sat up, then leaned his head heavily into his hands. Bertha, the cook, came out from the kitchen, looking sympathetic, and poured him a cup of coffee. "Do you want breakfast, Fitzhugh?" she asked quietly.

"No thanks, Bertha," he said, "I'm not staying." Then, turning to Wendell, "Come, let's go next door."

Wendell followed the barefoot man out onto the sidewalk where Fitzhugh garnered nary a glance for his bedroom attire from sophisticated New Yorkers. They climbed the next stairs over and went in without knocking. At the dining table, which was still askew from the previous night, sat a thin-nosed mustachioed humorist for the *Sunday Mercury,* Bob Newell, and the three-mustachioed ne'er-do-well, Macaroni, both fully dressed and disheveled since they'd not yet been to bed. Sections of newspaper lay about with dirty coffee cups. "Don't bother with the news," said Macaroni, barely looking up, "it's all local fluff and filler – it seems the celestial display last night knocked out all the telegraph signals worldwide."

"Interesting," said Fitzhugh, as the two sat without invitation.

"No news is the news, and fascinating in its implications regarding the aurora."

"So," Wendell pressed Fitzhugh, "who is it Rosalie says you should marry instead? Are you seeing someone besides your wife?"

"Certainly not," said his friend. "Rosalie was referring to Miss Opium, for which I can hardly blame her."

"Hmmm," said Bob Newell, "face forward into the pudding, as I heard it."

Fitzhugh frowned, "It's not just my abominable behavior last night, for which I blame the wine…"

"Aye," said Wendell, "it's quite dangerous to consume wine and opium together."

"…she also does not appreciate my writing."

"Well, you do write about *hallucinationem narcoticum*," commented Newell.

"But my writing is my soul, my life! Where would I be without it? Were she truly beholden to me, she would at least pretend to understand." Wendell saw the dilemma and felt a pang for his good friend.

"She doesn't understand, or doesn't approve?" asked Macaroni.

"Neither understands nor approves! Nor does she bother to read my book – she condemns my words as insane without ever reading them! When I married her, I fancied it my fame as a writer that won her heart, so how can she not even read it?! Alas, if my words are insane, then I am just a homeless bummler ranting to myself on the street corner!"

"Perhaps that's what any of us is," said Newell, "Perhaps people only pretend to understand anything we write or speak, or take our meanings altogether differently than we intend. How are we to know?"

"For an experience so ineffable as the deeper trance states of hasheesh, no language was yet invented till yours," observed

Wendell.

"But that is the point, is it not?" responded Fitzhugh. "I am the one who invented the language, who described the state where no one had before. I am the one who gave them the vicarious journey so they would have no need to actually consume the stuff. I would think I had made a great contribution, and I have been rewarded handsomely with fame. Do I sound insane to you in my writings? If I have sacrificed for its sake, am I to be condemned as unworthy to have a wife or be a husband?" He was looking quite distraught.

"Humans would be better off intuiting each other magnetically, as do animals," muttered Newell.

"I understand the lure of hasheesh," said Wendell. "But, pray, why opium? Are you doing research for a second book?"

Fitzhugh sighed deeply. "No," he confessed, "I don't understand why opium myself." And he hid his face in his hands.

Just then, Henry Clapp descended the stairs. "I warned you, Ludlow'" he said with amusement, having overheard most of the conversation, "a wife by definition can't be sympathetic to bohemianism, as the institution of marriage is inimical to it. If you want to keep her, you will have to get up in the mornings and don a banker's suit."

"Nay," said Fitzhugh, flushed as he raised his face, "Rosalie is far too romantic to want a banker for a husband. And she cares not a stick for money."

"Hah!" said Newell. "She'd rather be with it than without it, I assure you!"

"It seems," said Wendell, being irritated now with the lack of sympathy for his old friend, "that opium has become a problem on its own, quite apart from Mrs. Ludlow."

Fitzhugh tried to explain. "Opium is a muse like no other – beyond even the effects of hasheesh."

The other writers were suddenly sympathetic and nodded in assent. "I feel that way about alcohol," admitted Macaroni. "How can a man of the arts forsake his muse?"

"She is a vicious mistress," moaned Henry Clapp.

Wendell suddenly felt very grateful to Dr. Paschal Beverly Randolph for his own benign and effective muse, his magic mirror.

Lillian was back briefly, for Adah Menken's small and secretive wedding, which was celebrated afterward at Ada Clare's house. It was a happy time, and the couple seemed genuinely in love, inspiring a warm feeling of domesticity between Wendell and Lillian.

Lillian shared few of her lyceum adventures. She was soon gone for another two weeks, returning for the celebration of Anna Mary's wedding, with plans for an additional hasty departure. Wendell began to suspect that something was afoot with fugitives from the South and the school she funded in the Five Points. Once again, he was afraid for her. Hoping for some insight, he asked after Tuck and Ruby, but Lillian denied having seen them. The night before she was to depart again, she asked him to leave, though he had hoped to spend a last night together. On saying goodbye, she burst into tears.

"Are you afraid you might be with child?" he pleaded, holding her close.

"No," she said, "I am but weary and need sleep. I will see you in November, when I return."

He felt an old familiar fear of abandonment, a twisting in his stomach. "Will you not at least give me your itinerary – perchance I could catch a performance." Again, she shook her head.

"Are you never going to trust me?" he asked quietly.

She hugged him tightly, and trembled. "Wendell, please. I am sworn. Do not pressure me so. I do dearly, dearly love you. It is you who must trust me." The kiss she gave him satisfied his doubt, and he felt reassured that he, at least, was not the cause of her alarm. But that did little to assuage his helplessness to protect her.

"I will see you in November," she repeated as he departed into the hall and she closed her apartment door behind him.

Wendell put on his hat, thinking what he really needed was a drink. Instead of leaving, he made his way quietly up the stairs and knocked on Fitzhugh's door. His old school chum let him in and Wendell collapsed onto the sofa. "Harte, old man, you look positively done. Are you in romantic difficulties?"

"I would thank you for some whiskey," Wendell replied. Rosalie already had it in her hand and sat down next to him, smoothing Wendell's brow with concern. "Ah," he rued, "she leaves in the morning till November, and not even anywhere to reach her. I am most concerned that she is not safe."

"Why not safe?" Fitzhugh asked, surprised. Now Wendell realized his trouble, how close he had come to revealing something of her secrets. No wonder she could not trust him to know!

"I'm being the fool," he said hastily. "It's just she is a lady traveling alone." He sipped his drink, in which Fitzhugh joined him, taking the armchair opposite and regarding his friend through squinted eyes. 'He knows me well,' thought Wendell.

Fitzhugh changed the subject. "I saw Sam today. He has really gotten crazy about this militia thing. He goes weekly, forsaking even his legal studies."

"There has always been something of the solid citizen in Sam," rejoined Wendell. "Someday he'll run for office."

"It's a good thing, I think," said Rosalie.

"Do you wish I were more the solid citizen," Fitzhugh asked his wife, "and less the bohemian?"

There was a silence, and Wendell rose to go. "Thank you for the drink – you saved my life. I don't want to keep you up." His friends did not protest as he picked up his bag and moved to let himself out. But as he stepped across the threshold, he heard the door below close and footsteps on the stairs. "Fitzhugh," he said with an urgent whisper, "Lillian's leaving tonight!"

"Do you want to follow her?" asked Fitzhugh excitedly. Wendell did not need to answer as the two men ignored the disgust on Rosalie's face and crept down the staircase. Out on the night sidewalk, they saw Lillian hail a cab and quickly commandeered one to follow. Wendell was sure she would be headed to the Five Points, but instead her carriage turned north. "What is it you're suspecting?" asked Fitzhugh. "Do you think she's seeing someone else?"

"No," said Wendell. Once again he was in a precarious position, and silently condemned Lillian for having placed him so. If she'd trusted him, he would be with her, not following furtively behind. Now his friend Fitzhugh, in turn, was aggravated that Wendell seemed to be withholding something from him.

They followed Lillian's carriage up Fifth Avenue to 35th Street and watched as it entered through the gates of a large mansion. Both men knew the place – it was the mansion of Henry Ferguson. "Well," said Fitzhugh with a hint of exasperation, "isn't this where the lady lives? It is her house, right?" Wendell found this factual pronouncement very strange, as he had never thought of her as living anywhere but at the Household.

"I'm sorry," said Wendell, "I don't know what's been in me lately. But I thank you for coming – you are a true friend and I am indebted."

"You would be indebted," rued Fitzhugh, "were I not needing an escape from Rosalie just then. If I seem perturbed, it is at the prospect of going back so soon."

"Then come with me to the Studio Building, and we'll continue our nightcap there."

The carriage had not gone but a few feet in the new direction when Wendell bid the driver stop. "Hush, who's that?" Wendell whispered. Another carriage had pulled up in front of the mansion, close enough to be seen in the lamplight. Three men got out and proceeded with furtive haste through the gate on foot. Wendell easily recognized the first two: Gerrit Smith and the well-known colored orator, Frederick Douglass. But it was the third man, tall with slicked back white hair and streaming beard, that made his hide bristle, for he looked quite like illustrations Wendell had seen of the notorious John Brown, the brutal abolitionist who made Kansas bleed and put fear into the hearts of Missouri slave-owners.

Fitzhugh, behind him and unable to get a good look, asked again what Wendell suspected. "Nothing, really," breathed Wendell. "Pray don't speak of this to anyone – she would not like it that we followed her."

The next several weeks, Wendell worked diligently on the Gerrit Smith commissions, intent on collecting his money and sending some to his father. They were decently large canvases, and he reveled in the many shades of green he could employ. Finally, having largely finished, he decided he'd earned a break at Pfaff's and found himself sitting down with Walt Whitman. "Everything all right between you and Lillian?" the older man asked, leading Wendell to wonder what was being rumored now.

He had just begun to answer when they were interrupted by an excited newspaper boy who came running into Pfaff's yelling, "Extra! Extra! John Brown leads raid on arsenal at Harper's Ferry. Fierce battle rages!" The boy continued to yell, even though he was instantly mobbed. By the time Wendell pushed his way through, drenched with sweat and forcing down the fear that rose in him, all the papers were gone.

Chapter 14

A nation on the brink of civil war waited and watched as the drama continued between John Brown's small band and the federal army sent to arrest them. Lt. Col. Robert E. Lee led the soon victorious forces, killing two of John Brown's sons along with colored and white compatriots, and wounding John Brown. Brown was quickly bound over for trial, charged with inciting insurrection and murder. His plan had been to liberate the arsenal at Harper's Ferry, Virginia, for use by escaping slaves.

Debate over the incident flared at Pfaff's while Wendell listened quietly, sketching Henry Clapp as they sat with the group in the alcove. Wendell had come to admire the bohemian king's calm, and was trying to capture in the portrait the wisdom that seemed to emanate from Clapp's ancient-looking grey eyes. "'Tis a spirited defense the Concordians Thoreau and now Emerson make for Mr. Brown," Clapp was saying, "'*John Brown will make the gallows glorious like the Cross.*' Their deification of him will surely bring on a war."

Fitzhugh disagreed. "I doubt there'll be a war. President Buchanan will continue to appease the South by hanging him."

"That's what the abolitionists want," Clapp pointed out, "to make him a martyr."

"You know they are searching for accomplices," put in Ada Clare, which made Wendell's *crayon* slip. Shakily, he wondered at Lillian's whereabouts.

Tom Aldrich spoke with a touch of admiration. "It's new that white men should band together with colored to free slaves – it strikes more violent fear than Nat Turner's slave uprising or even the slave rebellion in Haiti. Southerners now apprehend that there are whites who will act forcefully on their anti-slavery sentiments." They continued on about the events in Virginia, so potent that even news of a fragile peace over Italian unification went almost unnoticed.

Wendell had written to Gerrit Smith that the paintings were done, but no word returned. It was now November, All Saints Day, and it seemed that darkness came early and the weather turned abruptly cold. There was still no word from Lillian, and he even worried that she hadn't taken warm enough clothes on her lyceum tour. In the 14th Street parlor with Fitzhugh and Rosalie, Wendell overheard Bertha at the door tell someone that Mrs. Ferguson did not live there, and wondered who wanted to know and why they called her Mrs. Ferguson.

A few mornings later at the Studio Building mess, the artists were stirred over revelations in the morning papers. John Brown was sentenced to hang a month hence – Wendell read his response, *"I believe that to have interfered as I have done, as I have always freely admitted I have done, in behalf of His despised poor, I did not wrong but right. Now, if it is deemed necessary that I should forfeit my life for the furtherance of the ends of justice, and mingle my blood further with the blood of my children and with the blood of millions in this slave country whose rights are disregarded by wicked, cruel, and unjust enactments, I say let it be done."* Among the men being sought for possible complicity were Gerrit Smith and Frederick Douglass. Mr. Douglass, the colored orator whom Wendell had seen at the mansion, had fled abroad to Canada along with others accused. Gerrit Smith, who had given John Brown land in the failed colored experiment at North Elba, had suffered a mental breakdown and was confined in the asylum at Utica, New York. To Wendell's tremendous relief, there was no mention of Miss Lillian Flax, Mrs. Henry Ferguson, or any woman.

Wendell watched a weak sun come in through the high basement windows and cast a grey light on the morning faces in the mess. He sat with Thomas Read, Sanford Gifford, and Ted Winthrop, trying to feel some semblance of normality with potato pancakes and coffee. But he felt queasy and unable to eat. "Gerrit Smith owes me my commissions," said Wendell, as if that were the true source of his agitation. Knowing Lillian's passions against war, he was sure of her innocence, but worried that the stealthy meeting in her husband's house might attract accusation.

"What do you intend to do?" asked Thomas.

Wendell considered. "Go to Utica." Having resolved the matter to himself, Wendell felt better. He rose amid well-wishes, waved his goodbyes and hurried up the stairs. As he passed the entrance on the first floor, George came out of his concierge office.

"A colored woman to see you, sir," said George.

"A lady to see me," Wendell corrected him with a hint of irritation. He followed George to his office where Ruby stood waiting. Apparently, George had not offered her a seat. "Mrs. Robinson!" Wendell held her proffered hand in both of his, squeezing it warmly. "I have been so anxious to see you. Please, sit down." He glared at George who gave a little bow, and left the office. "Would you like tea?"

"Please, call me Ruby," she said, "and I'd prefer coffee with cream if you have it."

Wendell searched around the hot water brazier in the corner, and not finding coffee, offered to retrieve some from the mess. Ruby looked grateful and allowed herself to be waited on. Wendell quickly returned, bearing coffee for both of them, and sat down across from her. He politely inquired after her family and how the recent news was being received.

"We are as anxious as everyone," she said. Then, "I have come with a message – Lillian has met with a delay, and begs you forgive her that she will miss Thanksgiving with you."

"Thanksgiving! Oh Ruby, something is so wrong! Shall I not go to her? How am I to reach her?" He had already risen, ready to rush off that very instant.

Ruby remained seated and sipped her coffee. "I don't know

myself how to reach her, but trust that she will be in touch." Now she grabbed his arm and pulled him close to look him straight in the eye, always disconcerting from a woman, and he understood with a shudder that she meant him to comprehend her words exactly. "There have been inquiries made, from federal agents, of her whereabouts," she spoke in a whisper. "If they should contact you, pray tell them nothing, and let me know at once." Holding the gaze, he exhaled his shakily held breath with an audible sigh and nodded.

"Can you tell me nothing more about what difficulties beset her?" he murmured back. Ruby shook her head and let go his arm, her dark fringed eyes softening with warmth and sympathy as he straightened.

"I'm sorry, Mr. Parry," she said. And not surprisingly, "I am sworn."

He smiled wanly at her. "Call me Wendell." His own dark eyes were softening as he surrendered to the situation. "And really, Ruby, how is your family?"

She brightened. "Tuck has a job with horses at the local livery," Ruby replied, "and except that we are hardly able to see each other, we are well."

On board the northbound train, Wendell sat in consternation by the window and picked up a Rochester newspaper that was lying on the seat. He read with disinterest about Mayor Wood's re-election. Then, as he leafed through, his heart suddenly raced. In addition to a rehash of events in Virginia was a letter from the fugitive former slave, Frederick Douglass, writing from Canada in defense of Gerrit Smith:

"His is a mind that has never known the fetter, and those who have fettered him must take the responsibility for the present affliction (God grant that it may have, ere this, passed away) and disturbance of mind. Mr. Smith has done nothing in his relation to dear old Osawatomie Brown for which posterity will not bless his

name and memory."

The courage of this public sentiment made Wendell even more apprehensive for Lillian, lest her name be linked. Was she in Canada with Frederick Douglass and the others accused? But since John Brown's raid itself, the number of voices defending the action had increased, and John Brown was changing in the North's public verdict from criminal to hero.

As the mighty steam engine broke loose of the city's harness and hastened to the countryside, dramatic hues of autumn foliage flanked the Hudson River on either side. For once in his young life, the artist did not notice. He had not even brought a sketch pad with him, an oversight so uncharacteristic as to make anyone who knew him wonder if he, like Gerrit Smith, had gone mad. In a stupor of uncertainty, rocking with the swerving rails, Wendell stared helplessly down at the newspaper. One maddening thought predominated over the jumble in his mind and mocked him: How much of a man was he that he could not protect his lady when she was in danger. How much of a man?

Wendell rose and began to stagger up and down the length of the car, not caring that he incurred anxious glances when the train lurched, launching him drunkenly toward some passenger's lap. Within minutes, the train was passing Washington Irving's house in Irvington. Wendell glanced up at it, marveling how long ago the *Rival* had stopped there at the dock. For a moment, he almost imagined that he saw the venerable old writer sitting atop the hill, the only remaining symbol of a young and hopeful America. Then, with a rush and a blur of dense orange and yellow foliage, the vision was gone.

Finally Wendell did what he'd always seen other passengers do but had never wanted to do himself – he sat down and sagged against the window, closing his eyes till he too was gone.

Three hours later, the conductor woke him. "Last stop, sir. This is Albany." Wendell picked up his carpet bag and climbed down onto the platform. He had not seen Albany since before his trip to Europe, and the mighty city looked to have doubled in size. Smokestacks belched as far as he could see, smelting iron and coal for shipment to Manhattan, and extending to the steel mills across the river in Troy. The young artist was already coated with a thin layer of black soot as he hurried to catch the train to Utica. Soon the engine was chugging along the edge of the Erie Canal, where Wendell watched barges being towed by horses from one lock to the next. In just a few decades, the Erie had given both New York and America manufacturing prowess surpassing much of Europe's. But now, the mighty railroads rushed past laden with goods, portending imminent monetary collapse for the wondrous antiquated canal.

It was dusk when the train squealed to a stop on Utica's busy canal front. A light rain had begun to fall, warming and cleaning the soot from the air. Wendell hurried across Bagg Square to the large brick edifice of the Northern Hotel and checked in. It was a nice place, the sort of place he could order a bath. After a light supper and a hot soak, Wendell retired early.

In the morning it was still raining, rendering the town soggy and dismal. Wendell was nervous as his carriage turned off Genessee Street and made its way up the rise to the impressive asylum with its massive Grecian pillars and sweeping lawns – "Old Main" the carriage driver called it. Wendell felt sorry for the driver, as his mackintosh had been uncomfortably breeched at the neck by a stream of water which ran freely off the rim of his top hat. "Would yer want me to be waitin' fer ye, sir?" asked the miserable man.

As Wendell considered, a flash of lightning lit up the distance. "No need," decided Wendell, handing the man his pay and a good tip. "Perhaps you could go home and dry off, then return for me here in two hours. I would be most appreciative." As the man assented, a delayed clap of thunder told Wendell the heart of the storm was still far off, and he hurried into the building. He was greeted in the grand entrance by an orderly who bade him sit until Mr. Smith's availability could be determined. Left alone there, Wendell waited with growing agitation as he peered through a cavernous archway into a long corridor and heard the scream of an inmate echoing along it.

After awhile, a rather portly and pleasant gentlewoman emerged and came straight to him with her hand outstretched. "Mr. Wendell Parry," she said.

He rose and took the hand, "Of whose company do I have the pleasure?" he asked with a small bow.

"I am Mr. Gerrit Smith's cousin, Mrs. Elizabeth Cady Stanton. And I believe you are the young artist whom Miss Lillian Flax so admires."

"I am pleased to make your acquaintance," said Wendell.

"I am so sorry that my cousin is not up to more company at the moment. I'm afraid I have worn him out. Perhaps you could come back later." The orderly had returned and nodded in concurrence with her assessment.

"Are you rushing off? It would be an honor to sit and talk with you. You have garnered my sincere admiration for your efforts on behalf of women's suffrage."

"Why thank you. But alas, would you believe an old lady like me has a new-born to attend – and not to mention the toddlers! But I am pleased to have met you."

"Before you go – Pray, have you news of Miss Flax's circumstances? I have had cause for concern." His anxiety showed and Mrs. Stanton looked at him sympathetically.

"Don't worry your head about Lily Ann," she assured him, "I have no doubt she'll be home soon. However," she paused, choosing her words, "be careful should her husband return. He ships cotton and will not approve of her abolitionist leanings."

She left him alone and Wendell, not knowing what else to do, sat back down to wait. The idea that Mr. Ferguson could return from Europe leant additional chill. The orderly busied himself at his station, leaving Wendell to listen to the growing storm outside, which frequently sent flashes thundering through the high arched windows in eerie syncopation with the screams from down the darkened hallway. The orderly looked up. "Some of our inmates are afraid of storms," he explained. Wendell nodded, but was not deterred from his unease. He dearly wished he had a sketch pad, and finally begged paper and pencil from the orderly. He made minute scribbles, drawing nothing in particular, and so passed the time. Then the screams grew louder and a man in a white lab coat appeared at the far end of the corridor, and hastened into a room where the screams abruptly halted. The white coated man came out and strode down the hallway toward the entrance hall. He had a quiet conversation with the orderly, and turned to Wendell.

"Mr. Parry? I am Dr. Gray, Mr. Smith's attending alienist. If you'll follow me, he can see you now. I am not sure he will know you, but his cousin vouched for your identity." As Wendell fell in beside him down the corridor, the doctor continued, "He is not clear on who a number of people are that he should know. I will leave you with him and his servant, but should he become agitated, please depart immediately."

"Thank you," said Wendell, and entered the room as the door closed again behind him.

Gerrit Smith stood before him, shaven clean and bald for lice and almost unrecognizable. He was thinner and wearing a blue inmate's uniform of lightweight cotton, his sunken face red and blotched. Wendell put out his hand to him, "I hope you remember me, Mr. Smith. Wendell Parry, the artist from whom you commissioned paintings of Ithaca?" Gerrit Smith grabbed the hand and pulled Wendell into the room, then pushed him into an easy chair. His servant stood in the background, watching uneasily.

"Are you here to get me out?" Mr. Smith hissed in a

conspiratorial undertone.

"Are you not here of your own volition?" Wendell said surprised.

"My own volition?" Gerrit Smith stuck his face within inches of Wendell's, leaning over and bracing himself on the arms of the chair. The great temperance fighter's breath smelled of brandy and cannabis, the medicines of the institution. "Who are you?" he hissed again. Wendell's heart sank.

"I have done some paintings for you, for which you had agreed to pay me $1000. Do you not remember? I was in Fishkill Landing at the Eagle Hotel, with Miss Lillian Flax." The man was staring wild-eyed at him and drooling. Wendell grew increasingly anxious, "Do you not remember?"

Gerrit Smith's eyes went blank, then the light came back into them. "You are here to get me out!" he declared. "I should be in Virginia, I should be going to the gallows with Captain Brown."

"I am sure you are guilty of nothing, sir," cried Wendell in dismay, "nor is Mr. Brown! You are doubtless here for your own protection, placed here by people who love you."

"Love me? They tricked me. They said they were taking me to Virginia." Now the man stood up, giving Wendell room to breathe his own air. "Of course I am guilty of nothing. I tried to talk him out of it. Oh woe is me that it should come to this." He sagged forlornly into another chair opposite and covered his face with his hands.

"And Lillian Flax?" Wendell asked quietly.

Gerrit's head snapped around and he let out an unearthly affrighted roar, at which Wendell jumped up, looking to the servant in alarm who came running. "You're after her! It was you! You were spying on us that night! You're from the government!" The servant had run from the room and came back with Dr. Gray and the orderly. Gerrit Smith turned to them, shouting, "He's after me! You said you wouldn't let anyone from the government in here!

You have betrayed me!"

They each grabbed one of Gerrit's arms. The alienist was talking to him in soothing tones as they forced him toward a man-sized baby's crib by the window, "It's all right, Mr. Smith, it's time for your nap. You'll be safe in your crib – no one can harm you there." And to Wendell's horror, they lifted the weakly struggling man into the caged bed and lowered a slatted lid, locking him in. With a loud peal of thunder, lightning flashed through the windows, rendering Gerrit Smith alight and owl-eyed, lying on his side in fetal position behind the bars. Wendell stood transfixed, his pulse pounding wildly, until the doctor pushed him out into the cavernous hallway and closed the door.

"Time for you to go, Mr. Parry," said Doctor Gray. There was a great squall of sympathetic screams and commotion coming from the rooms as Wendell ran down the corridor, footsteps echoing, and out past the Grecian pillars of Old Main into the heart of the crashing storm. Fortunately, his get-away carriage stood at the ready, and Wendell was soon, but not soon enough, hugging himself on the train seat as the infernal tempest pursued him down the tracks to Albany, and enveloped him on Albany's platform with its thundering deluge.

It was well after midnight when Wendell finally crept back to the relative calm of his atelier, soaked and shivering to his core. He was glad for the company of Cat in his bed and, still chilled, resolved to get himself a heavier quilt. Ah, he thought – but with what money? For he realized suddenly that, without Gerrit Smith's commissions, he was quite broke.

Chapter 15

A dejected Wendell Harte Parry sat in the alcove at Pfaff's, nursing a beer that Fitzhugh had been kind enough to buy him. He dared not think of Lillian – she was doubtless in Canada, with some wealthy abolitionist who had participated with her in their worthy adventures, and now acted as her rescuer. Wendell could see them, lost in a snowy cabin and huddled next to a fire, her hero soothing her fears beneath a blanket of fur, planning a future together in France. He felt the fool – not for loving her, but for allowing her to keep her secrets. Or perhaps, for not being a man to whom she could confide. Ah, there it was – for not being a man. His breath shuddered through him from his hidden depths of despair, as the old fear of being abandoned crept again into the pit of his stomach.

He swallowed hard on a head of foam and forced himself to rejoin the conversation – Fitzhugh was, a week hence, to take examinations for the bar!

"Sam assures me I will pass," Fitzhugh was saying, "he tested me all night."

"But you had studied medicine in college," gasped Wendell. "How long have you been preparing?"

"Since yesterday," his friend admitted. "But it all comes back. You may remember I studied awhile in my uncle's law offices. I had been considered quite the genius, and I would have Rosalie likewise think me so."

"Ah, what a man must do to prove himself worthy to a woman." Henry Clapp shook his head. "Best keep a woman a friend and be quickly done with a lover, or she'll soon have you playing the contortionist."

"*Au contraire,* Mr. Clapp. I thank my lovely wife for urging me forward," Fitzhugh defended her, "to finish something that had once fired my enthusiasm. And also to prove that my intellect has not been adversely affected by what she calls, 'mind obliterating pharmaceuticals'."

"Hear, hear!" said Tom Aldrich and led a chorus of mugs drumming on the table.

"You would think it enough," continued Fitzhugh, "that I have numerous articles and a new short story appearing this month in *Vanity Fair*. But as I can't commit her to read it, I must pass the bar also."

"It would seem she is actually good for you," chided Aldrich.

Mr. Clapp directed his attention to Macaroni. "So what's in that newspaper, Mr. Arnold, that you've been so assiduously hoarding?" inquired Henry, with an imperious puff of his pipe.

"Abject fear runs throughout the South, of a raid to free John Brown," exclaimed Macaroni dramatically. "I say 'tis time for the Feds to assert some authority, and do the hanging themselves."

"Nay," protested Aldrich, "let Virginia make him a martyr – let the South hang him."

"It seems to me," said the bohemian king, "that he should be hung between the two thieves." This bit of wisdom got the mugs drumming appreciatively. "Let us be done with Virginia," he shushed them. "There must be other news."

"Hold, I shall peep the inner pages," Macaroni said. He continued, reading aloud, "Stock markets were down on threat of France invading Britain."

"France invade Britain?!" Wendell was incredulous.

Henry sneered. "The Royals' chess game continues. Pray, there must be something new afoot? No aeronauts crossing the oceans in balloons, no high-wire artists above Niagara Falls?"

"A ring of counterfeiters has been arrested in Jersey City."

"Government persecution," protested Clapp. "If criminal counterfeiters do no good, they also do no harm, except to the regular counterfeiters on Caterwaul Street." This got a 'Hear hear' from Aldrich.

"Survey for a Panama Canal continues apace," Macaroni went on hopefully, "Hmmm... Several ships have foundered with the attendant pleas of the widows, and cetera... Murder and mayhem in the usual places... The stock market rallied as rumors of France invading Britain were dispelled... Rumors of Kit Carson's death were likewise dispelled – a good thing, that. I ask you, where would the West be without Kit Carson? The Mormons threaten secession of the Utah Territory and the Indians are yet a problem..." He looked up, "I reckon that about covers it – Oh wait, the biggest news of all!" He paused meaningfully and had their attention. "John Heenan is training in England for his title bout next June, while early betting favors Sayers. Heenan expects to weigh in at 190 pounds!"

"Fie!" exclaimed Clapp. "Are they betting already?! And nothing else in there but advertisements?"

"Where is Mrs. Heenan?" Wendell asked. "Is she abroad with her husband?"

"No. The Menken is touring with a production of *The French Spy*," said Henry Clapp. "I believe she is in Ohio."

Now it was Ted Winthrop who spoke, in reverent tones. "Adah's become quite notorious, has she not? I'll wager her fame will someday surpass her husband's." He raised his mug, "Well, here's to her, our good friend, may she delight her audiences everywhere." And the gentlemen joined him in a toast to the wonderful and scandalous Adah Menken Heenan.

Wendell, whose mind was yet on his woes, thought that ere the day was done, he should try to sell a painting. He tipped his hat by way of goodbye, and rose to leave. As he passed Walt Whitman, alone with a book in his usual spot, the good man bade him pause, and pressed a two-dollar gold piece into his hand.

"I thank you, Walt, I will repay you," at which Whitman merely shrugged and, as was his wont, looked back down to his book – and so Wendell departed.

Back at the Studio Building, three new residents were in the entrance with their luggage intending to move in – the long awaited friends from Europe – Emmanuel Leutze, William Stanley Haseltine, and Worthington Whittredge. "Hey, Parry!" called Emmanuel Leutze extending his hand, "We've arrived at last intact. Does the place live up to its vaunted reputation?" Wendell assured them that the Tenth Street Studios' reputation was greatly enhanced by their coming, as other artists gathered excitedly.

"Ah, the German School has arrived! Düsseldorf at last!" happily exclaimed Thomas Buchanan Read. "The Italians and French have all hurried home to war, and left the field wide open!"

"There will be a new Italy soon if the French have their way – unified, democratic and free!"

"Well," laughed Sanford, "Let us not trust Emperor Napoleon that far!"

They were soon all gathered in laughter and discussions at Jervis McEntee's atelier, where Gertrude McEntee bustled about waiting on them from her tiny kitchen stall. Anna Mary's atelier had been given up upon her marriage and now Mrs. McEntee was quite alone as the only woman at the Studio Building, not considering Mrs. Winter. She put out a fine array of treats for the men, and seemed pleased with her impromptu party. Wendell imagined having such an arrangement with Lillian, and wondered again at her whereabouts.

Naturally, the new-comers wanted to know whether the New York art market was lucrative, and soon there was a lively discussion. Thomas inquired what Wendell intended to do with his Ithaca studies, and the abridged and sordid story of his journey to Gerrit Smith's current abode prompted utterances of shock and sympathy. "When Church's *Heart of the Andes* is finished, let us hold a gallery exhibit of Parry's Ithaca canvases," suggested Sanford Gifford. "What had we scheduled there next?"

"Please," begged Wendell, "That's very kind, but I don't want to follow Fred's triumph. My work would surely suffer in comparison."

"You're too modest," suggested Fred Church. "Your Ithaca pieces are splendid, and deserve a showing. Indeed, we could arrange dramatic lighting upon the four of them, and your show would be quite as much an acclaimed spectacle as mine."

"Yes," enthused McEntee. "We'll bring in some large potted trees and dapple the light around the canvases to resemble a forest floor."

"I like that," admitted Wendell, beginning to catch the possibilities. "But is the space available?"

Louis Mignot spoke up. "I am scheduled for a six weeks show. I will happily yield my first two weeks to Mr. Parry, as I also don't wish to follow Mr. Church." This was greeted with laughter, and some consideration on Wendell's part.

Finally, he said, "It's a more than generous proposition, but three things militate against it. First, it's too rushed for timely notice; second, the country will be distracted by John Brown's hanging; and third, Monsieur Mignot's notices have already been published. And too, Louis, sweet friend, you will want the time before Christmas, as your small paintings make handsome Christmas presents."

"Why not have a private showing in your atelier?" proposed Worthington Whittredge. "There must surely be art collectors who would come."

"Truly," agreed Thomas Read, "Mignot can direct some of his traffic upstairs, and we can all recommend your exhibit to buyers whom we know. 'Twill take short notice."

"And let us play with the drama of the light in your atelier," enthused Church. "You have that wonderful skylight."

"Alright," said Wendell. "It's done! But I will not wait for Fred's exhibit to end. We can start directing the traffic upstairs immediately, beginning tomorrow, and invitations will be delivered before the week-end!"

"Hoorah!" said Leutze. "That's the spirit we came to America to find!"

Forthwith, all the artists went about converting Wendell's third floor studio into a handsome exhibition space. Gilded frames were commandeered from various apartments, which Wendell and Thomas efficiently put to use, and easels found for all the canvases. McEntee brought up potted trees, and Fred Church placed foliage against the skylight where the shadows would pattern the floor and not the paintings. Sanford and Thomas did the same on the windows. Gentle gas spotlights were mounted along the railing of the small balcony, and more plants and foliage placed about. The effect was to enter into a verdant world, lush and wet as Ithaca itself. "Now all it wants is the sound of flowing water," Wendell said. "But if my schooling serves me, it would be impossible without the offending sound of a motor."

"Ah, your schooling serves you ill!" spoke Thomas. "I will return shortly."

Thomas returned with a small Christmas pinwheel that spun around when the warmth of candles beneath it created a whirlwind. Wendell watched as the tiny flames soon did their magic and admitted that the resulting whoosh from paper striker on tin and tiny tinkle bell was watery. And so the scene was complete and Wendell went to bed that night with a hopeful heart and warm feelings for his fellows.

The camaraderie continued next morning during breakfast in the mess, with the newcomers full of stories about Europe and promises of treasures to trade when their crates arrived. Fred Church was waiting impatiently with a cup of coffee for the gallery to open. "*Heart of the Andes* created a sensation in England," noted Emmanuel Leutze. "If touring be so lucrative, how do you dare to sell it?"

"Ah," laughed Church, "it has been sold, and the sum should please you, for it will drive up the price of paintings everywhere. And the owner has made a magnificent bargain – I may continue to tour it for two years, and should anyone offer me double, I am free to accept it."

"Amazing!" Sanford Gifford dabbed his chin. "We hold our breath as we await the sum."

Fred stood and a big grin spread across his affable face as he smoothed his bushy mutton chops in preparation for the grand announcement. His throat made clearing noises. "Gentlemen," he declared after a suitably suspenseful interval, "I am finally to build the mansion I have always dreamed of. I have received…" another pause, "$10,000!" He bowed slightly, clearly gratified at the gasps and exclamations at this, the largest sum ever garnered for the sale of a new painting. Wendell put his hands together in applause, and the entire mess joined in. The excitement was electric, a new level of respectability for American art.

Now Wendell was anxious, too, for the doors to open – since Fred's painting was no longer for sale, he knew Fred would send any disappointed buyers upstairs to his showing. And Ted Winthrop would again be selling his *Companion to the Heart of the Andes* booklet outside the gallery and would certainly direct people up.

As Wendell departed to begin his day, he noted crowds assembling outside and a bright sun that was auspicious for the dappling effect of his windows. He climbed the stairs with some excitement and breathed in the ambience as he entered, pretending to see it for the first time. Yes, the leafy shadows flooded the floor around canvases that were quite pleasing: multiple shades of green surrounded the deep and dramatic Ithaca gorge; in another, white ripples cascaded merrily into the cool and rocky pools of Buttermilk Falls; Cayuga Lake was, but for a lone sail, as pristine as if man were viewing it for the first time; and the farmland in the fourth canvas stretched away across rocky rolling hills, past shady woods and small farm houses with neat fences – a green and tempting paradise to the cows that munched there beside the little brook.

Wendell lit the candles under his pinwheel and waited for what he hoped would be a good turn-out. The excitement in his stomach now turned uneasily to dread, as memories of his previous showing and his first week-end with Lillian came flooding back. Was she safe? Had she abandoned him? Why had he not heard from her? He had not much time to rue before possible patrons appeared at the door.

The ladies came first, always eager to see an artist in his studio, and tittered behind their gloved hands while, to Wendell's chagrin, they showed more interest in the artist than the art. Then came several gentlemen, who made knowledgeable remarks about lighting and composition, and shook his hand with promises of further contact.

Shortly before noon came a young woman, very pretty and dressed in the highest fashion. She clearly had a great deal of money. Her husband soon caught up to her, himself attired with top hat and the finest light-weight wool. They surveyed the lovely scene, over which she uttered sounds of absolute delight, then she whispered something to her husband and he back to her. Their heads turned expectantly to Wendell, who offered his hand and seated them along with tea and cookies.

The man introduced himself as Mr. John McClure, the agent who handled *Heart of the Andes* for Fred Church. Wendell was astonished. Indeed, he had never heard of an artist having an agent. "There is a great demand for captivating tours," the man explained. "Mr. Church has begun a craze that your display could stimulate to greater frenzy." His wife leaned over and whispered something behind her gloved hand, beaming at Wendell when she finished. "My wife," he explained, "would like for me to buy all four pictures outright and take them on tour myself, with you making an occasional appearance to drive the delirium of the art fanatics. You have the youth and good looks to become a star. But alas, I have been too successful in getting a high price for Mr. Church's work, and now cannot afford the price which you could surely get following an exhibition tour."

"You flatter me," said Wendell coolly, though his heart raced. "What would be the terms were I to engage you in exhibiting the canvases for me?"

"I believe an advance of $100 for each canvas, and I would take a 20% cut of any sale made while on tour. The buyer would naturally not take possession till the tour was complete. Meanwhile, I would claim whatever receipts I garnered at the gate, and pay your expenses for any appearance you could make." Wendell wanted to say yes immediately, wanted the $400 with a chance for more, but sat with his mouth open, unsure if he could believe what he was hearing. Mr. McClure stood and handed Wendell his card. "Please think about it. And congratulations on a stupendous show."

"Thank you," said Wendell, standing. He bowed to the lady and gentleman. "I will contact you, on either possibility. You have given me much to consider."

An older couple had entered ere the first couple left, and stepped up in turn to talk to the young artist. "I say, good sir," the man said with the stilted tones of English aristocracy, "would you be so kind as to sell me the one titled *Buttermilk Falls?* My wife desires to have it upon Our Lord's coming birthday."

"What is it you wish to offer for it, sir?" asked Wendell, reeling with his good fortune.

"Would you take $600?" Wendell looked at him – that would have been a good price yesterday, but today Fred Church had got $10,000. Not that he compared himself to Church! Again, it was tempting to take it. His needs were pressing, and he imagined the needs of his father and sister were as well. And six hundred was better than four hundred.

"I had planned to take it on tour," Wendell heard himself responding. "Would you be willing to spare it for the duration of six months?"

"No, no," the man blustered. "Sir, that is quite out of the question. I depart for England in a fortnight and fain would bring the picture with me."

"I am sorry then," said Wendell, again surprised at his own words. "My tour has a prior claim on it."

"Then perhaps you will consider $800," countered the man. Now Wendell's heart was truly beating wildly – it was but $200 shy of what Gerrit Smith had originally offered for all four!

"Again, my apologies. If you wish to purchase the painting, you must agree to take possession only after the tour, which I assure you will not happen before Christmas." He could not believe he had said it. Was he so committed to a tour which was not yet certain, which in no way guaranteed a sale, that he would walk away from $800? But when he looked at the four paintings together in so pleasing an arrangement, his heart told him there was greatness in them – he was right not to let one go.

The man shook his head, and handed Wendell his card. "As I said, I am sailing. If you change your mind, please contact me. I am so sorry, my dear," he said to his wife. He tipped his hat to Wendell and they left. Wendell quickly scrawled a note to leave on his door, 'Back in five minutes,' and hurried down the stairs to Thomas' room.

"Thomas, 'tis I," he called while knocking loudly on the door.

"*Entrere!*" came the answer, and Thomas Buchanan Read welcomed him with a quizzical expression. "I am unable to discern your mood," said Thomas, "whether 'tis alarmed or elated."

"Ah, 'tis both! You discern my mood correctly." Wendell flopped down on Thomas' sofa, sprawling in mock exhaustion. "I am a jackass caught between two bales of hay!"

"Truly an appalling predicament for a jackass!" laughed Thomas. "But out with the story quickly, I must finish this sculpture and arrange for its delivery." So Wendell told of the two offers, and what his considerations were in accepting either.

"Clearly," said Thomas, studying his friend more closely, "you wish to do the tour. As would I! To allay your fears, you have only to ask Mr. John McClure for a larger advance. Be audacious, like Church! Require that he not sell the paintings for less than $1500 apiece, and that he include you on the entire tour with a share of the gate. Afterall, without your paintings, he has nothing for himself, so command a hard bargain." Wendell found this advice enhanced his already elated mood, and he determined to close the studio and go straight away to visit Mr. McClure. He left with effusive expressions of gratitude.

As Wendell headed back again toward the staircase, George the concierge came after him with a letter. It was from Lillian at last! Now his elation gave way to almost unbearable anxiety. He headed up the stairs to find privacy for its reading, and seeing folks waiting patiently before his door, quietly let himself out onto the balcony above 10th street, where a crowd below was being ushered in to see *Heart of the Andes*. He discerned no eyes lifted towards him, and opened the letter postmarked Canada with an eager trepidation.

"My Dearest Wendell," it began, *"I pray this letter finds you well but missing me as dearly as I miss you. These few weeks have surely been some of the longest and coldest of my life. Even now I cannot return, as the fate of a Dear One whom I tried to dissuade from a doomed course is not yet final. You cannot believe how heavy is my heart for my sad friends and for want of seeing you! To be in your arms – aye, my Love – your bed! 'Tis the only dream that now sustains me. Were it naught but a dream!*

"I have been so foolish, and only hope you will forgive me for

my rash actions which even now I may not confess to you, but which you have surely guessed. Please don't forsake me, my Heart, my precious Wendell. It will not be forever though it may seem so. I will write again soon, with news of how you can come to me that we may be the sooner together. I love you. Your Lillian"

Wendell folded up the letter carefully and slipped it into the watch pocket of his vest. She loved him! So great was his relief that he was shaking and his knees had gone weak. He slumped down on the floor of the balcony, buried his face in his hands, and wept like a child above the unseeing throng.

Finally, having expended himself, Wendell rose and regained his composure. The crowd before his door had disappeared, save for one man in a rumpled suit of modest cloth and a small pinched hat. "Mr. Parry?" said the man, not extending his hand, "I am Mr. Carlyle, federal investigator. Might I askee a few questions?"

Chapter 16

"I can offer you some tea," said Wendell jovially as he unlocked his studio door. He was amazed at how his voice, so very detached from him, landed just the right casual note, and hoped its tone would belie a pallor creeping from his scalp down into his cheeks.

"That's a kindly offer, but not while on the job, thankee," said Mr. Carlyle, doffing his hat as he entered. Wendell closed the door behind him and motioned the investigator toward one of the chairs beside the little table. The man's "I'll stand, if ye don't mind," sent shivers along Wendell's spine, "but feel free to sit your own self." He was offering Wendell a seat in his own house! Wendell shook his head, and remained standing, leaning for support on the chair's back.

"What is it you want?" Wendell felt his composure slipping – no doubt, just what the son-of-a-bitch intended.

"Ye follow the news, Mr. Parry?"

"Seldom," said Wendell. "As you can see, my life is devoted to creating beauty and extolling Nature."

"But ye've heard of John Brown and that recent business at the federal arsenal in Virginy, haven't ye?" Wendell nodded. "And do ye know a 'Miss Lillian Flax'?"

"Sir, I will not answer questions about anyone other than myself. If you wish to know something about Miss Flax, I suggest you ask her directly." He breathed a sigh, relieved that he had handled the matter so well.

The man squinted his beady eyes. "And where might I find Miss Lillian Flax, Mr. Parry?"

"I assure you, sir, I do not know." And now he was very glad that he did not. The sincerity was in his voice, and the investigator clearly found him believable.

"Well then," said the man, handing Wendell his card, "if ye do see her, tell her I'm looking for her, will ye?" He put on his hat, "I'll let meself out, and I thankee for yer time."

Wendell braced himself as his weight sagged heavily on the back of the little chair. Fearing his legs would give out from trembling, he sat down, his mind demanding action but giving no clue as to what. Finally, his thoughts arranged themselves into some coherence. He needed to see Ruby, he knew that. But what if the investigator was waiting to follow him? What if there were fugitives at Ruby's apartment building and he, Wendell, led this Mr. Carlyle right to them? He shuddered. Best sit tight for a time.

Wendell heard some giggling outside the door, and a little knock. Yes, act normal, let in some art lovers. He opened the door and welcomed in two elderly ladies who tittered behind their hands and were clearly having a wonderful time. "Ladies, come in, come in! Welcome to my atelier." He spoke loudly and effusively should Mr. Carlyle be loitering in the hallway, and ushered in the women with an extravagant bow and kisses to the hand. As he entertained them with his lavish display and offered cookies all round, a plan began to formulate. He excused himself to the ladies and sat down to write up his new tour proposal.

Seeing that the handsome young artist had withdrawn his attention, the two women left. Wendell sealed his envelope and searched for the card Mr. McClure had left him. If Carlyle followed him, he would be led to McClure's business office, and likely not wait to follow him further to the Five Points.

Wendell pulled the door closed behind him and sauntered casually down the stairs, stopping to inform the exhibition below that they need not send others up. Then he walked to Broadway, and hopped on an omnibus – carriages being currently beyond his means! – and headed downtown toward the financial district. Throughout, there was no sign of the federal investigator.

Once again, Wendell had forgotten his sketch pad and *crayons*.

Now, as he looked out the windows of the wood-paneled conveyance, his thoughts were whelmed with the day's events – and the day not even over! An exhibition, an offer of a tour, Lillian's letter, a visit from a federal investigator, and a furtive visit to the Five Points – 'twas almost too much! Suddenly, he wanted to go to church. Perhaps Sam would welcome him to Beecher's church on Sunday – he would ask. It had been too long since he'd seen Sam anyway.

Wendell got off the horse-drawn bus at Liberty Street and looked around at the cavernous buildings looming overhead. A salt wind was blowing up from the bay, and with it came snatches of a tune sung by a boy.

> *"When they hang John Brown on high*
> *They will let his spirit fly*
> *We'll keep his name alive and not forgotten.*
> *I will fight for Uncle Sam*
> *And be proud because I am*
> *Fightin' to get paid for pickin' cotton.*
>
> *We'll be fightin' to get paid,*
> *We'll be fightin' to get paid,*
> *Fightin' to get paid for pickin' cotton..."*

Wendell looked around and saw the ragamuffin just as a Met was shooing him off. "Wait!" yelled Wendell. He sprinted after the little singer and grabbed his shoulder. "Wait!" he said again as the boy jerked around to look fearfully at his pursuer. "Where did you learn that song?" The waif eyed him suspiciously until Wendell produced a coin. "Please."

"Everyone knows that song," proclaimed the boy triumphantly, pocketing the prize. "My friends was singin' it down by the wharf." Then he turned and ran away.

Thanksgiving found Wendell at Sam's parents' house in Brooklyn. He had been gratified by an invitation from Ada Clare who was hosting the bohemians at her 42nd Street home. But he wanted to be with Sam and his extended family's normal lives. There was comfort in the familiar old brownstone and large dining table, set with revered coin silverware and carefully handed-down china, beside the warmth of a grand stone fireplace. He had also been invited to Ithaca, but on a sadder note – Catherine had suddenly moved in with the older woman who was Hyenwatha's "lover", and the elder Harte Parry was by himself and desperate for money. Wendell had sent $200 of the $600 he'd received for his tour advance, and promised to send more after the tour, now scheduled for spring. He very much hoped that, appropriate to the subject matter of his paintings, Ithaca would be included as a venue.

Sam's mother took off her apron and sat down at the foot of the table, signaling the elder Stockard to begin Thanksgiving grace. After "amen", Wendell helped himself and passed along the serving bowls, heaped high with sweet potatoes, minted cabbage, cranberries and turkey. It was the servants' day off, and everything had been cooked by the women themselves. Wendell looked around the table. Besides John and Martha Stockard, there was Elizabeth, newly pregnant and radiant, sitting across from him and Sam. Next to her sat Elizabeth's younger sister, Margaret, whom Wendell suspected was meant to lure him away from Lillian and into marriage. She glanced shyly at him, always lowering her pretty eyes modestly when he smiled into them. She had wispy blonde curls that escaped a pile on her head and fell against a delicate pink neck and sweet lace collar. Then there was Martha Stockard's mother, known to everyone as Grammy Ellen, of whom everyone said she was much the gregarious lady since her husband died. Her glum son Lionel, recently widowed, rounded out the company.

"I was so happy to hear that Fitzhugh passed the bar," said Martha Stockard jovially. "You boys have always been so dear, it gives me almost as much pleasure as it will when Sam finally passes his." There were sniggers at the thinly veiled dig, for Sam had been taking his time through school.

"Fitzhugh could not have done it without Sam's help," Wendell defended him. "He drilled him nightly."

Sam's father spoke, "If Sam would drill himself in his studies half so much as he drills himself with that infernal regiment, we'd soon have a senator."

"Is that what you want, Papa," asked Elizabeth, "for Sam to be a senator?"

"Certainly," proclaimed Mr. Stockard. "His grandfather was a senator, now Sam should be one also."

Sam was not enjoying this repartee at his expense. "Mayhap Sam's son will be the senator," Elizabeth deflected brightly.

"Nonsense!" proclaimed Grammy Ellen. "Not my grandson, nor my great grandson, will enter that den of thieves – lest it be to burn it to the ground!"

"Grammy!" laughed Sam, "Your opinion is most welcome, as always!"

Grammy continued, "Any government that would allow John Brown to hang is not worthy of allegiance." The table fell into awkward silence, the weight of the hanging scheduled but a week from the morrow falling heavily on their thoughts.

"Amen," spoke pretty Margaret finally, and blushed becomingly as Wendell smiled at her daring. The conversation returned then to safe territory throughout dinner and dessert, after which the gentlemen retired to the den for a smoke and a drink.

"You seem to have taken a shine to Miss Margaret," said Sam, lighting a Havana and puffing grandly.

"She's comely," agreed Wendell.

"And intelligent, too," insisted John Stockard, pulling

thoughtfully on his prized meerschaum. "Has quite a dowry. If you married her, you could find more leisure to paint."

"I would ask for her hand myself, were I your age," Lionel added lamely. They were ganging up on him.

Wendell spoke quietly, looking at Sam. "I am not done yet with Lillian," he said. Suddenly it seemed only he and Sam were in the room, and Sam was somehow a doppelgänger of himself, in an intense internal debate.

"If you wish a family," said Sam, "I don't see she will ever leave her marriage. She is beholden to the money, whether for reasons noble or ill."

"I love her, Sam. She is family enough without marriage."

"…were she ever home." Sam looked at him and knew he'd hit a mark. The room refocused as the other men joined in.

"Who is this Lillian?" inquired the elder Stockard with some irritation. "You're not involved with a married woman, are you, young Parry?"

"Indeed, one would hope not!" chimed in Lionel.

"Alas, there is nothing to be done about affairs of the heart." Sam was trying to rescue him.

Wendell looked at John Stockard. "It's something I have to resolve," he said apologetically, "and leaves me unfortunately unable at the moment to entertain other, uh, attractions."

"Hell, that explanation is as dense as a rock!" proclaimed Mr. Stockard, "Must I pray for you on Sunday?"

Wendell said sincerely, "I'm wondering if I may accompany you on Sunday."

"To church?" Mr. Stockard softened. "Of course you may, my boy. You know you are always welcome."

Sam prevailed on Wendell to take a walk with him, ere the sun should set. They crossed to the park that ran along the normally busy river, quiet now for Thanksgiving, and gazed out at Manhattan where the gas lamps were beginning to blink on.

Sam huddled, his hands dug deep in his coat pockets. "War is coming – you know I have been training with the 14th Brooklyn." Wendell nodded, bracing against the chill and breathing steam into the wet-smelling wool of his muffler. "Train with me, Wendell," urged Sam. "I have sore missed your company. It's not so different from our college sports."

Wendell was touched. "The intention makes all the difference. Yet I have missed you, too, and will consider it."

Wendell sought only solace in attending Plymouth Church with the Stockards that Sunday, but no solace awaited him – he should have known John Brown would be the topic. The organ music swelled as it had before, and the congregation sang from its hymnals. Then Reverend Henry Ward Beecher strode purposefully to the pulpit.

"An old man, kind at heart, industrious, peaceful, went forth, with a large family of children, to seek a new home in Kansas."

The pastor's voice rose as he described how pro-slavers from Missouri had ridden into Kansas and stuffed the ballot boxes for slavery, burning and killing those who opposed them, including John Brown's first-born son.

"The shot that struck the child's heart crazed the father's brain. He goes to the heart of a Slave State. One man; and with sixteen followers! He seizes two thousand brave Virginians, and holds them in duress!

"When a great State attacked a handful of weak colonists in Kansas, the government and nation were torpid, but when seventeen men attacked a sovereign State, Virginia, then Maryland arms, and Virginia arms, and the United States government arms, and they three rush against seventeen men.

"Let no man pray that Brown be spared. Let Virginia make him a martyr. Now, he has only blundered. His soul was noble; his work miserable. But a cord and a gibbet would redeem all that, and round up Brown's failure with a heroic success."

Hardly an eye did not betray tears and righteous anger when Beecher finished, and the great hall sat hushed. "Let us pray," said the preacher quietly, and though each parishioner mouthed the familiar words, inside was turmoil as a hanging and a holocaust loomed unstoppably ahead. Feeling alone among them, Wendell silently screamed 'No! Lillian, come home! Turn back the clock, 'tis not yet the season for such folly!'

But the clock would not be turned back. That America's idyllic childhood was irrevocably ended became achingly apparent next morning with an early rapping on Wendell's door. Sanford Gifford was followed in by Ted Winthrop. They sat down on the edge of Wendell's bed and plopped a newspaper under his chin. The stark headlines read: "*Washington Irving Dead.*"

Wendell sat up and looked at his friends. "I am stricken by this news," he said. "'Twas so shortly ago that Durand visited him." It seemed the end of an era, the end of America's youth and hopeful beginnings, the end of God's favor upon the land. 'I pray I don't live to see such a thing as this country torn apart,' Irving had said.

"The timing of it," opined Ted, "half between Thanksgiving and a hanging that will take us all to war, has put the entire nation in a nostalgic melancholy. Especially we knickerbockers here in Gotham, who have embraced those enduring nicknames he gave us."

"Enduring and endearing," agreed Sanford.

Said Ted to Wendell, "There will be extra trains Thursday bearing mourners hence to Irvington. We plan to go and fain would have you with us."

Then Sanford handed Wendell a letter. "George bade me bring this to you. Shall we leave you while you read it? We'll see you in the mess for breakfast."

When the door had closed behind them, Wendell tore open the envelope. It was from Lillian.

Chapter 17

Wendell was sitting beside Sanford Gifford, Ted Winthrop, Asher Durand and his son John Durand, a reporter with the *Crayon*, when the crowded train pulled into the station at Irvington. Across from the platform was the dock where they had come by the sloop *Rival* just a few short months before. "I wonder how is old Captain Collyer," said Ted.

"Perchance we'll see him here," spoke Asher Durand hopefully. The men stood as the passengers began to detrain, and each turned to give Wendell a squeeze on the shoulder and a handshake. "Give our regards to Miss Flax." Through the dirty train windows, Wendell watched his friends enter carriages bearing mourners to Sunnyside, the house where America's first great writer had lived and was now laid out.

Almost alone on the train, Wendell sighed his relief that the federal investigator did not seem to have followed, and took out his sketch pad. The whistle blew and he felt the awesome power of the engine as it picked up speed, squealing its metallic song, sending him to Lillian.

It was the next morning, Friday, December 2 that Wendell arrived in Concord, Massachusetts. The air was frosty, with a mild nor'easter bringing in threat of snow. He tightened his muffler and pulled his hat low as he hastened along the sidewalk to the Thoreau House hotel, the only place to get a room in this tiny village north of Boston. A small sign said this was where the armory had been that sparked the Revolutionary War.

Wendell set his carpet bag down before the faded yellow door and knocked. A blonde matronly lady in modest dress opened it, beaming her pleasure at his expected arrival. "Well, I'm sure you must be Mr. Parry," she said, holding wide the door. "I'm Aunt Sarah." She called into the further reaches of the house, "Oh Liz,

Wendell's here."

A voice called back, "Wendell Phillips?"

"No dear, Wendell Parry, Lily Ann's friend." A second matron appeared, a brunette, with a grin as she removed her apron and held out her hand. "This is Auntie Liz," pronounced Aunt Sarah. "That's what everybody calls us. We'd be honored if you did likewise." Wendell was somewhat nonplussed at this greeting, and bowed over the proffered hand, declaring his pleasure at meeting her.

"Oh, such fine city manners," tittered Auntie Liz with a curtsy. "You may kiss it if you like." This started the women giggling, particularly when Mr. Parry declared his delight at doing just that, at which Aunt Sarah offered her hand to be kissed, too. "Lily Ann has splendid taste in artists as well as art," she flirted. "But come, dinner awaits and is getting cold."

"Perhaps, Sarah, Mr. Parry would like a chance to see his room first and freshen up from his trip."

"Indeed, Ladies, I would like a moment, but only a moment. I am much overtaken by your generous hospitality."

"Well then," said Sarah, "Your room is the first up the stairs to the right, number 3 – the key is in it. Now mind you, only a moment. You look fresh as a daisy already." He bowed again and ascended to room number 3, a sizable country room with four-poster bed and mauve flowered wallpaper. A gracious window overlooked a small apple orchard. He stowed his bag, used the chamber pot hidden under the bed, gave his face and hands a quick rinse from the pitcher, and checked himself briefly in the mirror. Then he hastened downstairs to the dining room where the two ladies waited, at a table laden with wonderful harvest smells reminding him how hungry he was.

There was a brief and heart-felt grace in which fervent prayers were offered for John Brown on this, his hanging day.

"Do you mind if we call you Wendell?" asked Aunt Sarah,

when they had commenced eating. "Afterall, darling Lily Ann does go on about you – Wendell, Wendell, Wendell. It seems you are part of the family."

"I would be honored. I am embarrassed to confess, however, that I don't know your relationship to Lillian."

"Oh, of course you don't," said Aunt Sarah passing the biscuits, "this is your first time here. You know that when Lily Ann was small, she lived at Brook Farm, the transcendentalist community?" Wendell nodded. "That's where her mother became dear friends with Sophie Hawthorne. She and Lilly Ann visited Sophie here often, particularly in the summer whilst school was out, and Lily Ann could play with Lizzy and Louisa May Alcott – young Ellen Emerson was another friend. Lily Ann was often left here all summer."

"Alas, poor Lizzy Alcott passed to Heaven last year," put in Auntie Liz.

Aunt Sarah continued. "The Alcotts live just across town from here, in Ralph Emerson's old house, and that's where our nephew, David, also lived for a spell, and the Hawthornes just across, with the Emersons nearby. So Lily Ann was very frequently around, you see, and all we Concordians are quite close."

Wendell realized with some excitement that the lady was referring to family members of Bronson Alcott, Nathaniel Hawthorne, and Ralph Waldo Emerson, all of whom he held in the highest regard. "Is this the house in which Henry David Thoreau grew up?" he asked, impressed.

Auntie Liz tisked and tutted, declaring, "Oh, I know he went and changed his name, but he'll always be David Henry to us."

"So where is Lillian now?" Wendell asked the question with such affected casualness that he came close to speaking with his mouth full.

"She has been staying with Louisa May at the Alcott house," responded Aunt Sarah. "She will doubtless be by soon to see if you are arrived – she had already been twice today. But I told her, and I should tell you, that we are happy for the happiness she has found with you, but this is not New York City, and we will not have illicit relations going on under our roof. It's the house rules, we run a clean establishment."

Auntie Liz chimed in, "We have been hoping she would someday leave that sham of a marriage and marry for love. So you see, Wendell darling, we are pulling for you."

"Thank you, Auntie Liz," Wendell blushed. "I wonder, can you tell me how long she has been in Concord? I know little of her lyceum schedule."

"Well, how long is it, Sarah – several days since she returned from Canada?" The two women looked at each other, wordlessly deciding how much they should tell him. Sarah nodded and Auntie Liz proceeded. "It's nothing everybody doesn't know, I guess. She went to Canada for fear of being asked about the involvement of herself and Gerrit Smith in what the papers call the 'Secret Six.' Of course, there were a lot more than six, I think all the abolitionists supported John Brown. I know I did! But the papers named who they named, the ones whose names were found in John Brown's effects. Alas, the only one of them that didn't run away was Thomas Higginson – what a fearless man he is! You know someone all your life, but don't have any idea what he's made of till there's a crisis. Poor Frankie Sanborn is still in Canada, and so are Samuel Howe and George Stearns. Frederick Douglass was not named, but fled to Europe with our Reverend Parker. They fear to return till John Brown can no longer claim them as accomplices."

Now Aunt Sarah got angry – Liz had clearly gone too far. "Fie, Elizabeth! What a terrible thing to say. John Brown is above all an honorable man, and has repeatedly exonerated the so-called Six. They gave him money, but knew not what he would do with it. Anyway, Wendell dear, if you are worried for Lily Ann, the lawyers have said she need not answer questions and

Massachusetts will not extradite anyone to Virginia. That's why she's here instead of in New York."

Lawyers? Extradite? Was that the same as arrested? Wendell's head reeled.

"Well," huffed Auntie Liz, "let's hope they don't question Gerrit Smith. It seems quite the rational move on his part to check into an asylum."

"I visited Mr. Gerrit Smith in the asylum," offered Wendell. "He is indeed quite alienated."

"Well, 'tis still an effective defense, real or unreal," proclaimed Aunt Sarah. "Aye, it's he you must worry about talking out of school, not Old Brown."

Suddenly, they heard the front door open and footsteps dart eagerly across the floor – and then, there she was! She was noticeably gaunt and thin, which was magnified by black funereal dress. But her eyes were bright and her heart full as Wendell stood and she threw herself into his arms. Now, they were both laughing and crying, and covering each other with kisses.

"Liz, I need you in the kitchen," said Aunt Sarah, and winked. "You two remember the house rules," she admonished as the aunts went out and closed the door, leaving Wendell alone with Lillian in the dining room.

"My God, Wendell," she said. "You're really here." She was laughing and crying at once. She covered her face with her hands and choked back a sob.

Wendell put his arms around her. "It'll be over soon," he promised.

"They're going to hang him, Wendell. They're going to hang him."

Lillian backed up against the wall and pulled Wendell close as she drew his mouth down to hers – she seemed as one starving. "Lillian…" he murmured tenderly in her ear as her arms encircled his neck and her feet left the ground. Her breath was hot against his cheek, and he found himself moving rhythmically against her as she fumbled with his trouser buttons.

Of a sudden, she pushed him away and stood, smoothing her skirts, just in time before Henry David Thoreau walked into the room. "Hello Henry," she greeted awkwardly, "I'd like you to meet Mr. Wendell Parry."

"Henry Thoreau," was the response as he offered his hand. He was a rustic plain man with sad eyes, a scraggly neck beard that ran along his chin-line, and a large off-centered nose.

Wendell coughed, and shook the hand self-consciously. "I am delighted." His thwarted passion had left his beard sticky and a button undone on his still tumid trousers.

"Lily Ann tells me you are a friend of Walt Whitman," continued Thoreau intensely. "A most remarkable poet. He would have achieved great stature for *Leaves of Grass* were he not made scapegoat for his sexual frankness." The reference to sexual frankness at such a time left Wendell speechless and blushing. But Thoreau seemed quite oblivious, and Lillian was suppressing a giggle.

On hearing Henry's resonant voice, the aunts re-emerged from the kitchen. "Oh David," said Auntie Liz, "Thank goodness. We had been so worried. Did you get the man safely across the border?" Thoreau gave her a warning look and glanced at Wendell; Auntie Liz hastily changed the subject. "We have pulled an apple pie from the oven. Now, now, 'tis a morbid day, we know, but the apples could not wait and the pie is hot. There is just time to eat it before we need leave for the service – we will dedicate the pie to him and wish him many such in heaven. Now do sit down, all of you."

"If you don't mind, Auntie Liz, Miss Flax and I were just contemplating a walk," spoke Wendell hastily, "though the offer of still more of your delectable cooking is quite tempting."

"Not so tempting as 'Miss Flax', heh? Very well, but let me

remind you again, you are in the land of the Puritan, so behave yourselves," warned Aunt Sarah. "There are those who are still of a mind to brand with scarlet letters."

They bundled up in their wraps by the front door and he slipped his arm around her as they stepped out into the frosty air. "What did she mean, about Thoreau going to the border?" Wendell was trying hard to understand just how deeply immersed in the troubles these people, and Lillian, were.

She seemed anxious for once to tell him. "One of John Brown's men, a Negro, showed up in town, seeking protection. Our dear brave Henry hid him in his buckboard and drove him to Canada."

Wendell felt her frail body tremble against him. "Ah Lillian, we should go back, you need that apple pie. You have grown so thin."

"But I want you to understand, my Heart, where I've been, why I've been away from you so long."

He took her hands and faced her, staring into her soft viridian eyes, wide with pleading and innocence. "I do understand, Lillian." He shifted his weight uneasily, "I have a confession," and took a breath, his own eyes pleading. "The night you left the Unitary Household, I followed you to your mansion. I saw who entered there."

Her eyes grew wild with alarm, giving his stomach a lurch. "It was you! We thought Gerrit was crazy when he said someone was spying on us!"

"A harmless spy, surely!" he defended himself, remembering the same accusation from Mr. Smith when they had locked him in the crib. "It's not I that drove him mad!"

Lillian's eyes softened. She hugged him with forgiveness, snuggling against his warmth, begging forgiveness in kind. "I gave him money to free slaves," she said miserably. "We all did. Captain Brown is the most compelling man I ever met."

"But now a federal spy comes round asking for you," Wendell

continued fiercely, holding her close. "Oh Lillian, will you never be able to come home?"

She pulled away and took his hand. "I'm cold, Wendell. Come, let's go to Louisa's house. She's eager to meet you."

It was a mile walk over to the Alcott's Orchard House past the already overflowing churchyard. Wendell told her about losing his commission from Gerrit Smith and the pending tour he had garnered in its place. And he told her of the amazing price Fred Church had got for *Heart of the Andes*. Lillian laughed, happy for him. "I shall not now be able to afford your art, at such lofty prices!" she said, teasing.

He stopped and pulled her close. "I would not sell it to you anyway," and kissed her mouth fully, causing shocked looks from two women passersby.

"Uh oh," whispered Lillian, flushed. "They know me, and that I am married." She nodded to the women who looked at each other uncertainly before hurrying off. "Oh Wendell, I do so want to go home – to be free again from such stares!"

The Alcott household was in a fluster of preparation. The Emersons had arrived in their carriage, all five of them dressed in black, and Bronson Alcott was hitching his own team to a buckboard to accompany his next door neighbors to the church. It was already almost 2pm and the hanging was to be at three. "It's as well you did not arrive yesterday," declared Mr. Alcott on meeting Wendell. "The town's few copperheads were so angry at our vigil that they burned an effigy of Mr. Brown." It was clear that he feared more trouble, and there was something of an anxiety along with shocked dismay that no rescue seemed to be coming for their doomed friend – several large regiments and the cessation of Virginia rail traffic saw to that.

"At least it wasn't an effigy of you, Papa," declared Louisa May earnestly as she threw on her cloak and muff. Ellen Emerson climbed down to be with her friends while the rest of the Emersons departed. Bronson helped his wife and smaller girls up onto the seat of the buckboard. "You don't mind if we walk, do you Papa?" asked Louisa. Bronson looked uncertainly at Lillian, so frail, who expressed her desire to traverse the mile on foot with her two girlfriends and Wendell. Bronson relented and drove off.

The young women were pleased to make Wendell's acquaintance, but would not lower themselves to flutter over him on this most serious of days. The black of their dresses made them appear particularly somber. Of the two, Louisa May seemed more grim. "I have written a poem about Mr. Brown," she said, and without waiting an invitation, began to recite. As they walked, their sad footsteps fell in cadence with her words.

"No breath of shame can touch his shield,
Nor ages dim its shine;
Living, he made life beautiful,
Dying, made death divine.
No monument of quarried stone,
No eloquence of speech
Can grave the lessons on the land
His martyrdom will teach.
No eulogy like his own words,
With hero-spirit rife,
'I truly serve the cause I love,
By yielding up my life.'"

They marched on past the fine old colonial houses with lovely lawns and the several shops that became more numerous as they approached the little town's center, where a graceful belfry on First Parish Unitarian Church rang its congregation to the special service. Thoreau was to act as pastor since Reverend Theodore Parker, one of the named "Secret Six" conspirators, was in Europe. Nate and Sophie Hawthorne were also abroad. Louisa, Ellen,

Lillian, and Wendell slid into the second pew while the speakers – Alcott, Emerson, Thoreau, and others – took the first pew in front of them. The rest of the pews rapidly filled up as a massive outpouring of emotion overtook the little town in this, Old Osawatomie Brown's last hour.

"Are you not going to speak?" Wendell whispered to Lillian. She shook her head. She could have her own platform at the Lyceum, she whispered to him, but could not easily share one with the men, nor Louisa May recite her poem; for the men were absolutely progressive in their politics but ever so conservative in their civility – they were New Englanders.

The service commenced in a dream-like state of unreality. Thomas Higginson, alone of the "Secret Six," had vowed to rescue Captain Brown and there was still a prayerful hope for some miraculous news. The words from the pulpit were stirring indeed, but wove in and out of the imagination each parishioner had of what must be happening in Virginia: The brave old man writing his last letters to his wife and children, saying goodbye to his fellow captives, strolling toward the gallows with dignified calm – perhaps stooping to kiss a slave child held up to him as the downtrodden clamored for one last look at their champion. And then…

Thoreau from the pulpit was saying, "…Such do not know that like the seed is the fruit, and that in the moral world, when good seed is planted, good fruit is inevitable; that when you plant or bury a hero in his field, a crop of heroes is sure to spring up. This is a seed of such force and vitality, it does not ask our leave to germinate.

"A man does a brave and humane deed, and on all sides we hear people and parties declaring, 'I didn't do it, nor countenance him to do it in any conceivable way. It can't fairly be inferred from my past career.'"

Mr. Thoreau was looking from face to face as he said this, and they squirmed under his gaze. "Ye needn't take so much pains, my friends, to wash your skirts of him. No one will ever be convinced that he was any creature of yours. He went and came, as he himself informs us, under the auspices of John Brown, and nobody else.

"'All is quiet in Harper's Ferry,' say the journals. What is the character of that calm which follows when the law and the slaveholder prevail? I regard this event as a touchstone designed to bring out with glaring distinctness the character of this Government. We needed to be thus assisted to see it by the light of history. It needed to see itself. When a government puts forth its strength on the side of injustice, as ours, to maintain slavery and kill the liberators of the slave, it reveals itself simply as brute force. It is more manifest than ever that tyranny rules.

"This event advertises me that there is such a fact as death, the possibility of a man's dying. It seems as if no man had ever died in America before.

"It is the best news that America has ever heard. It has already quickened the feeble pulse of the North, and infused more generous blood in her veins than any number of years of what is called political and commercial prosperity. How many a man who was lately contemplating suicide has now something to live for!

"Some eighteen hundred years ago Christ was crucified; this morning, perchance, Captain Brown was hung. These are the two ends of the chain which is not without its links. He is not Old Brown any longer; he is an angel of light. I see now that it was necessary that the bravest and humanist man in all the country should be hung. Perhaps he saw it himself. I almost fear that I may yet hear of his deliverance, doubting if a prolonged life, if any life, can do as much good as his death."

As they at last tearfully filed out of the church into the bright sun, Wendell heard a song begun in the crowd, and others began to take it up:

"When they hung John Brown on high,
They let his spirit fly.
We will keep his name alive and not forgotten.
I will fight for Uncle Sam
And be proud because I am
Fightin' to get paid for pickin' cotton.
Yes, we're fightin' to get paid,
We're fightin' to get paid..."

Wendell looked at Lillian whose face was flushed as the voices swelled. "I heard it in even in New York," he told her, wondrous.

She filled with emotion. "I didn't write that verse," she laughed through tears, "it happened of its own."

The others caught up to them and they were soon all aboard the conveyances, headed back to the Alcott's Orchard House. Wendell thanked his hosts for inviting him to share their pew, and left to spend the night at the Thoreau House hotel. He had not gone beyond the yard when Lillian came running after him. She flew into his arms, and looked at him with wet eyes through her steamy breath. "Oh Wendell," she said, "Come what may, we can no longer be apart – we'll leave for New York in the morning."

"Come, walk me to the hotel," he begged her. They walked the mile discreetly arm in arm, then pushed open the yellow front door and entered the Thoreau House. Auntie Liz met them.

"Oh Lily, I'm so glad you're here. There's a gentleman to see you," she said, handing her his card. Lillian looked at it and, as she passed it wordlessly to Wendell, he heard her breath constrict: Anthony Carlyle, Federal Investigator. "He's in the parlor, dear."

Chapter 18

Lillian was shaking. She held tight to Wendell's arm as she steadied herself toward the parlor on the shadowed side of the house where a little gas lamp could not undo the dimness. A dark presence sat in the easy chair and now rose. "Miss Lillian Flax?" the presence inquired before their eyes adjusted and they saw the menacing little man who introduced himself as the investigator. "Me topic is of a private nature," Carlyle said, nodding toward Wendell.

"I have no secrets from Mr. Parry," she answered stiffly, as Wendell, fearing her knees would give out, slipped his arm around her. At this moment his heart burst open in his chest and his love for her grew fiercely protective – she had no secrets from him!

"Good enough. Sit ye down, I have questions for ye about a friend o' your'n." Once again, Wendell bristled at the arrogance of the man – it was for Lillian to invite him to sit! She seemed about to resist, but Wendell urged her to the couch where she perched precariously on the seat's edge while Wendell stood protectively beside her. "I would ask ye about Mr. Gerrit Smith and his association with Mr. John Brown, what was hung today."

"Mr. Gerrit Smith has gone mad," Lillian said. "It would be unseemly for me to speak for him, when it is his lawyer whom you should address."

"Yes, I see," said Mr. Carlyle. He paused, "Does yer husband know of yer affiliations?"

There was dead silence in the room. Wendell started, intent on the man's throat, but Lillian put an urgent hand against his leg. "The marriage is a business arrangement," she said icily. "My husband leaves me to my own affairs."

"And do ye have a lot of affairs?" the man asked cheekily. The hand on Wendell's leg stiffened, in desperate restraint. She stood and moved between the two men.

"I do not know why you are goading Mr. Parry, nor indeed, what you want with me, Mr. Carlyle," Lillian scolded.

"Well, I'll leave ye then," leered the federal investigator. He rose and put on his hat. "But mind ye, if ye are summoned to appear before a congressional hearing, best ye go. I would not want to drag Mr. Ferguson into yer affairs – unnecessarily." Lillian had her fists clenched as the man showed himself out. Neither she nor Wendell spoke, nor was there any breath audible.

Finally, Wendell let out a long sigh and said, "At the least, we know what they want. Mayhap it is safe for you now to return to New York."

"Aye. And on our way, let's stop and see Gerrit – I wish to know for myself his condition of mind."

She turned and kissed him. "I must be back for supper at the Alcott's. I'll see you after breakfast, packed and ready to go!"

Wendell settled up with the Thoreau House sisters and arrived at the platform early. Lillian showed up shortly after in the buckboard with Louisa May Alcott, come to see her off. The day had a frosty brilliance to it. "I am sorry I hadn't more time to get to know you, Wendell," Louisa May said sweetly, and handed him the picnic basket Abby Alcott had put together for the trip. "But then, I am selfishly happy that I had Lily Ann to myself for at least a few days." To Lillian she said, "Thank you for coming, dear sister, it was almost like we were still kids. Let's make it again on some happier occasion."

"Yes," said Lillian, embracing her, "and soon. Perhaps you could visit me at the mansion." Wendell felt ever so slightly dismayed – he had never been invited to the mansion! Was the Unitary Household too unsavory for Lillian's New England friends? But he brightened quickly at the arrival of the train and the prospect of finally bringing Lillian home. How long had it been – two months? It seemed rather like two years – until now when, settling down next to her in the seat, it seemed they had never been apart. She sighed as she waved to Louisa May through the window and laid her head thankfully against Wendell's coat, snuggling the wool. Wendell put his arm around her, enjoying her womanliness, while he smelled her hair and remembered gardenias.

It was late that night when the train arrived at Utica Station and they arranged for a porter to take her steamer trunk across Bagg Square to the Northern Hotel, where they checked in as Mr. and Mrs. Wendell Parry. Lillian had slept most of the way, yet seemed pale and tired. She explained that her menses had begun to flow, and she felt faint. So he ordered her a bath and gently washed her back, marveling that a woman could lose so much blood and live – he was sure he could not! Discreetly behind a dressing screen, she wrapped herself in rags, and in a soft flannel gown came to bed, where she fell instantly asleep in his arms.

Wendell was overcome with tenderness toward her. For a long time he lay in the dark, listening to her deepening breath, happy for every moment he could be with her. Remembering how truly afraid he had been that he'd lost her, his lids grew heavy with grateful tears until they finally drooped and closed – he slept better than he had since before Old Osawatomie Brown had ever raided Harper's Ferry.

She woke late, and to Wendell's relief, seemed somewhat recovered. "Come, *Mon Coeur*," he insisted, "we are going to find you a steak for breakfast."

Lillian pinned her hair up and smiled, touched by his concern. "Indeed," she said with amusement, "my New England friends had fed me nothing but vegetables. Not only do the Alcott's not eat meat, they eat no tuber that grows pointing down – towards hell, I suppose."

"Then let us find you some hellish tubers as well," offered Wendell with amusement. "I am prepared to provide you with all the sin the puritans denied."

"If the devil is temptation, you are he," she said, and tested her theory by kissing him lustily.

They found a lovely place on the rise above the town, overlooking Bagg Square with the railroad station and busy canal just beyond. Buoyed by steak and good red beets, Lillian began in a hushed voice to tell him something of her strange journeys over their time apart. "I was in Boston as a guest of my friend, Julia Ward Howe, between lyceum engagements," she said quietly, after ascertaining that the few close-by diners couldn't hear her, "when I was approached to travel north and alert a certain house to expect fugitives. This I did, and stayed on to help in acquiring clothes for the unfortunates. It was while I lingered there that I received an urgent telegram from Julia that Harper's Ferry had been hit and that all correspondence relating to John Brown should be destroyed. Of course, I wired Ruby straight away to go through my desk and burn my letters."

"Are there not servants at the mansion?" whispered Wendell with alarm, "Are there not spies and enemies within its walls?"

"It is manageable. There is an Irish gardener who is sympathetic to the cause, and who is charged with protecting the place. He lives in his own cabin behind. The maids come twice weekly, and often Mr. Ferguson's accountant uses Henry's office during work hours – he is a potential enemy, but suspects nothing. Rather seldom does Henry's sister arrive with her husband, and on such occasions I hire a cook and keep to the house, playing the good hostess. I like them, and so am not too troubled by their visits, which are announced well in advance."

Wendell looked around uneasily as their voices had risen, but there was no longer anyone at the nearby tables. Lillian needed no urging to continue her story, "Ruby did not get my message straight away as the telegram boy was afraid to venture into the Five Points. I had to pay an extra two dollars! I stayed put where I was, desperate for news, growing more alarmed at what I read.

Julia Howe wired me again to wait there for her husband, Samuel, one of the named 'Secret Six,' who took me thence to Canada. Alas, he and George Stearns are still there, and Gerrit Smith gone mad!"

Her eyes were wide with the horror of it, and a note of despair crept into her voice. "Oh Wendell, what have we done? All any of us sought to do was liberate slaves, and now we may have gone and started a war."

Wendell reached across the table and took her hands. "Nay Lillian," he soothed, "it's not you or John Brown either that will start this war, but slavery itself. When doing what is clearly right leads to war, then perhaps war is also right."

"Fie Wendell, you speak like a man!" Then sadly, "Nay, you speak as everyone is speaking, male and female, clamoring for battle. If it comes to it, promise me you won't go." Her green eyes brimmed with fear.

He tried to reassure her. "Believe me, I am not inclined to fight, Lillian."

"Then promise me." There was a silence. Wendell had already agreed to practice with Sam's regiment, but that didn't mean he would go to war – there wouldn't be a war. And now here was Lillian, returned to him at last, her distress tearing at his heart.

"I promise," he said finally.

She sighed, satisfied, and continued with her story. "Being in Montreal with Sam Howe and George Stearns came nigh to being a war in itself. At first, Frederick Douglass was with us and, he at least, I find tolerable to women. But he soon left for Europe, and I was not permitted by those puritans, in whose charge I apparently was, to check in as anyone other than Mrs. Henry Ferguson! And there they talked endlessly of plot and intrigue while they discouraged me from adding to the discourse." She sighed, "But then, Dr. Samuel Gridley Howe, the great suffragist, treats his wife Julia the same way. She is smart and talented, and would use her voice on behalf of abolition and suffrage, but he ever shuts her up."

"Such treatment of women is hard for me to comprehend," said Wendell, "when it's your unfettered mind and free spirit which bade me fall in love with you."

"When I first saw *Sands of Morocco*," she remembered fondly, "I saw in its creator a man who was free in spirit, and I knew that spirit to be kindred to my own."

Soon they were on their way by carriage to Old Main. Sitting beside Lillian in the bright sunlight, Wendell could appreciate the care and thoughtfulness of the luxuriant grounds, designed specifically to soothe the troubled soul. They entered the asylum together, though outside Gerrit Smith's door, Wendell stepped aside and let her visit the man without him. Somehow, Wendell didn't think that Mr. Smith would welcome him.

As he stood somewhat tensely outside the door, Smith's man-servant came out and spoke to him in hushed tones. "I have found this, sir, and am in need of advice how to best dispose of it." He handed Wendell a crumpled piece of paper with scrawled penmanship on it:

"The great and the good go to the noose, only the mean and the treacherous avoid it. Do those serve also who helped prepare the martyr to shed his righteous, cleansing blood? Do those serve also who now stand aside, who hide and are silent? Are they guilty of abandonment who, like him, are bound and fettered? I make this a day of fasting, meditation, and prayer – all I can do within the bars that hold me. The one who dies has nothing to fear. God will gather the beloved, his fierce defender, to him. It is we, the rest of us, who need ask mercy. We who will be left – it is we whose blood will flood tomorrow to follow today's rivulet."

"When did you find this?" asked Wendell, alarmed.

"The day of the hanging, sir. It is in Mr. Smith's hand."

"It's best destroyed," concluded Wendell, handing the paper back. "Pray, let none but his lawyer see it," for it came nigh to being a confession. He decided not to mention it to Lillian, for all he wanted – were it possible! – was that he and she should soon be back to normal.

"How is he?" he asked her when she came out.

Lillian seemed shaken. "He babbles – if he goes before Congress – he will prove unpredictable – you know that."

Wendell put his arm reassuringly around her shoulders. "But you are guilty of nothing," he said quietly.

"Yes," she mumbled uncertainly. Then, "He is quite morose, but we all are. We loved Captain Brown, who is only just martyred. Surely a time of despondency and fear of the forces unleashed is justified – not insane."

Finally, they were back in Greenwich Village, emerging from their long nightmarish sojourn and returned to normality. Excited friends took the couple to see the controversial play, *The Octoroon*, at the opulent Winter Garden on Broadway, and life returned to painting, parties, newspapers and Pfaff's Saloon in pleasurable routine. Christmas at Ada Clare's apartment was a revelry of all the friends together again, a moment of nostalgic bliss ahead of an uncertain future.

Now that it was winter, Lillian no longer travelled to lyceums, and spent much of her time with Ada Clare writing for Henry Clapp's *Saturday Press*. She was assigned to cover events at the Academy of Music across from her Unitary Household, and so she and Wendell frequented that grand opera house for many delightful concerts. There was little pay in it, but she was encouraged to do more writing and so began a book of poetry and songs. Once, she asked Wendell to do look-out for the school in the Five Points, sketching street scenes out front so Tuck and the other men could attend the classes taught by Ruby. Tuck, however, said Wendell was attracting attention rather than deterring it, and placed young Willy in the role while he took Wendell finally to Almack's. There they both danced heartily the juba jig when Tuck wasn't playing his fiddle for the tap dancers.

Mostly Wendell spent his time fulfilling minor commissions and practicing with Sam's regiment while telling Lillian that he and Sam were simply attending a "gentlemen's club". He did not consider this a lie, for there was as much talk as practice, and many a fine cigar sampled with new friends.

Wendell was at the armory enjoying a Cubano when the prototype of the new uniforms arrived. "At last," said Sam, "a uniform worthy of an artist's brush." And indeed it was, modeled beautifully on the French Zouave uniform, but more the Alpine *chasseur*, its red trousers less billowing, its waist-length navy blue jackets adorned with red trim and gold buttons and, rather than a fez, a red-trimmed military hat with front brim. Indeed, it looked much like the uniform of the Hungarian freedom fighters who had excited such passion and admiration in their recent failed uprising against Austria. No other American militia had just such a uniform, and it made the wearer look quite smart, especially when a sword was added alongside the leg. Wendell was proud of his hand in the design and ordered two for himself, straight away modeling it for Thomas. He ached to wear it for Lillian, but knew that he could not lest she become fearful. Meanwhile, Sam beamed proudly as he posed for a painting at Wendell's atelier – a handsome soldier and soon father. Come summer, he would even take his exams before the bar.

One day at Pfaff's, Lillian invited Wendell to spend a night at the mansion. "Why so?" asked Wendell surprised. "You had not invited me before."

"It's not a place I wish to stay. 'Tis empty, cold, and ghostly. But I'm bound to hold no further secrets from you, my Heart. And you will at least enjoy my art collection." Wendell was pleased that since their return from Concord, he had been fully included in everything she did. But his pledge to her made him come nigh to confessing his ruse with Sam, for the new uniform gave the "gentlemen's club" a decided military feel. It was he who was keeping secrets from her! No matter, it was none of his business how she spent her time with Ada Clare and her lady friends, and none of hers how he spent his time with his men friends. Besides, he would keep his pledge not to go to war.

They arrived at the mansion on a cold and rainy Sunday afternoon, a day when Henry Ferguson's accountant would not happen by. A short flight of stairs mounted to the large front door through massive two story pillars, flanked on either side by a graceful wrap-around porch. The fireplaces had been lit ahead of their visit, but most of the furniture remained covered with white dust cloths. An empty cavernous entryway echoed their voices and bade them speak in softened whispers. She took him by the hand, moving uncertainly as if she were trespasser rather than owner, and led him behind the large banistered staircase which swept upward from the entrance. Toward the back of the grand house was a solarium filled with lonely but living potted plants, and through it a parlor with a viewing bench and every inch of wall covered in paintings.

Awestruck, Wendell sat upon the bench, as before him loomed the rival of Durand's National Academy of Design. The mansion was no longer empty but filled with old friends – every artist Wendell knew from the Studio Building and beyond was represented: Fred Church, Sanford Gifford, Asher Durand, Jervis McEntee, Louis Mignot, Samuel Morse, Josephine Walters, Anna Mary Freeman, Thomas Buchanan Read… And she had even added the Tenth Street Studio newcomers: Emanuel Leutze, Worthington Whittredge, William Haseltine, and Albert Bierstadt who had only just moved in. The men in the mess had not been joking that Lillian was their benefactress. Wendell slipped his arm around her waist and smelled her hair, content to sit silently with her surrounded by such inspiring pieces – for surely she had picked the best, and it was a delight to look upon them, lit carefully by gas and all in one place. "They are truly magnificent," he said finally, murmuring in her ear.

"Yes," she agreed happily, "and have appreciated considerably in value, thanks to Frederic Church. Pity they belong to Mr. Ferguson. The secret is that neither Mr. Ferguson nor his accountant has art awareness, and so one or two can disappear and not be missed."

"And that's how you pay for your abolitionist activities?" Wendell guessed. If so, it was a dangerous game.

"Yes, but not all of it is stolen. I have my allowance and lyceum money, which are thankfully mine."

Lillian stood and led him to the kitchen. The aroma of roasted pork and cinnamon apples assailed his nostrils. "Where is the cook?" he asked, looking around. "I had thought we were alone."

"Indeed we are," Lillian laughed, "for you are looking at the cook. But certain things must be done and you need don this apron and help me." Wendell donned the apron and pulled the heavy roast gallantly from the oven. After an excellent meal, he was assigned duty washing pots. He found it enjoyable working side by side with Lillian, and especially when she smiled and said, "It is quite arousing for a woman to see a man doing dishes."

"I am grateful to know that," Wendell laughed. "Such a simple truth to have eluded men for so long." At which she looked at him suggestively, took his hand, and wiped it dry on the inside of her dress.

Chapter 19

Wendell was sitting with Tuck, Ruby, young Willy and Lillian in the Great Hall of the Cooper Union. As Wendell listened to the lanky politician who held the stage, he felt his face flush with anger.

"You charge that we stir up insurrections among your slaves," Mr. Lincoln was saying. "We deny it; and what is your proof? Harper's Ferry! John Brown!! John Brown was no Republican; and you have failed to implicate a single Republican in his Harper's Ferry enterprise.

"This is all Republicans ask – all Republicans desire – in relation to slavery. Let it be marked as an evil not to be extended, but to be tolerated and protected only because its actual presence makes that toleration and protection a necessity. Let all the guarantees our forefathers gave it, be, not grudgingly, but fully and fairly, maintained. For this Republicans contend, and with this, so far as I know or believe, they will be content."

Wendell's disappointment was acute, for the new Republican Party had been the one hope for change. But Mr. Abraham Lincoln seemed to offer only appeasement, and no relief for those in bondage.

Afterwards, Tuck fumed, "I thought the Republicans was on our side!" A wet snow was falling as Wendell and Lillian waited with the Robinsons for the Harlem Railcar to come.

"'Were'" corrected Willy, "'were' on our side."

Tuck ignored him. "An' he don't say nothin' bout us who is free havin' our citizen rights or havin' a vote."

"Fie! It matters not what politicians do," proclaimed Lillian forcefully. "Slavery must be ended through insurrection of the slaves themselves. They should refuse to work."

"Then once again," protested Ruby, "it would be coloreds

alone who are killed."

"I believe it could work were it coordinated," offered Wendell, "but that seems the difficulty. It was for lack of a simultaneous uprising that John Brown failed."

"Captain Brown never meant for folks to just sit down and refuse to work," said Tuck, "he meant they be armed."

"I have seen sit-downs used in the factory, and a small victory won each time," insisted Lillian.

"How so?" Wendell asked, perplexed.

Lillian continued casually, "I worked in a factory. After my mother left, I ran away and became a *grisette*."

Wendell was surprised. "You had not told me."

She smiled at him and squeezed his hand. "Two years later my father found me, at the start of the '57 depression, thin almost to starving. That's when he arranged my marriage to Mr. Ferguson."

"Yes," nodded Ruby. "But even in those harsh conditions, the color of your skin protected you. A *grisette* is not beaten and sold."

"Surely the tactic could work," Lillian persisted. "There is too much investment in slaves to kill them."

"Lillian, I knows you mean well," said Tuck, "but they just sells your chillun. They don't have to do no more than that."

"So what are you saying?" Lillian asked with dismay. "Is there no alternative to war?" Seeing her distress, no one answered, but looked at her helplessly or looked away.

After the Robinsons had departed, Wendell and Lillian walked back to Pfaff's, where the always cynical bohemians had not attended the speech. Henry Clapp, in particular, opined that all politicians are an affront to free people – already, this Lincoln was raising money from whatever unworthy rascal wished to be owed a favor by the next president. Yet there was a stir of excitement that Mr. Lincoln had just gone into Mathew Brady's new photography studio in the same building. A large crowd gathered outside to gawk at the candidate while the bohemians stayed in their seats, feigning disinterest.

"I feel sorry for Mr. Brady," observed Henry Clapp. "Mr. Lincoln is too coarse for the lens, and rather needs a flattering brush."

Wendell's laugh was bitter. "Perhaps the man deserves to be seen in an unflattering light."

Still, Wendell was curious to see the photograph, and excused himself to go upstairs and pay Brady a visit. To Wendell's delight, Mr. Brady remembered him and invited Wendell through his busy factory to see the just printed portrait of Mr. Lincoln. "I believe he looks rather presidential," Brady said proudly, his hands stuffed into the pockets of his lab coat as he gazed at his new creation. "I have an order for it already, from *Atlantic Monthly,* and my lithographers will soon be at work reproducing it for printing." Wendell agreed that the image was surprisingly handsome.

He looked around in awe at Brady's 'operating rooms,' only recently relocated from further down Broadway. Drapes were slung across the ceiling on a movable wooden frame with which the window light could be directed, while handsome wooden boxed cameras rested on sturdy tripods. Along the opposite wall were glass cabinets full of photographs made by Brady and the other 'operators' in his studio: small daguerreotype portraits, tintypes, ambrotypes, as well as large portraits the size of paintings, gilt framed and printed on canvas, that Brady said were called 'Imperial' portraits. These Imperials could cost as much as $700 and were made from a giant camera that held 16" x 20" plates. His chief operator, Alexander Gardner, also had a secret of enlarging from wet plate negatives, and Wendell gawked as Brady showed him his Woodward Solar enlargers, which swiveled during long exposures to catch the moving sun.

There were also cases of the albumen print *cartes de visite,* little cardboard likenesses now being carried in purses and wallets, and mailed to relatives for photo albums. Wendell saw portraits of

Edwin and John Wilkes Booth, Laura Keene, Edgar Alan Poe, P. T. Barnum and his midget Tom Thumb, the prizefighter John Heenan. He loved the emotion the images evoked in him. No matter that the head was affixed from behind to a wooden brace to keep it still for the long exposure – here was not an artist's flattering interpretation, but a real moment in time with all the subtleties of expression impossible to hide. Among the many daguerreotypes presented were *New York Tribune*'s editor Horace Greeley, Edwin's father Junius Brutus Booth in stage costume, artist Asher Durand, President Buchanan and Wendell's old mentor, Samuel F. B. Morse. "To him I owe my painting career," Wendell commented.

"And to him I owe my photographic career!" laughed Brady. "I had been a painter, and he showed me a daguerreotype!" Wendell liked the handsome innovator's confidence and heavy curling dark hair above a closely trimmed and pointed beard. He wore little spectacles on an aquiline nose that heightened his mystique of being an intense observer. Even better, Wendell liked the feeling of excitement that came over him as Brady led him into the mysteries of the darkroom with its chemical smells and strange devices.

"Would you teach me?" Wendell asked suddenly, "I have been wanting to learn for curiosity and to use in my work. Many painters employ a camera to save their subjects from a long sitting."

"I would be delighted," enthused Brady, "if you will limn for me a simple backdrop. I quite admire your landscapes."

"I will limn you several!" laughed Wendell, "You have but to describe your preferences." By the time he left, Wendell was glowing with anticipation.

Back at Pfaff's, raised voices alerted Wendell to a fracas. The bohemians were in a fluster around Mr. and Mrs. Heenan who both had bruised and blackened eyes. "Be fair!" the battered Benicia Boy was saying, from a chair that tilted back dangerously. "My face is beaten, same as hers. That should prove my innocence." He pointed to the cut still weeping on his cheekbone and did look to have gotten the worst of it.

Ada Clare was standing over him, half spitting in a spirited defense of her friend. "You are a pugilist! Reputed the best in the world! And you would dare to hit a woman?! No sir, there is no justification."

John Heenan jumped up, knocking the chair over as he did so, seeming on the verge of hitting the surprised Miss Clare. Wendell and the other men tensed, balling their fists. The boxer, thinking better of his attack, shoved his hands in his pockets and stormed out of Pfaff's, leaving his wife slumped over and asking for whiskey.

Lillian held the Menken's hand and stroked her hair, "You must leave him, you know."

Adah nodded. Then she jumped up with a strangled "No!" and ran out the door after her husband. Before Wendell could even alert Lillian to his presence, Adah was back, weeping and demanding another drink. She sank into her seat wearily and, ever the dramatist, expressed her woe with her own poetry:

> *"Leaves pallid and sombre and ruddy,*
> *Dead fruits of the fugitive years;*
> *Some stained as with wine and made bloody,*
> *And some as with tears,"*

then downed her drink like a tosspot. This time it was Ada Clare who comforted her, pulling her head onto her shoulder, while Walt Whitman stood over them with fatherly concern.

Meanwhile, many a man had gathered round and Wendell knew what they were thinking – 'Damn, she looks good even with her eyes blacked.'

"Listen Menken," said Ada Clare, "what Lillian said is true.

Next time he'll kill you."

"True," added Walt, "this is just the beginning."

"Alas," Adah sobbed, "the papers say I am a bigamist, that I am not divorced from Mr. Menken. One even said I am not divorced from Mr. Isaacs, which would make me a trigamist!" This last actually made her laugh, as there had been a Mr. Kneass, but only one Mr. Isaacs Menken.

"Fie," said Lillian. "If John Heenan loved you, he would not care for legalities. It is with him you live, not Mr. Menken."

Adah Kneass Isaacs Menken Heenan screwed her face in distaste. "It's because Johnny has 'handlers', as if he were a fighting cock or dog. They wish boxing to be made legal, and seek to give it a savory face. Johnny fears the scandal with me has hurt their vaunted purpose."

"Perhaps 'Johnny' thinks that hitting Adah will make boxing more savory," mumbled Walt Whitman to no one in particular.

While Wendell watched, he felt sad for Adah's difficulties, but even sadder that the Benicia Boy's fascinating muscles might no longer be available for him to sketch.

Then, as if to confirm the charges against her, the Menken pulled a mangled cigarette from her skirt and begged a light. Matches flared as Ted Winthrop, Tom Aldrich, Macaroni, and the comic writer Bob Newell huddled protectively around. With her blackened eyes, boyish haircut and cigarette dangling from pouty lips above a sweetly trembling chin, Adah looked deliciously disreputable. That she was a Hebrew rumored to be of the Negro race only heightened her mystique.

It was Bob Newell who knelt before her and took her hand. "Adah, Adah," he said dramatically as she exhaled smoke in his face, "your blackened eyes excite your adoring minions even as John Brown's hanging excited his. Now, 'tis your own growing legend will doubtless convulse the newspaper's columns."

The Menken looked at him quizzically. "I sense it is not me

you mock."

"Aye," he said tenderly, "it's not you." A passional look passed between them. Though Wendell dared not admit it, a small part of him felt sorry for the hapless John Heenan who had, it seemed, met his match.

The stars were evidently crossed that week. Fitzhugh confessed his suspicion that Rosalie and the recently arrived artist, Albert Bierstadt, were sweet on each other. Walt Whitman had been taunted by Macaroni about joining a gentlemen's romantic club, and was avoiding Pfaff's. Henry Clapp announced that the *Saturday Press* was in imminent danger of demise.

Worse, the John Brown affair menaced Lillian again. Sam Howe, back from Canada, was called to testify before the Senate Committee investigating Old Osawatomie – Wendell worried what he might say. Others were subpoenaed and refused to appear, placing themselves in contempt of Congress. In Concord, it was reported that federal marshals had attempted to arrest Frankie Sanborn, one of the named 'Secret Six,' in his yard, but the good people of the town had risen up and prevented it. Strangely, the committee said they would not call the recently released Gerrit Smith, which Lillian took to mean that she herself was safe – Wendell was not so sanguine.

All this, and the threat of Lillian's husband becoming aware of her involvement, put Wendell of a mind that Lillian should straight away divorce Mr. Ferguson and marry him – he waited only the right moment for asking.

Daily, he visited Mr. McClure, mapping out the tour that would make him wealthy. It was planned to last the entire summer, and would visit all the major cities in North America and Europe. If he and Lillian were married, she could travel with him to Ithaca, a current impossibility.

Following a particularly lovely sojourn with her at the Unitary

Household, Wendell pulled out his magic mirror and began to plot his proposal in earnest. "Lillian," he practiced aloud, "would you do me the honor of…" No, too formal. "My Dearest Lillian, I cannot bear to be apart from you. Will you accompany me on my tour – as my wife?" This he liked, but rehearse as he might, he could not trust himself to say it in her presence. At last, he penned a fine looking card, with a lovely sketch of hearts and gardenias, held his breath, and posted it.

Several days passed. Wendell was standing in his red painter's smock before a giant canvas, breathing the linseed oil as he limned yet another backdrop for Mathew Brady, when a light rapping came at his door. He opened it. Lillian smiled joyfully at him and gave him a delicious hug and lingering kiss, making his heart soar.

"My Heart," she said, "I see you are busy. You have made yourself somewhat scarce of late."

As he kicked the door closed and they stood in their embrace, Wendell did not know what to say next. Finally, he ventured timidly, "Did you get my letter?"

She stepped back and looked at him, her green eyes wide with innocence. "A letter? No. Whatever was it about?"

Caught! Nothing to do but say it out. "It was a proposal of marriage," he gulped. A look of confusion crossed her pretty features, so he cleared his throat and clarified, "I want to marry you, *Mon Coeur*." Now the look was one of shock and his heart sank.

"But everything is so perfect as it is. Why would we want to do that now?" she asked with alarm.

"I want you to come with me on my tour," he explained.

"But I have my lyceum tour," she protested. "Had you forgot?" and it was Wendell's turn to look shocked and perplexed – indeed, in his excitement about his own tour, he had quite forgot hers. There was a moment of panic as he tried to salvage what he could of his proposal, for he was intent that the marriage should occur.

He grabbed her roughly and clung to her.

"Lillian, *mon coeur*," he begged, "I don't want to be apart from you again – I want to keep you safe – Mr. Ferguson could come home. Forget the lyceum. Come with me!"

She pushed him back with an uncomfortable laugh, "Don't be so rough with me! I had already planned to accompany you to Paris – I would not miss it! But you know the lyceum is important to me."

"Lillian, we can't travel together unmarried! My tour will be in all the papers, and any gossip about me would be unwelcome by Mr. McClure."

"Stuff and nonsense!" rejoined Lillian. "Look at Adah Menken. A good scandal does nothing but pique the public interest. Mr. McClure is in it for money, not for sainthood. Besides, I must consider my own schedule. Now I need build a career for myself, and you for yourself. If I were to divorce Mr. Ferguson, we would not have enough to live on."

Wendell was becoming desperate, his voice getting louder as he determined that she should see things his way. "You have no faith in me, Lillian! This tour will make me rich."

Lillian's voice was also rising. "Mr. Parry, you are reckoning your chickens well before they're hatched. I will not work in a factory again!"

"I would never let my wife work in a factory! You insult me and my work!"

Lillian looked frightened at the tone their discussion was taking. "Wendell my Heart, I am happy as we are, I've never been happier. I had thought you were also."

There was much that had been festering inside of him that now pushed its way out in a feverish tumult. "You are happy because of Mr. Ferguson's money!" he shouted. A bead of sweat sprouted along his brow. "You are choosing his ill-gotten gains over me. My God, Lillian, he ships cotton picked by slaves!"

"It is not Mr. Ferguson's money I spend," Lillian defended herself, "'tis my father's! My father did not ship cotton!" She was almost screaming at him. "Where do you think your money comes from, Mr. Parry – it's all filthy lucre. I spend it for good, Wendell, for good! And how would you dispense money to your wife – would you give her an allowance? Or wait until she batted her eyes and asked you for it? Marriage is slavery, it is unequal between man and woman."

Livid, Wendell shouted, "I insist you put aside Mr. Ferguson, Lillian, and marry me!"

Lillian's green eyes flashed a warning. "You insist?! You would own me outright or not have me at all? Is that what you just said?"

"Yes," said Wendell recklessly. She had already jerked open the door and was headed down the stairs. "Lillian, you are treating my proposal as an insult!" He yelled his parting shot after her, "It is not an insult!" and slammed the atelier door.

The studio was suddenly quiet but for distant echoes of their words. What had he just done? He jerked the door open and ran down the stairs after her, stumbling in his haste, his red paint smock flapping. Outside, Wendell saw the carriage pulling away from the curb. He sprinted across the street and grabbed the door. "I'm sorry, Lillian," he called out to her, "I don't want to marry you!"

"Drive on!" Lillian commanded the coachman, who gave his horses their head, knocking Wendell away.

"But I don't want to marry you!" Wendell shouted after it, believing that it would stop, that she would come running back. As loud as he could, he yelled again, "I don't want to marry you!" Alas, the carriage continued to pick up speed and finally turned the corner onto Fifth Avenue. Lillian was gone.

How could this have happened? Wendell was in shock as he walked back up the middle of 10th Street. Now he noticed people had stopped along the sidewalk and were laughing at him. Only an elderly Negro seemed sympathetic, sitting on his stoop where Wendell had oft seen him before. He shook his head as Wendell passed. "'Twere me," he said, "I'd want to marry her."

Chapter 20

Wendell dragged himself forlornly to Thomas Read's atelier and knocked on the door. *"Entrere!"* came the reply as the door opened, and *"Buon Dio,* Wendell, you look utterly deflated!"

Wendell threw himself down on the well-worn sofa. "You discern the look correctly. Alas, this time I am a jack-ass caught between two piles of shit." His voice was strangled and he blinked hard as Thomas handed him a whiskey bottle. Wendell took a swig. "I have made the mistake of demanding Lillian marry me," he confessed, "and now she is unlikely even to speak to me."

Thomas looked alarmed. "While I sympathize with your dilemma, I am rather glad she declined! She does, after all, give support to many of your fellows in this building."

Wendell heaved a giant sigh. Was his mistake to have ramifications beyond Lillian? Would his friends now shun him and call him traitor? He handed the bottle back to Thomas and got up to leave.

"Wendell, stay," said Thomas, placing a friendly hand on his arm. "I spoke rashly. Forgive me. Had she said 'Yes', I would gladly be groomsman at the wedding." Wendell sank back down into his seat and put his head between his hands.

"Alas, Thomas, what am I to do? 'Twas my fear of losing her that has now driven her away."

Thomas sat down on the chair opposite and crossed his legs, stroking his goatee thoughtfully. He tipped his beret. "I truly doubt that she's done with you," said Thomas. "The besottedness of your relationship has been quite mutual. Give her a few weeks, then if she has not returned, take a bunch of lilies to her. I'll wager she'll be back in the sack by month's end."

Wendell took Thomas's advice and for the next several weeks stayed away from places he might see her. He had hoped she would come to him, but by month's end and desperate, he finally determined to pay her a visit. On a frosty morning he arose early to walk to her apartment in the freshening dawn. Lilies would betoken peace, but at the little flower stand on Broadway, his eyes fell on romantic red roses. It was the rising sun which lit them in the most breathtaking way, casting a halo around each soft red petal – ah, to capture that upon a canvas, and give such a limning to Lillian. He stared for a long time in his admiration, till the flower girl, anxious for a sale, begged his attention. Wendell paid the handsome price and crossed over Bowery to 106 East 14th Street.

As he approached, he was most alarmed to see all four of the Unitary Households boarded up and empty. He ran to catch the man just pounding the final nail. "Hold, what goes here? What has happened to the tenants?"

"Don't yer read the papers?" said the man, "They've been given the boot. 'Twas a duel over one of them 'free love' ladies, way I heard it."

"When?" asked Wendell with great agitation, "How long since they've gone?"

"Not more'an a day or two," the man said kindly, eyeing the flowers. "Thar be friends of yer'n, huh?"

"Yes. Was anyone hurt?" Wendell imagined the worst, Fitzhugh and Bierstadt killing each other over the flirtatious Rosalie.

"Nay, thar be too drunk to hit thar marks."

Wendell retrieved a *New York Times*, which said the Unitary Households had been closed for bills unpaid and had been a scandalous continuation of Henry Clapp's Free Love League, shut down five years earlier by Mayor Wood's Muni Police – no mention of a duel. The paper somehow managed to implicate dreaded communism, as well as Horace Greeley and even long-dead Margaret Fuller. Wendell read of the Households,

"Unblushing adultery was no uncommon circumstance. The

serving-maids were debauched; children of tender years fell victims to the arts of accomplished seducers; lust raged, and decency was banished...

"It was no uncommon occurrence for brother and sister, cousins, and other relatives, to associate together as man and wife. To ruin a child was regarded as a pleasant deed. To seduce a wife was considered no wrong to the husband...

"In the presence of deeds such as these, it was not wonderful that none but the utterly depraved finally remained to sustain the fortunes of the 'Household.'"

Wendell was not surprised that the staid *New York Times* would go on a rant about the Unitary Households – it was not the first time, to which his father had alluded when Wendell was in Ithaca.

When he arrived at Pfaff's shortly after, Wendell was still carrying his red roses, and dearly hoped she would be there. Alas, she was not. But Fitzhugh, Henry Clapp, Macaroni, and Bob Newell sat in the smoky haze of the alcove and welcomed him over. "Where have you been?" they greeted him.

Wendell countered with his own query. "Where are you living, now that the Unitary Household is no more?"

They had moved into apartments on Waverly Place. Lillian was visiting Josephine Walters – they knew not where or for how long.

"Surely you have not bought those flowers for Lillian," said Macaroni. "She says you are parted."

Wendell's stomach went quite queasy. "Nay, I bought them for you," he said angrily, throwing the flowers down on the table. He turned around and left.

Wendell was more hopeful next morning when George the concierge knocked at his studio, announcing a letter. Wendell threw on his djellaba and opened the door – surely the letter was from Lillian. But alas, it was from Mr. John McClure, and worse! His wife had taken ill and the tour was cancelled! Enclosed were $200 in bank notes and a plea to hold onto the Ithaca canvases another year in hopes that a tour could commence the following spring. Of course, should Wendell sell the canvases in the meantime, the entire of the $800 thus far advanced should be repaid.

This was indeed a blow. Wendell had been still entertaining a hope that Lillian would change her mind and marry him – there was surely no way now he could support her. His chagrin was almost unbearable, and suddenly he was glad she was gone – he would feel shame to face her. In his obsessed mind, Henry Ferguson's money became his bitter rival, and he would not see Lillian again until he had bettered it – even if he had to rob a bank!

For the moment, rather than plot a robbery, Wendell went downstairs to Thomas's atelier. Thomas welcomed him in, and once again, Wendell flopped down on his sofa. "The lilies didn't work," observed Thomas.

Wendell did not answer, his mind deep in cogitation on his money woes. "Thomas," he said at length, "what are your plans for the summer?"

"I have two commissions that will keep me here," said Thomas. "Why do you ask?"

"I would like to buy your remaining faceless paintings." It was more a confession than a request, for he had no money with which to do so.

Thomas stroked his goatee thoughtfully, "I would be happy to make you a consignment of them," said Thomas. "You can pay me at summer's end for those you don't return."

Wendell brightened. It would not be cheap, for shipping the boards upstate was dear in itself. He was suddenly glad for the $200 that McClure had sent.

Thomas continued, "I am quite naturally short of pretty young women – there is always need for more of them – paintings, I mean."

"Understood," said Wendell, finally smiling. "I will stop in

Ithaca and add to your collection there."

And so it was decided. Lillian would have two weeks to come crawling back, and then Wendell would be gone for the summer, and let her stew over him. This time, it would be she who would not know where he was!

Despite his determination that she would come to him, Wendell continued to look for her daily at Pfaff's and even ventured to the school in the Five Points. There it was said that she visited Anna Mary Goldbeck, but they knew not where Anna Mary lived. Vainly he wondered what Lillian had said of him, and if their Pfaffsian friends laughed behind his back. He could just hear them – "How foolish of him asking her to quit her husband's wealth to live with a starving artist! As if any woman would even consider such a thing!"

Sam, meanwhile, was delighted that Lillian seemed to be gone. The 14th Brooklyn militia were at Washington Park on The Hill at 'Fort Greene,' practicing the light infantry maneuvers they had seen done by Elmer Ellsworth's impressive Zouave drill team. "It's not that I don't very much adore Lillian," Sam explained as they huffed their packs and rifles up The Hill in their handsome uniforms. "You were right to insist she marry you – without marriage, she offers no future by way of family," he paused to catch his breath, "and since Lillian's now given you the mitten, I fain you would give Elizabeth's sister a second look. It would be a great comfort to have you for a brother-in-law."

As Wendell reached the crest, saw his mark and took aim, he thanked Sam kindly. "It's too soon," he opined, and added out of politeness, "I might consider the comely Miss Margaret later if she's still available."

He was by now quite anxious to leave for Ithaca. Thomas's faceless boards had been shipped ahead and Wendell's Ithaca paintings placed on display at the New York Academy of Design by invitation of its president, Asher Durand. Wendell did not understand why he yet lingered. Still, his heart ached as he copied the bodice of Lillian's portrait to make a faceless board. He was so deeply engrossed in each detail that he almost proceeded to put the face in, without needing even to look at the original. It was as though she stood before him, her skin alive beneath the folds of her gauze blouse, the scent of the gardenias she'd worn that day mingling with the smell of his linseed oil. He could almost embrace and kiss her, so strongly did he feel her presence. And so, when the knock came at his atelier, Wendell was sure 'twas she at last.

Suddenly full of gratitude and forgiveness, Wendell pulled open the door. It took a moment before he realized that it was not Lillian who stood before him, but the Comtesse de Clairmont.

"Monsieur Parry!" exclaimed the Comtesse as she swept her voluminous skirts imperiously across his threshold. She held out her hand to be kissed, and pulled it away as he bowed over it.

"Comtesse, pourquoi on me donne ce plaisir?" he inquired politely, trying not to look disappointed.

"Mon Cher, vous me devez un portrait avec un tit." Oh no, was she returning the painting? *"Mais non!"* she answered his question, *"Le Comte est très heureux."* Ah, she was offering him another commission then – he could use one and she paid well, in gold coin. *"Avez-vous le temps maintenant?"* He assured her he did have time right now, and she looked back out his door to inform her attendants that she would be awhile. Wendell heard the men depart down the stairs as she pulled the door closed.

Wendell invited her to sit at his little table and offered tea, which she accepted. She smelled of an exotic perfume that wafted towards him enticingly from the cleavage above her tightly bound bodice. He tended the brazier, realizing with some excitement that he was being hired not just to paint her, but to fuck her. Well, if Lillian had said they were no longer together, what was the harm? As the water heated up, he sat down opposite his guest, and, resting his ankle on his knee, allowed his crossed leg to fall widely open as he tipped back in his chair. A knowing smile passed between them.

"Vous êtes loin de chez eux, Comtesse," he said. Indeed, she was far from home.

"J'en suis venu à voir Amérique," she explained with relish, *"New York, Chicago, San Francisco, New Orléans, Québec, les grandes plaines, les montagnes Rocheuses."*

They drank their tea slowly, making such small talk as Wendell could master, then she rose and gestured towards his dressing screen. Ah, she was going to be coy. He set it up for her in the room's center and she disappeared behind it, coming out with her hair flowing to have him help with first her stays and then her stockings. Soon she was quite naked and clutching a rich velvet drapery as she sat demurely upon the posing bench. *"Vous avez froid,"* observed Wendell, noticing her goose bumps. *"Je vais allumer le chauffage,"* and he turned up the gas on the heater. Wendell gazed at her with his painter's eye, thinking how much better she looked without the trappings of aristocracy – almost sweet. He approached her to adjust her pose. *"Juste un peu taquiner, de révéler le tit,"* he said, and stroked her nipple as he pushed the drapery aside.

The Comtesse sighed, looking at him with lustful longing. *"Vous n'êtes pas chaud?"* Yes, he nodded, he was hot, at which he let drop his trouser braces and began to undo his shirt. Soon he stood bare-chested, aware of the effect his chest curls had on her, and now she ran her finger along the top of his trousers, and stroked the bulge beneath them. As she began to undo his trouser buttons, he pulled her up and onto the little bed. He sighed as she kissed him, feeling such pleasure in the physical purity of it, the lack of emotional attachment. He was not afraid of losing her, he didn't care if she came or went or what she thought of him. He just laid back and felt her kisses upon his chest and her hand reaching deliciously down inside the bib of his breeches.

There was a sound at the door and a sharp gasp. Wendell looked over to see Lillian standing there with her mouth hanging open, staring with an expression of utter horror. He threw the startled Comtesse aside and stood up hastily, fastening his trousers with a pleading look at Lillian.

"I thought you wanted to marry me," she said with a strangled voice. Then she slammed the door and he heard her footsteps running down the stairs.

Wendell fumbled with his clothes, and grabbed his smock as he jerked the door open and ran after her, pushing his arms through the sleeves as he flew. Beyond the Comtesse's waiting carriage, he saw Lillian's coach fast pulling away across the street, the coachman urging his horses to a gallop.

"Lillian, I do want to marry you!" he shouted as he gave chase with all his effort. "I do want to marry you!" He continued to chase her all the way across Fifth Avenue till the carriage turned precariously to merge with the busy traffic of Broadway. "I do want to marry you!" he yelled finally, in hopeless defeat.

The breath went out of him completely and he almost swooned. As he turned up 10th Street, he didn't care that people were once again laughing. He felt the nausea rise, the familiar fear of abandonment he knew so well from childhood. He had truly done the unforgivable this time. The old Negro was sitting on his stoop, opening his mouth to say something, then simply closed it and shook his head sadly.

As Wendell climbed the studio stairs, the hastily dressed Comtesse was coming down. *"Je suis tellement désolé,"* she said miserably as she brushed past him. She pressed a coin into his hand. *"Pour votre temps,"* she murmured, and kissed his forehead before she continued down in a waft of French perfume, disappearing out the heavy door.

There seemed no reason to linger in Manhattan – he had seen

the look on Lillian's face. If there was ever anything a lover would not forgive, it was surely the sight of such betrayal. Had she only heard about it, there might be a chance, given that they were parted. But to witness it…

Even Cat's mewling concern was no comfort to him as he slept lonely that night upon his bed and wept bitter tears. There was now no hope he would ever marry, for indeed he could not conceive that he would ever love again. Was there no woman that had not left him? First his mother, then his grandmother, now Lillian – only Catherine was still faithful. "Catherine has sacrificed much for your sake," his grandmother had said, "Mrs. Ferguson has not." And then, "You must give her your hand." As he finally fell into a fitful sleep, Wendell dreamed he was lost, choking in a desert sandstorm, while all about him buzzards wheeled and waited.

And so Wendell Harte Parry arrived at the train station in Ithaca, Upstate New York, on April Fools Day, 1860. This time it was his father who picked him up at the platform and drove the buckboard through carefully maintained dirt roads to the familiar farm house, where the chickens scattered and the shutters banged forlornly against the attic dormer.

"Welcome home, Son," said the elder Parry, glancing up at gathering clouds. "It surely does look like it's going to rain."

Chapter 21

Catherine's departure had left the little farm house in a most downtrodden state. When they opened the door, clumps of dust came alive and scurried like spiders across the wooden floor. Dirty dishes were piled high on the kitchen counters and scattered through various corners. There was a smell of cooked cabbage and old onions, while fruit flies hovered in the pantry. Wendell's voice betrayed his distress, "Had I not sent you enough money to hire help?"

His father placed his cane in the corner and sagged wearily into the kitchen chair. "I reckon I'm not much of a maid-servant," he confessed guiltily, making a bare spot on the table to lean his elbow. "Fix yourself some coffee or tea, if you're wanting it." He reached across to pick up a dirty half-full wine glass and downed the remainder with a swallow.

"Do you not have any help?" Wendell asked again, stoking the stove with wood for hot water.

"Your sister's living with a female lover. You are aware of that, are you not?"

"That they are lovers? No, though I had guessed at it." Wendell sat opposite the elder Parry and eyed him with concern. "What has that to do with my question?"

Mr. Parry was becoming agitated and Wendell could smell old wine and tobacco leaching through his sallow skin. "Does that not rankle you? What kind of daughter leaves her father for lust of a woman? And a poor woman! Catherine should marry a man with money to take care of me, or else stay and see to it herself."

"Father!" barked Wendell for attention, "Had you not gotten the money I sent?"

His father looked at him mystified. "She takes it. Any money you send, Catherine takes. She takes it and gives it to that woman."

Wendell was becoming quite alarmed. Was his father babbling? He seemed almost alienated. Wendell gripped Harte Parry by the shoulder and met his eyes as he asked again, "Dad, do you have any help here?"

There was a pause, and the older man's chin began to tremble. "No," said his father, "I have none."

Wendell rose and headed toward the door. "It's starting to rain. I'll see to the horses."

Outside, the horses were restless as the first drops splattered the dirt. Wendell examined them closely and was relieved to find them well cared for. He undid their harnesses and led them to the barn, in which lowed several healthy looking cows with plenty of hay and clean bedding. The chicken coop was likewise in good repair with happy chickens. Tiny plants came up in neat rows in the garden. Even the pigs and pen seemed adequately tended. Surely his father had not done all this.

Wendell hoisted his steamer trunk up to the little dormer room and by the time he came down, the rain was coming hard. His father had risen and was leaning heavily on his cane.

"What do you mean you have no help?" asked Wendell. "Everything seems ship-shape, as near as I can reckon."

"Damn and tarnation, I've no help in the house. I am left to cook and clean for myself, and do all the women's work. Then that woman comes and does the man's work outside and Catherine gives her all my money."

Wendell looked at him surprised. "Catherine's lover is helping you?"

Harte Parry lit his pipe even as he leaned heavily on his cane. Wendell could see his hands shake with incipient palsy. "More a hindrance than a help. She costs too much, and can't do half what a man can. Won't come inside at all, like she's scared of me." He sighed, "I guess I should be glad of her," as he sat back down heavily into his chair. "Thing is, Son, I'm needing a lot of help these days, more than she's willing to give. I tire easily."

"Have you talked to Catherine about it?" Wendell was feeling relieved that Catherine was still about and handling things, even if she was in the background.

"Nay, she keeps to herself these days. I don't think she sees anyone but that so-called Seneca Sue."

"What of her meetings? Surely she must still lead the meetings."

The elder Parry started to guffaw cruelly, happy to convey Catherine's comeuppance. "There are no more meetings. Your sister was found to be a fraud." Now Wendell sat tentatively, shocked and curious. His father went on, laughing gleefully. "Some guest from Canada spoke to old Hyenwatha in Onondaga language and Hyenwatha didn't understand a word of it!" Harte Parry doubled over with mirth, until his laughter caught on the smoke and turned to a spate of uncontrollable coughing.

With something akin to revulsion, Wendell regarded his father and vaguely recalled why he had been so anxious to leave home for college. Mixed with his disappointment was something like pity and a sense of duty. "How long since you've eaten?" Wendell asked when his father had caught his breath.

"Oh, I eat, I eat!" Harte insisted defensively, "I can still crack an egg or two."

Wendell rose. "Then why don't you get some rest. The rain has stopped and I fain would visit my sister."

"You won't need the rig," offered his father agreeably, "Catherine's cabin's just a short walk through the woods – the old Patterson place."

After a change of clothes and washing up, Wendell went along a shallow deer path that led through the still dripping trees. He knew the way – he had walked this way many times as a boy going to Tommy Patterson's – whatever happened to Tommy Patterson? He breathed in the fresh air and was glad to be out of the city.

When he came at last to the old Patterson Pond, luminous and green in the rain's afterglow, Wendell thought how much he'd like to paint it – viridian, Hooker's green, azurite – and how much Lillian would like such a painting. The ducks on its surface ignored him and quacked loudly over some rare and tasty morsel, while beyond, a deer munched contentedly on new spring growth. For a moment, Wendell felt Lillian's presence so palpably that it almost seemed she was not lost to him. And then the emptiness overtook him, and he sagged with the realization that, alas, she was lost. Sorrow and confusion overwhelmed him. It had not been his intention nor Lillian's to end the relationship, so how had it happened? Now, he saw her face again as she stood last in his doorway, and remorse ripped through him, doubling him over such that he had to grab a nearby tree for support. Truly, he was a fool. He looked up toward the little cabin in the distance with smoke curling out its chimney. "Your sister has sacrificed much for your sake, Mrs. Ferguson has not," echoed his grandmother's voice – and yet his sister was a fraud. How had she known of Mrs. Ferguson? Did it even matter anymore?

Briefly, Wendell considered leaving, until he saw Catherine Cayuga come out of the house and begin to hang laundry round the back. She looked his way and he waved. "Ho, is that you, Little Deer?" called Catherine, and seeing it was, ran to meet him.

He was surprised at the eagerness of her greeting. She led him into her tiny cabin, one room with a rough table beside a wood-burning cookstove, two small beds in the corners surrounded by shelves, and a large mirrored armoire which Wendell recognized from her bedroom at home. Seneca Sue, who introduced herself as simply Sue, sat at the table wearing a coarse brown work dress which seemed to embarrass her. "I'm sorry," she explained, "I had been working in the field and did not expect visitors." It was Wendell's opportunity to discuss his dad.

"You do a good job in your labors," said Wendell. "I'm pleased to see Father's place looking so well cared for. Do you work there frequently?"

"I work there as much as he'll allow. Sometimes, he chases me off," she admitted. "I don't think he likes me very much."

"Then why do you stay?" asked Wendell, admiring the woman's forthrightness. He guessed she was in her early forties, and wondered what her life had been before Catherine.

"We need the money," answered Catherine for her. "As you might imagine, Brother, work is not easily found for such as us."

"And what are you doing for money?"

Catherine placed tea in front of him and sat down with a wry smile. "Alas," she said, "I am still the domestic, keeping the home-fires burning. At the least it's my own home now. As for money, I manage with what you send to pay Father's bills as well as ours. And I still garner donations from the spirit meetings at the lodge."

Wendell looked surprised, and she shook her head. "I see Father has told you of what he calls my 'come-uppance'. The incident did cause some discord, but Mary Jane Randolph said that often spirits pretend to be someone they are not, and that I would have no way of knowing that the entity was not Hyenwatha. As her husband is Dr. Paschal Beverly Randolph and famous for communing with spirits, her pronouncement was well received. I now make no claims for who the spirit is that is coming through, and my congregation is more cautious. It has actually grown larger since it is no longer restricted to Indians."

Wendell was fascinated. "And does the spirit still claim to be Hyenwatha?"

"No," said Catherine, "that spirit has not been heard from again. Now it's an assortment of men and women – I never know who's coming, and have little ability to call forth a particular one."

Wendell remembered the thin dark woman who sold patent medicines and had a sorry connection to Gerrit Smith. "How is Mary Jane Randolph and her little daughter?" he asked.

"She is no longer in Ithaca, and we haven't yet heard of her whereabouts. I believe she organizes her husband's writings which are indeed prodigious. Do you still have his magic mirror?"

Wendell nodded and Sue spoke up excitedly, "Can you tell us something of how you met Dr. Randolph and came to have the mirror?"

Wendell shook his head apologetically. "The magic around the mirror, how it was charged and where, is knowledge to which only its owner is privy." Both women looked disappointed, but he wished to press his original topic. "Father says he needs more help in the house, and indeed, neither he nor the house looks well. Is there no money for that?"

"Nay!" said Catherine, "He drinks! He and the house would look fine but for that. He should clean his own mess!"

"Still," said Wendell alarmed, "he is a grown man and Patriarch. He should have some say over how his money is spent."

"Wendell, you don't know what you say," insisted his sister. "He drinks his money lest he's smoking it. If we allowed him to be frivolous, there would simply not be enough to maintain both our households. And while you have been most generous, we are never sure when more will arrive and how much."

"If Sue or you could work somewhere else," reasoned Wendell, "I would not have to maintain two households. I had never expected that."

"Fie, Little Deer! Folks may come to us furtively by night to speak to their dead, but do not hope they will hire us by day. They have their high and righteous morals – indeed, we are both hell-bound in their eyes."

It was now becoming clear to Wendell that supporting his strange and alienated family was going to be far more expensive than he had hoped – Lillian had been right that he could not afford to marry her. Suddenly Wendell was afraid that his lot in life would be to live always as a poor bachelor.

He rose to leave, and had yet one more question. "So is Grandmother's spirit real?" Wendell realized how much he wanted to believe it was, that she had not abandoned them, though he felt almost silly thinking it.

His sister looked at him closely, with hope that matched his own. "I believe she is real," Catherine said and seemed to him utterly sincere.

Over the next few weeks, Wendell found himself frustrated with having not time enough to paint. The farm and household chores of cleaning and preparing daily meals for himself and his father proved surprisingly burdensome. Contrarily, his father had time to drive into town daily to see if any news of the John Heenan/Tommy Sayers fight had arrived from England. He had been quite excited to hear that his son knew the American champion. Apparently, the elder Parry had found money to wager on it as well as money for wine and tobacco. "Wendell! Heenan has been incarcerated in England!" he proclaimed one day with great consternation. "His crime was intending to disturb the peace. Damn that Sayers was not similarly arrested!"

The elder Parry's interest was so piqued over the coming fight that Wendell suspected he had a great deal of money riding on it. When Wendell got the confession out of him, he was shocked – should Sayers win, his father would be deeply in debt and the farm lost. "If you lose the farm over this, I will not send you a penny!" Wendell railed. Finally came the news that the boxers had fought forty-two rounds to a bloody draw and each awarded a belt – no bets were paid and no money lost.

At last, Wendell sat down in a curtained off section of the barn to limn. It was Lillian's body that confronted him in side by side versions, five in a row, with clothes and backgrounds varied only slightly. In each one, the empty face taunted him with its reflection of his own empty heart. Nay, 'twas not emptiness he felt, unless despair could be thought so – were his heart truly empty, he would be spared the pain of knowing that he could never touch her again save with a brush.

One day his father surprised him while he painted and, leaning over his shoulder, commented, "Here you sit, painting the same lady over and over, while neglecting to put a face on her. I can only guess that she turned down your proposal of marriage and you are now gone quite mad."

"Perhaps madness runs in our family," Wendell demurred.

"Hmmm," considered the elder Parry, "you may be right, Son. Your mother always was a strange one."

It was almost a month before Wendell was ready to depart, his father's buckboard loaded with crates of the faceless torsos. He was leaving the house in better order than he'd found it, but had not much hope that it would stay so. Catherine sat beside him as he yelled his final goodbyes and urged the horses toward the train station. "Sister," he offered, his heart full, "I have garnered new respect for the work of women. If you have sought to torture father for his ingratitude, I pray you reconsider and show him some mercy – he will not last without a woman's help."

"Fie," said Catherine bitterly, "he does not respect me. Let him be the one to beg for mercy." As they parted, Wendell could only give his sister a hug and hope her revenge would not go too far.

Wendell had chosen as a destination little-known Monticello in Sullivan County, where he could hire a wagon and disappear into the Mongaup Valley, well off the beaten track of fellow artists and New York City's summer sojourners. His plan was to find a cabin and live a life of quiet contemplation as Thoreau had done at Walden Pond, with only his limning subjects coming by to have their likenesses imposed on the pre-painted bodies. At this he succeeded rather well, landing in Bethel at a care-taker's cottage which looked out upon vistas of untamed woods and creeks. He hung Lillian's picture in the window of the General Store, with a notice of his hours and his price, and a place to sign up for the appointment. The sign said *Portraits in the Mode of the Old Masters.* In one short week of settling in, his appointment ledger started to fill up.

It was a perfect little town for Wendell's purposes, shades of sepia and aureolin, and just large enough to have modestly well-to-do business owners with friends who aspired to be like them. When Mr. Wynkoop Kiersted, owner of a tannery that made boots of Brazilian and Basque leathers, found enough satisfaction with his portrait to make an appointment for Mrs. Kiersted, the rush was on. Soon Dr. Purdy and his wife were limned, along with their darling child whose torso was close in size to one Thomas had been wise enough to paint. Next the shop owners, and the mill owners, and the owner of the carding factory added their names for appointments, which led to the less-wealthy school-teachers and town constables wanting portraits as well.

Wendell took sittings three days per week, three per day, fleshing out each likeness with carefully ground batches of the finest pigments, layered for durability to last millennia. To keep wood smoke away from the slow-drying paint, he cooked the occasional fish or rabbit he caught over an outdoors fire, and washed up thoroughly in the pretty creek which also found its way into his sketches. On warm nights, he sat under the stars with the lightning bugs and talked to them for company, wondering if Lillian, too, were looking up at the sky. When Wendell had time, reading Cooper's *The Last of the Mohicans* assuaged his loneliness more than even Thoreau.

He had been in Bethel for almost two months without being questioned as to his identity or having much discourse with the townsfolk, when a young woman sat down behind his paint panel and smiled shyly. She looked so like Lillian! She had of course chosen to be limned upon the bodice that was Lillian's, the one wearing the very outfit that Lillian had worn. Now as Wendell painted, he felt himself aflame with passional hope again. How grand that the nature of his work invited him to stare at her so freely. Parmelia – Parmelia Gillespie. "You have a beautiful name," he said, "to match a beautiful face."

She flushed. "Excuse me, sir, but what is your name?" she asked. "I had not heard it spoken."

"You are the first to ask it," he said. "Just call me the limner."

"An itinerant artist? My father says there aren't any more limners, not since daguerreotypists began knocking on doors."

"Aye," said Wendell, "I'm the last one."

He reached over and swept back an errant lock from her pale neck and guessed from her retreat into shyness that she was a virgin. She spoke not again till he had finished the skin's underpainting and sketched her features. "A second sitting would be advisable," he said, "to capture the light in your eyes correctly." She made an appointment for the following week, then left him feeling alive as he had not all summer. As he lay in bed the following nights, her image merged in his mind with Lillian's, whom he once again was holding close – kissing luxuriously to the smell of linseed oil and honeyed lemons.

When Parmelia returned, she was bolder in her dress and manner, as though having made up her mind to have him. "Have you been to Paris?" she asked almost wistfully as he wetted his brush.

"Indeed I have," said he, taking a stroke, "and will likely return. It is a great and romantic city. Do you wish to go there?"

"Oh yes." She flushed becomingly. "Are French ladies so different from American ladies?"

Wendell laughed. "Why is it that ladies always ask about the ladies? Do you not wish to know about the men?"

She looked down, embarrassed. "I don't really know much about men," she confessed.

"If you could please purse your lips just a little," Wendell suggested, lifting her chin. It would be so easy to kiss her now, he thought, and they both sighed. He painted in silence awhile, noting how her lovely breasts rose and fell with her breathing.

"In town, they say you are a famous artist in hiding."

"And what say you?"

Again, she flushed. "I think you're hiding from a lover's angry husband." She evidently found the thought delicious and almost giggled as she said it.

Wendell colored, vividly imagining Henry Ferguson's return. "Nothing so romantic as that, I assure you!" he said hastily, breaking their spell. "Well, I am done with you. It should be dry enough to pick up in a week or so."

She was hesitant as she rose to go. "My parents have asked me to extend an invitation for you to dine with us this Sunday noon."

They both stood in silence, looking at each other across some deep and unfathomable divide. "There is another, Parmelia," he murmured finally and took her hand. "Please thank your parents for me and give them my regrets. I leave for the city at month's end." He bowed deeply and kissed her hand before letting it go. "I hope you get to Paris."

She nodded impassively, though he thought he saw a hint of relief. "Thank you, sir. I wish you well." With that, she turned and left, plunging Wendell's heart once again into lonely despair. Almost, he ran after her. But the truth of the matter was he could no more afford to court Parmelia than to court Lillian. Nay, the real truth of the matter was that Parmelia was not Lillian. And now for the first time since he'd arrived, Wendell went out on the town, looking for the town's drunks with which to commune and wondering whether such a place had any prostitutes.

Chapter 22

When Wendell finally arrived at the Tenth Street Studios, he had $2500, a needy family back in Ithaca, a depleted stock of paints and large debts to Thomas. He took care of it all cheerfully and felt good about the thousand still left. This from just the one small town, and the few who had come the five miles from Monticello – Thomas was indeed a brilliant marketer. Their friends were also returning from summer adventures and the artists admired one another's new sketches. Wendell had limned lovely vistas of the landscapes near his cabin and thus his secret was safe – he had simply spent the summer as they had, capturing Nature's loveliness.

He was back but a week when he saw her. She was coming out of Sanford Gifford's atelier with her hair askew. Wendell went pale, wondering if she and Sanford were passional, when their eyes met and she quickly looked down. "Hello, Mr. Parry," she muttered, as they froze in their tracks in the hallway.

"Hello, Miss Flax," he gulped. "I trust you have been well?"

"Yes," she said, "and you?" Wendell found he could not answer, and stood staring at her with tight lips.

After an awkward moment, she continued, surprising him, "I have some business that may interest you. Might you be free in an hour for lunch?"

As his heart soared with hope, his voice inexplicably stiffened. "Certainly. Where shall we meet?"

"Do you know the French place on the corner of Bleecker and MacDougal?" Wendell nodded. "Well, see you there, then." He was dumbfounded as she left him standing, wondering what business she could have with him. Did she want to sell *Sands of Morocco*? It could be something like that – best not to read anything too auspicious in it. Afterall, she was asking to meet him in a public place, perhaps as protection against him saying something too personal.

Still, a freshly groomed Wendell was cautiously excited as he strolled by Washington Square and made his way to Bleecker. "Don't react to anything she says," he told himself, "just listen." He passed up the temptation to buy flowers, and urged himself to be nonchalant.

She was waiting already seated at a small table by the window. Her hair was tidied with a hat pinned atop it, and she had a satchel that gave her a business-like air. Wendell noticed that she had finally regained some curves lost in Canada. As he sat down opposite her, he was grateful that le garçon came over quickly to announce the spéciales.

They were both very quiet as they sipped their waters and waited for their orders to arrive. "You are looking well," said Wendell, then immediately regretted it. Too bold, he thought.

"Thank you," she said, then sipped again in silence. The food arrived and they both nibbled at it, making small comments about how good it was. The time seemed long till Lillian finally took an envelope, addressed to Henry Ferguson, from her satchel. She opened it and spread out the letter before Wendell's unfocused eyes. "This is a letter to Henry Ferguson asking for a divorce," she blurted. "Shall I send it?"

He was completely taken aback. Was this a test? "Oh no," he said hastily, "No, please, Lillian. You do wonderful things with his money..." He grimaced at his mistake, and lamely corrected himself, "with your money."

She looked down at her lap and they both fell silent. His heart slammed, trying to make sense of what she'd asked. Did she want him back? If she divorced, surely she did not expect him to support her. He thought he saw her chin quiver.

"Could I ask you a question?" she said at last. She looked up as he waited. "Did that countess pay you to sport with her?"

This was indeed a test, and though his life depended on it, he did not know how to answer. Either solution would be wrong. After an interminable minute, he managed a strangled, "Yes."

Lillian flushed and once again looked down. When she looked back up, Wendell was shocked to see her teeth bared and venomous. "You would sell your paintings to her and not to me," she hissed. "You would sell your body to her."

Wendell's mouth fell open. How could she have such an idea of him? "Lillian, no!" he cried, "I don't do that!" He was genuinely appalled.

Tears began to spill down her cheeks. "So what do you do, Wendell?!" Looking franticly around for escape, she shoved herself from the table and ran out onto the sidewalk. Suddenly, he comprehended her meaning. She wanted him! She was willing to get divorced to have him! She wanted him!

Wendell chased after her and caught her by the arm, but she kept her face averted and strained to get away. "Lillian, please. Oh my God, if you want me, take me! Please, Lillian, I'm yours for free!"

She kept her face averted, embarrassed as she wiped her tears.

"I'm yours for free, Lillian," he said again. "Yours and no one else's. I swear it."

The manager of the restaurant had stepped out onto the sidewalk and stood with his arms folded, waiting. "Though I could let you pay for the lunch," Wendell added for levity.

She sniffled, looking down at the sidewalk. "Please don't sport with her again," she begged. "Please, I couldn't take it."

They went inside and paid the tab, then arms entwined and fully restored to each other, they made their way over to Waverly Place, the new unitary household.

Over the next few weeks, Wendell was astonished at how much news he had missed during his summer retreat. There were the big stories of Adah Menken's quick Indiana divorces from both Mr.

Menken and Mr. Heenan, Elizabeth's and Sam Stockard's new baby boy, and Ned's honeymoon in Niagara – he had married with only Adam Badeau and John Wilkes in attendance, cheating his friends of a celebration.

In addition, the election was in its full momentum, consuming everyone. Many of the artists had been away from civilization, so Ted Winthrop attempted to explain the summer's salient happenings as they all sat about Sanford's room. So many were crowded in that most had to sit on the floor.

"Since becoming the Republican candidate," said Winthrop, "Lincoln has declined to give another speech. Thirty thousand marched upon his home demanding it, and he referred them to his published debates. He sits on his porch and shakes hands, speaking substance only to those who give him money."

"He wishes to avoid the question of slavery," commented Sanford.

Someone asked who the powerful but unofficial Know Nothing Party would support. Ted answered, "The Know Nothings, or Native American Party, divide along geographic lines, effectively ending their anti-immigrant movement."

"Who is running for the Democrats?" asked Wendell.

"The Democrat Party has split, running Douglas for the North and Bell for the South. Yet most Southern Democrats had already defected to the new Constitutional Union Party."

"Such a split will leave it wide open for the Republicans," observed Sanford.

McEntee nodded. "And the South threatens to secede should the Republicans win."

There was silence as everyone considered the implication. Finally Wendell spoke what they were thinking. "There is no hope then, to avoid a war?"

"The devil!" said Winthrop with more certainty than he felt, "'Twould be suicide. The pols are bluffing. You know they have less heart than a half-penny slit!"

Said Sanford, "Ted and I are training with the 7th New York Militia. It would be welcomed to have some of you join us."

"I have not the pedigree to join" Mignot laughed. The 7th was known for the illustrious lineage of its members. Winthrop himself was grandson of the puritan John Winthrop, a governor of Massachusetts and founder of Boston.

Assured that dead ancestors would not matter, there were promises to consider it from men who had never thought of themselves as warriors. "And what about you, Parry?" asked Sanford.

"It would be an honor, truly," responded Wendell, "but I am committed elsewhere." It was time, he thought, to tell Sam he would no longer train with the 14th Brooklyn. He did not want to jeopardize the harmony he had restored with Lillian. Besides, planning for his Ithaca paintings tour had commenced in earnest and would open after New Year at the Studio Building Gallery. "My tour is scheduled to begin, with New Orleans in February."

Thomas shook his head. "You may have to cancel the South and go straight to Europe. 'Twill be a good time to be abroad. Is the West Coast on your list?"

"No," said Wendell. "I don't fancy taking the paintings for weeks on a stage coach through Indian territory. Or Mormon territory either! The Republicans promise a transcontinental railroad – perhaps when it's complete, I'll finally get to Frisco."

Now Albert Bierstadt spoke up. "I am planning another trip west, to paint the Rockies."

"What?" said Church surprised, "You've only just returned from there."

Bierstadt smiled, puffing up his large chest, his blue eyes steely. "My canvases will rival yours, Fred, in size if not in grandeur. I am working on one now." Wendell did not like the arrogant "Hun," a name many of the artists called Bierstadt behind his back.

Church laughed. "I'm not afraid of a little rivalry." Indeed, Church seemed unassailable as America's grandest artist. "I have my own good news," Church continued. "I have bought a small farm on the Hudson and will soon take Isabel there as my bride." The artists all cheered and congratulated him – Isabel had been his greatest reward for *Heart of the Andes*, just as *Sands of Morocco* had brought Lillian to Wendell.

Meanwhile a new gallery had opened on 10th Street, just down the block on the corner of Broadway. It belonged to Mathew Brady, who had moved out of his Bleecker Street studio and into a large and elegant building that befit the famous photographer. Everyone who wanted to obtain a photographic image insisted on a *Brady*. Wendell and Lillian went to see it and were staggered by its grandeur. Hand-tinted Imperial Portraits on canvas of celebrated people covered the lavishly appointed walls, while graceful chandeliers, green silk furniture with gold trim and green plush oriental carpets completed the look of opulence. Mathew Brady greeted them himself, and pointed out how many of the photographed subjects sat in front of Wendell's painted backdrops.

In mid-October, Wendell had joined his friends around the common dining table at their "unitary household sans servants" on Waverly Place, to read accounts of Prince Edward Albert's New York visit. "All this fuss," said Rosalie, blowing bubbles. "One would think the country still British."

Henry Clapp laughed. "Young Prince Bertie wishes to see New York," he pronounced. "Has anyone really seen New York until he has visited Pfaff's? No! Fellow bohemians, it is up to us to issue an invitation to his R.H. and steal him from the Grand Ball for a beer."

Wendell checked his fascination with Rosalie's bubbles as his ears perked up, "Ha ha." Then, "You're not joking."

"Have you a plan for such a thing that won't get us arrested?"

asked Fitzhugh.

"It appears that yours truly and several other journalists have press passes for the ball," responded Clapp confidently. "If you will wait at Pfaff's this evening, mayhap you will find yourselves rewarded."

At the appointed time, expectant Pfaff's patrons sat at the table in the alcove. They had dressed normally for the occasion, wanting to appear nonchalant. Lillian had her guitar and was tuning it, Rosalie was blowing bubbles from her pipe. Wendell saw the door open and a darkly cloaked royal entourage enter furtively, Clapp in the lead. "Please make yourself comfortable," said Clapp affably, and took the young man's hooded wrap, revealing a clean shaven boy with hair parted and coifed, in elegant and conspicuous attire. His bodyguards huddled uncertainly by the door, but Bertie seemed not the least dismayed. The young Prince took a chair in the alcove next to Wendell and nodded to the bohemians. 'How novel, hey,' thought Wendell, 'to be sitting right next to the future emperor of the world!' Prince Bertie had just passed his first year at Cambridge and doubtless felt at home in the somewhat collegiate atmosphere, even when Ada Clare was introduced as the "Queen of Bohemia."

"There is a suspicion abroad that your R.H. drinks," Clapp offered with a wry smile.

"Yes, thank you, we'd like your best American ale, if there is such a thing. It is a relief to be out of the ball. We had to profess a headache to get away."

Charles Pfaff had come over to greet his visitor. "Vassar Ale! It is the best American ale, but are you sure you vould not vant a good German beer?" The Prince responded with a dismissive flick of his hand, and Charles rushed to accommodate him.

"We are sorry," said Bob Newell, "that the boxing match went so badly for your country."

The Prince grinned, taking the bait, and dropped the royal

'we.' "I was there, sir, and left just before the police arrived. I saw the whole thing, all forty-two bloody rounds of it. And indeed, the lion was the winner, not the eagle."

"Well, we won't tell your mother of your indiscretion," teased Mr. Newell, "Did you know that the Benicia Boy himself sat there in Your Highness's very chair not six months ago?" The Prince opened his eyes wide in only partly feigned reverence, and gasping, clutched his hand to his heart. His audience was delighted.

"How does Your Highness like American women?" Ada Clare flirted, then lost her nerve and blushed becomingly. The prince winked at her over his ale.

Wendell asked, "Seriously, how do you think on Americans?"

The Prince leaned his chair back and raised an eyebrow. "We think Americans have not much respect for the British mind."

"But Americans do have respect for the British mind!" protested Clapp. "We just wish they would exercise more control over it."

This earned a brief laugh and a royal retort. "You lot are making quite a muck of it, with a civil war looming. Perhaps you had been better off British." Bertie waited, and when no rejoinder came, continued, "Mind, if you Yanks do mix it up, better come out looking strong and unified, lest you tempt someone from abroad to see you as a ripe plum."

There was a moment of dumbfounded silence. "Is that a threat, sir?" Newell asked, astounded.

"Of course not. I do not speak for the Crown. And you must be aware that there are other empires than Britain."

Clapp nodded. "We Americans remain quite hopeful that we can still avoid a war."

By now, the rest of Pfaff's patrons were aware of the young royal's presence and gathered round. To ease the pushing, Lillian picked up her guitar and asked the Prince to teach them English drinking songs. Soon, the Crown Prince was singing.

"I'll drink up my drink, and speak what I think,
Strong drink will make us speak truly,
We cannot be termed all drunkards confirmed,
So long as we're not unruly.
We'll drink and be civil, intending no evil.
Let every man have his due,
To save shoes and trouble, bring in the pots double,
For he that had one had two."

It went on for interminable verses, and each time the massed audience would sing the extra drink, "And he that had two had three!" "And he that had three had four!" with great merriment.

Finally the young prince, more than a little inebriated, was pulled off of Queen Ada Clare's lap and whisked surreptitiously back to the ball.

A month later was election day. Voter lines stretched along the sidewalks as throngs of men turned out to support Mr. Lincoln and his Republicans. Wendell and Lillian made their way past the mayhem to the Stockard's door. "Hello!" Sam greeted them excitedly as the first chill of winter gusted into the house. "Have you voted yet?" Voting was a sore subject with Lillian. After a warm greeting, she excused herself to see the baby and Elizabeth, who were still abed.

The men removed to the drawing room for a smoke. "The polls are stupendously crowded," commented Wendell, "I waited hours for my turn."

"As did I," said Sam. He sat in his leather easy chair and crossed his legs. In dress and manner, he was looking every bit the lawyer that he now was. He laughed, "The wait is enough to keep anyone from voting twice, no matter how much Tammany tries to pay them. But tell me, are you busy? You have been notably absent from the armory."

"I will not be returning," Wendell confessed, feeling bad to be letting his friend down.

Sam sighed; he had evidently been expecting this. "I know you too well to blame it on Lillian," he said. "I have been struggling with it myself. There is always the question, 'Why would a man give up his own happiness and comfort to do what's right?'"

"You mean go to war to free someone he doesn't know?"

"Yes," said Sam. "Why would he?"

Wendell winced. "Is this some gauntlet you are throwing at my feet?"

Sam sighed. "You are an artist, not a soldier – I know that. Still, it's a question we must all ask."

"'Am I my brother's keeper?'"

"Aye, that question." Sam sat back, looking resigned. "I and the men shall miss you, and comes the war, you may be of a different mind. You know I'll keep your gear for you."

Wendell flushed. "I am going abroad in the spring and unless my paintings sell quickly, I may be gone some time." He was happy for the excuse, but it rang hollow. He was saying he would be out of the country while his comrades went to war, and it bore a taint of disloyalty, if not dishonor.

Sam smiled and drew on his pipe. "Your tour's coming together this time, eh? Wonderful! I always knew you'd be a success, Parry – though the timing could be better."

Wendell changed the subject, "And how do you like being a father?"

Sam laughed. "'Tis a true miracle that will take some getting used to, particularly, I think, for the baby. What a miserable little cuss! My mother assures Elizabeth that a few months are needed before we feel ourselves the fabled family. Dammit, Parry, we have had no sleep! Thank the Lord for my mother and Margaret coming over to cook and clean." Sam lowered his voice and leaned towards his friend. "Between you and me, it's hard. Now that Elizabeth's a mother, she's hardly a wife if you get my meaning. I've been half a year without."

Wendell regarded his friend with amusement. "Patience, dear fellow! You have prospects for the future, which is more than many men can boast."

"Indeed," Sam grinned, "I can always count on you to put things in perspective. And how are you and Lillian? Will there be wedding bells?"

Wendell shook his head. "I no longer feel an urgency to marry. We have agreed to remain as we are till I can support her," and added mischievously, "or she me."

Just then Lillian entered the room and the gentlemen stood. She was smiling in the transported way that women have around babies. "What an adorable son you have, Sam! He is sleeping, so your wife begs to sleep, too, whilst there is opportunity."

"Good, good. I encourage that." She gave him a kiss on the cheek and wished the family well, signaling time to leave.

Outside, the weather was indeed blustering and a chill fog crept in from the harbor. Despite this, people gathered with intense excitement as newspapers already proclaimed a victory for Lincoln and his new Republican Party. Lillian gripped Wendell's arm and shuddered. "If there's a war," she said, her eyes glistening, "promise me again you won't go."

They stopped walking as he turned to look at her, wondering if she had guessed his conversation with Sam. "Is there no cause for which you would have me fight?" he asked softly, and added, "I am not a Quaker."

"There is no need for war! The Quakers are right. There is never a need for war."

"Yet you gave money to John Brown."

"For liberation of slaves, not for war! Sweet Jesus, how I wish our government would just declare slavery illegal. Their masters should simply be arrested for failing to pay them or for treating them poorly."

Wendell shook his head sadly. "You know it's not going to happen that way, Lillian, not while there are Southerners voting in Congress. Men are going to fight and die, and thus will the evil system of slavery end. Don't hold back for fear of what evil may replace it. We must take each evil as it comes."

"But you are not a warrior," she begged. "You are an artist, necessary to remind the world of beauty, and more so in the midst of war."

Wendell sighed, uncertain of her assessment. "I'll make you a bargain," he said finally, then smiled suggestively, "a hard bargain, if you like." She didn't take the bait, but softened as she listened intently to what he would say next. "Should it go badly and I feel I am needed – not till then will I go to war."

Chapter 23

Wendell was enjoying a gay Thanksgiving at Ada Clare's apartment. He was grateful for this moment of repose before the tragedies that loomed. Alas, in the elegant light of the candelabra that graced the table, Henry Clapp sobered the occasion with news that the *Saturday Press* had again lost readership. "No one wants to read art and literature anymore, only news of impending war," he rued.

"So why not write about impending war?" asked Aldrich.

"Because I am a bohemian," Henry responded, "by temperament and by creed. You may not know it, but in Boston I had been a well-known temperance fighter and abolitionist." This was greeted with sounds of disbelief, but Clapp went on. "My time was spent in advocating, always engaged in angry and heated rhetoric; not against drinkers and slave owners, mind you, but against those that should have been allies. We cut each other mercilessly for being too soft or too hard. I was miserable. I finally found peace when I went to Paris and shared a drink with a bohemian. I swore then that I would never again engage in the politics of certainty."

In December, the *Saturday Press* ceased to print. Five days later, on December 20, South Carolina seceded from the Union. Mr. John McClure warned Wendell of possible cancellations on the tour, and said he would know more after the holidays.

Wendell had been drinking at Pfaff's when he found the privy occupied by someone being sick, and decided to relieve himself against the brick wall in the alley. He finished his business and turned to go back when he flushed to see Ada Clare and young Aubrey sitting on the stoop. "Pray, forgive me, Ada, I did not see you there."

"Tsk, tsk, Wendell, what would Mrs. Grundy say?" She was

trying to hide it, but she looked to have been weeping and pulled her son and her shawl close against the chill December air.

"Indeed! What would Mrs. Grundy say about a lady hiding out in a back alley? Are you not well?"

Now the tears sprang freely. "Fie!" she cried, "Our comrades inside forget that South Carolina is my homeland! The war for which they clamor would be fought against good people I've called friends and family." Wendell sat down next to her and put his arm about her shoulders, hugging her like a sister.

"I'm so sorry," he said. They sat a moment in silence. "What is this paper you clutch in your hand?" She opened a well-worn page of the *New York Traveller*, dated March of 1860, and handed it over for Wendell to read. In the center was printed a poem titled *Ada Clare:*

> *O, blessings on this quiet hour!*
> *My thoughts in calmer currents flow –*
> *She is not conscious of her power,*
> *And hath no knowledge of my woe.*
> *Perhaps if like yon peaceful star,*
> *She looked upon my burning brow*
> *She would not pity from afar,*
> *But kiss me, as the breeze does now.*
> *~Aglaus*

"A friend of yours?" asked Wendell.

"I knew him in South Carolina. We perhaps would have been better friends were not our politics so different." She sighed, "Perhaps he is only using the notoriety of my name for his own advancement."

Wendell had not before perceived the gay and indomitable social hostess as lonely. "No," Wendell assured her, "the poem is heart felt." Then quietly he added, "As I am sure the tunes composed to you by Louis Gottschalk were." She was about to protest that Louis' name was not to be mentioned in front of Aubrey, but Wendell's intent was sincere and she seemed comforted that her son's famous father had once loved her. "Come," said Wendell, "the weather will soon chill Aubrey, if not yourself."

He helped her up and led them back inside Pfaff's where a rowdy discussion of how to punish South Carolina was at full volume, with many of the fellows defending her right to secede against a louder majority who wanted war. Only Walt Whitman seemed sensitive to Ada's feelings. "Stop!" yelled the venerated poet, standing upon his chair, "Stop!" The throng quieted. "The Queen of Bohemia is from South Carolina. Show her some respect."

Henry Clapp stood and the abashed debaters raised their drinks. "To Ada Clare with our apologies." The men saluted and drummed their tankards on the tables. Ada Clare nodded acknowledgement, then took Aubrey's hand and departed by the front door with the few other women following along behind her. As soon as they left, the debate was back in full sway.

Christmas was gloomier almost than anybody had remembered, with hostess Ada Clare's South Carolina trust fund cut off from her. Shortly after New Year, which was lamented more than celebrated, five more states seceded including Louisiana. John McClure wrote to Wendell that the tour through the South was now definitely off, but would be opening in Paris in March. Wendell had hoped to sell exhibit tickets before having to pay for passage to Europe, and did manage some from a lackluster exhibition at the Studio Building. He had an offer which he declined for two of the paintings, at $600 each. Then it was announced that the *Crayon* was insolvent and would soon cease printing; people were just not interested in reading anything that didn't have to do with war.

By now, Waverly Place had descended into bickering because

the women, Lillian and Rosalie, seemed always to be cleaning up after the men. Lillian felt guilty to leave Rosalie alone as the only female, but became quite happy at the Studio Building in Wendell's fine-arts atelier where dust and debris were disparaged. They had found a little couch and bigger table, and a nice-sized feather bed which they often shared with Cat, who had finally grown quite fond of her. In the mornings, they had breakfast with the artists in the mess, and frequently she visited Mrs. McEntee at tea-time.

"Gertrude McEntee," she informed Wendell, "is an excellent landscape artist, but keeps her paintings in the closet and will not sell to me, for fear of showing up her husband."

Over the next short months, Lillian wrote diligently in the atelier while Wendell rendered his favorite sketches into oils. In this way, they were quite content, working late into the night by gaslight with Lillian frequently playing a new song for Wendell on her guitar. Some nights, some of the other artists would drop over to visit and hear her play. Afternoons they took long, luxurious, sensual naps before going to Pfaff's for supper.

Such was their pleasant routine. When she or Wendell needed time alone or with their friends, she would disappear, returning to Waverly Place or the Mansion, or the school in the Five Points. There were nights when she didn't return, but Wendell trusted her now and anticipated their coming trip to Paris with excitement. Her lyceum schedule would resume after their five weeks away – if the Ithaca paintings didn't sell by then, Wendell would go on to London without her.

She often seemed so lost in her tunes that Wendell frequently turned the attention of his sketch pad upon her. One evening, she perched on the chair with flowing hair and bare feet, one foot tucked under her in a way that hiked up her skirts, and her bodice loosened carelessly exposing her camisole. She leaned over her guitar with intense concentration. *"La bohèmienne,"* thought

Wendell appreciatively as he sketched.

Then she began to sing a tune she'd composed, in slow and tremulous voice:

"John Brown's body lies a-mould'ring in the grave
John Brown's body lies a-mould'ring in the grave,"

He recognized the tune as *"Say Brother Will You Meet Us, On Canaan's Distant Shore."* Lillian flushed when she looked up to see him watching, then went on, sending shivers up his spine.

"John Brown's body lies a-mould'ring in the grave
His soul is marching on!
He's gone to be a soldier in the army of the Lord,
His lambs will gather to him at River Jordan's ford,
He sacrificed his body 'cause slavery he abhorred,
His soul is marching on!
Glory, Glory! Hallelujah!
Glory, Glory! Hallelujah!
Glory, Glory! Hallelujah!
His soul is marching on!"

"Beautiful," breathed Wendell when she had done. *"C'est beau, Lillian. Vous êtes en train de devenir un morceau remarquable écrivain."*

They spoke French as much as they could now, since they would soon be going together to Paris and Wendell's French was far more certain than Lillian's. It would be her first trip abroad except to Canada.

"Simplifiez, s'il vous plait." She laughed, though he saw a hint of a tear in her eye for her martyred friend.

Wendell rephrased it, *"Vous êtes un auteur des chansons magnifique."*

"Merci," she said gratefully. "The lyceum has no interest now in my anti-war sentiments, so I will offer only *chansons politiques."*

They set sail on the steamer *Arago* on March 5, 1861, one day after Lincoln was inaugurated. News of troop movements and hostilities inflamed the populace, even as the new government strove mightily to quell the crisis. Wendell and Lillian stood along the railing of the luxury liner and watched their divided country recede into unreality, all news of her to be shut off for the duration of the voyage. As mighty engines urged the side paddle wheels to speed, the distance between ship and shore increased until home was at last utterly consumed by the sea's cold and hungry horizon. Now the 300 foot vessel with its 350 passengers seemed alone and small, lost upon a vast and empty ocean with the awfulness of not-knowing. The engines vibrated noisily beneath their uncertain feet in counterbalance to the deeply undulating waves, while acrid coal smoke whipped their faces. It was then that Lillian threw up.

Wendell held her as she leaned over the railing, vomiting till nothing but the sound came. It was the signal for a shipboard community to make itself known, and passengers came over to offer advice and sympathy.

"She'll be all right in four days," said one woman, taking the liberty of talking to Wendell as Lillian was clearly beyond communicating. "It takes awhile to get your sea legs." Lillian groaned and looked helplessly at Wendell, her silent message clear: 'Four days! This was to have been a romantic voyage, we were going first cabin!'

"Whatever you do," the lady continued, "don't go to your cabin. You need the fresh air." More passengers came over, and others heaved at the rail, till the whole ship was either seasick or conversing about seasickness. When the dinner bell finally rang, the sufferers were deposited next to buckets in their berths while the healthy went to dine.

As predicted, four days later Lillian joined them with a ravenous appetite, and from there on the voyage was fun. Wendell sketched and Lillian entertained the guests with songs, many of whom had interesting stories of their own. When suddenly the crew unfurled the mighty sails and turned the engines off, there was magic, with all sense of self lost to the overwhelming ecstasy of wind and sea.

A week later, the port of Southampton rose up out of the waves, dirty and unsavory. Though they were ready to feel themselves on land again, they were glad they didn't have to get off – and then, in short order, Le Havre, France, utterly attractive, a busy harbor alive with sails of every size before a picturesque town. Debarking upon the stone jetty, awash with the incoming tide, they were excited but wet and dirty, and felt the unfamiliar land move beneath their feet. Up close, the buildings seemed quaint and exceedingly old. Wendell was pleased that no passports were demanded, nor did gendarmes search their luggage as had happened on previous visits. The new law was just in effect, and their timing couldn't have been better. Wendell and Lillian made their way by carriage through narrow mud streets to a hotel where, after a warm bath and hot meal in a light and charming room, they both fell fast asleep.

The diligence to Paris left at dawn, a giant stagecoach with compartments of varied cost. Wendell enjoyed watching Lillian's enthusiasm, almost girlish, as she got a window seat. She leaned out, sighing gratefully, as the green valley rolled away in tamed and tasteful farms through which the Seine River flowed, a wide silvery stroke of nature's brush, dotted here and there with islands.

The roads were comfortable and paved and the intérieur companions friendly – they hailed from many places, happy to share their victuals at mealtime and help the ladies down when there was pause for personal needs. By late afternoon, they were ready for a longer delay, and the road complied by entering the narrow cobbled streets of Rouen. Now the new-comers gasped for the picturesque and ancient grandeur of gothic spires among graceful wooden buildings, white with much contrasting trim. Here, in the 15th century, Jean d'Arc had been martyred, and the ville looked scarcely to have changed. The carriage stopped before the Cathedrale Notre Dame de Rouen, ablaze with the setting sun, the tallest, oldest, and most ornately beautiful building they had ever seen.

"I fain would go in and light a candle, in thanks for our safe deliverance from the voyage," said the transported Lillian to Wendell.

But once inside, it was not religion that brought them to their knees in the nave, it was art. Indeed, the overwhelming transcendence of art, its soaring gothic arches, statues and stained glass, inspired them both to tears. How were such labors possible of mankind but through the love of God?

The rest of the way to Paris was passed in the dark, and they slept leaning against each other till uneven cobblestones shook them awake and the conducteur shouted *"Voilà Paris!"* The sun was just rising, setting off church-bells and street vendors who rattled in noisy carts as the city woke with a cacophony that rivaled New York's – and on a Sunday! They passed narrow winding streets, black with soot and dirty urchins, to cross into the heart of the city where massive street renovation was taking place.

The diligence left them off near the Jardin de Tuileries, on a wide tree-lined promenade rich with statues and fountains. Wendell and Lillian could only marvel briefly at the scene, before the necessity of getting their luggage off the street and into a cab took precedence. Statues and inspired ornate architecture greeted them at every turn. Shortly, they made their way past the grand Roman-columned church, L'église de la Madeleine, where the sound of organ music swelled onto the rue, competing with rumbling carriages, as a richly dressed parade of Parisiennes entered the church for Sunday service. For Wendell, imagining the city through Lillian's dazzled eyes was like seeing it all for the first time. Everything was grand, everything was classical, everything was art – tout était magnifique! Just behind on a tiny crowded street was their hotel, the Victoria, at 6 Rue Chauveau-Lagarde.

"Ah," said Lillian as they finally made their way wearily up narrow stairs to their room, "I can see why artists come here."

"I fain would show you why lovers do," said Wendell.

They slept first, wrapped naked in each other's arms. Then, as the setting sun lit the city golden outside their chamber, they expressed their passion. Soon, the gas lamps of Paris began to flicker on. Wendell stood behind Lillian at the window, his arms around her, and they looked out upon la ville l'amour at night. Even on a Sunday, its much vaunted night-life of restaurants, theaters, and cafés beckoned. "Come," said Wendell excitedly, "I have places I want you to see."

They boarded a crowded horse-drawn omnibus and sat on top, where they were afforded the best view of lights from the myriad temples and bridges reflecting on the waters, and crossed the River Seine to the Rive Gauche, the Left Bank. They got off in the Latin Quarter, named for the language taught at the many surrounding colleges, and as he sought out his favorite café, Wendell led Lillian by the hand through sidewalks crowded with étudiants et étudiantesses.

"Hey, Lillian! Miss Lillian Flax!" an American voice called out. A tall wiry man with fair hair and beard was standing by his chair and waving.

"Oh, look, Wendell, it's Bill Stillman of the *Crayon*! 'Twas his atelier you moved into at the Studio Building!" She waved back and they made their way through the labyrinth to his table.

"How are you, Lillian? And Wendell Parry, is it? I haven't seen you since our interview." He pumped Wendell's hand excitedly.

"By God, it's good to see Americans."

"Oui, Il est bon de voir les Américains," laughed one of the students at the table, introduced as Alphonse. Lillian looked surprised that he was Negro. The women, too, seemed to be students. Since the men stood and kissed Lillian's hand elaborately, Wendell kissed the hands of the ladies and sat down.

"Tous les Américains sont allés chez eux à la guerre," explained Alphonse affably.

Wendell was alarmed. *"Ce que la guerre?"* and in English, "We hadn't heard about a war."

"Yes," said Stillman. "All the Americans have taken off in anticipation, drawn like moths to a flame. I have been left alone among the Gauls, easy prey to their garrulousness."

"Que signifie 'garrulousness'?" asked one of the students. There was an aside in French, and everyone laughed.

The newcomers explained their presence in Paris, and asked Stillman why he yet remained. "I am shortly on my way to Rome," he said, "where I am to serve President Lincoln as his consul." At their expressions of surprise, he told a long and amusing story about his previous political involvement in the Austro-Hungarian conflict, his failed effort as a secret courier to secure the Jewels of St. Stephen from their hiding place and crown the rightful king of Hungary. The Frenchmen laughed, evidently having heard the story so many times that they could easily follow along even in English.

During the course of the telling, Wendell and Lillian ordered food. "I believe I had met your sister in Ithaca," Stillman surprised him. "A most remarkable woman."

Wendell dropped his fork. His heart-beat quickened. "Did you tell her of my relationship with a Mrs. Ferguson?" he asked.

"I may have," Stillman flushed at the possible indiscretion. "She naturally wished for news, and that was all the gossip I'd heard of you – aside from your legendary painting prowess."

Wendell's thoughts fluttered uncertainly. Seeing the impatience of the students, he switched the conversation to Paris and its splendors, speaking in French. It was an easy enough topic for even Lillian to follow along, and thus they spent une très agréable soirée.

Early the next morning, golden light illuminated the room, awaking them with an urge to love. Silky sheets caressed silky bodies, as hands reached out to caress silky skin. They were served a continental breakfast of croissants and café au lait in bed, then went attired magnificently in search of Le Petite Hall des Fine Arts, where Wendell was to meet Mr. McClure ahead of his exhibit opening. They had left themselves plenty of time to stroll down Rue Royale to Jardin des Tuileries and thence up the broad expanse of Champs Elysée. Like the elegant couples around them, they found the endless promenade through this grand garden park most pleasurable, and were altogether entranced by the intoxicating romance of it. As a gentle spring breeze blew off the nearby River Seine, Wendell was elated by the passional look on Lillian's face and the possessive way she took his arm. Champs Elysée was a sumptuous lovers' parade, and they were proud to be with each other and show each other off. Everyone smiled and nodded and tipped their hats, as if to say, "You are so fine, we are so fine – is this not the perfect place to look and feel our finest?"

The lovers turned at the Grand Palace and found John McClure waiting for them in a sidewalk café outside Le Petite Hall des Fine Arts, on Avenue de Marigny across the street from the park. The hall was not as petite as Wendell expected, but was indeed dwarfed by the monuments and palaces around them. A line was beginning to form in front of it in preparation for the noon opening. As Wendell and Lillian sat down with Mr. McClure, they felt excitement for the show.

"How was your voyage?" and "Where are you staying?" Mr. McClure wanted to know. But when Wendell alluded to an agreement that he and Lillian stay with John and his wife, Mr. McClure pulled him aside. "Excuse us, Miss Flax, while Mr. Parry and I discuss some business."

"I'm so sorry, Wendell," he said when she had gone to find a cabinet de toilettes, "but the wife won't have Miss Flax, too. She says it would be unchristian of her, since Miss Flax is not your missus." This was indeed a blow, unexpected but not surprising. Wendell remembered telling Lillian that Mr. McClure would not wish them to travel together unmarried. There was a further blow. "I have promoted you as a bachelor artist, and as you see, it is the mademoiselles who are lining up to see you. I feel it would be bad for gate receipts if you had Miss Flax with you in the receiving line. Please allow me to show her Paris whilst you greet your admirers."

"Anything else?" inquired Wendell, stiffly.

Mr. McClure sighed. "The usual patrons of such shows are Americans. They are all going home in advance of war. I fain would go home myself and am hoping for a quick sale. A private reception is arranged for tonight at the apartments of the Duke de Beauchamp, to which important art collectors are invited. I would have no problem with you bringing Miss Flax to that soirée – she is most charming and may prove an asset." They rose as Lillian returned, and they all made their way around to the side entrance of the Petite Hall. Inside were hung many of Wendell's pieces including, to his surprise, *Sands of Morocco*. The Ithaca display was mounted impeccably, with gaslights throwing dappled light through deep green foliage. A viola played watery-sounding music from the corner. Wendell squeezed Lillian's hands and whispered a thank you for *Sands of Morocco*.

"Well, good luck," Mr. McClure said before opening the main door, "and one more thing: It may be wise to lower our expectations of what a good offer should look like."

The exhibition went well, with a satisfactory number of gate receipts. Mr. McClure had been right that they were mostly enamored young ladies whose primary interest was the artist. It was beginning to seem a very long afternoon indeed, with much flattery and hand kissing. Wendell was relieved when his two benefactors finally returned and John chased everyone out to close the door. Back at their hotel, a chagrined Wendell explained to Lillian that their accommodations with the McClures had fallen through, and that his situation was not the best for their continued stay.

Lillian laughed and fingered his cravat. "Alas, Wendell! A fine bohemian you turned out to be, who will not accept money from his mistress!" And so they ended the matter with a much-desired romp and then dressed for the evening's recreation.

The elegant apartments of Le Duc de Beauchamp were on the grounds of the Grand Palace. Wendell and Lillian were both quite impressed at what Mr. McClure had managed to put together, for the Grand Palace was the ultimate in magnificence and prestige. After their wraps were taken by a servant in almost medieval dress, they descended a staircase to an ornate ballroom where a chamber orchestra played a Strauss Waltz and elegant men squired their partners around the dance floor.

The names of *"Monsieur Wendell Harte Parry et Mademoiselle Lillian Flax"* were announced and the dancers paused, turning to applaud the young artist in whose honor they were gathered. Wendell, flattered in the extreme, felt his face flush. What mattered that his mistress kept him if all Paris was at his feet? He looked at Lillian, whose admiring gaze was nigh worshipful, then bent and gallantly kissed her hand. "Thank you," he whispered, his eyes glistening.

They continued down the steps, when suddenly, from the midst of the throng, came a familiar voice. *"Wendell, Mon Cher! Monsieur Parry!"* Wendell cringed. He did not have to look to know who it was.

Chapter 24

He smelled her before he saw her. He was looking at Lillian, whose face had gone quite frozen, when the odor of exotic perfume grew strong and he glanced into the eyes of the Comtesse de Clairmont. Wendell took the hand that was held out to him, but did not bow over it or kiss it. *"Comtesse,"* he acknowledged her, then pulled his hand away. He turned awkwardly to Lillian. "May I present my betrothed, Miss Lillian Flax." The two ladies stared at each other, till Wendell spoke again in French, *"Puis-je présenter ma fiancée, Mademoiselle Lillian Flax. Lillian, La Comtesse de Clairmont."*

"Yes, I know who you are," said Lillian stonily. The comtesse looked at the fierce young woman with uncertainty, then a smile broke across her face.

"Elle est charmant, Wendell," she tittered brightly, hooking her hands through his elbow. *"Viens, j'ai patrons des arts pour vous à satisfaire."* Before Lillian could protest, John McClure was standing in front of her, presenting his own elbow. The couples were dancing again, and as the comtesse led Wendell over to the punch bowl, John squired Lillian out onto the dance floor. Wendell glanced back at her to see a vexed Lillian brushing away Mr. McClure's straying hands from her person.

"Excusez moi, Comtesse," said Wendell and left her as he went to cut in. "John, could you please handle the comtesse? I believe she has a deal to negotiate."

As he took Lillian into his arms, she murmured, "Please, Wendell, don't sell your pictures to her. She would extract the same price she had extracted before, and I could not take it." He realized then that she was trembling, and stroked her hair soothingly as he held her close. Soon she was recovered, and the duke came over to introduce Wendell around the room, while a bevy of Frenchmen huddled around Lillian. When last Wendell looked, she seemed to be having a good time.

Back at the hotel, Wendell wished to make love before they could converse about the evening, but Lillian's female prerogative prevailed. "If you would not sell the canvases to me, why would you consider selling them to her?" she asked. "You may deny it, but she would demand your pound of flesh."

Wendell tried to jolly her, and cupped the protuberance in his trousers. "My flesh weighs more than a pound," he joked, and regretted it when she threw herself face down upon the bed and bid him go away.

"Lillian, please, trust me," he begged, sitting next to her. "She only seeks to introduce me to buyers."

Lillian sat up on the bed and looked at him angrily. "Fie, Wendell. You can be bought, you've proved that. Any sale through that woman would be contingent on your cock in her!"

Wendell stiffened. His voice was low as he asked, "Is it because I am kept by you that you think so little of me?" He rose and went out down the stairs into the midnight streets. Angrily he paced the sidewalk, then leaned back against the wall under the deep eves of the hotel. He sighed and lit a cigarette as a light rain began to fall.

The distant sounds of the city dampened and lamplight danced upon wet cobblestones. The dark carriage of a high-priced dame de la nuit came by. She was dressed in red lace and, opening the door invitingly, leaned out and said, *"Voulez-vous la société d'une dame?"* Wendell shook his head and exhaled a cloud of smoke as the carriage rumbled on, leaving behind a steamy quiet.

And then Lillian was there, dress and hair straggly with rain, tears trailing down her face. She sniffled back the mucous that dripped freely from her nose, giving her the appearance of a child badly in need of a mother. Tossing aside his cigarette, Wendell put his arms around her and she buried her head into his chest. "I'm so sorry," she confessed. "You did not deserve that. I'm so sorry."

"Nay, Lillian," he soothed, "I had once betrayed your trust and am grateful that you've tried so hard to forgive me."

"And now?" She looked up at him and shuddered against the damp.

"I don't know that you will ever truly forgive me," he said miserably. "Indeed, if it were the other way around, I have doubts that I could." He lifted her chin and pledged with all sincerity, "I swear I will not betray you again, Lillian." And then he kissed her, dripping nose and all, and put his coat around her shoulders and her wet velvet dress. "Come," he said, "I would get you warm," and they went back to their room where Lillian did all in her power to prove him forgiven.

When Wendell had to be at the exhibit, Lillian spent her time happily on the Rive Gauche, playing music with Alphonse and his friends; and when he didn't have to be at the exhibit, they spent long hours at the Louvre, watching the many art students taking pains to duplicate the surrounding grandeur of the Old Masters. Lillian's collection at the mansion seemed tiny next to these endless and elegant hallways, filled floor to ceiling with works of astonishment. But she predicted of her collection, "Someday students will sit before the paintings of the Hudson River artists, trying in vain to copy their techniques." Wendell didn't comment, but a satisfied expression appeared and he sighed with contentment – this museum, and now with Lillian by his side, was truly one of his favorite places in the world.

All too soon, it was time for Lillian to depart for her lyceum tour. Wendell had offers for his paintings, and had sold a few of the lesser ones. But for the Ithaca exhibit, Mr. McClure always seemed to have another fish on the hook, another possibility for a better deal. As Wendell accompanied Lillian to Le Havre, he assured her that a sale would be closing shortly and his departure would not be far behind.

"My Heart," she said passionately as she stood her last with him upon the quay, "there are worries that ships home will be hard to find should war break out. If you don't get your price, please don't go on to London. I can buy the paintings for the $1500 each you had originally hoped to garner." With that assurance, he kissed her and said goodbye.

He stood a long time upon the stone jetty, watching the smoke of her steamship disappear beyond the horizon. The cold incoming tide damped his trouser hems, but he stood deep in thought till a nearby church bell reminded him of the time and his need to catch the diligence back to Paris. Mr. McClure had said he had a sale lined up and fain would have Wendell there to sign papers on the morrow.

He was tired when he arrived next day at the Grand Palace and the apartments of Le Duc de Beauchamp for his appointment with Mr. McClure. The servant took his coat and directed him up the staircase to the chambers above. Wendell knocked on the assigned door which cracked open – a delicate hand reached for his sleeve and pulled him inside.

It was the Comtesse de Clairmont. She laughed brightly and threw her arms around his neck, pressing her body against him and sending a waft of her perfume into his nostrils. Wendell disentangled her gently, pushing her away. *"Non, non!"* he pleaded, *"Je suis engagé pour être marié."* She stepped back from him and sighed, shaking her head.

"Ah, mon pauvre Monsieur Parry," she said. He relaxed a bit and asked where Mr. McClure was. Upon hearing that he would be yet another hour, Wendell begged to wait in the foyer. The Comtesse shrugged, and before he left to go downstairs, he asked if she was the buyer.

"Mais non," she insisted, she was only acting on behalf of the Marquis who had empowered her to offer two thousand apiece for the pictures. When he paused in astonishment, she stepped

between him and the door. *"J'ai un sac d'or, sous ma jupe,"* she confided, raising her outer skirt and revealing layers of lacy crinolines and hoops. The Comtesse laughed and opined that she had so many skirts, she didn't know where that sack of gold had got to. She pouted prettily, blocking his way and lifting her petticoats, begging him to help her search. Wendell flushed with shame, a sickening feeling growing in his groin. It was against his nature as a man not to reach out and grope for the gold and whatever else he could get. For a conflicted moment, he felt queasy. Finally, he shoved the comtesse aside and went down the stairs.

He was shaking as he reached the foyer and asked the servant for his coat. Above him, he could feel the comtesse's eyes longing after him, and he dared not look back at her. Now he begged the servant tell Mr. McClure that the deal was off and he would be taking his paintings and sailing for home.

John McClure found him packing in his hotel room. "What is this, Parry? It's already in the papers that the Marquis has bought the paintings and scheduled an exclusive showing at which you are to be present."

Wendell spoke with agitation, "So sell him the paintings! But I will not wait around for it – it's a trap set for me by the comtesse." He tossed the last of his things in his steamer trunk and buckled the lid emphatically, then turned to look at Mr. McClure. "You should come, too. It's said that once war breaks out, American steamships will be commandeered for the military. If need be, I have a buyer for the paintings at home and I'll see you get your share."

"What? Is it Lillian? I wonder why you didn't sell them to her in the first place."

Wendell sighed heavily and sat down on the bed. "'Twas my pride. I wanted a grand tour. I wanted to be Fred Church."

"Alas. And it would have been indeed grand, but for my wife's illness and this infernal business with the South. But you have made quite a splash in Paris – $8000 for the four pictures is a magnificent amount. I beg you not to turn up your nose at it." They sat for a moment, then agreed that John would once again see the Marquis with apologies that Wendell could not attend his showing.

John McClure returned that evening with the sad news – the Marquis was no longer interested in purchasing the paintings. "I begin to perceive that it is not my skill at painting alone that makes my work popular," said Wendell. "Woe! 'Tis a despicable business. Well, at least now we can go home."

"Have we enough money?" asked John.

"I had sold some of the lesser paintings," was the response. "Come, let us make arrangements for the canvases to be shipped and quit this place."

When the *Arago* finally arrived at South Harbor, Wendell was amazed at how normal everything seemed. Even in the midst of a thunderous downpour, it was unimaginable that anything so dire as civil war was in the offing. The Confederates had fired on Fort Sumter and evoked a strangely unresponsive lull. Wendell said his goodbyes to the McClures, and promised John that he would see Lillian straight away about purchasing the Ithaca paintings, which he arranged to have delivered to the Studio Building. The money would be split between them, $3000 apiece, a more than satisfactory sum.

Back at his atelier, Wendell was glad to sleep with Cat in his own bed, and join his fellow artists for breakfast. He sat down with Thomas, Sanford, and Ted Winthrop, who were surprised to see him back so soon, and still more surprised that Lillian was to buy the paintings.

Thomas looked at Wendell fearfully, not daring to speak.

"What is it?" Wendell asked alarmed.

"You do know that her husband has returned, don't you?"

Thomas's question exploded on Wendell like a howitzer shell.

He shook his head, his heart racing, his mouth dry. Seeing that his poor friend knew nothing, Thomas continued regretfully, "Only days ago. He moved her out of Waverly straight away, and closed her accounts. I went by the mansion yesterday, thinking she was being held against her will and, Wendell, there's a small army encamped on the grounds. I don't know how a rescue could be affected." He sat poised, waiting to take action should his friend request it.

Wendell's head was reeling. She would, of course, now ask for a divorce and would likely be unable to buy the paintings. He had waited so long for this moment, and now felt so unready. He kicked himself for bungling the marquis' offer. "She is doubtless making arrangements to leave him," he responded cautiously. "There is much to settle and will take some time."

With a lot more aplomb than he felt, Wendell took his leave. Soon he was in a carriage headed up Fifth Avenue toward Ferguson's mansion. His plan was to knock on the door and inquire about delivery of the paintings, and assume the deal would go through. Perhaps he would be able to see her.

The coach pulled up to the front gate and Wendell paid the coachman to wait. Surprisingly, rather than the small army Thomas had described, there were no guards anywhere and the gate was open. Wendell got a creepy feeling and had the coach pull into the drive, then got out to walk. He still had seen no one when he mounted the steps and stood before the door, hat in hand, wondering with a panic if anyone was there at all.

Just then he heard voices inside, and on an impulse, ducked under the window and peeked through. Lillian and Henry Ferguson emerged from the solarium and stood in front of the sweeping staircase. Heart pounding, Wendell strained to hear.

"As you have requested," Mr. Ferguson was saying, "I have sent the guards away. They will no longer be peeping in the windows at you." Wendell flushed at the reference, and noticed how surprisingly handsome this Henry was, a virile man in his forties with muscles bulging beneath impeccably tailored clothes.

Now Lillian was talking to Ferguson, and Wendell was shocked at what he heard. "Thank you, my darling. We are alone at last." She leaned into him, raising her chin. "How many years have I longed for this moment."

"Why Lillian, you surprise me," Ferguson spoke with pleasure. "In my new career as blockade runner, I fain would have a fiery young wife beside me." Wendell's stomach lurched uncontrollably, and he ducked just as Mr. Ferguson looked toward the window. "Did you hear something?" he said.

Lillian threw her arms around his neck and drew him close. "Nay, husband, nothing but the wind. Kiss me," and she put her mouth to his as Wendell's breath caught in his chest and he was unable to breathe. The kiss became more passional, suffocating Wendell and churning his gut, but he could not turn his eyes away. He was frozen in place, magnetically compelled, as one might be witnessing a train wreck.

Now Henry Ferguson's hands were all over her, running over her clothes and under her skirts. She offered no stiffness, no resistance. Suddenly, he scooped her joyfully into his arms, "By God, Mrs. Ferguson, I will do more than kiss you," and carried her up the sweeping staircase.

Wendell gasped for breath as a physical helplessness overtook him. He pulled himself up and tried the knob, bashing his fist weakly against the door, thinking there must be some mistake.

When the coachman reached him, Wendell was choking, his hand slapping the door helplessly. "Shall we leave, sir?" the coachman asked alarmed, "There seems to be no one home."

"Nay, I will not leave," whimpered Wendell. He was breathless as he continued his helpless slapping and the cab turned to go. Then realizing it was useless, he cried, "My life is over, 'tis over. She's played me for a fool!" The carriage waited as he pursued it lamely and pulled himself inside, then curled up in a fetal position on the seat, gasping, and let out a plaintive wail that echoed down the length of Fifth Avenue all the way to Greenwich Village.

Back in his atelier, Wendell drained his brandy flask and paced the room, trying to deny what he had seen. Knowing Lillian's politics, he thought, it made no sense that she would stay with her husband lest she were spying on him for the North. Then rage overtook him. *"Merde à l'enfer!"* he said aloud. "What care I for what lofty cause she keeps her husband's money and his cock in her. It's all the same and I'm done with her."

Wendell tipped the empty flask up and sagged onto the bed they had shared. Then, despairing that life could ever again be worth living, he cried himself to sleep.

There were vague impressions of buzzards squawking above when Wendell woke groggy and sick next morning. Slowly his awareness turned to the sounds of pandemonium coming from the hallways and through the windows. His eyes focused till they made out Sam, sitting in the chair. He was wearing his 14th Brooklyn Militia uniform and stood when he saw Wendell wake.

"It's war, Wendell," Sam said. "Lincoln's called for us. Do you want to go?"

BOOK 2
The Rival

Saw I your gait and
saw I your sinewy limbs
clothed in blue,
bearing weapons,
robust year,

Heard your determin'd voice
launch'd forth again
and again,
Year that suddenly sang
by the mouths of the
round-lipp'd cannon,
I repeat you, hurrying,
crashing,
sad, distracted year.

~ Walt Whitman
Excerpt from <u>1861</u>

Chapter 25

Two young chasseurs of the 14th Brooklyn Militia stood on steps in perfect weather to better see the parade as it came down Broadway. The men marching were the 7th New York Militia, called by the papers the "silk stocking regiment" for their many illustrious pedigrees. So loud was the crowd's reception that nothing of the regiment's singing or rumbling howitzer wheels could be heard. The mighty crowd roared its approval of the troops and pelted them with gifts – gloves and handkerchiefs and flowers, as well as money, tobacco and food. It seemed the whole city spoke as one in support of these first boys heading for the nation's capital to rescue Massachusetts militias and a beleaguered President Lincoln.

Sam tugged on Wendell's elbow. "There they are," he pointed, "marching beside the caissons." And the two began calling their names, "Sanford Gifford! Ted Winthrop! God be with you – we'll see you in Washington!" After the troops were swallowed from view, the camp followers came, women, children and colored volunteers who would not fight, but went along to support the troops.

Long after the parade had passed, Sam and Wendell stood gazing after it. The throng had dispersed, and they needed to be about their own business, readying themselves for orders they knew would come.

Wendell went alone to Mr. McClure's office, to make him a settlement of the Ithaca canvases. It had been but a few days since the matter at the mansion, and Wendell was yet loath to tell his story. So he simply said that Miss Flax's offer had fallen through and he wished to convey two of the canvases to McClure as settlement of his debt. This information was received in a stiff yet gentlemanly way. Then, still in his uniform, Wendell stopped at Pfaff's.

"Fie, no uniforms in here," greeted Henry Clapp from his perch in the alcove. "This is free territory."

"Hear hear!" drummed the tankards on the table.

"'Tis your freedom I am bound to preserve," responded Wendell wryly.

"Does that uniform permit you to drink?" asked Clapp. Not wanting a drink, Wendell shook his head, and Henry said, "Then you have not preserved your own freedom. Ha ha. But sit, if they will at least allow a doomed man his coffee. Our table has too many empty seats of late."

"Coffee sounds good," Wendell sighed, taking the proffered chair. He wished he felt more dashing in his colorful uniform with its gold buttons and red trousers. "Alas, there are lice in the camp – they have threatened to sheer my hair and beard."

"Of that I approve," said Clapp, "'twill leave a cleaner corpse." Indeed, Wendell's hair and beard were in disarray, and his face puffy from crying and lack of sleep. Clapp continued, "How was the parade? I will miss Winthrop and Gifford, who have at least an honest calling. These other empty chairs were lately occupied by writers who have rushed off to make dishonest names for themselves, even taking government jobs."

"You can't blame a man for wanting to profit from misery, can you Henry?" asked Tom Aldrich with a grin, who would himself be leaving soon for the front as a war correspondent for the *Tribune*. Next to him, Fitzhugh sat with half-shut eyes, oblivious.

Henry raised his mug to Wendell in mock salute, "You fight for glorious and immortal memory, that future generations may practice avaricious Mt. Vernonism at your grave."

"Hear, hear," rang the table.

"And what will you be doing, Mr. Clapp?" asked Wendell.

"Don't worry," Henry assured him, "there will be someone left behind to put a candle in the window for you."

"I hope you don't march off before my new play opens,"

purred Adah Menken from the far end of the alcove. Her now constant companion, Bob Newell, sat beside her. "I have the leading role in *Mazeppa.*"

"Then you will once again be wearing men's clothes," observed Wendell, familiar with the Byron tale.

"And less!" laughed the Menken. "The scene wherein Mazeppa is stripped naked and tied to a horse, I shall be wearing naught but flesh-colored tights. And unlike previous stagings, the horse I am strapped to will be real."

Fitzhugh opened his eyes blearily. "I believed you as a man, Menken, but a naked man? Forgive me for asking, but how do you expect to be convincing?" The table laughed and pounded mugs.

Wendell shook his head. He was beginning to doubt the wisdom of women's freedoms, with behavior more outrageous even than the men's.

"My enlistment is up in three months – perchance I will see *Mazeppa* then." Wendell was amazed at how normal his conversation seemed.

Tom Aldrich spoke, "Might you be going tonight to Laura Keene's Theater? There is to be a benefit performance of *The Seven Sisters,* to aid families of the war volunteers."

"I have not leave to go." Wendell had none of his usual appetites anyway.

Now Ada Clare spoke up with concern in her voice. "Wendell, I have not seen Lillian since her husband's return. Pray, what has become of her?"

Here he flushed. "I'm sure there is much business that keeps her occupied," Wendell said.

She looked at him suspiciously. "Did you have a nice time in Paris?"

He said nothing. Finally he stood and thanked Clapp for the coffee. "I must get back to the base," and with that he departed.

The weeks went by slowly, gloomy and wet. Those beards and

hair without lice were left intact, and life at camp became a series of endless drills and meeting new recruits. They had set their tents in Washington Park at Fort Greene with its stunning view of Wallabout Bay at the mouth of the East River, the Naval Shipyard and Manhattan beyond. The men had to request leave to go even nearby to their homes. The change of scene suited Wendell, and the excitement of men going to war for the first time. He was becoming far closer with Sam's "gentlemen's club," especially Augustus and Frank, than they had been over cigars, though he found it hard to join whole-heartedly in their good-natured conviviality. Even Sam remarked on the melancholy in his friend, who now almost never sketched and avoided any mention of Lillian.

One day, Colonel Wood called Wendell over to the armory. "There's a lady to see you, Private Parry," he said. Wendell drew in his breath and went to the reception area where, seated, was Ruby Robinson. He shook her hand in a formal, awkward way, far different from the warmth he had once offered her. She seemed shaken almost to tears.

"How are you, Ruby?" he asked.

"Alas, not well," she said, despairing. "Tuck has lost his job to the war, for the owner of his business signed up with the army and left. Then Willy ran off following the 7th New York to Washington, so Tuck went after him – he's not even twelve, but looks so much older!" She looked away, embarrassed at her list of woes, and Wendell softened towards her, wondering about the purpose of her visit. She continued, barely above a whisper. "And Lillian has been thrown out on the street by Mr. Ferguson, and with her my job and funding for the school. She has asked me to give you this letter." She handed Wendell an envelope and heaved a shuddering sigh.

Wendell put the letter in his pocket, too polite to tear it up in front of her. It was further proof of Lillian's betrayal that she hadn't come herself. He stifled a conflicted rush of pleasure and sorrow at her misfortune – if Henry Ferguson killed his faithless wife, it would serve her right. "I will look for Tuck and Willy when I get to Washington," he said. "Hopefully, they are both on their way back to you already. With so many men leaving, I am sure Tuck will be able to find work."

"Thank you," said Ruby, standing to go. "May God be with you and your regiment."

Wendell took the proffered hand warmly in both of his. His voice shook with emotion as he wished her well and then watched her back, so small, so strong, so vulnerable, disappear toward the wharf.

The next day, Colonel Wood informed the men that their period of enlistment would be three years rather than three months, and each was given the chance to withdraw – not a man did. A brief leave was granted to accommodate the extra preparations and goodbyes needed to be gone so long. Wendell stored his belongings with Elizabeth Stockard and went back to bid the Studio Building farewell one last time. Except for the furniture he and Lillian had bought, the room looked much as it had at his arrival two full years before – the same patina of dust and the same nails protruding from the walls. The only thing left that he'd brought with him was his muse, the magic mirror on the floor leaning against the wall. A sudden fury overtook him and he kicked it, and watched dispassionately as it fell over with a clatter and cracked. Then he went down to say goodbye to the other artists and to Thomas, who would try to see him in Washington where he hoped to find commissions for paintings of the war.

On May 18th, 1861, a month behind the New York 7th, the 825 men of the 14th Brooklyn broke camp, heading for Washington City. Crowds gathered to watch them, growing ever thicker as the militia approached the ferry and continued on the Jersey side. Sam's parents and Elizabeth pushed through to the front of the crowd and tossed flowers at their feet.

As they marched, Company C's drummer struck a beat and to Wendell's horror, the men began to sing *John Brown's body lies a mould'ring in the grave*. It left such a lump in Wendell's throat that he could only gasp for air and pray that he would soon be dead on the battlefield. 'Her greater service to country will be to turn me into a killer,' he thought viciously, refusing to think her name, 'for upon every enemy I'll see Ferguson's face – and her own.'

The regiment went by train along tracks that had been heroically repaired by 8th Massachusetts and 7th New York, militias that had pacified Maryland to prevent her from seceding and isolating the capital. Occasional angry civilians still lined the track, waving banners that bore Virginia's rebellious motto, Sic Semper Tyrannus, "Thus Always to Tyrants," the South's equivalent of "Don't Tread on Me." On board, the levity of lads on the adventure of a lifetime was unfazed, and Wendell finally joined in their singing and excitement. In Washington, they boarded a steamer for Camp Cameron at Fort Monroe and Meridian Hill where, it was said, the 7th New York Militia would greet them.

Indeed, Sanford Gifford and Ted Winthrop, already toughened and turned into soldiers, were there waiting when Sam and Wendell debarked. "Stockard! Parry!" they shouted from the pier. With hearty handshakes all round, Sanford said, "You're a sight for sore eyes! We trust your journey was easier than ours had been!"

"Fie!" said Sam, "We were anxious to make the battle. You had tamed the trip too well for us."

"'Tis true, we did!" laughed Ted, "Maryland was lousy with traitorous plug-uglies when we arrived. It probably still is, but they daren't show themselves again!"

Letters from home awaited them at their new camp – Wendell and Sam laughed to see how alike they were, full of worry, saying nothing. They read in both: *"Are you getting rest?" "Do you have enough food?" "We're very proud of you," "We miss you,"* and *"Come home safely."*

That day, the friends visited at the 7th New York Militia's camp and shared their adventures. "The worst part," said Winthrop, who was a veteran trekker from his journeys with Fred Church in the Andes, "is that half the men marched in gentlemen's shoes and had their feet rubbed raw by Philadelphia. Their agony was excruciating, making light of mere rain, snipers, and lack of sleep." Then they extolled the northern skills of fixing a rail or a locomotive and reminisced of the celebration that had occurred when they reached the capital as heroes and camped in the Representative chamber.

Nor were all their thoughts of war. Sanford had done a lively painting of camp life, and Ted revealed that *Cecil Dreeme* was accepted for publication. This brought a hearty round of cheering and congratulations. Ted soon spoke wistfully of Adah Menken and was saddened to hear she was still seeing Bob Newell. Despite the look of woe, Sanford clapped him playfully on the shoulder, "Not to worry, Ted old boy – she'll be free again when you get home."

Winthrop took heart. "She is the wild one," he said with admiration, then saluted with his coffee cup. "Here's to me, that I be the man to tame her!"

Now Wendell opined, "For myself, I'm done with untamable bohemian women! When I return – if I return – 'twill be to marry a virgin!" This was the first he had acknowledged the rift with Lillian, even to Sam, and his comrades looked at him with surprise. Seeing him flush and grow quiet, they simply accepted it without further question.

"You can marry my sister-in-law," said Sam hopefully, "guaranteed untouched."

"And I have a sister!" offered Ted, and so jollied their friend into good humor.

The evening, too, was spent in camaraderie, reminiscing around a campfire. Sam and Wendell related many frolicking adventures at Union College, including hilarious accounts of imbibing hasheesh with Fitzhugh. Sanford and Ted told tales of their own wild derring-do on separate wilderness treks out west. The storytelling drew them close. When they ran out of stories, they sang songs till late at night, unable to get enough of one another in a life each secretly feared would be cut short.

The next day, the 7th New York Militia departed for Arlington to help build a fort, after which Sanford would head back to New York ending his three months' enlistment – the early departure of the 7th from New York had, for the moment, preserved their shorter obligation. Winthrop, now a committed soldier and made captain, would be heading for Big Bethel, Virginia. As for the 14th Brooklyn, they were to remain a month without much to do but drill and survive.

Now that Wendell felt better, he remembered Ruby Robinson and his promise to help find her son and husband. The Negro supporters were handling the camp kitchens and clean-up details at Fort Monroe, with more coloreds arriving daily, runaways who had heard news of a war to secure their freedom. Rather than send them back south, Major General Butler had declared them contrabands of war, thus getting around the property laws of the Fugitive Slave Act. Wendell went among their tents, inquiring for Tuck or Wilberforce Robinson, and was directed toward the officers' tents where he found Mr. Robinson tending the horses. Tuck brightened at seeing Wendell and grasped his hand eagerly. "Whewee!" he said laughing, "Don't you look fine! That's a right pretty uniform you're wearin'." Wendell shook his hand, happy to see a face from home. "I hope to be wearing a uniform myself," Tuck went on, "'fore this war's over. This here is the black man's war, and they don't let us fight."

"I saw Ruby, Tuck. She's worried after Willy and wants you both home," said Wendell.

"I goin' home, soon as Willy be well." Anxiety crossed Tuck's handsome face. "He's poorly," he explained as he brushed a filly's flanks, "He been laid low with a sickness that been spreadin' through the colored side of camp. He's recoverin', but they's others tain't so strong."

"What does the camp physician say?" asked Wendell, concerned.

"He just shrug and say somethin' about it bein' 'endemical' in these parts. Hell, I don't need no white physician." Here he dropped his deep voice conspiratorially. "I smuggled into Virginy last week and found me some healin' herbs."

Wendell was impressed. "How did you get past the guards?"

Tuck grinned. "They was encouraged not to notice – it sure do help to pick some tobacco along the way. Anyways," he went on, "I'm surprised to see you here, since Lillian be doin' so poorly herself. Seem like you'd be home with her."

Wendell went silent. Finally he said quietly, "Lillian ceased to be my concern when she went back with her husband."

Tuck looked at him, surprised. "That what you think? Who told you that? I just know she put up a whole lot of distraction so's me and Ruby could get the runaways out the basement without him noticin'. Guess he beat her up bad for it, too."

Wendell stood for what seemed a long time, his heart stopped, trying to digest this revelation, trying to reconcile it with what he'd seen. "How bad is she?" he asked at length.

Tuck shrugged. "Don't guess I know. Last I hear, she still recoverin' at my place."

Wendell wanted to ask more, wanted to assuage the growing anxiety in his stomach, but the bugle was blowing to muster his regiment. "How long before you leave?" he asked.

"I gone try to get Willy out of here tomorrow."

Wendell gave a farewell wave and choked back conflicting emotions as he broke into a sprint to Camp Meridian. At his first opportunity, he fished the rotting letter from Lillian out of his pocket and carefully pulled apart the stuck folds. There was nothing to read, only a wet sea of wavy black lines where once had been sentences.

After the regiment's smart drill, Wendell collapsed in the tent he shared with Sam. "Oh Sam," he groaned as they lay on cots next to each other, "I fear I have made a very grave error."

Now he told his story, to which Sam listened attentively. Upon its conclusion, Sam laid the back of his hand across his eyes in contemplation. "The lawyer in me says if she were a man, using her body in the service of saving lives would be almost laudable. But she is not a man, and I don't think it is in a man to forgive infidelity, whatever the cause. 'Tis a pity it should end this way. I always liked Lillian, I even liked you and Lillian together." He rolled over onto his side to look at Wendell in the deepening gloom of the tiny tent, lit only by a small oil lamp. "Truth be told, I envied you. But she being married to someone else bode ill from the beginning."

"You envied me?" Wendell was surprised at the confession. "You never showed it."

"Not in wanting her for myself," corrected Sam, anxious not to mis-lead. "I rather envied the passional quality you displayed with each other. Such intensity is fired by uncertainty and being apart, and thus not available in the married state. How does Tom Aldrich's poem go, 'Will of the wisp, that I may still pursue?'"

"Do you not feel passional towards Elizabeth?"

"Of course – at times." A fond memory flickered across his face and brought a smile. "The night she conceived – it was nigh ecstatic. Never had I thought a woman could open to me in that way. Wendell, I truly felt the smile of the Creator as I filled her womb with every ounce of my essence." He straightened, returning to his point. "But most of the time, lovemaking feels dutiful and devoted – a good feeling, but leaves a longing for wilder days." Wendell watched as Sam rolled onto his belly and laughed, full of memories. "Do you recall that girl, what was her name – Katerina? We met her on a summer break below Greenwich Village, at the Ornithorhynchus Café." He stumbled over the word.

Wendell was enjoying Sam's stories, feeling as they were still roommates at college, and thought back fondly to the "platypus" café made famous by Poe. "That girl who fancied Fitzhugh," Wendell remembered.

"Yes, that's the one," Sam continued. "Believe it or not, she told me she fancied you! With her I lost my virginity – I believe Fitzhugh did as well, though he never would admit it."

Wendell laughed. "How well I remember! But had you relations with Elizabeth before you married? You never did tell me, and I was gentleman enough not to ask."

Sam derided the question. "You're teasing me. Nay, I was so besotted, I was afraid I would embarrass myself with her, and needed to be married for guarantee of a second chance should I spoil the first. There was a girl right before her who quite unnerved me – I forget her name. I was so excited that I soiled her dress before she even had a chance to lift her skirts. She never spoke to me again." Now they were both laughing heartily.

Finally they quieted and Wendell grew serious. "But you and Elizabeth are to be apart three years. Can you both deny yourselves intimate companionship for so long?"

Sam snorted. "Wait till you have a kid!" he said. "Elizabeth loves the little bugger more than she loves me – she is content. Indeed, he has replaced me in her bed! As for me, I dream of the day when I will return to a woman whose womb is welcoming, whose body is taut, and whose tits are no longer sticky with sour milk. And a son who is no longer a mama's boy! 'Twill be a most blessed homecoming. Aye, the thought of it will sustain me, even through three years. Anyway, I am certain the war will not last so long."

There was a rapping on their tent and a command for lamps

out. They complied, and soon Wendell heard Sam in easy snoring next to him. Endless camp life with slogging and drilling lay ahead – he supposed the exciting part of war to be sporadic at best. Three years seemed an awfully long time. He took a deep breath and determined to send a letter with Tuck to Lillian, pleading with her to wait for him. But then he saw her again in his mind, the easy way she had invited her handsome husband to carry her up the stairs. She could have found some other ruse, some other distraction!

When Wendell finally had a chance next day to look for Tuck, he and Willy had already left. Wendell had wanted to tell Tuck to ask Lillian to write to him, to explain herself. But perhaps it was better to let sleeping dogs lie for, indeed, Sam was right – he could never forgive her.

A long asked-for outing to Washington City was finally granted, and along with other New York regiments including the German-speakers, the 14th Brooklyn boarded a steamer to the capital. They had hoped for a few hours of liberty, but instead were mustered into parade lines to march in front of the White House. Scaffolding for the new Capitol Dome loomed in the distance.

The navy band played as the 14th Brooklyn lifted their red knees in unison – the time spent designing the uniforms had been well worth it. Past the reviewing stand, Colonel Wood, most dashing on a fine stallion, ordered their heads right, so they could see Generals Winfield and Scott standing beside a tall top-hatted figure. Wendell heard Sam beside him say reverently, "Look, 'tis Lincoln himself," and felt a hint of pride. He laughed as he envisioned the cynicism on Henry Clapp's face were he to see them now.

Following that brief outing, it was back to routine. Sam and Wendell both wrote letters to their families, and again, both letters sounded the same, saying nothing: *"Life at camp is tedious," "We had a good trip down," "So glad I'm here with Wendell," "So glad*

I'm here with Sam," "We paraded in front of Lincoln and 'twas a grand affair," "We're anxious for the battle," and "I miss you."

After innumerable boring days, the big excitement at camp was the arrival of the *Atlantic Monthly*. It contained Ted Winthrop's harrowing account, told hilariously as only Ted could, of the 7th New York Militia's journey from Manhattan to Washington City and their taming of the Maryland "plug-uglies." It was passed around eagerly.

The hilarity had barely died down when Major General Butler called the men together. "Men," he addressed them once they had assembled and stood at ease in the bright sunlight, "I have the sad duty to report to you that we have finally engaged the enemy in battle at Big Bethel. Unfortunately, the secessionist side has prevailed, with some loss to our forces. It was a but a short time ago that those brave men were among us, and our grief is felt the more profoundly for it. A list of casualties is posted." There was a buzz of consternation, a realization that war might be a serious affair after all. Major General Butler went on, "It is of particular personal regret to me that among the deceased is Captain Theodore Winthrop, the first Union officer to be lost in battle." A gasp went up from those assembled. Wendell and Sam sagged against each other, their knees suddenly weak, as they tried to square the impossibility of it with what the General was saying. "As you may remember, he volunteered for General Pierce's staff when he could have mustered out. Captain Winthrop fought bravely. Commanding his company, he leapt upon a fallen log and shouted, 'One more charge men, and the day is ours!'" Butler paused to clear his throat, then went on huskily, "That's when he caught a musket ball to the heart, killing him instantly. His is one of the names that shall be remembered to history as a valiant hero who died preserving our Union."

Three weeks later, pulsing with sorrow and vengefulness, the sobered 14th Brooklyn joined General McDowell's 35,000 men at

Arlington, the largest army ever assembled in North America. They were bound for Manassas, Virginia, and the 25,000 rebels that lay in wait across the Bull Run.

Chapter 26

"This is beginning to not be fun," opined Wendell as he and Sam awoke on the rocky ground. It was the fifth day since they'd left Arlington and neither had gotten any real sleep. They quickly tied their blankets and shoved their arms through the harnesses of their haversacks. The dawn was not yet open, but word was about that they were to rise quietly and march to where they could cross the stream to the battle. It was imperative that they get there before the rebel General Johnston could merge his army with Beauregard's and spoil their numeric advantage.

Wendell looked out at the brilliant moonlight dancing across thousands of polished barrels and raised bayonets, silver-edged and glowing, a great phosphorescent river spreading up Warrenton Pike as far as the eye could see. For a moment, the aching damp of his body disappeared as a thrill of awe rose in him. This was history. There was fear of what lay ahead, but for now it was a mesmerizing sight, larger than anything he'd ever known – something of God in it, and he was glad he was here. "If things turn out badly," he said quietly as he and Sam joined the moonlit march, "I want to thank you for bringing me. 'Tis truly something to behold."

Now the companies split off in the darkness, their boots quietly tramping in their different directions. They marched awhile and, as the sun rose red along the horizon, the 14th Brooklyn reached the Bull Run. "Red sky in the morning, sailors take warning," thought Wendell reflexively.

The excitement of the undertaking was wearing off and fear was replacing it. Colonel Wood road up ahead, and bid the 14th Brooklyn keep their powder dry as they raised their muskets and stepped off the muddy bank at Sudley's Ford into a surprisingly strong current. Several men in the front lost their footing, and each step now seemed to undermine their confidence. Up ahead, they could hear the sounds of battle, musket shot and explosions of cannon, growing louder. Colonel Wood mustered them at the opposite shore, had them form their lines and ram a ball into their muskets.

"Look there, lads – the ladies and gents of the government in Washington have turned out for the show." He gestured at a distant mound to their right, lined along its ridge with fancy carriages and parasols. The enemy, he went on, was dug in ahead of them atop Henry Hill where they had captured a battery of cannons – the objective would be to charge up the hill and retake the battery. "Wait till you have a clear shot," he admonished. "Reloading is difficult during a charge." Now he had the boys give a spirited yell, and seeing the spirit was lacking, cried, "Don't worry, Lads! The fear goes out of you once you kill your first, then the fun begins!" He let the stallion rear up and shouted, brandishing his sword, "May God be with us! Hoorah for the Union Army!"

The 15 year-old drummer struck a beat, and the 14th Brooklyn marched ahead. For a moment, their courage was up, and pride in the dauntless way they moved forward in perfect lines onto the yellow smoke-filled battlefield, orderly and in time to the drum. Their chasseur uniforms with red trousers made them dashing figures as battered regiments around them cheered their arrival.

The first men fell in the front row. Wendell's stomach lurched and he was glad he and Sam were several rows back. Now came the bugle and the command to charge up the hill, straight into the enemy's fire. Wendell and Sam exchanged a look that encompassed all the history between them, and wonder that their lives had come to this. Then they turned, and with a yell, joined the headlong rush to ruin or to glory.

A volley of musket fire met them, with so much smoke and dust that suddenly Wendell felt alone on the hill. He could not see Sam, could only dimly discern the flashes of red around him, in noise so deafening he thought his head would burst. He continued in what was the uphill direction, stepping over bodies, some alive and some not, but he dared not look at them. He was in a grove of pines when he saw Frank go down, yelling for the men to save the colors. A clear shot at the enemy was proving elusive. Wendell's stomach tightened until he was unable to breathe, the old familiar feeling of abandonment taking him over. Then suddenly ahead of him, the smoke cleared and he looked directly into the eyes of Johnny Reb.

He shot him. Wendell felt the power of the hammer bear down on the powder, felt the blast and the recoil, saw the look of surprise on the rebel's face as, vignetted by the smoke, he gripped his chest and sank to the ground. Now the air rushed back into Wendell's lungs with life-affirming triumph, and his voice rose up in a powerful howl. The chaos of the battle around him re-entered his awareness, and he was quick to look to Sam, and see that Sam, too, was the victor. Eagerly, he rammed another musket ball home and turned to find another victim. He was aware of musket balls flying past his ears and each one that missed him was elating, convincing him of his own invincibility. With a puff of wind, the smoke cleared and he saw them all ahead, just yards away, young boys in tattered gray, reloading their muskets. Easily, he shot another, hit the ground, reloaded, and without getting up, shot a third. He rose, accepting as his due this god-like power over life and death. As the line continued to rush upward over the crest, the objective of the battery came in range, while in Wendell's surrounding view more companions fell.

Suddenly, the battery flashed with earsplitting thunder. The volley of cannonballs exploded in front of him, and men, blue and red against a bright orange background, flew into the air and landed in pieces at his feet. The shock threw Wendell to his knees, where his god-power abandoned him and his breath rushed out, seizing up his chest so he could not breathe. Sam appeared beside him and grabbed his arm, pulling him to his feet as the Colonel called out, "Fall back! Fall back!" Union men ahead of him were running down the hill, their faces crazed with fear. Then Augustus fell, and Wendell, too, turned and ran.

The rebels were cheering and, with a rebel yell, pursued. "Reform your lines," called Colonel Wood at the bottom of the hill, "Reform your lines!" They kept running, across the field, stumbling over rocks and bodies, tossing aside their haversacks and blankets. "Reform your lines!" Then to a man, the 14th Brooklyn turned and stood, their backs against the Bull Run. Seeing them take a stand, the rebels thought better of their chase and slunk back to the safety of their hilltop. Now the 14th Brooklyn raised a cheer, which echoed across the wide expanse of the battlefield, rallying their side.

The sun was climbing, and the day growing hot – smoke, dust and sweat stained their handsome uniforms. Death and gun-powder hung in the air like the devil's laundry. Other companies, New York and Massachusetts boys, were sweeping up the hill on the further slopes, drawing fire, and the rebels' cannons turned away to train on them. The re-ordered ranks of the 14th Brooklyn loaded their weapons and once again marched ahead to the drumbeat. A volley from their howitzers flew over their heads at the enemy, numbing their hearing and giving welcomed cover.

Colonel Wood galloped his horse ahead of them, his sword raised in the choking heat, leading the charge. When he neared the crest, they were horrified to see him fall, the horse rearing up, and a cloud of dust billowing where the rider had been. Wendell and Sam joined their comrades in trying to cover his escape, but they were too far away and his wound too severe – the rebels quickly surrounded him and bore him away to their side.

The capture of their beloved Colonel rallied the men as nothing else. "Charge, Lads, charge! Let the Rebs pay for it!" They were no longer individuals but a unified army holding high the Stars and Stripes as they swept with a vengeance all the way to the crest, and now it was bayonets and swords that did the fighting. Wendell thrust his bayonet through the heart of the first rebel he met, and was surprised at his own lust for the blood that spurted hot and red upon his face. He and Sam grinned at each other – they were musketeers on a mighty mission. Their fury quickly routed the Rebs, and suddenly the battery was theirs. They'd won the day! They scurried to secure the cannons when they saw the Rebel commander Jackson, astride his horse, unmovable as a stone wall. "Stand your ground, men! Stand your ground! Here come those red-legged devils again." He was referring to the 14th Brooklyn and their pride swelled.

Another company of Rebels suddenly appeared on the hill, rushing up to staunch the flight of their comrades who turned and joined them, charging the chasseurs with renewed and overwhelming force. "Retreat!" came the call, "Retreat!" and the Union bugle sounded reluctantly as this time the 14th Brooklyn backed down the hill under heavy fire.

Once again they reformed their ranks, General Wadsworth giving the orders, and once again they began to move forward to the drum, across a field now littered with dead and dying. The day was too long – the men were growing drowsy in the heat. Overhead, buzzards circled.

Back and forth they went to the top of the hill, they and other regiments, trying to recapture that battery, their ranks growing thinner each time. Suddenly the flanking brigades to their left began to panic, dropping their packs and scrambling downhill towards the Bull Run. "Stand fast," yelled Wadsworth, "Hold your positions!" And to their horror, a great wave of gray came over the hill, as trains had brought in Johnston's army to merge with Beauregard's, and now the Rebs had cannon, cavalry, and solid lines of infantry. Across the field, they heard General McDowell, commander of the Union forces, yell, "Fall back," and "Retreat," as the cannon volley began and the rebels charged down the hill.

"Give the retreat cover! Stand your ground and give 'em cover!" yelled Wadsworth to the 14th Brooklyn as the Union rout began, bodies falling everywhere, haversacks and muskets thrown aside, splashing, drowning, wagons overturning.

Wendell met Sam's eyes, surprisingly calm and tired, a scary look of surrender. "No Sam! No!," he cried as they turned to the onslaught, standing their ground and exchanging one last volley before the rebels swept into them with bayonets and swords. From the corner of his eye, Wendell saw Sam fall and instinctively stood over him as an enemy lunged with a shrieking rebel yell. In a desperate effort, Wendell caught the bayonet with his hand and turned it aside from Sam, the searing pain of severed flesh and bone ignored as the Reb let go the gun. Enraged, Wendell threw down his own gun and seized the secessionist around the neck, who gripped Wendell's neck in kind. The battle was all around them, the smoke, the bugles sounding retreat, screams, wagons running, cannons booming, musket balls whizzing by – still Wendell and the Reb were locked in a death grip, each trying to strangle the other, circling like wrestlers. Above his battered hands, Wendell saw the rebel's face begin to puff up big and blue, the eyes bulge out from fear as much as pressure, pleading to no avail. Still, he gripped Wendell's neck, holding on, and neither man had gotten a breath in some minutes. Wendell was becoming faint as he watched with fascination the blood begin to bubble from the corner of his assailant's mouth. He had a vague impression of wanting to paint his picture, paint the red blood against the blue skin, the bulging eyes, the beads of sweat, the few hairs that tried to be a beard. Smalt, Prussian, vermillion. He was a kid, maybe eighteen, this confederate soldier who wouldn't let go even near death. They were weak in the knees and sinking to the ground, when suddenly a cannon's burst blew the kid out of Wendell's hands and lifted them both heavenward.

Wendell felt a moment of panic and excruciating pain,

followed by ecstatic bliss which seemed to last forever – he was flying away, flying apart. Then all went peaceful, white, and silent.

A white haze still lingered when the pain returned, a haze that alternated between searing heat and unbearable cold. Wendell heard a voice calling for water, and vaguely realized it was his own. The sounds of moaning and muffled screams seemed distantly to penetrate. For a moment, he fancied hell's fire reaching for him. "'Tis doomsday,' he thought with alarm. Then, 'No – doomsday was yesterday.'

His sticky eyelids slit open with a will, and he became aware of faint images moving through the whiteness. Now the whiteness brightened, as if a cloud were lit by the sun, and from the middle, emerging towards him, came an angel dressed in green. As she approached, he could see her familiar features and felt his heart stir in his chest. She knelt and leaned herself across him gently, hugging him, magically abating his pain, and he could feel her body shake. "Don't die," she begged, "Wendell, please don't die." Unaware that he moved only a bandaged stump, he reached his hand to stroke her hair, and felt the silkiness of it. Then he smiled and drifted again into unconsciousness.

Days later, the fever still raged. Wendell felt himself sway and heard wheels turning, as he opened his eyes to find his head cradled on Lillian's lap, in a bunk aboard a train. Around them were other occupied bunks and numerous flag-draped pine boxes. Loved ones, dressed in black, sat on them and wept.

"Is Sam in one of those?" he asked.

"Yes," she said.

Sadness and regret fell on his chest, a huge weight, with so much heaviness that he could not cry, but only gasp for air. His hand ached and he held it up to look at it. After several moments, he realized it was gone – it was just one more thing, one more thing along with Sam. The implications of not having his right hand, of not having Sam, were too much now to consider. Even his anger at Lillian was beyond him. There was no reality to anything anymore – only the pain was real.

Wendell was trying to escape, trying to drift away again into unconsciousness, when he heard his sister's voice. "Is he awake? Thank the Lord." Now a hand pushed up the tender flesh behind his battered neck, sending a wave of pain screaming along his spine, as his head was lifted and a flask of water pressed to his lips. He groaned and heard the groans of the men around him and the women weeping over coffins, merging with the clickety clack of the rails in one undifferentiated rhythm, rocking him back to sleep.

When he woke again, he was lying on the seat in the passenger compartment, leaning against Catherine, dressed in civilian clothes. The train was straining steeply up, threatening to stall and roll back down. Wendell recognized immediately that they were on the train to Ithaca. "Where's Sam?" he asked.

"He and Lillian got off in New York City," she said. He felt a pang, and determined it was for Sam and not for Lillian.

"My hand is missing," he stated dully. His grandmother had said, "You must give your sister your right hand," and his whole body convulsed with shivers.

"Yes," said Catherine crisply, putting up a brave front. "And by the looks of your neck, you're lucky it wasn't your head."

Now he saw the puffed blue face with bulging eyes and blood bubbling red from the mouth. This time the mouth was leering at him and he was being strangled. He began to struggle, arms flailing.

"Sshhh, Wendell – Sshhh Little Deer," soothed his older sister, stroking his head, though he felt her alarm. The familiar gesture relaxed him and the visage faded. "We'll be home soon."

His father and Seneca Sue met them at the station to help him into the wagon. Moving that short distance was agony. He was amazed at how easy the battle had been, compared with coming home – he almost longed to be back there, where he felt like a god, where he felt invincible – where he still had his hand and Sam was still alive. But now the reality hit him – he had let his friend down, and he himself was a useless cripple who would never again be able to paint. More than that, he was a monster – he had taken pleasure in the killing, and longed for that pleasure now.

They put Wendell in his own little bed in the downstairs room that had been Catherine's. They were offering him water, trying to get him to eat, fussing over his bedding and bandages. He wished they'd go away and let him die or at least cry. Finally, once he'd consented to a few spoonfuls of broth, they left him alone. He lay there for hours, perhaps days. In the lengthening rays of the afternoon sun which lit the dust and made it sparkle, Wendell began to see faces hovering over him. He saw Sam and Ted, his mother and grandmother. He was having a deep and wordless conversation with them when he saw Lillian.

"Lillian, these people have come for me. Why are you here? Are you dead?" he asked with alarm.

"No," she said, "I have come to make sure you stay alive." And he felt her warm body slip into the bed next to him and felt her arms around him, her breath soft in his ear. Again, her touch seemed to abate his pain. The others nodded approval and began to fade, his fever broke, and Wendell knew that, for better or for worse, he would not die.

He had thought she was a phantom or a dream, but when he woke in his djellaba, she was there, sleeping peacefully beside him. Wendell looked at her still form, her reposed features – so brazenly innocent, as if nothing had happened. But a livid scar across her temple bespoke her foolishness with Ferguson, and his mind re-enacted the scene as it had a hundred times. His heart said let it rest, you need her now – you've got her now. But his pride spoke the louder and he recoiled from her in the bed. Angrily, he shook her awake.

Chapter 27

She woke with a start, her eyes wide, gasping at his rudeness. She tried to get out of the bed, but he found surprising strength to pin her roughly, and force his mouth furiously onto hers. She was beneath him, struggling, and making a strangling noise in her throat as though unable to catch her breath. Alarmed, he backed off, and she slid from his grasp onto the floor where she clutched at her throat pleadingly, then stood and stumbled toward the door, yanking it open. The labored sounds of suffocation flew into the house and Catherine appeared quickly, grabbing Lillian as she slumped.

"Breathe with me," ordered Catherine. Catherine made the same rasping sounds, synchronizing her breath with Lillian's efforts – then Catherine slowly calmed her own breath to normal and, miraculously, Lillian's breath followed.

Wendell was shaking as peace returned with the measured sound of their breathing together. Finally satisfied that the crisis was over, Catherine faced him. "She has asthma," she admonished. "You'll have to learn to do that yourself."

"Do what?" Wendell cried weakly. "What happened? How, Lillian? Whence came you to have asthma?"

Lillian was still slightly breathless, "I had told you," she said, "in the note Ruby gave you – that Mr. Ferguson had…" she paused and gasped before going on, "…raped and tortured me."

Catherine flushed. "I should leave you two to talk." Lillian nodded and Catherine left the room, closing the door behind her.

"Ah Wendell," Lillian said, keeping her distance across the room, "do you think the less of me, that I am ruined?" Tears welled in her eyes.

Wendell sat on the edge of the bed, dizzy from confusion and exertion. There was anger in his voice when at last he spoke. "Fie, you would call it 'rape'? I was watching, I saw it. I regret the violence of his response to your treachery – but seduction is not 'rape.'"

Her eyes grew wide, this time with comprehension. "Ah, 'twas you at the window. I thought it was the runaways. Is that why you went to war without even a goodbye?" He didn't answer, just stared at her accusingly, "…and did not read my letter?"

Quietly he said, "What would the letter have told me that was different from what my own eyes said?"

She was beginning to sob. Her breath rasped again on the intake and she looked fearful. "I must calm myself before I speak of it," she managed, and left the room.

He lay back exhausted, while the late horror of his life swept over him in a wave of pain and pity. Ted… then Frank, Augustus, and Sam… and how many others with the killing still ongoing? Oh Sam, Sam… Damn Lillian! There was no solace in coming home – the flower patterned wallpaper closed in oppressively. Finally, he lurched himself out of bed and managed to make it on unsteady legs to grasp the door frame, the missing hand reaching uselessly to support him. Then he willed himself beyond it into a chair at the kitchen table.

"Look who's up," said the elder Parry from a seat where he sipped from a pint of whiskey. "That's good, that's a good sign. The doctor said 'twould take longer. Welcome back from the dead, Son." He got up and went to the dormer stairs and shouted up, "Hey girls, Wendell's arisen and looks a might hungry!" Harte sat down again beaming as Catherine and Lillian rushed excitedly down the tiny steps.

"There are letters for you, from your friends," said Catherine, "They've been quite worried."

"Yes," said Lillian, "Fitzhugh and Rosalie, Ada Clare, Walt, Jervis and Gertrude, Asher, Sanford – all have written. And Elizabeth blesses you that you were with her Sam."

Wendell did not feel their excitement. "Why am I not with my regiment?" he asked bitterly.

Hearing him, Catherine slammed a bowl of stew before him and responded with a huff. "You have been mustered out – the miasma was upon you. You'd have died if you had stayed in that hospital."

"I would fain be with the men, to kill and to die as they do. I am no longer fit for civil life." He picked up his spoon with a shaky left hand. Everyone else fell into a stony silence while Wendell ate noisily and hungrily, the good stew taking the edge off his morose thoughts. "Still, I should thank you," he mumbled into his food.

"Son," said Harte soberly, "we're proud of what you did. There would be no civil life but for soldiers."

"Fie, you speak as a politician speaks." Wendell was weary of them, weary of life. The meal was good, but his stomach had grown small and unused to food. If he ate more, it would make him sick. He did not want to go back to the bed, but knew not what else to do. His every movement pained him.

"I'm going home," said Catherine, pulling off her apron and tossing it on the counter. "Better company awaits me there."

Wendell suddenly felt sorry for his sullenness. "Thank you, Sis, truly!" he called after her, but she was gone, slamming the door. Now he tried for better cheer.

"Do you have a newspaper?" he asked.

"Perhaps it's too soon to see a paper," cautioned his father. Wendell was about to protest, but his mind was on Lillian standing silently in the kitchen. When he glanced up at her, she flushed and lowered her eyes.

"I have *Cecil Dreeme*," she suggested quietly. "It has given me solace to hear Ted's voice in it. Perhaps you may want me to read it to you." Yes, he thought, that's exactly what he wanted. He should resist going back under her treacherous spell, but for now it soothed him.

Wendell relaxed back into his bed, with Lillian reading on the chair beside him, and he could see Ted in the story as if he were still living.

"Home!" she read, *"The* Arago *landed me at midnight in mid-winter. It was a dreary night. I drove forlornly to my hotel. The town looked mean and foul. The first omens seemed unkindly. My spirits sank full fathom five into Despond.*

"But bed on shore was welcome after my berth on board the steamer. I was glad to be in a room that did not lurch and wallow, and could hold its tongue. I could sleep, undisturbed by moaning and creaking woodwork, forever threatening wreck in dismal refrain."

As Wendell listened, he could almost hear Ted's voice, and took comfort. Lillian continued, *"It was late next morning when a knock awoke me. I did not say, 'Entrez,' or 'Herein.' Some fellows adopt those idioms after a week in Paris or a day in Heidelberg, and then apologize,–'We travelers quite lose our mother tongue, you know.'"*

Here they actually began to laugh, and their hilarity built as witticisms poured from the late Winthrop's pages. When Lillian reached a part about "deciduous" white flakes of paint falling from the tracery at NYU, their laughter turned to sobs. Somehow, Wendell was not embarrassed to cry with her. When their tears were spent and their noses cleared, Wendell reached for her with his missing hand, then waved the bandaged stump and moved over in the bed. "Will you not take off your clothes and lie with me?" he entreated her.

Lillian nodded and stood, unbuttoning her dress as he watched. But just when she was about to reveal herself, her breath caught asthmatically. "Breathe with me," he said with alarm, and did as he had seen his sister do, breathing with her until at last she could breathe with him. He was surprised at how well it worked. She looked regretful and began to redo her buttons.

"I am so sorry," she said tearfully.

"What is it, Lillian? What plagues you?" He reached to touch her, but she backed away. "If I breathe with you, will you not be able to tell me?"

She sat back down on the chair and slowly matched her breath to his. Finally, a look of calm settled on her features and she began to tell her story. "I had given him tea cake laced with laudanum and left a key in the bedroom door. My plan was to drug him and lock him in. Beneath the staircase, my bags were packed, with the money I had promised you and anything else I could fit." She had to stop here and breathe with him some more, and now he felt shame for condemning her – she was not guilty after all, and he knew not whether to laugh for joy or cry for his stupidity. Lillian went on, "He had guessed my ploy. Indeed, he knew everything. When we reached the bedroom door, he took the key and turned to lock it from the inside. 'Your darkies were always free to go. I never cared a wit about them or any of your abolitionist adventures, even John Brown,' says he. 'But this,' and he drew the drugged tea cake out from his pocket… "

Now she was gasping, and once again Wendell calmed her with his breath. "Oh Wendell," she managed at last, "I struggled, but he put a pillow over my face." Here she began to sob. Wendell rose and put his arms around her and pulled her to him, but she startled violently and went into a full asthmatic fit, then hurled herself out of the room.

His heart beat wildly as he heard her in the kitchen, straining for breath and Catherine calming her. Wendell roused himself and managed to make it into the kitchen chair opposite where she sat, looking at him with unbearable sorrow and regret. "The asthma comes when I approach you with passional intent?" he asked, his voice breaking. She nodded, tears streaming down her cheeks. "Oh Lillian," he moaned, "and I had felt sorry for my hand!"

A moment went by before she could speak again. "When he had finished with me, he threw me naked down the stairs." Lillian reached to touch the scar on her temple. "He said that I wouldn't find my suitcase, that everything in the house was his, then tossed my torn dress after me saying I could take the clothes on my back. When he passed me bleeding on the stairs, he threw $200 at Ruby as if spitting on her, and told her to take me to the hospital."

Wendell felt exceedingly angry. "He knew all this before he carried you up the stairs!" he cried. "I could sympathize were it a fit of anger, but this is premeditated rape."

"No court in the land would convict him," said Lillian.

"Aye," agreed Wendell sorrowfully, "but mayhap the divorce will go more in your favor."

"I am sure neither one of us will bring it up. I am hoping for an annulment, as he had effectively abandoned me all those years."

"And your father's property? Is all of it lost to you?"

She nodded. "I have no right of inheritance. The two companies were merged. What rights I had while married were but a gentlemen's agreement."

Wendell looked confused. "Do you mean, if your husband were to die, you would have no right of inheritance?"

"Oh," said Lillian startled. "That's not what I meant, but I suppose it's true. If we were still married and he died, I would inherit."

There are thoughts a man must not dwell on, lest he find himself acting on them willy-nilly. Such a thought went through Wendell's mind, and he suppressed it reluctantly.

Now they became aware of Harte sitting at the table with his mouth hanging open and Catherine in similar mode in the kitchen. A silence of embarrassment overtook them, with the only sound being Catherine rustling about pretending distraction with the dishes. Wendell got up and staggered back to the bedroom, Lillian following. They closed the door.

"Woe is me," cried Wendell falling backwards onto the bed and throwing his bandaged stump across his brow, "I should have trusted you. I was right outside your door! Damn me that I didn't bust it down! Perhaps I would not have gone to war nor lost my hand! Now, how am I to care for you?"

"Do you even want me now, Wendell, that I am damaged?" Her voice was small and pitiful. And for the first time he noticed, as he looked at her in the soft sunlight that lit the room with a summer glow, that she had once again grown frail as she had been in Concord.

"I admit Lillian," he said quietly, "it will be very hard on me not to touch you. But yes, I want you even so." And he realized with a rush of pain that he himself was damaged, and was overcome with gratitude that she also wanted him.

That night, she slept again curled up against his back, magically abating his agony and soothing his dreams. He awoke next morning to find her dressed and with her bags packed. "I am going to the city to make some money," she informed him. "Indeed, your father and sister have not the means to feed me further." It was an emotional blow too many, and left his heart in a turmoil. Still, he nodded. "If you would sign me as agent for your remaining paintings, I will try to sell them."

"Alas, Lillian, your signature will work as well as mine," Wendell reminded her morosely, "my left hand is not recognizable." Yet he penned her a note giving her agency, and stood looking after her as his father's buckboard bore her away to the train station.

As the months went by, she wrote regularly, and he gradually became better at writing back. She had sold some of her writings and a song, and was paid once to sing at lyceum. And she was having success in selling Wendell's pictures, occasionally sending back the welcomed proceeds. She stayed with both Ada Clare and Elizabeth, who were most grateful for her company.

She had gone to see Ruby and Tuck in their new home in Auburn, at the top of Cayuga Lake. They had been invited to move there by Auburn's famous resident, Harriet Tubman – "Moses" – who had aided so many runaway slaves to reach Ruby's school in the Five Points. Tuck was now Reverend Robinson, the minister of Auburn's colored church.

Lillian wrote, too, how their other friends were doing: Tom Aldrich had been covering Bull Run for the *New York Tribune*, and "saw you, Wendell, literally blown apart by a cannon. He was most surprised and gratified to hear you are still alive. Indeed, it shook me badly to hear his description, and knowing Sam lay just behind." Thomas Read was enlisted, and employed in boosting troop morale, traveling the country with actors and speakers. Elizabeth was desperately trying to hang onto her house and memories, but would most likely be moving to Brooklyn with Sam's parents.

The rest of them led lives that seemed unbelievably normal. Henry Clapp was writing theater reviews under the name "Figaro;" Adah Menken's play, *Mazeppa*, had been such a sensation that Edwin Booth had congratulated her onstage; and Horace Greeley came by Pfaff's to meet her. Edwin was now acting in London where Molly was expecting a child. The Laura Keene Theater was readying itself for the summer season. Those who were still around sent their greetings and best wishes to Wendell.

Each day Wendell went to the post office, hoping for word from Lillian. One day, as he sat beside his father on the buckboard, leafing through the mail, he came across an envelope from the Department of War addressed to Catherine. "What do you think this could be?" he wondered aloud.

"It's your pension check," explained the elder Parry to the flummoxed young man. "Catherine gets them regularly." Seeing the look on his son's face, he added, "Damn good thing, too."

Wendell ripped open the envelope. Inside was a check, written to Catherine, for $8. "Why was I not told of this?" he asked.

Harte shrugged. "She is your guardian, you know. You were quite maimed when the doctor attested your incapacity."

Wendell flushed with humiliation. "Am I then considered completely unable to care for myself?"

Harte nodded uneasily. "We need the money, Son," he said. "Don't be too eager to attest your good health. It would be hard for you to find a job that pays that much."

Wendell did not reply, only sat on the seat feeling anger rise inside him. He did not begrudge his family the money, indeed he was relieved to hear of it, but he would find a way to make more than a paltry $8 a month. He was Wendell Harte Parry, he had once been offered thousands for a single painting. Surely a missing hand would not condemn him to dire poverty and dependence forever – he was not incapacitated.

Chapter 28

With Catherine's excellent nursing, Wendell was slowly recovering. His stump sealed itself and healed, and he became increasingly proficient with his left hand, even at firing a pistol. Catherine grew less begrudging as he hunted rabbits and managed to take over the cooking and fire-tending for himself and his father. An additional burden for all was the elder Parry's drinking, grown worse since his son's injury, but that too seemed better. Harte complained of pain in his missing toes and had a hard time walking. Wendell was grateful that Seneca Sue still tended the farm, taking home a share of milk and eggs.

But as Wendell's body grew stronger, so too did his demon. It had begun as vaporous dreams of Sam. At first the dreams were comforting, with Sam still alive and smiling. But after awhile, the dreams had become ghoulish, full of explosions and dead faces.

The first time he dreamed of the young Rebel with the blue face, he had been startled awake by the vivid sensation of those hands about his throat. And then it began, night after relentless night, the blue face becoming clearer, more distorted, grotesque in its suffering, Wendell's own hands useless as his assailant's hands pressed tighter. So regular and real did the dream become, that Wendell grew fearful to sleep at all. Not wanting to upset his family or Lillian, he told no one, and slowly descended into his personal hell, struggling daily to conceal it.

Lillian returned at Thanksgiving and at Christmas, but fearful to be touched by Wendell's barely restrained desires, she left all too quickly. Fortunately for the little Ithaca family, Lillian was getting good money for Wendell's paintings – news of his career-ending martyrdom had boosted their price.

That winter, the weather turned its usual bitter cold. January brought a new tax on income, and the government took 3% of earnings over $600. Wendell now accompanied his father to the town saloon whenever the roads were passable. Here the workers from the various mills gathered and complained, their work made harder by the snow and ice. They worried endlessly about the war, dragging on longer and bloodier than anyone had foreseen. Several blocks to the east of the saloon was the town square, and there Wendell could find library books and get copies of his favorite publications and the *Ithaca Journal*. He was surprised to find in the *Atlantic Monthly* new verses to Lillian's song, *John Brown's Body*, penned by Julia Ward Howe and dubbed *The Battle Hymn of the Republic*.

In May, Lillian wrote that she had gone to Concord, sadly, for Henry David Thoreau's funeral. Thoreau's death saddened him, and seemed a grim omen. "He started this war and now fails to finish it," Wendell thought, as if the war had lost its leader.

It was a great relief and blessing when, as spring blossoms turned to fruit, Thomas Buchanan Read came to call. Wendell had been stacking wood when the wagon drove up, unannounced, into the yard. "Thomas! What a pleasure!" Wendell greeted him. "I had thought you were in the capital."

"I have lately been in Kentucky. Alas, entertaining the troops does not pay well, though General Wallace has made me Major, my heroic deeds implicit in the title." Thomas climbed down and habitually reached his hand out to shake Wendell's, then finding none to shake, grabbed him and gave him a quick squeeze about the shoulders. He continued, "I am taking a break from it to make some money." As they walked inside, Thomas gestured toward his wagon, and Wendell understood that it contained his secret headless portraits. "I had heard you were in need of a hand," he explained further, "and while I can't give you a painter's hand, I can give you a hand made by a painter."

Wendell flushed with humility as he realized what was being offered. "You would sculpt a hand for me?"

"Indeed," said Thomas. "I have brought with me the best wood for the job, and finest whittling tools."

They gave Thomas the upstairs room and Wendell slept almost peacefully that night. Now Catherine, to Sue's dismay, began to come over almost daily, offering to cook and clean and delight in Thomas' good company. Often when everyone was abed, Wendell could hear them talking quietly in the dormer room above him.

As the sculpting continued and the elegant hand took shape, Wendell's demons returned nightly with full ferocity. First came the distant sound of cannons, almost as soon as he closed his eyes. Then, moments later, the sounds of marching boots and drumbeats as the cannon fire grew closer. If he failed to wake himself then, the shouting and screaming would start and the smoke would close in around him as musket balls flew past his head, and Sam would clutch at him even as Sam's killer grabbed Wendell about the neck. Slowly, the blue face gained almost complete control of their nightly battles, and continued to pursue him briefly even after he woke. The demon had become so real that Wendell resisted sleep as long as he could, and took to placing his pistol by the bed lest he should be tormented into waking hours.

When he raised his stump for the first fitting of his new hand, he was shaking visibly, his dark eyes red and sunken. "You have been growing more tense over the time I have been here," Thomas observed. "Are you not able to sleep?"

"Sleep?" admitted Wendell, "I hardly know the word."

"I had seen you are sketching again," Thomas slid the cuff onto Wendell's wrist and gently buckled the leather straps in place, "a strange blue shape of dark and indistinct content. Is that the image that haunts your dreams?"

"Nay," said Wendell, "I have not the skill with my left hand to render him accurately. Yet I do think the drawings contain something of his madness." He had meant to say "menace," but now that the word was out, it hung over him like Damocles' sword.

He held up his new hand, beautifully shaped to accept a handshake or hook an object, and saw it as something alien. The word madness reverberated through the room and the leering blue face appeared before him, laughing loudly enough that Wendell was sure Thomas could sense it.

"Do you hear that?" cried Wendell with a spasm. He swung the new hand at the phantom, but Thomas grabbed his arm to stay him.

"Who is it, Wendell?" asked Thomas alarmed. "At whom do you strike?"

Panic set in as he looked at Thomas, his vision confused and unfocused. After a moment, compos mentis returned and Wendell shook his head. "No one," he said. "There's no one there. Pray forgive me."

Catherine had not invited Wendell to her gatherings, but she was excited to invite Thomas, so Wendell joined them and Seneca Sue in the buckboard. Wendell was sure it would be quite like his last visit, which he remembered now with unease. After they made themselves comfortable on the tiny wooden benches which filled and left many standing, the lights lowered to the beating of drums, and fairy lights flashed about the room. Two persons sat on the stage, Catherine Cayuga and her guest, a man of Delaware Indian blood through whom it was hoped that the great Delaware chief, Saint Tammany, would speak.

This time it was Catherine who clothed the man for his transformation, and when he rose from his throne crowned with a feathered headdress, Wendell shivered. He no longer trusted Catherine since he'd found that Bill Stillman had told her of "Mrs. Ferguson." Yet he wished very much to ask Saint Tammany to make contact with his grandmother and find out why it was ordained that for Catherine, his right hand had been given over. The saint spoke first in Delaware language, then greeted the throng with a wish for peace and began to take questions. When came

Wendell's turn at last, the saint did not answer his question, but said mysteriously, "Your right hand is not gone, and he whom you think is undead yet lives." And he said that Sam and Ted were at peace.

That night, Wendell and Thomas spoke till late of the meeting, in which Thomas had received greetings from his dead wife and children. He had been urged to find another love and assured his dead wife would stay with him as his muse. He was deeply moved. As for Wendell, the saint's pronouncement had left him more anxious and disturbed, though Thomas had a better interpretation of it. "It was meant to reassure you that all is well in the spirit realm," he said. When asked his plans after the war, Thomas got a faraway look. "Now that Italy is united, I wish to go back there."

The next day, Thomas took his leave. The Parry family stood in the yard, all of them, to watch him go, as if he were the last guest they'd ever have. Wendell felt dread at Thomas' departure, that he was truly left alone with his demon. He wondered if he would ever see Thomas again.

After the wagon pulled out of sight, Wendell went behind the house with his pistol for more practice – he felt he was still at a disadvantage shooting with his left hand. He drew the gun and leveled it at the target, hitting it just left of center. Satisfied, he was putting the gun back into its holster when he noticed the target moving towards him. His stomach lurched, and he pulled the revolver out again, shooting at what was no longer the target, but was transmuting into a shade of blue with a distinct flash of red in the corner. Then the specter of the Rebel appeared, bloated and disfigured, a visage of grotesque suffering as it came towards him. Wendell shot again, hitting it directly, but the demon was impervious and kept coming faster, lunging and grabbing Wendell's throat as he fell backwards, firing wildly.

The demon had him so close it threatened to merge with him, the revolting smell of death coming from its leering mouth and pulsing blue temples. There was no sound, it was muffled – only a heartbeat pounded in his head. Time itself paused long enough for Wendell to examine the details of his enemy's face – the dark eyes with long feminine lashes, the stern brow and strong jaw through beard and mustache. He was so familiar. He recognized it gradually as his own, when suddenly it changed into the scraggly chinned kid that wouldn't let go. Wendell was struggling to reach his own hands around the demon's throat, but his right hand was missing and this left one weak. He could feel the immense dead weight of his nemesis on top of him, crushing the air out of his chest, his own face bloating horribly as he struggled for breath. Then a blast blew them both to pieces and what had been Wendell Harte Parry surrendered itself again to the blissful white light of nothingness.

Wendell did not know how long he floated in that whiteness – time had long ago ceased to exist. When he came back, he was lying in a crib behind slatted wooden bars, looking into a high-ceilinged room lit by sunlight that streamed through large arched windows. From out the room, he heard plaintive cries – screams and squalls – and briefly remembered thunder and lightning. Wendell knew where he was.

Trying to move, he realized he'd been drugged – probably hasheesh and brandy, or laudanum. He was dressed in thin blue cotton, and his head and face had both been shaved clean. Above him, the slatted bars continued across the crib, closing him in. "The Utica Asylum," thought he, "Old Main." Wendell knew, of course, why he was here, and hoped he hadn't hurt anyone. The demon was his and his alone, yet he could not bring himself to say it was not real. Indeed, reality made no sense to him now.

The door opened and an angel floated in, looking around her in confusion – Lillian. There was no one he'd rather see, even under such humiliating circumstances. If Gerrit Smith had gone mad, how much shame could there be in it? Surprised to see him in the crib, she threw her carpet bag down and rushed to his side.

"Oh, Wendell," Lillian swooned towards him, gripping the bars. "Wendell my Heart."

"Lillian, I am so glad you're here. Are you come back to me, or have you come to say goodbye again? No matter, you're here now."

"Alas, I am not come back, Wendell," she told him, falling to her knees to look him level in his eyes. "I have enlisted as an army nurse, and am stationed in Washington. I am shipping out tomorrow." He reached through the bars to touch her cheek, but she backed away and picked up the heavy carpet bag. "Sanford had found this in your atelier and wanted me to bring it to you," she said, and drew out his magic mirror. He looked at it with the crack across the top, and could not explain the happiness he felt on seeing it again.

Lillian slipped the mirror back into the bag and pulled at the hasp on his cage. "Look here, Wendell, it's not locked. You can come out."

"Nay, Lillian," he said. "For now, it's the right place for me. I feel safe somehow in here, as if perhaps I could even sleep." He sighed wearily, "I sometimes think that's all that is needed – if I could but sleep a few days, I should recover."

"Aye, I feel the same," she said, though he did not know if she meant about him or about herself. Then she lifted up the lid of the crib, kicked off her shoes and standing on the little step provided, she climbed in. He moved over for her and she slid in behind him, lowering the top down, and curled against his back with her arm around him.

Now Wendell felt his safety assured, and lying together thus, they both fell fast and peacefully asleep.

How long it was before he woke, he could not guess. It had been a blessed sleep, black without a hint of dreaming. He pushed himself over in the cramped space to face Lillian, who still slumbered soundly beside him. As he gazed at her lashes lying lightly upon pink cheeks, the red bow of her moistened mouth, and the soft rise and fall of her breast, a fierce passion came over him. Surely he could take her and once entered, her panic would subside and their lovemaking would be as it had always been – he had but to force the issue, persist until she could break through her resistance.

It was with excitement and some trepidation that he brought out his stiffened member from the slit provided in his asylum uniform. Lillian moved once and sighed as he carefully lifted her skirts. His heart pounded as he saw the prize through the slit in her pantaloons, so wet and inviting, so easy. Without touching her, he managed to maneuver himself for the plunge. Then with a prayer, he pushed himself into her, ignoring the sudden gasp and wheeze as her eyes flew open. She tried to push him off, struggling for breath.

"Breathe with me," he said in her ear, but she could not. Her eyes were wild with fear, and she was not managing any breath at all, nothing for him to breathe with. Alarmed, he was yet overcome by a convulsive urgency that forced him to continue – surely she would come through it. Now to his horror, her face was turning blue beneath him, and he was atop the bloated and suffering visage of his demon. For a moment, he thought he was strangling it, and the room's colors seemed to brighten while the muffled silence came upon him – the only thing he could hear was his heartbeat amplified in his head.

As the demon's eyes began to roll back, Wendell's trance abated. Horrified, he pushed himself off of her, forcing the lid of the crib up with his head, and shaking her by the shoulders. "Lillian!" he screamed through his deafness. "Lillian!" She was flopping about spasmodically like a fish thrown up on the beach. He threw open the crib top and jumped out, shouting for help.

Two male orderlies burst into the room and grabbed Wendell

by the arms, forcing him back toward the crib. They paused in confusion when they saw the limp body of Lillian there, her skirts still up and clearly ravished. "Hurry, she can't breathe," Wendell managed.

With practiced movements, they had her on the floor and were lifting her arms repeatedly above her head. At last she gasped and drew breath, pink flooding back into her face. Then they forced Wendell back into the crib and this time, they locked it.

Lillian was crying as she sat up. Her hand clutched at her throat. She was the picture of suffering when she looked at Wendell, then staggered to her feet and ran from the room.

Chapter 29

The next days were spent in drugged stupor. Wendell was only occasionally allowed out of his cage, and no one came to visit. He had heard stories that people once confined were unable ever to get out. He didn't deserve to get out. He was mortified at what he had done. More than that, he had lost Lillian, finally and irrevocably forever – he was sure of it.

The door opened and Catherine walked in with Dr. Gray, the alienist, and a tall well-attired dark gentleman whom Wendell recognized as someone he had known, but could not now place. After a moment of staring, he brightened with amazement and delight – Dr. Paschal Beverly Randolph, the magician in the Levant who sold him his magic mirror.

"Look whom I have brought with me, Little Deer! He has agreed to take you as a patient in return for some of the patent medicines in my cupboard."

"In truth, you are more an apprentice than a patient," offered Dr. Randolph. He thrust out his hand, then seeing Wendell's hand missing, flushed and lowered it. "It is my delight to meet you again," he said.

"Thank you so much for coming, Doctor Randolph. I can think of no one else who could offer me such hope, for indeed it will take magic. I knew 'twas an omen when Miss Flax brought the magic mirror back to me."

Beside Randolph, Dr. Gray shook his head uncertainly, perhaps frightened by the magician's mysterious prescription and exotic dark complexion.

"Dr. Randolph, up till now, I had not seen fit to question your credentials," said Dr. Gray, "But I must confess that all this talk of magic unsettles me. It is unusual enough to release a patient to another's care – particularly a patient with extreme delusions and proclivity to violence."

Now the magnificent Dr. Randolph, with strong and dignified bearing, worked his magic on the alienist. "Let me assure you, Dr. Gray, of not only my credentials, but of my vast experience with patients such as Mr. Parry," he said, his voice deep and resonant. "While you may quibble with the unscientific sound of the word 'magic', surely you are Christian, and it is important that my patients see me as able to work God's magic on their behalf. As Mr. Parry has just attested, he had been otherwise left without hope."

"Well," considered Dr. Gray, "If the family is agreed to release this asylum from liability…"

"Of course we will," said Catherine, proud of her part in it.

Wendell had not been sure he wanted to come home – he had felt safe in his crib. Dr. Randolph had left him with instructions to take the patent medicine if needed to calm himself, and begin again his nightly rituals with the magic mirror. But the magic mirror gave him only Lillian's image, terrified, gasping beneath him like a fish. He wrote letter after letter full of long apologies, begging her to at least remember him fondly. He assumed she was now nursing troops in Washington City and he sent to the hospitals there, but heard nothing from her. She must hate him.

He soon stopped writing, and upped his dose of the patent medicine, which rendered a muffled stupor in which he could keep his demon always hovering at a safe distance, unable to catch him unaware. Vacillating between ecstatic relief and unbearable remorse at the demon's apparent suffering, Wendell kept a wary eye on him, afraid to take his attention away even for a moment. He felt connected to this demon, and to nothing else. Conversations bypassed his comprehension and interest – most of the time he was unaware of the people around him except to step out of their way, or to go through the motions of sitting and eating with them.

The summer heat was oppressive. Wendell was now known about town as a violent lunatic, a crazed casualty of the war. When he went with his father to the tavern, the men seemed to shy away from him in fear and awkwardness. Seneca Sue unabashedly ran.

He often thought he might take his life and thus end his misery – indeed, he knew Catherine was worried for it. The ghost was always hovering just at the edge of his vision. Their small hope was that Dr. Randolph would work his magic, in return for some of the medicine in Catherine's amply stocked cupboard. But the doctor was a busy man and they were full into the harvest when he finally appeared in the yard, wearing a top-hat and astride a handsome horse.

"Mr. Parry," he greeted him, surprised when Wendell extended his beautifully carved hand. "Your hair and beard are back. And a wooden hand – it is quite agreeably shakable."

"Thank you," Wendell flushed, "I am fond of it."

Lodging for Dr. Randolph had been found with a parishioner of the little temple, the same that had cared for his now estranged wife and child. Catherine prepared a nice meal in her father's house, and over supper, the war's progress was discussed around the small kitchen table.

"The war was supposed to be over quickly, yet Washington is still besieged," rued Randolph. "The South's new commander, General Lee, that same blasted man who stopped John Brown, is more capable even than the wounded Johnston. Once again, our forces are pushed back to Washington from Bull Run."

Mention of Bull Run penetrated Wendell's stupor.

"Merde à l'enfer!" Wendell swore, "It's where we started a year ago!" The idea that Sam would be dead for nothing was almost too much. A fierce sadness welled up in his chest, pushing through the haze of his medicine. Suddenly he blurted, "I must return to what's left of my regiment." Tears sprang to his eyes and

he grabbed for his father's brandy bottle with his wooden hand, knocking it over into Catherine's dinner, splashing her dress with vile alcohol and gravy.

There was an embarrassed silence, broken when Catherine stood abruptly and cried, "Go back to your regiment, Wendell? What good would you be, you can't even eat your supper!"

"I am sorry," said Randolph, standing in respect to the lady. "It was insensitive to speak of the war. Please forgive me." The other men stood as well, and helped Catherine clear the table. The dinner was clearly over. The men then left her with the dishes and retired to the front yard for a smoke. Feeling a pall from his continued presence, Wendell excused himself and went to his room where he retrieved a bottle of brandy from under his bed, and proceeded to drink until he fell back against the pillow, his eyes closing helplessly into whatever hell he might descend.

The next day, Wendell met alone with the doctor in Catherine's cabin. As per instructions, he had brought the magic mirror. The magician lamented over the mirror's crack, but was not as angry as Wendell had feared. "'Tis a shame and a lesson for you," said the doctor kindly. "The magnetic force has escaped and the mirror is quite useless. As the mirror was consecrated to your painting, its crack is not unrelated to the loss of that art."

Wendell was silent, remembering. The ritual had been sexual – he had been roused to ecstasy by nine masked and dancing virgins, said to be the nine Muses, who all gave thanks with him at the climactic moment for his vision in the mirror – the vision of himself as a famous artist.

"Do you mean," said Wendell incredulous, "that I might not have lost my hand had I not first cracked the mirror?"

"It matters not that you cracked the mirror first – there is no before and after on the spirit plane," answered the doctor. "There is only your intention, and of that I am not privy. In any case, we shall have to get by without it." Wendell took this to mean his hand, then realized he meant the mirror.

He went on, "As for your demon, Mr. Parry, I have skryed my own mirror and believe that a simple ritual will put it to rest. It seems the poor devil is afraid of you, and must be assured that you and he are no longer locked in battle. At the fullness of the harvest moon, we will do what we can about it." Wendell was exceedingly grateful, and realized that the doctor was the first person he had actually felt a connection with since his release from the asylum. He didn't feel normal, for he no longer remembered what normal was, but he didn't feel crazy. The demon was not hovering, and seemed for a moment to be gone entirely.

"In the meantime, I recommend that you cease taking the patent medicine," continued the magician, putting on his top hat and giving it a thump. He held out his hand and shook Wendell's wooden one, his other hand grasping Wendell's forearm warmly. "And consume no alcohol. I will see you soon."

As the summer continued, so too did this new feeling of calm. Wendell became better adapted to using his left hand, and a much better help about the farm. He even found more uses for the wooden hand, and marveled at what a clever curve Thomas had made between thumb and fingers. For a time, the whole family settled into a pleasant routine. Seneca Sue began a hesitant acquaintance and the elder Harte drank less.

Wendell's determination grew that he would find Lillian and bring her to Dr. Randolph to be cured of her asthma. As though fated, a letter arrived from Sanford Gifford saying that his regiment had been recalled till September; if he survived, he would be with Fred Church in the Hudson River Valley till January – meanwhile, Wendell could use his room. As soon as Wendell's appointment with Dr. Randolph was complete, Wendell would leave for the city, and try to find work and Lillian's whereabouts. The world seemed suddenly brighter.

Now the crops were almost in, and the large harvest moon was at its full. Wendell saw the doctor's horse in the front yard and approached the door eagerly. He was about to enter the house when he paused at raised voices coming from the kitchen.

"You have spent naught but short days with him," Catherine was protesting, "certainly not worth that much of my cupboard's stock."

"Why is it that you of the white race always see fit to diminish my value," the magician was saying. "I, who have brought the Rosy Cross to America. I, who have counseled Emperor Napoleon and Queen Victoria, who performed séances for Mrs. Lincoln when her son died! There is no one, no saint even in the Orient, that can do what I do. You had promised me more, and I have spent considerable for tonight's magical effects!"

Catherine spoke with vehemence, "You would clean out my cupboard and leave me bereft, who helped your wife and child?! And just so you can make a better show of it, Paschal?"

"Showmanship is vital to magic. You know that," retorted the doctor, his voice rising.

Catherine was adamant. "You have ever suffered from the sin of pride. You forget that I am as great a part Indian as you are African, and I, too, am worth more than I am paid. It's the nature of the spirit business. But I will not fall victim to a spendthrift."

"Then I have done enough, Miss Parry. He is your brother – you rid him of his demon! I am done with you!"

Wendell stood before the door, his heart slamming as the doctor wrenched it open, Catherine shouting after him, "What I did for your wife should count for something!"

Wendell was blocking his path, and saw the wrath and humiliation in the doctor's eyes. "Please, Doctor, please. I beg you, let me talk to her."

"Yes, talk to her," Randolph said with sarcasm, giving his top hat a thump and heading around Wendell to his horse, "I leave you in her capable hands." With surprising athleticism, he bolted onto his steed, and spurred the animal down the road, scattering the chickens and leaving Wendell alone in the yard with sinking unease.

The wind, which had been blowing noisily, paused as if muffled, and the chickens opened their beaks, but no sounds came. Wendell looked around him into the sudden quiet, and saw his demon quite clearly, leaning against the fence. It was there but a moment, then vanished, and the sounds of the wind and the clucking in the little farmyard resumed their normality. Wendell's disquiet deepened. He then determined to leave for the city as soon as he could pack.

He had not many possessions now, a steamer trunk full and a carpet bag. Wendell sat down with Harte for a final breakfast.

"So, you're leaving me here with the vixens, are you?" muttered Harte, full of drink and self-pity.

"Father," Wendell said, placing his hand gently on Harte's arm, "you must find yourself a wife. A man drinks when he has no wife, and you do surely drink too much."

"It's my toes hurt. That's why I drink. I know they're missing, but they hurt all the same. Seems like they'd stop by now, but instead they just get worse."

"I know," said Wendell sympathetically, for he had felt the same in his missing hand, "but I'm sure they would hurt less if you at least were courting a lady." He was speaking for himself, and felt at one with his father as loneliness played across the older man's features and his jaw trembled.

"I will assuredly wind up in the almshouse," Harte lamented. "The banks'll take the farm soon enough. Family used to take care of family, but the corporations are set on driving able-bodied folks into factories, while the government offers almshouses for the rest of us. Hell, I expect that's where you'll be working, in a factory, if you can work at all."

Wendell sighed with resignation. "Aye," he said, "or mayhap I'll join you at the almshouse," and thought to himself, 'So long as it's not a madhouse.'

Wendell cleared the table, then the two men took the luggage to the buckboard. He went to the chicken house to say a brief goodbye to Sue. A lingering farewell to the tearful Harte was tendered in the front yard as Catherine waited in the wagon to drive Wendell to the train station. It had been more than a year since Catherine and Lillian had brought him home from the war.

Wendell was sullen as he sat by his sister, not having made his peace with her treatment of Doctor Randolph. He had never mentioned the pension checks, but had helped himself freely to the patent medicine in the cabinet and secreted jars of it in his trunk.

The medium, Catherine Cayuga, easily read his mood about the magician. "Fie, Little Deer," she chided, "Paschal spends money he needn't, to make an unnecessary show of it. He told you your demon fears you. Next time you see it, speak to it with reassuring words."

Wendell did not reply. It was hard for him to think charitably of the demon who had killed Sam and speared his hand, and whose death grip he could feel, even now, about his neck. Catherine sighed. "It's up to you," she said.

Finally Wendell spoke. "Randolph is a Sex Magician, Catherine. I have no other hope for Lillian and me. Pray, tell me where I might find him."

"If you must, he keeps an address in Utica."

As they stood upon the platform waiting the train, Wendell was suddenly sad for his hard feelings. Indeed, if he owed a debt to his sister before, he owed her more than that now. "Catherine," he said, "so help me God, someday I will make you glad you have sacrificed so much for my sake. I do truly thank you for it."

Her eyes flooded with tears. "Your thanks means more to me than any reward, Little Deer."

When the train came, they were still locked in close embrace upon the platform.

Chapter 30

When Wendell arrived at Sanford Gifford's atelier, the news spread quickly. Soon the artists were gathered in Sanford's room, clamoring for an account of the war and Wendell's injury. Wendell was happy to see Mr. and Mrs. McEntee, Leutze, Bierstadt, and Whittredge. Durand dropped by and even George the concierge crowded in along with Mrs. Winter. Sorely missed were Sanford and Thomas – and especially Ted Winthrop. Also absent were the Creole Louis Mignot who had moved to London, and Fred Church who was with his new wife in the Hudson River Valley. Wendell felt Anna Mary's absence, and acutely, Lillian's.

With great respect, the artists listened to Wendell movingly recount his last meeting with Ted, and the circumstances of Sam's death. They admired the hand Thomas had made for him, and over and over worried what he would do now he couldn't paint. Some offered to have him act as their agent, but soon saw this held no interest for him. Finally, to allay their concerns, Wendell ventured, "I am trained in photography. Mayhap Mathew Brady's studio will have something for me to do." He had said it without thinking, but now found the idea had great appeal, and even hope in it.

Finally alone to settle in, surrounded by Sanford's soaring peaks and luminous vistas, he sat on the bed and felt overwhelmed with nostalgia. Just then Cat came in, and rubbed himself against his legs. Wendell laughed and greeted him, "Ah," he said, "Now I'm home." His dreams that night were a confusion of packing and moving, but not unpleasant.

The next day, Mathew greeted him heartily and was happy to let him lend a hand, if not two. Brady was in dire need of more help. Glass plate negatives had piled up, ready to make albumen prints for display and the handful of men he employed could not keep up. Wendell eagerly pitched in, and proved slow but careful, a good craftsman. His work was appreciated, but alas, Brady could not now afford to pay him. Brady wrote Wendell's hours down in a ledger and promised to pay him when he should secure further funding for his project.

Wendell urgently wished for news of Lillian. He must see Fitzhugh. Not only would Fitzhugh know Lillian's whereabouts, but he would understand more than anyone how real was Wendell's demon, which only a morning glass of whiskey and a few draughts at night now kept at bay. Fitzhugh would not think him mad.

At last, Wendell caught the gang gathered in the alcove at Pfaff's. It was as if time had stood still for them and nothing had changed. Fitzhugh and Rosalie were both there, she blowing bubbles from her clay pipe, while next to her, Henry Clapp smoked his wooden pipe. Tom Aldrich sat beside a lady named Lil Woodman who was evidently besotted with him, and the newly wedded Bob Newell and Adah Isaacs Menken sat next to Ada Clare and Aubrey. Macaroni was in military uniform, and quite out of order with drink. Walt Whitman sat in his accustomed chair and waved a hand. The whole gang, save Fitzhugh, were nonchalant at seeing Wendell, raising a mug in greeting as if they had seen him just yesterday instead of a year and a quarter ago. But Fitzhugh stood at Wendell's approach and wordlessly grabbed him in a bear-hug, shaking and clinging like a child. Wendell understood his feelings and was silently moved.

"I am finally fed and clothed at government expense," laughed Macaroni in explanation of his uniform. "I have been stationed at a day job in Staten Island, but should the Rebs attack, I'm prepared to desert."

"What's your day job?" Wendell inquired.

"Getting drunk and writing poetry," replied he, and launched into his latest:

"A harmless fellow, wasting useless days
Am I: I love my comfort and my leisure.
Let those who wish them, toil for gold and praise,
To me, this summer-day brings more pleasure."

The bohemians laughed and Wendell said, "Ah, 'tis good to be home and find everything the same." Everyone raised a tankard and drummed on the table.

Wendell congratulated the Menken and Bob Newell. She laughed, self-satisfied, "You missed my show last week in the Bowery," she said. "I did creditable impressions of Edwin Booth and Horace Greeley, plus a spoof on my famous scene from *Mazeppa*." She rose then and before their eyes, transformed herself to Edwin Booth, and with somber baritone implored her upraised hand, "Alas, poor Yorick. I knew him, Horatio. He was fatter then, as I remember."

Wendell laughed, grateful that this small enclave was so untouched by war.

Aldrich looked up from his newspaper and stared wondering at Wendell. "Well," he said finally, "I believe you're the only one who hasn't heard my account of your demise at Bull Run. And I suspect you don't want to."

"Indeed," agreed Wendell, "I have dwelled enough on it. But what is this talk I hear of a draft? Would not that affect all of you? Henry?"

Clapp looked at him. "Some of my poverty comes from saving money to buy my way out should it come. I hear it may cost upwards of $300."

"Hah! That is nothing less than an outrage!" cried Fitzhugh, standing suddenly and beating his fist on the table. "It's not fair that the rich buy their way out while the poor must always pay dearly!"

"And if you are drafted, Ludlow, will you pay their price or will you go?" asked the cynical Clapp.

"I will take Greeley's advice and be long gone to the West," declared Fitzhugh, reseating himself.

Now for the first time, Rosalie spoke up. "But who is to fight this war? Now that it is started and the Emancipation about to be declared, should we not win it? I would hate to think of Sam and Ted dying for naught – or John Brown and his men."

"But how is war not coercion?" argued Clapp. "Has it not been the bohemian motto that we abhor coercion in any form?"

The Menken spoke up. "Fie! Slavery is coercion! Of the worst sort! How, Henry, can you square that?"

"Some things cannot be squared, Adah," he answered with genuine sincerity. "I don't condemn the war. But if you have a principle that you yourself should not coerce, then you must live by it, as do the Quakers."

"It seems" said Bob Newell, looking for the irony, "that you would coerce yourself into following your principles, even against your own heart."

"Once one begins to coerce," responded Clapp, "it does not just stop. Once coercive, coercion becomes habit."

No one responded and Wendell addressed Aldrich, "It's been awhile since I've heard news from Europe."

"Yes. Either Europe is extraordinarily quiet, or the papers are ignoring the rest of the world."

Fitzhugh added sardonically, "America is the world. Its war is all that exists – there isn't anything else."

"Indeed," said Clapp. "Even Marx, the Tribune's London correspondent, writes of the American war. He congratulates the British textile workers that, despite their severe suffering from the cotton blockade, they will not be used as excuse for Britain to come into the war on the side of slavery."

"Bravo for the British Worker!" said Wendell.

Clapp went on, "Even the London banks agitate for war against

Lincoln. He turned down their usurious loan offers and issued the debt-free greenback instead, which is backed by nothing but a green back!"

"Ha ha," laughed Fitzhugh. "I and everyone else have accepted the new currency without a second thought."

Announcing her need to depart for Aubrey's sake, Ada Clare stood, the signal for the rest of the women to depart with her. Rosalie and Adah Menken happily abandoned their menfolk, and flounced toward the door, skirts held high. The sight brought a pang of longing to Wendell, who remembered suddenly the acceptance he had felt among this group and his first kiss with Lillian. He wondered if he would ever again feel that he belonged somewhere.

His reverie was interrupted by a tug on the sleeve. "Come," said Fitzhugh, "Visit with me awhile."

As they walked out onto busy Broadway, Wendell asked why the city seemed to be thriving even while the nation suffered. Fitzhugh laughed and gave his shoulders a shrug. "New York grows rich from supplying the war, both sides of it where it can. As Karl Marx said, the bourgeoisie will sell the proletariat even the weapons with which to fight against them."

Deep in thought about the state of mankind, they reached the house at Waverly Place and entered in silence. Fitzhugh went to the cabinet and pulled a large hookah down, and set it on the kitchen table. Wendell sat opposite his friend, looking eagerly at the exotic pipe filled with bubbling water. Fitzhugh expertly puffed, coaxing the coals to life beneath his match. Hasheesh smoke curled around the ornate bowl, catching the light as it floated upward.

Wendell puffed on the stem of one snake-like hose and met Fitzhugh's softening gaze. All thoughts of not belonging began to drift away. No words passed between them, nor were words necessary. Wendell summoned his nemesis, to have a look at him, and when it appeared at a safe distance, Fitzhugh seemed to see it too, and smiled. Something in the smile struck Wendell as absurdly funny, and soon both men were laughing together merrily. The nemesis slunk away in seeming embarrassment, which was funnier still and they laughed the louder. Other funny visions arose between them, till their breath was almost gone in laughter and smoke. In this way the two friends passed the afternoon together, with not a care in the world.

As the sun sank into evening and the effects of the hookah wore off, Fitzhugh began to fret that Rosalie had not returned home. He bade Wendell stay when Henry Clapp and Macaroni returned, and the men scrounged a meal together along with some wine. The conversation turned to Edwin Booth, now back from Europe – Fitzhugh and Rosalie had been invited to join Molly Booth in her private box for *Hamlet* tonight. "If Rosalie does not show up soon, Wendell, I will ask you to go in her stead." The other men looked at each other, and Wendell surmised it would not be the first time Rosalie had been late, perhaps waylaid by Albert Bierstadt.

Wendell was so glad to be going to the theater with Fitzhugh that he almost forgot to feel badly for his friend's marital woes. Fitzhugh, too, found pleasure in his friend's company, and they had no trouble making a fine evening of it. They were especially pleased to find Tom Aldrich and his new friend Lil in the elegant box with the pretty and delicate Mrs. Booth. She was sitting next to her husband, who seemed not at all concerned that the curtain below would soon rise. Ned stood as they entered, looking especially handsome in his short tunic and sandal-laced legs.

The usually shy Booth was effusive in his greeting – his studied gestures and compelling expressions exuded a warmth to match his magnificent voice. "Parry! I had heard tidings of you! I hear you have a new hand crafted perfectly for shaking," and gripped Wendell's wooden hand while he also grasped his arm. A faint smell of alcohol exuded from his gently rouged lips. "You're looking quite well for a specter. Tom here had pronounced you dead some time ago." He turned toward his lovely wife, gesturing broadly. "Darling, this is Mr. Wendell Parry, the artist who limned the landscape Lillian sold us for our parlor, the same whom Tom had pronounced dead at Bull Run! He is by some miracle here in the flesh. Wendell, my wife, Mary Devlin."

Wendell bowed and offered the back of his wooden hand for her hand to rest on, which he swept gracefully to his lips. "Charmed," he smiled as he kissed it.

"Ned is too liberal, Mr. Parry. Please, I am Mrs. Booth, and you may call me Molly."

Fitzhugh offered a weak apology for Rosalie's absence. "Well then, Wendell can sit next to me," said Molly brightly, "and listen to me mouth all of Ned's lines."

Ned excused himself and Wendell sat next to Molly Booth as the house lights dimmed, and the curtain rose above a vast and sumptuous set, a veritable painting. 'Smalt, cobalt violet, aureolin, prussian blue,' painted Wendell in his head, feeling quite himself again – he especially appreciated the flashes of vermillion in the rich costumes. The audience sat rapt, as they would for a fine orchestra, not at all like the rowdy crowds he'd seen at other Shakespeare plays. Ned had reinvented Shakespeare's tragedy to be appreciated as fine literature and poetry. Wendell rather suspected Molly's part in that, and settled down for an evening of high culture.

As Molly mouthed the lines along with her husband, Wendell was swept away into the magic of another world. Ned's Hamlet was a complicated, nuanced man who drew his viewers into his agonizing dilemma and broke their hearts. Through four full hours, no one breathed save Molly Booth and the actors onstage. When the lights went up, grown men were weeping.

Wendell had been in the city a week, and his most dreaded responsibility could no longer be avoided. He announced his presence to Elizabeth, and asked if she would like to accompany him to Brooklyn to visit Sam's grave. She had not seen Wendell since he'd left for the war with her husband, and almost fainted when he stood suddenly at her door. "Seeing you here is like it were yesteryear, and my dear Sam still alive!" she cried, and gave him a most immodest and heart-felt hug.

Indian summer had all but ended as they made their way by carriage to the ferry where a chill wind warned of an early winter. Elizabeth, in veiled black mourning, cuddled her small son in her lap, staring with wonder all the while at Wendell, as if trying to see her husband's last moments on his face. In Brooklyn, their carriage picked up Sam's parents and Grammy, who were eager for the outing and surprised to see him, too – they poked at him like Doubting Thomases that Wendell was real and resurrected. The two older ladies were also dressed in mourning, though unveiled. They were quiet as the carriage rumbled across cobblestones past the blustery south bay where they could look out beyond the Battery and see New Jersey. Finally their cab turned away from the water and entered beneath the soaring spirals of the Green-wood Cemetery Gate.

It was a vast and serene park-like setting in which Sam had been laid to rest under a small gravestone in the family plot. As the women placed flowers and murmured their greetings, Wendell felt that same muffled quiet come upon him, where the wind stopped and the women's mouths moved but no sound came. He looked up and saw the demon, more pitiable than grotesque, a young man with straggly hairs trying to be a beard, staring at him from across the little headstone, struggling to breathe and turning blue. "Talk to it," Catherine had said.

'I don't know what to say to you,' he thought.

The demon's respirations grew loud inside Wendell's head and

Wendell heard words echo between his ears, 'We are both of us damned.' Then it disappeared and the sounds of the cemetery returned. Wendell shivered and, feeling suddenly nauseous, excused himself to sit beneath a tree and wait.

When they had finished their prayers, Mrs. Stockard came to him and bent over to feel his brow. "How are you?" she asked, filled with concern.

"I admit, it's hard being here. I would prefer to be in my bed."

"And not come to dinner?"

"Alas, Mrs. Stockard, you know it's not lightly I would miss such comfort. But right now, I truly want to be alone in Sanford's atelier."

By now the other Stockards had joined her and were shaking their heads. "My boy, you look poorly. Are you safe to journey back by yourself?" Wendell nodded and staggered to his feet.

Mr. Stockard gripped Wendell's wooden hand with his two in a warm embrace. "My son is at rest," he said quietly, "but you are my other son – it's for you I am concerned."

Wendell was moved. "Believe me, sir," he said, "I am better now than I had been."

Mr. Stockard shook his head in sympathy. "I was far from well when I returned from the Mexican war. 'Twas having a family that saved me. Would you not like to stay with us awhile? Miss Margaret is yet unclaimed."

Wendell shook his head. The thought of a woman other than Lillian stabbed at his heart – he could not abandon Lillian to live her life untouched, unable to breathe. Somehow he must find her, and bring her to Dr. Randolph.

After receiving assurance that Elizabeth and young Sam were in good hands, Wendell took his leave. And then, for reasons he could not pin-point, he had the carriage drive past Ferguson's sentry-guarded mansion.

Chapter 31

Wendell had acquired Lillian's Washington address and as he sat at Sanford's desk intent on writing her, he was not sure what to say. She had not responded to his prior entreaties. Finally he penned only, *"Lillian, I am in New York. I miss you. Pray do not fear me – I have learned my lesson. You will always and forever be my only love. Wendell."* He also wrote a letter to Paschal Beverly Randolph in Utica, begging his help for Lillian.

Wendell now worked regularly at Brady's studio, mesmerized by the ghosts of soldiers that slowly emerged beneath the glass negatives. No matter whether the sun was bright or faint, he had a knack for stopping the exposure at just the right place for the perfect print, and so wasted very little of the precious albumen-treated paper. He could tell that Mathew was happy with his work and was delighted to help Mathew set up a display of images from Antietam in his elegant new gallery. While the battle at Antietam had actually stopped the South and saved the capital, the numbers of war dead from both sides were staggering. Mathew was intent on showing the reality of war, hoping that the shock of such visceral pictures would somehow persuade a settlement. If nothing else, it would be the first thorough pictorial documentation – he had scores of Gardner's extraordinary photographs.

The show itself seemed modest in its billing, just a sign on the gallery door advertised it, but it was an overwhelming success. Wendell watched the viewers stream in, week after week, and rather than find the images repellent, they stood riveted for hours, gazing at the small black and white prints and staring through stereoscopes to see the war in three dimensions. At first, this was amazing to Wendell and to Brady, but then both men knew first hand the addictiveness of battle, the compulsion to understand this thing called death by having it close and sudden.

Wendell felt esteemed working for Brady, and was grateful for the job. Though most of his pay was delayed and promised, he did receive small amounts of cash. The free accommodations in Sanford's atelier made it possible to survive on such meager wages, along with the occasional sale of an old painting from Elizabeth's attic. Asher Durand continued to display the Ithaca paintings at the Academy of Design.

When Wendell wasn't working, he drank at Pfaff's with Clapp and Macaroni, or imbibed hasheesh at Waverly Place, smoking with Fitzhugh. He frequently drank fine wine to excess with Ned, who seemed to have taken a liking to him, joined by Molly, Tom and Lil at the restaurant below Ned's apartment on 5th Avenue. The only friend Wendell was temperate with was Walt Whitman, who engaged Wendell in deep conversation about Lillian, and Walt's own unrequited love. Walt was careful not to mention gender, but Wendell suspected that the object of Walt's affection was a man.

In many ways now, Wendell felt at peace. Only occasionally did he awaken to a full battle or see his demon lurking in the shadows. At such times, he drank heavily, and thus kept his nemesis at bay, though the absence of any letter from either Lillian or Dr. Randolph increased his apprehension that it might yet return.

As the holidays approached, Wendell regularly received invitations to join Molly and her other guests in the Booth theater box and the small after-theater parties at their apartment. Here, Molly would retire to tend the baby while Edwin unwound, promising her not to drink "too much," then winking as either Tom or Wendell pulled a bottle out of his coat. Ned was fun to drink with, and Wendell would go into paroxysms of laughter as Ned mimicked characters he had seen on the streets, or they all played out scenes in books they were reading.

Just before Thanksgiving, Ned pulled Wendell aside and promised a surprise should he come for a small dinner party. With anticipation, Wendell entered the modestly elegant hotel, where the

Booths maintained their now familiar apartments, and went up the stairs to the third floor. Ned answered his knock. After he shook Wendell's wooden hand effusively, Molly took Wendell's hands in both of hers and offered warm thanks for his coming. She had a look of mischief about her, and Wendell wondered why, hoping it hadn't to do with Margaret – he was not yet ready for that. The Booths were known for playing cupid; indeed, it had been they who had introduced Tom to Lil Woodman. As Molly turned to lead him into the well-appointed and already merry salon, there was another knock at the front door.

"Ah, Lillian, it's been too long," Wendell heard Ned say, and spun around to see her thin smile straining beneath a blotched complexion. She wore a spinsterly dress, long-sleeved and buttoned to the neck. Ned bowed over Lillian's hand to kiss it, then tenderly untied her bonnet and hung it by the door. As Molly approached to greet her, Lillian looked up at Wendell, who was standing with his mouth hung open and his heart slamming. She gave a curt nod and held out her hand to him.

Wendell pressed it carefully to his lips, searching her eyes – he saw the deepest sorrow and longing in them. Silently, she hooked her arm through his proffered elbow and they followed Molly into the sitting room and took their separate seats around a handsome bear rug where Molly's greyhound posed before a fire. A painting of the Hudson River, limned by Wendell, hung over the mantle. Lillian was quickly surrounded by her old friends, becoming the center of attention, and Wendell hoped that Margaret wasn't coming. Feeling suddenly shy, he downed his drink and asked for another. Finally Lillian rose and disappeared with Molly into the kitchen.

Fitzhugh nodded to Wendell from where he stood, his eyebrow arched curiously, leaning against the bookcase with his glass and hovering possessively over the seated Rosalie. She too nodded hello, blowing bubbles through her pipe and pretending not to notice the rather loud Albert Bierstadt, who had arrived unescorted.

Laura Keene came over and greeted Wendell warmly – she had not seen him since his return. "Yes," she said to questions about her demised theater, "I will be touring with my company, doing *My American Cousin* for a thousand nights! Literally, a thousand nights! I will be acting again! The final night will be at Ford's Theater in Washington City." She seemed quite pleased with the arrangement.

Thomas Bailey Aldrich came by to greet him, looking flushed and boyish, with his new fiancée in tow – Lil Woodman occupied the apartments across the hall and had become close friends with Molly. Rounding out the small gathering were the McEntees.

Lillian returned to her seat. To Wendell's relief and heartbreak, she kept her sad viridian eyes carefully averted the whole time. Finally, Ned held sway and after ascertaining that everyone had a drink, proposed a toast to the gallant men of the Union war effort, commemorating their dead friends, and thanking Wendell personally for his service. "Hip hoorays" were offered, then Wendell remarked that Lillian had contributed, and Tom Aldrich, prompting another cheer for the brave nurses, reporters, artists and photographers who daily leant support. Laura reminded them of the women at home, taking up the work, and keeping watchful prayers till their men returned or didn't. They were in the midst of a cheer for the women when there came another knock at the door and Ned's brother, John Wilkes Booth, unexpectedly joined the party. All mention of the war died abruptly for the evening.

Ned greeted his brother warmly, and introduced him to the few he didn't know. As a famous actor, everyone knew who he was. Then Ned responded to Molly's entreaty to tell about the skull that was used in his plays.

"Yes, Ned," seconded Aldrich, "where does one get a skull to take upon the stage? Had you robbed a graveyard?" Ned picked up the skull, and leaned on the mantel to look at it, assuming for a moment the character of Hamlet. Then he began his narrative.

"The story of this skull is that my father, Junius Brutus Booth, was traveling with his players through cattle towns and mining towns, where there is yet little to read and less to entertain. I was with him, a mere boy, as his manager. In those remote regions, people are hard-pressed to quote Dickens and still have not heard of Hawthorne. Yet even those who can't read know by heart their Bible and their Shakespeare."

Having set the stage, Ned dramatized the scene in a most entertaining manner. "So when my father was playing a particular town, and came the townsfolk together to hang a horse thief, the condemned man was asked his final wish. 'Please,' said he, 'I should like as my last request to play upon the boards opposite the great actor, Junius Brutus Booth – in the role of Yorick.'" Everyone laughed as Ned concluded, "His request was granted, and so came my father by this skull."

"Imagine," said Laura Keene as the audience applauded appreciatively, "a common horse thief."

"Or an uncommon one," put in John Wilkes. "My father actually knew the horse thief, as he had been in jail with him in Louisville."

Ned smiled, still commanding center stage. "Wilkes has more fondness for the family's dirty linen than I have."

"This horse thief is doubtless the first in all history to actually petition for the role," Laura laughed. "'Twould be fun to put out a casting call for the part. Pity I didn't think of it when Henry Clapp had his amusing paper."

Molly Booth picked up her guitar, and the guests all sang along with her and Ned, though quietly, as Molly and Ned together provided the sweetest voices.

While the host and hostess went to the kitchen to ready the food, Gertrude McEntee sat down at the piano. Tom Aldrich disappeared with his new love behind a diaphanous curtain. The others gathered around John Wilkes or Laura Keene, inquiring as to their recent adventures. Everyone was drinking rather heavily, and many in the group were tempted to do a turn as Hamlet opposite the hapless horse thief. The variations on "Alas, poor Yorick," leant endless hilarity, some mimicking Ned, some mimicking the Menken mimicking Ned.

Lillian was obviously tipsy, laughing hard and self-consciously, ignoring Wendell's gaze. Recklessly, she asked John Wilkes – whom papers had called the most handsome man in America – if he needed a Juliet to play opposite his Romeo. Wilkes took her hand with theatrical flourish and bowed low over it, swaying slightly from the effects of the alcohol. A wary Wendell joined the audience as Romeo's dark eyes looked meaningfully up at Juliet's and his lips brushed her fingers. Still holding her hand, he stood erect, and placing his other hand over his heart, spoke with such intensity of love that the ladies swooned with ecstasy.

"As daylight doth a lamp, her eyes in heaven would through the airy region stream so bright, that birds would sing and think it were not night." Then to the onlookers' great titillation and Wendell's horror, he reached out and pulled Lillian close, bending her back in passional embrace beyond anything that would happen on the stage, his lips planting themselves squarely on hers.

Surprised, Lillian at first resisted, and then began to wheeze. The actor let go with alarm and she twisted away, in the desperate throes of full blown asthma. Angst came over their audience, and she grabbed at Wendell's clothes as he caught her before she fell. "Breathe with me," he insisted urgently, and assumed her wheeze himself, bringing her quickly to rights, gasping and embarrassed.

"I am so sorry," she panted to everyone, and especially the thespian, "I get asthmatic at the most inconvenient times." Relieved, everyone joined in her laugh, and their hosts called them to the table.

Despite their smiles, Wendell and Lillian were both shaking.

Wendell sat at the table opposite the younger Booth who uncomfortably avoided his gaze. For a mad moment, Wendell envisioned strangling him.

But he soon forgot it as the food was good and the table merry. Now it was Fitzhugh who squirmed uncomfortably from the amorous glances of Bierstadt at Rosalie. Even Tom Aldrich, despite his new fiancée's presence, still seemed besotted with Fitzhugh's wife.

The dining was quite informal, with at-table readings of both literature and verse, and finally a call made to Tom Aldrich to recite the poem that made him famous, *Baby Bell.*

"When first I read it," said Laura, "I suspected a much older man had written it. Pray, where did you get your inspiration?"

The tipsiness of the gathering allowed him to squat upon his chair, and, with elbows propped on his knees, he answered, "A cold garret and an intense need to make some money." They all laughed knowingly.

"The muse loves a starving artist," said Wendell, and Tom began his recitation.

> *"Have you not heard the poets tell*
> *How came the dainty Baby Bell*
> *Into this world of ours?...*
> *She came and brought delicious May,*
> *The swallows built beneath the eaves;*
> *Like sunlight, in and out the leaves*
> *The robins went, the livelong day;...*
> *How sweetly, softly, twilight fell!*
> *O, earth was full of singing-birds*
> *And opening springtide flowers,*
> *When the dainty Baby Bell*
> *Came to this world of ours!"*

Tears had already sprung to young mother Molly Booth's eyes in anticipation of the poem's sad sentiments. Even that horridly handsome John Wilkes was moist of eye as the famous poem continued.

> *"...And for the love of those dear eyes,*
> *For love of her whom God led forth,*
> *(The mother's being ceased on earth*
> *When Baby came from Paradise,) —*
> *For love of Him who smote our lives,*
> *And woke the chords of joy and pain,*
> *We said, Dear Christ! — our hearts bent down*
> *Like violets after rain."*

Tom caught himself as, transported in his delivery, he almost fell off the chair. Lil Woodman watched him with adoration, and Bierstadt moved closer to Rosalie. After a pause, Tom went on, his voice quavering with emotion.

> *"...It came upon us by degrees,*
> *We saw its shadow ere it fell—*
> *The knowledge that our God had sent*
> *His messenger for Baby Bell.*
> *We shuddered with unlanguaged pain,*
> *And all our hopes were changed to fears,*
> *And all our thoughts ran into tears*
> *Like sunshine into rain.*
>
> *"We cried aloud in our belief,*
> *'O, smite us gently, gently, God!*
> *Teach us to bend and kiss the rod,*
> *And perfect grow through grief.'*
> *Ah! how we loved her, God can tell;*

Her heart was folded deep in ours.
Our hearts are broken, Baby Bell!"

By the end, only Laura Keene managed to keep a dry eye. There was silence, during which the women composed themselves and dabbed their faces. Suddenly, as the applause rose, Lillian got up and ran from the room. Wendell followed her to the couch where she was in the midst of another full-blown asthma attack, wheezing uncontrollably. He breathed with her until she calmed.

"What inspired this, Lillian? Did the poem upset you?" Wendell searched her fear-filled eyes, then returned with her to the dining room where the applause continued. Embarrassed at their own tears, the small audience had barely noticed the couple's absence.

Finally the evening came to an end. There was no discussion of where Lillian would go – she clung to Wendell's arm as they hurried along the sidewalk to the Tenth Street Studio Building.

Chapter 32

Once inside the atelier, Wendell shooed Cat out and turned on the gaslamp as Lillian sat heavily upon the bed, looking miserable.

"I would kill that John Wilkes Booth," cursed Wendell, "if history would not condemn me for it."

"Fie, Wendell," she admonished, "he was but playing."

"Lillian, why did the poem cause you to wheeze? Is your asthma grown worse?"

He waited. Eventually, the silence of the room pressed in. "The poem bothered me," her voice dropped to a whisper, "because I am barren. An abortion as consequence of the rape has rendered me so." She looked at him and held her breath, awaiting condemnation.

Again, the room grew quiet. The time lengthened. Wendell could almost hear his demon returning, hear him laughing through the gloom. Once again, visions of killing Ferguson flashed through his mind. He shivered, aware of the evening's creeping chill. Finally he said, with an edge to his voice, "Why hadn't you told me?"

Lillian stiffened and did not answer. Then he asked, as gently as he could, "Are you sure?"

She looked in his eyes. "Oh, Wendell," she wailed, and fell into his arms.

Wendell held her tight and cried with her for their loss. Soon their affections turned passional and she began against all her will to wheeze.

Reluctantly, he pulled away. "Nay, Lillian, we cannot." She sat down again upon the bed, and Wendell sat beside her.

They were quiet, each lost in thought as she struggled to catch her breath. "Are you sure you're barren?" he asked at length. "How do you know?"

"A judgement came upon me in the form of fever," she said, seeming glad for confession. "It lasted three days. The abortionist said the closing of the womb is certain in such cases." She sounded forlorn as she continued, "I didn't mean to deceive you. I had little hope then and less now that we can ever be passional with each other, so what did my sterility matter?" When she spoke again, shakily in the gaslight, it was of her deepest fear. "Despite that it was Ferguson's, I feel sorry now. I have destroyed my only chance at having a child." She was silent a moment, then added in a whisper, "I am a monster."

Those words. Had he not said the same of himself a thousand times? "I too have called myself that." His voice was barely able to escape him. "I took pleasure in killing," he confessed. "Nay, I reveled in it." He waited now for some nameless judgement to fall on him, then realized it was her judgement that he feared.

She shuddered. "You are not different from the other boys. They come in with entrails hanging out, limbs and faces missing, parts of torsos even, shaking and feverish and barely alive. Their suffering is excruciating. The papers all say how they miss home and family, and they do, but most wish to be back on the battlefield. I patch them up and send them out again, those that don't die." She hid her face in her hands. "Truly, I don't understand men. So brave and so silly."

She paused and he heard her whisper, "I came here to tell you, Wendell, you must find somebody new."

"No! Lillian!" he panicked. "Believe me, your childlessness is naught to me. I just want to be with you. Please, have faith, Lillian, this asthma will pass. I know a doctor, a Sex Magician, who can help us."

She looked at him with something akin to pity, and he guessed she still doubted his sanity. "A magician, Wendell? Will he cast spells and make us drink love potions?"

"He uses ritual mesmerism," Wendell insisted, feeling suddenly insecure in what he was saying. "He is the doctor who sold me my magic mirror."

Her look was indulgent. "Is he here in the city? May we see him tomorrow?"

Wendell had heard nothing from the doctor and shook his head sadly. Lillian placed her hand on his knee as if he were a child, urging his careful attention. "I don't much believe in magic, you know that. As you may imagine, I have been to every doctor who would see me for my asthma, and I have tried every folk remedy besides. Nothing helps." Her eyes were moist. She cleared her throat – what she was going to say was difficult. "Wendell, there is someone else who loves you. I have given her my blessing."

Wendell was stunned. "Margaret?" he asked, incredulous.

Now it was Lillian's turn to look stunned. "Margaret – who's Margaret?"

Wendell flushed and said quickly, clearing his throat, "Perhaps you don't know her. It's Elizabeth's sister – she cares for me, far more than I care for her." There followed an awkward silence.

"No, it's not Elizabeth's sister," said Lillian finally. "It's Ada Clare." The name struck him with pleasant surprise. He had not known Ada Clare liked him in that way.

Jealousy suddenly flashed across Lillian's green eyes and the look roused him dangerously. She went on hastily, ignoring the sparks that flew between them. "It's my small redemption, Wendell, that I don't cling to you unfairly when you can still find happiness with another. You once wanted me to be a wife and give you a family. Cursed am I that I didn't when I had the chance. Now you must seek what you want from another."

Wendell rose and loomed over her where she sat on the bed, the bulge in his trousers pointing at her like a pistol. "Fie, Lillian! It's you I want. You are more to me than either Ada or Margaret could ever be. When first I bed you, without dint of signature or ceremony, I held myself as married to you. For better and for worse, married to you! I don't want another."

He was breathing hard and she shrank from him, tears starting in her eyes. "What I say is true," Lillian cried. "You know it. With all your passional words, you stand before me wanting what I cannot give."

Wendell smacked the offending member, wincing in pain. "Truly, I will cut it off – what I want is to be with you. Lillian, I love you."

She covered her face, not daring to look at him. "Will you take me home now?" she begged, beginning to wheeze. "Please, it's not safe for me here."

Wendell's frustrated desire went dumb and damp. With effort, he calmed himself and submitted. "Where are you staying?" he asked reasonably.

Her look was pitiful. "At Ada Clare's," she said.

They were quiet in the carriage. When they arrived at Ada Clare's graceful home in the park by the reservoir, a cold sleet was descending. Wendell had the carriage wait as he helped her down and saw her to the door. "How long will you be in town?" he asked on the front porch.

"I must return to my duties tomorrow." There was a look of fierce determination about her as she added, "Wendell, don't feel sorry for me. I am needed in Washington. You," she faltered, "you wouldn't have believed the suffering Antietam brought. We are the fortunate ones, you and I. Please, you must accept it, it's over. I will not read your letters or see you again."

His heart fell to his feet as, with nary a backward glance, she went in and closed the door behind her.

When the sun rose, he was still in the bed, his arm hanging carelessly over the side. There was a ferocious pounding in his brain. He opened his eyes painfully and saw the daylight, along with slushy snow sliding down the window. He was becoming a drunk, he knew it. Wendell sighed and let his heavy lids droop closed – it was a day for sleeping in.

Before heading to Mathew Brady's studio, Wendell stopped in Pfaff's at Walt Whitman's table. He sat down quietly and waited to be acknowledged.

"Yes, I know," said Whitman kindly, looking up from his paper, "Lillian was here."

"My own demons have been considerable," Wendell explained, "yet with time they grow less troublesome." With time and with alcohol, he thought, but did not say it. "Will not Lillian's asthma also abate?"

"It's a question a young man could waste a lifetime trying to answer," advised Walt. "Do you know why Lot's wife crystallized into a pillar of salt?"

Wendell sighed as he grasped the point, "Because she looked back."

"Quite," said Whitman. "I know how it pains you, and indeed pains all of us who love you and Lillian. But yours is not the greatest tragedy in this war. Meanwhile, should you look ahead, you may find that the future is not so bleak." Whitman nodded toward the alcove where the bohemians were gathered in animated hilarity.

"Ada Clare?" asked Wendell. Walt nodded and, with an air of dismissal, went back to his reading.

Wendell rose and smiled woodenly towards the several at the alcove who had seen him, including Ada Clare. With a wave, he pushed out Pfaff's heavy door, and hastened up Broadway to Mathew Brady's 10th Street studio.

Brady was gone frequently, covering the war and managing his own massive army of photographers, working on all fronts. The other workers in Brady's studio knew Wendell well by now and appreciated his abilities. Even in their boss's absence, they designated work for the artist's careful eye. But Wendell had no permanent arrangement and worried constantly about his dearth of finances.

When Brady arrived back from Washington City, Wendell was greeted eagerly. "Mr. Parry, I've a pile of negatives for you! Indeed, they are so horrible and moving that once seen, the public will demand a quick end to this war." They went together to the darkroom where the pile loomed, threatening to fall over.

After a few moments of pleasantries, Brady left Wendell alone with the printing. The images revealed twisted wrecks of humans that lay in scattered pieces upon a familiar battlefield. Many of the distinctive uniforms, blood-soaked tatters blowing in the wind, were yet recognizable as his own regiment, the 14th Brooklyn. His stomach churned as he strained to see the faces. Was that one Joe? Harry? Was anyone still alive? He looked at the label – the pictures were from first Bull Run. Wendell felt like he was choking on the bile that rose in his throat. As he continued to print, his mind began reliving the battle, charging up the hill visible in this photograph, firing his first shot and seeing the ball hit its mark, just there beyond that tree where Frank had fallen, and he had turned to see Sam triumphant behind him. A strange elation came over him, and vengeful blood-lust burst his heart. "Brady!" he heard himself shout. "Brady!"

Mathew came running at the alarm, only to find Wendell ripping off his labcoat with transported anticipation. "I'm going back!" Wendell yelled excitedly, "I'm going back to the war. I'm going to rejoin my regiment!" His excitement bordered on a delirium. "I am sorry to leave you with so much work, but I must go, I must go now! I owe it to the men! I owe it to my country!" He did not mind at all that he might die, it would be a heroic and useful death. A pleasant picture formed in the back of his mind – when death came, he would be lying in Lillian's lap at the hospital in Washington.

Brady grabbed him by his arm and restrained his leaving. "My God, Wendell! You have but one hand! They won't take you back with a left hand!"

Wendell stopped in his tracks. For a moment, he had forgotten his dismemberment. Now the sudden remembrance jarred him, deflating his ecstasy. "Please," said Brady, "I need you here."

Wendell pressed his eyelids to force back the tears. "Hell," he said when he could contain himself, "I should have died instead of Sam." Brady suggested he take the rest of the day off.

At the atelier, Wendell threw himself on his back upon the bed and looked around at all of Sanford's paintings. He wanted to talk to someone, but felt not a lot in common anymore with the other artists who discussed commissions and luminosity and pigments. He missed Thomas.

There was a knock. "Letter for you, sir," called out George. At last, a reply from Dr. Randolph. Wendell opened it eagerly.

"My Dear Mr. Parry, I must apologize that my reply is so late in coming, but I have only now received your letter. I am in San Francisco bringing the Rosy Cross to such as will have it, and meeting with some small success. It is gratifying to be able to share my education and ideas with a receptive audience.

"I will not be returning to New York until early February, and have only a few days there before departing for Europe and the Orient. Might I assume that your sister's efforts on your behalf have proved inadequate? If so, I feel some remorse at having abandoned you to her. Therefore, with appropriate recompense, I will endeavor to fit you into my busy schedule. I will write again in January with precise details for our proposed meeting. A response from you is not now possible, as I am traveling. Yours Sincerely, Dr. P. B. Randolph"

There was another knock. It was John McEntee. "I have been instructed by Gertrude to bring you to dinner at our apartment and she won't take no for an answer." That and the letter were enough to put Wendell to rights again, and he happily let the kindly McEntee take him in hand. When they reached the apartment on the first floor, Wendell was grateful that Ned and Molly were there as well, and the conversation would not be solely about painting.

For the next days, Wendell worked long hours for Mathew Brady, avoiding Pfaff's and a possible meeting with Ada Clare. It wasn't that he was afraid of her, it was quite simply that he wasn't sure how he felt and, too, he needed to regain Brady's trust. For his part, Brady seemed not to doubt Wendell's sanity, but only to fear losing him for lack of payment.

On Thanksgiving, Wendell declined invitations to the Stockards' and Ada Clare's by pleading ill. Then he got drunk and went to bed.

The next day, Brady found him again at work in the darkroom. "Parry, I have a proposal for you," he said. Wendell fished the print out of its fix and gave Brady his attention. "Do you still want to rejoin your regiment?" Wendell nodded. "I'll be going with Gardner up the Rappahannock River where the Army of the Potomac is massing. I imagine the 14th Brooklyn is with them."

Wendell's heart leapt. He looked at Brady and waited for him to continue.

Mathew adjusted his spectacles. "When the army engages Lee, Timothy O'Sullivan and I will be there. I could pay you to print the resulting negatives. Most of my printing is being done in Washington and so will be less to do here." He paused and read Wendell's positive reaction before moving on. "And I would welcome you if you wanted to come with us as our field apprentice."

"Why yes," Wendell declared, all eagerness. "Where do I go?" He was poised to rip off his labcoat again and Brady laughed.

"Wait, there's more. In my Washington livery is a small itinerant's wagon with a decent horse. The wagon is set up for *cartes de visite*, with camera and portable darkroom. They're not much use to me and I could let you have them in settlement of my debt. It would be a chance to set yourself up."

"The whole rig including the horse?" Wendell was amazed.

"Precisely. And you could buy your plates and supplies through me at my discount."

"I don't believe I've ever had a more welcomed offer," said Wendell, overwhelmed with gratitude, "on both accounts. I would love to own the wagon and love to join you in the field as your apprentice."

"And Wendell," Brady said, clearing his throat. "the work you've done is greatly appreciated. I'd have been lost without you."

"Truly," admitted Wendell, "I'd have been lost without you, too."

Fortune was smiling on him at last. He was going to Washington. He would not only persuade Lillian to see the doctor, but eventually he would open his own studio and have a means of supporting her. Suddenly, he had everything to live for.

The next morning, he rose early for breakfast in the basement. The other artists were happy for his good fortune and insisted there was room in the building for photographers should he decide to return. Wendell was moved by this, and felt a deep nostalgia as he hailed his farewells. He left a long letter for Sanford, thanking him for use of the room, then he and George hefted his steamer trunk and carpet bags into a carriage which took him to Elizabeth's house. Wendell left the steamer trunk in her attic along with what was left of his paintings, then said goodbye to Elizabeth and Margaret. Here, too, he was cheered onward to his good fortune.

Next he caught Ned, Molly and the baby at breakfast with Lil Woodman and Tom Aldrich in the restaurant below their apartments. As Wendell entered, he noticed young women giggling outside, a common sight now wherever Ned went. Inside, an early Merry Christmas was wished to all, and entreaties to stay safe.

Lastly, Wendell took his carpet bag and walked the several blocks to Pfaff's, where he was lucky to find the bohemians gathered for midday conversation and carousing. "Harte, old chum," greeted Fitzhugh, "you've got your bags packed. Brady says you've signed on as his photographer."

"Yes," laughed Wendell, "It's better than that. I'm to have my own equipment and wagon – to own!" He seated himself and smiled fearlessly at Ada Clare.

"Alas," rued Clapp playfully. "Honest work has paid off, has it? Again, I have been proved wrong."

"I'm sure I'll prove you right yet," offered Wendell sympathetically, which evoked laughter and the pounding of mugs on the table.

Clapp handed him a limp sheath of the thinnest rubber Wendell had ever seen. "What's this?" asked Wendell perplexed. Everyone burst out laughing.

"What do you think it is?" asked Fitzhugh.

Wendell examined it a moment, noticing Ada Clare had averted her eyes as he did so. It suddenly occurred to him what it had to be, and he flushed rather than say it. Bob Newell spoke up. "'Tis a capote!" he explained. "Rather clever, don't you think?"

"Tsk, what would Mrs. Grundy say?" said Wendell, dropping it onto the table. "I trust it's not been used."

"Of course not," spoke Adah Menken, "we've been saving it for you and Ada!"

Wendell sucked in his breath as Ada Clare flushed deeply and swatted her friend's shoulder while the table roared. It would be too ungentlemanly for the men to say it, but they were delighted the Menken had.

"Fie on all of you!" shouted Ada Clare, standing and making an angry fist. The table quieted and everyone looked at her expectantly. "All I said to Lillian was I think Wendell handsome, and she has made all these fantasies about it." Wendell flushed while she paused, regaining some composure. "She knows Wendell wants a wife and I will never marry. I believe in her heart, she's trying to prevent him from marrying Margaret by arousing his interest in me." Here she looked at Wendell, her chin raised undaunted. "Of course, we all know, save that foolish Lillian, that he still loves her and will have no other."

"Who's Margaret?" asked Adah Menken, setting off another round of hilarity.

Wendell felt a flood of relief to have it all out in the open, and his heart leapt at Ada Clare's assessment of Lillian's motives. He was more than a little grateful to Ada, and in fact, he had to admit, he was truly fond of her.

By now, Walt Whitman had drawn up a chair and waited patiently for a chance to change the subject. "Parry," he said, seizing an opening, "You say you will be with the boys on the Rappahannock?"

Wendell nodded. Walt went on anxiously. "My brother George is a first lieutenant with the 51st New York. If you happen upon him, please, tell him how worried I and his mother are – it's been too long since he's written." The deep concern in Whitman's voice suddenly sobered the bohemians.

Wendell placed his left hand comfortingly on the older man's arm. "I surely hope your brother is alright. I will see to him as best I can."

Chapter 33

December 2nd found Wendell huddled in the chill beside photographer Timothy O'Sullivan against the railing of a military transport ship. A freezing mist rose off the placid Potomac against which the heated violence of the engines seemed incongruous. The chill bit through their lungs like ice daggers and Wendell expected that he, Timothy, and Mathew would have almost as rough going as the soldiers they would be photographing.

Wendell liked Timothy. He was soft-spoken, a man younger than himself, with reddish hair and a walrus mustache that hid his mouth but for the fog that came out of it. His clothes were massively too big except across the shoulders, and Wendell guessed he had lost a lot of weight. Having recently mustered out of service in South Carolina, Timothy spoke wistfully of the warmth of the Sea Islands and highly recommended that Wendell visit there. He was also interested in Wendell's views on photography as art, for he very much wanted to be taken seriously as an artist.

"My views have been changing," laughed Wendell. "When I was painting, photography seemed an upstart, threatening to replace by machine what is carefully rendered by heart and hand. I haven't yet decided whether my evolution to more favorable views is simply self-serving." He paused and added, "Photography seems an art almost in itself, the images captured on the battlefield. Certainly they evoke what no painting ever has."

On the deck behind them, impatient mules harnessed to innumerable side-by-side army caissons snorted and blew more steam into the foggy air. Mathew Brady emerged from the back of one of his two covered "whatsit" wagons and compulsively paced the deck. He was likely going over again every aspect of his massively complex undertaking which included some twenty photography units, one at least in every theater of the war. The two whatsit wagons held numerous cameras, supplies and a portable darkroom.

They were forty miles south of Washington, heading for Aquia Landing and thence were fifteen more miles by rail to Falmouth and the federal army. It had been a long time since Wendell had seen battle and he anxiously awaited his chance to test his reaction.

At Falmouth, they were greeted by a vast field of snowy log cabins housing the more fortunate soldiers, and a vast field of conical tents which housed the less fortunate. Their own small tent did little to shield the cold. The temperature dipped down to zero degrees, and all they could do was huddle and be grateful for one another's body heat.

Finally asleep, Wendell had a strange and vivid dream. In it, he was sleeping outside on the hard ground, underneath the whatsit wagon, on a hill overlooking a tiny farmhouse. He awoke to see two farmers coming up the road towards him. Wendell's hand went warily toward the handle of his gun, then he thought better of it and stood, raising his hand and his stump into the air. Best they see he was harmless.

"Hello, Gentlemen," Wendell hailed them affably. "Do you know where I might find a battle? I'm looking to photograph one for history's sake."

The men eyed him suspiciously, and the older one trained a musket on him. He was a gruff man with a full grey beard. The other was young with a straggly beard and hat pulled low over his face. He looked familiar and walked on a peg-leg. They consulted. Then the older one said, "We'll let you pass for a photograph."

"Delighted," said Wendell. "But just one picture of the two of you. I have to save my plates for the battle." They watched as he pulled the wooden camera with its tripod out of the wagon and set it up. He was getting ready to pose them when the younger one pushed back his hat with a bewildered look of recognition.

Wendell's heart panicked.

"Well, I'll be. It is you! I knowed you looked familiar. I thought sure you was dead, the way you haunted my dreams. You ain't a ghost, is you? Pa, this here's that demon I been wrestling with."

The old man pulled back the hammer of his musket, and Wendell's mouth opened wordlessly, his scream of terror caught in his throat. There was a moment of searing regret when he thought he was dead. Then the demon pushed the rifle aside and Wendell knew he was dreaming.

The demon went on, "Name is Pervis. I've had me some real sleepless nights when I wrestled with your shade. How is it possible you're alive?"

"You killed my best friend," hissed Wendell, his own voice far away. "You cost me my hand and my art career."

"You done got some of my friends, too," Pervis said matter-of-factly. "I lost my leg, but I reckon that was more the fault of the cannon then yourself. I don't hold the cannon no grudge, don't even know whose it was, but we'd have killed each other sure if it hadn't blowed when it did." His smile took on a look of almost ecstatic relief.

Wendell awoke to snow. His tent partners were outside having breakfast by the fire and the army was beginning to move out. He was alarmed that he had slept so late, then the dream's strong images floated into his half-sleeping brain. Had it been a visitation or was he still crazy? Did his demon yet live, and in that little farmhouse? They were obviously poor country folk who had never owned a slave, and for whom the world would be a better place if they could "get paid for picking cotton." So what were they fighting for? he wondered.

With Lillian's song singing through his brain, Wendell rose. He felt magic afoot, a healing effect from the dream wash over him. He chose simply to believe in it, believe that "Pervis" was alive and leave it at that. Hadn't Saint Tammany said as much at Catherine's church? "He whom you think is undead yet lives."

The still-thick fog felt more like a suspended mass of ice crystals as Wendell and Timothy followed Mathew in the whatsit. Sporadic gunfire sounded from below. They paused at the edge of the rise to look down on the Rappahannock River with the city of Fredericksburg rising through the fog on the opposite bank. Spread out beneath them in a vast multitude was the Union Army of the Potomac, under the command of General Burnside. Wendell could discern men trying to lay pontoon bridges across to Fredericksburg and getting hammered by secessionist resistance.

Timothy and Wendell set up the large Anthony camera with the 16 inch Harrison lens. Mathew ducked under the focusing cloth, where he adjusted the camera's angle, adjusted the bellows, and tried to fine focus with the lens pin. It was too foggy to get any pictures, until the sun poked through, lighting up the camera's long brass lens like a cannon barrel. Suddenly, one of the Confederate's big guns, which had been aimed at the bridge builders, tilted up and fired straight at the camera. The cannonball hit just feet away, scattering debris in all directions while photographers and mules ran for the trees, overturning one of their wagons and leaving the camera behind. A fierce barrage commenced below and, as the photographers crept back to look, the entire town seemed to crumble before them. Buildings toppled with a dull roar. Wendell's heart raced as he heard screams coming from across the river, saw dust and smoke and flames rise up, heard cheering on the Union side.

Mathew pulled the unhurt camera back to a safe position and all three men righted the wagon, then spent precious time cleaning the toxic mess of chemicals and broken glass from its floor.

Below them, the building of the bridge commenced in earnest, continuing on into the afternoon. Suddenly a hail of grapeshot and rifle fire felled the bridge builders to a man. Again the big guns of the Union trained on the city and again buildings exploded and crumbled. Wendell choked with emotion as he watched. He prayed the civilians had been safely evacuated, but knew from the dots of color scurrying about that they had not.

Now there were big guns from the other side firing on the bridge builders, and the Union side crept back to wait for cover of dark. Wendell and Mathew blanketed the mules against the cold, and they all crawled inside the tent to sleep. As Wendell ate his jerky and snuggled into chemical smelling covers, a wave of guilt overtook him – below, men were not sleeping.

Early in the morning, the sound of explosions and rifle fire penetrated the tent. Alarmed, Wendell scurried out. Fredericksburg had been leveled. Bridges were in place and the entire Union army was crossing over to where streets and houses were filled with desperate house-to-house battles.

Wendell was amazed that he felt no emotion, until he wavered unsteadily and realized he was about to faint. Suddenly, he was throwing up.

When he recovered, he entered the darkroom wagon and watched O'Sullivan mix collodion with acetone and ether in just the right amounts. He wore a labcoat to protect his clothes, but his ungloved fingers froze from contact with the wet chemicals. "The secret is to not put it in the silver nitrate solution until it reaches just the right degree of sponginess," Timothy explained, letting light in through the upraised flap so Wendell could see. He then slid the coated glass into the silver nitrate box and lowered the darkroom's tarpaulin wall. Total darkness ensued except for a red patch in the corner which was supposed to let red light in but was useless in the gloom. Wendell could hear Timothy loading the wet plate into the holder. Timothy opened the flap and Wendell took the holder out to Mathew at the camera. Working with plates in the field was quite different from working with the albumen prints in the studio and the intensity of attention Wendell gave to learning the details helped him to avoid feeling what was going on below.

The sky had darkened again and Brady's exposure was taking a long time, but there was no hurry as the freezing weather kept the emulsion from becoming brittle for the better part of an hour. As long as everything remained still, they should get something. After the first plate was developed, Brady decided it was time to move on down to the entrance of the town. They covered the mules' heads and on foot led them toward the burning city.

The ice on the Rappahannock was red with blood. Seagulls and buzzards were already feeding on the torn bodies of men and animals that floated up on the frozen banks. Wendell was alert for the red trousers of the 14th Brooklyn, but otherwise avoided looking too hard. When the sounds of fighting moved further into the distance, they led the wagons gingerly across the pontoon bridge.

The scene that greeted them in the city was staggering. Not only were there destroyed buildings and dead soldiers, but bodies of women and children along with signs of pillaging, ransacking, and even rape. A deep shame colored Wendell's face and he could feel Brady resist taking out his camera. Then a woman, torn and bloody, ran out from the rubble, screaming hysterically, "You make some photographs, Yankees! You make some photographs and you make damn sure that people see 'em, you hear? Folks should know what happened here." She sagged onto the ground and hid her face as she sobbed. Wendell got out his canteen and offered her some water which she gulped desperately, then he prepared a plate for Mathew as the sounds of cannon and gunfire echoed off the mountains in the near distance.

Stopping now and then to take pictures, the photographers made their way through the debris. Fredericksburg was slowly coming back to life as the living came out of hiding and began to dig out the dead and wounded. Few paid Mathew's company any mind, but the slowness of the plates in the gloom allowed only a couple of successful exposures. As darkness fell, the Union army fell back to bivouac in the streets, and once again the locals escaped into the shadows.

The soldiers shared their rations with the photographers and rolled out bedding under the sky. They were not allowed tents or fires. O'Sullivan and Brady crawled into the wagons and Wendell slept beneath. His muscles cramped from the unrelenting cold, and he barely slept.

Just before sunrise, the photographers rose and followed the Union Army to where it spread across a vast field to the southwest of the city. The photographers took cover as the Secessionists were freely firing Robert E. Lee's heavy artillery from above on Marye's Hill. It was too dark and too dangerous to take any photos. Brady ordered the photographers back to an abandoned house where they climbed to the roof for a good vantage point. Here they stayed with their field glasses, staring with disbelief at the ensuing carnage.

Wave after wave of General Burnside's Union army tried to storm the Confederate position above them, falling like bowling pins as they did so. Still, they kept charging up the hill, marching forward to the drumbeat in orderly lines, then running ahead before falling in great clouds of flying limbs. Wendell clutched the field glasses, wanting to run into the battle screaming, "Stop! Stop! What are you doing?" This was the most colossal foolishness he could imagine, very reminiscent of Bull Run.

All day they continued, cannons and howitzers throwing up dust and bodies, obscuring and then revealing a much smaller Union army. It was shocking, the extreme of folly. The army was a fraction the size it had been, and yet they were still charging up the hill.

Idiots! A deep malaise swept over Wendell and he sagged against the roof. What was it all for? What was any of it for? For the life of him, Wendell could not understand how what he was seeing had anything to do with freeing slaves or even preserving the Union. Perhaps Henry Clapp was right, war was nothing but man's fondness for coercion. And, he admitted guiltily, bloodlust – the erotic ecstasy of killing.

Finally towards evening, the retreat was sounded. Another rout. "My God, where art Thou?!" Wendell's strangled voice pleaded beneath the bugles' urgent call, "Thou art not on our side!"

The photographers sat helplessly and wept as the tattered remains of what had been men streamed below in unruly dismay. They could hear the sounds of the Rebel cheers coming from Marye's Hill.

As the chill winter winds came down from the north and the Federals retreated for the night back to Fredericksburg, the photographers lingered, grim and speechless. When they, too, fell back to the city, human scavengers were picking through the dead and dying bodies as if picking through garbage.

Before anyone could turn in, a red glow showed in the northern sky and several of the soldiers wondered aloud if the capital was on fire. Wendell recognized it at once – Aurora Borealis. Way down here in Virginia, it was the aurora. The army around them began to come alive with awe and wonder as the whole sky turned as bloody as the ground beneath it. It backlit the broken ruins of a church tower whose black and jagged silhouette hovered like a judgement against the rising flames of hell. Finally, even the heavenly or hellish wonder ceased to be important as weariness caught them up, and the surviving soldiers slept like the dead beneath the dancing sky.

For awhile, Wendell lay awake, trying to make sense of meeting Pervis, to interpret it in terms of reality. That Pervis was somehow alive was redeeming, but also meant he was not a ghost, and therefore Wendell had indeed been crazy. Perhaps alienation in war was normal. And why not? – War itself was crazy. He closed his eyes and acknowledged the wrath of the Almighty. When he finally slept, he had a strange dream, filled with the contradictory images of a smiling Pervis and burning buildings falling into rubble.

By morning, there was no more stomach for battle. Before the photographers had warmed themselves and finished breakfast over a small campfire, those of the Union Army that remained had entrenched themselves at the far end of the field and wouldn't move. The very heavens were against them and they knew it. The photographers fell in behind, taking pictures of the tense, exhausted line. All day the two enemies watched each other and waited. Except for the inevitable Union withdrawal, the battle was over.

On the fourth day, Burnside asked for a truce to pick up the dead and wounded. As trenches were dug, Brady's men moved among the bodies, Brady carrying the camera, Wendell and O'Sullivan hefting the portable darkroom. They stepped gingerly among the grotesquely rigid corpses, slowly recording the gruesome sight, intent on leaving a legacy for anyone who might wonder what war was like.

By the time the remnants of the dead men were buried out of sight in the trenches, and a brief entreaty made to God on their behalf, the weather had warmed and a fierce wind began to blow. The photography equipment was hurriedly stowed, and as the storm raged, retreat was sounded. Once again, it was a pitiful Army of the Potomac that slogged back to Falmouth.

The photographers were silent as they followed the army through the storm. Wendell was thinking of miracles and of Lillian – brave sweet Lillian who fought so tirelessly for her cause. He had not tried to see her in Washington, reasoning that when he returned to the capital near Christmas, she would be more open to seeing him. He needed to talk to her. Truly, it did not matter that they could not make love, he just wanted to talk to her, to be in her company. If only he could persuade her of that. But he had to admit, 'twould be even better if she would see Dr. Randolph and be healed.

"I would like to find my regiment," Wendell commented to Brady sitting beside him.

Brady nodded. "Take a couple of days to relax and look around. Then I'd be obliged if you took one of the wagons back to Washington and made some prints. Gardner is there and will introduce you to your own rig." Wendell nodded. "The stable is paid through March, and you're welcome to make use of it."

Following breakfast, Wendell departed from his fellow photographers with a fond feeling and a fervent wish for their continued safety.

Chapter 34

A solemn scene, filled with despair, greeted Wendell at the Union Camp in White Church not far from Falmouth. He drove the reluctant mule forward into smoke from hundreds of campfires, which mercifully masked the odor of death that had been growing since the weather warmed. Rows of neat tents and teepees huddled around the tattered remnants of men eating stoically by the fires. Beyond the camp and around their own fires, colored and white washerwomen struggled over barrels of torn and bloodied uniforms. Once Wendell would have noticed vermillion, Egyptian brown, cobalt yellow, and an overall wash of deep azurite – now all was reduced to tones of black and white. Perhaps it was the influence of the photography, or perhaps it was that the war itself made the world devoid of color.

The men ignored him until one looked up and said, "We'd be obliged if ye didn't git yer photographs here, mister. Wait at least till we've won somethin'."

Wendell nodded. "I'm looking for the 14th Brooklyn. Used to be with them, at Bull Run, so I know something of what you're feeling."

Now various of the men considered him. "First Bull Run or second?" asked one.

"First," said Wendell holding aloft his stump. "I lost my hand there."

"Tough luck," said the first man. "Sorry what I said about taking pictures. You go on ahead and get whatever you need. This here's the 51st New York, seen action at 2nd Bull Run and Antietam. Been a hot fall, you might say. Don't know where the Red Legged Devils are, but they're around somewhere. Damn good regiment."

The name 51st New York wakened Wendell's memory. "You got a Lieutenant George Whitman?" he asked.

"Yessir. He's in the hospital tent. Caught himself some shrapnel from one of those percussion blasts, but 'tain't serious. Ye can park your rig over with the horses and yourn'll get took care of."

"I'm obliged to you, sir." Wendell tipped his hat and turned the mule's head toward the corral near the teepees. "God bless you," he said, and heard one of the men announce to the others excitedly that "That there is Mathew Brady." He smiled. Perhaps the man would get a chance to see the real Mathew Brady, but meanwhile it wouldn't hurt to let him think he had.

Wendell took a photo of arms and legs piled by the tree outside the hospital tent. He'd become impervious to shock. Inside, the stench of death grew more oppressive. Stoical groans and mutterings arose from hundreds of bloody cots. Wendell soon encountered Walt Whitman's brother sitting calmly in a chair while a medic removed a piece of percussion ball from his cheek and dabbed at the wound with bloody water. "Lieutenant Whitman?" Wendell inquired, saluting with his handless limb to keep from having to deal with the embarrassing handshake.

Whitman nodded curiously.

"Wendell Parry, photographer. I have been obliged by your brother Walt to ask after your health." A big smile spread across Whitman's features.

"Ah," he said jovially, "what an unexpected pleasantry in the midst of our travails. I am assuming, of course, that my brother is well?"

"Very," Wendell assured him. George Whitman seemed to await more news, so Wendell added, "His *Leaves of Grass* has acquired a positive notice from Ralph Emerson, and so has become somewhat respectable."

"Wonderful," exclaimed George. "I had been reluctant to brag about him to the men as his name has a salacious ring in their ears."

"Which should make you very proud of him, sir. 'Tis proof the men have read his poetry, though they won't admit it. Just as they hide *cartes de visite* of Adah Menken in their knapsacks."

Whitman began to laugh openly now, raising spirits throughout the tent. That the lieutenant continued to laugh until he almost couldn't stop was telling of the strain he'd been under, and of his own well-loved image of a nudish Menken hidden in his knapsack.

Finished with his surgery, George rose, offering to accompany Wendell's search for the men of the 14th Brooklyn. Outside, the sun was setting, shooting streaks of aurelian and cobalt yellow through the smoke of the campfires. A Negro stood beside the closest fire, and began to sing in a deeply timbered basso the plaintive words of *Shenandoah.*

> *"O Shenandoah, I long to see you,*
> *Far across that rollin' river,*
> *O Shenandoah, I long to see you,*
> *O roll, O roll-er-ee*
> *Across the wide Missouri..."*

"The man has an amazing voice," said Wendell quite moved. "Who is he?"

"He's the slave of one of the Maryland men," Whitman confessed.

"A slave?" It was a startling revelation.

George nodded. "Indeed, his owner has been sore pressed by the men to release him. He says he will at Christmas, and a sizable amount has been wagered on whether the poor soul will stay on as a hireling or skedaddle up north. Most of the money is on skedaddle." They laughed, then joined in as the camp began to sing along. Soon, the song could be heard around other campfires, some so far away that it delayed as if an echo, the sad longing for home pulling at every man's heartstrings. Wendell decided to wait until morning to find his regiment and George returned to his duties, promising to write his mother and brother.

Wendell sat down in the nearest firelight to warm himself, next to a civilian of his own age with a sketch pad. "Nice drawing," complimented Wendell, peeking over the man's shoulder.

The man looked up from his work and a slow smile of recognition spread across an affable face. "Wendell Harte Parry, isn't it?" he asked.

"Do I know you, sir?"

"I met you at Pfaff's and asked that you put my name on the waiting list for a Tenth Street studio. Name is Winslow Homer."

"I do remember!" said Wendell delighted. "You had once sat in the alcove and Clapp introduced you."

"That's right. But what are you doing here?"

"I'm a photographer now," said Wendell, holding up his stump, "for Mathew Brady. I'm not fit for painting anymore, or for soldiering. And what are you doing?"

"'Tis a shame." The illustrator shook his head sympathetically. "I truly count *Sands of Morocco* and the Ithaca studies among the greats. I'm on assignment for *Harper's Weekly.*" Winslow flipped through his sketches, showing them off. They were mostly of camp life, some humorous and some plaintive. Wendell looked on admiringly, especially at the ones to which color had been added. He knew Homer had been passed over on the Studio Building waiting list many times for more intimate friends. "I'll speak to the concierge again, if you're still wanting a studio," he promised.

Wendell spent the short trip up the Potomac by steamer exposing more plates and hoping some pay awaited him in Washington. He had not found his regiment, but by now, he didn't care. He was tired and just wanted to see Lillian.

In Washington, fully forty ambulance wagons took the Fredericksburg wounded from the steamer. Wendell followed them to Union Hotel in Georgetown, a large 4-story brick recently converted to the army's use, where they were delivered into the

"Ballroom." Just inside the door, he set up his camera and tried not to gag at the smell. The large ward looked to be full already, but the orderlies claimed there was room enough for all in the mosquito netted beds. Nurses in white bonnets and long bib aprons stood at the ready, and an efficient operation seemed to take place. Wendell was scanning the room anxiously for Lillian when a voice called, "Mr. Parry, Wendell Parry!" and he looked around to see Louisa May Alcott.

"Miss Alcott!" he greeted her, delighted. "I had no idea you were here."

"I have just arrived," she said, looking anxious. "This is my first incoming load of wounded. I am surprised to see you, and especially so soon after seeing Mr. Whitman. He was here searching for his brother who is listed as wounded."

"Mr. Whitman? Walt Whitman? Why, I have just been with his brother, near Falmouth. I will be delighted to tell him his brother is well."

"I'd love to visit with you further but I'm on duty," Louisa apologized. "Lillian is in the next ward, but I have doubts she'll see you now either. It looks like we'll be busy all night. If you're still in town in a few days, mayhap things will have settled."

"Perhaps I can visit further with you then. Do you know where I might find Mr. Whitman?"

"He's probably inspecting the wounded as they come from the ambulances," she said.

Wendell thanked her and took his leave. He did indeed find his friend outside, and hailed him heartily. "Walt," he called out.

The bearded poet turned his haggard head and brightened at the sight of him.

"Wendell, how be you? I had hoped to run across you."

Wendell approached with his carved hand outstretched, grinning. "I have just come from your brother's camp. He wishes you to know he is fine and will write forthwith to your worried mother."

"Oh, that's great news!" rejoiced the relieved Mr. Whitman as he pumped his friend's wooden mitt. "But what of reports he'd been wounded?"

"A scratch on his chin only. I doubt 'twill leave a scar."

They mounted the whatsit wagon, and went up Bridge Street in search of a cheap rooming house where they might spend a night or two.

The streets were alive with troops, chickens, wagons, pigs, and fancy government types. Freedmen, who had been emancipated in the capital fully eight months earlier, were everywhere in evidence in every kind of occupation.

"I hope you are better situated than I," Walt said, "and are inclined to be charitable. I had my wallet stolen en route and walked all the way from the train station. I have arrived quite penniless and with my feet pitifully blistered."

"And hungry, I'll wager," observed Wendell sympathetically. "I'm hungry, too." After grabbing a bite for which Whitman blessed Wendell again and again, and the fortune of their meeting, the two decided to spend what was left of the daylight in seeing the sights. The wagon proceeded down Pennsylvania Avenue, one of the few paved roads, toward the half-built Capitol Dome that loomed in the distance. As they approached, the attire of the inhabitants became increasingly ostentatious, a parody of Paris, with women in 3-story hats and men with all manner of dramatically contrived military 'uniforms' – high boots, scarlet-lined capes, ornate swords along the leg, and plumes in the hats. That the city had been under siege non-stop for a year and a half seemed not to perturb them, nor did the muddy side streets strewn with garbage. Perhaps the clothes and airs were in heroic defiance of the capital's coarseness.

"I come to like Lincoln's plainness more and more," commented Whitman as he watched the gaudy parade. They passed the Statue of Freedom on the Capitol lawn, destined to crown the Capitol Dome. Birds had built their nests between her helmet and sword, giving her a nature goddess countenance. But it was the White House, with its elegant carriages coming and going, that commanded the greatest admiration, the one building that had enough gravitas for the nation's true situation. The man who lived within its graceful walls labored under a tremendous burden. Wendell was especially solemn. He had been here once before, marching past Lincoln with Sam Stockard at his side.

On H Street, the two friends pulled up in front of a likely-looking place to spend the night – the Surratt Boarding House, an unimposing townhouse on the corner of 6th Street. "Even this modest place will likely not be cheap," said Wendell, "but you'll share my room and we will count ourselves lucky."

Once again, Whitman declared his gratitude to Wendell and to Providence. "I thought I would be spending the night in a hospital ward, starving, and still looking for my brother."

The landlady, Widow Mary Surratt, was a hefty, plainly dressed woman in partial mourning for her recently departed husband. She managed to convey both gentility and disapproval of the two comrades. Walt Whitman's name had evidently preceded him and she found it disagreeable. The idea that each could not afford his own bed dismayed her even more, but she had sympathy with the loss of Walt's wallet – the high price of one dollar per night clearly made two rooms unaffordable. Finally in need of their business, she consented to give them a small room on the top floor.

With winter solstice approaching, the sun set early. Wendell felt the full weight of his fatigue as he crawled into the one small bed beside Walt. "Did you see Lillian at the hospital?" Wendell inquired casually.

"I did," said Walt. "Alas, she looks unwell. The job wears on her, as does her asthma. She seems to me to have developed a persistent cough."

"What shall I do?" cried Wendell dismayed, rolling onto his side to look at his confidante. "By God, Walt, I love that woman to distraction. 'Twould be the death of me should something happen to her."

"Have faith," said Whitman, and reached over to turn off the gaslamp. "What you cannot do, Providence can. I was convinced of that today." He was quiet a moment, then added with a stirring in his voice, "What I saw in the hospital, Wendell – it changed me. I don't think I will be returning to New York. I very much feel I am needed here." In the dark, he bent over Wendell and, finding his lips, gave him a tender kiss. Then he turned his back and went to sleep.

"Well, Wendell, I'm off to Falmouth," said Whitman next day, emerging from the army clerk's office with permission to travel to the camp. Wendell gave him a few dollars on their ride to the steamer, and with white beard blowing, Whitman waved a last goodbye from the deck before the ship's smoke obscured him.

At Mathew Brady's studio, things were in disarray. Manager Alexander Gardner, whom Wendell had met in New York, was quitting and taking his son with him. He had been Mathew's right hand man for years and now wanted to open his own studio. Wendell got the impression that a precipitous move was prompted by some perceived slight on Mathew's part, but Wendell had no further clues. Until Brady got back, the studio was closing.

"Please," Wendell begged him. "I had promised to print these plates and am in sore need of the money. I have also the title to a horse and rig in your livery."

"Mathew Brady doesn't own the livery," corrected Gardner with irritation. "Just take the papers to the stables and they'll give you your rig. That, at least, is paid for." Finally, he looked at Wendell's fallen countenance and took pity on him. "OK," he sighed, "do your prints. I'll pay you for them, but make it fast."

Wendell did what he could ere the sun should set and the livery close. Neither he nor Gardner engaged in conversation before Wendell ran out the door and traded in Mathew's whatsit for his own lovely little itinerant wagon, emblazoned with Mathew Brady Photography on its leather sides, and a sweet horse named Hidalgo.

The closing of Mathew's studio depressed Wendell. It would be a few days, surely, until Louisa May or Lillian might provide him some company. Usually happy to be on his own and with new creative tools, Whitman's departure and Lillian's likely rebuff left him forlorn – there were too many disturbing images to plague an unoccupied mind. Wendell went in search of entertainment.

On passing a modest hall, he saw the newly posted playbill,

> *"Readings Tonight From the Famous Poet*
> *Who Inspires Our Warriors to Victory,*
> *And Soothes Their Sorrowing Breasts*
> *Through the Agonies of War –*
> *Major Thomas Buchanan Read."*

Feeling infinitely better, Wendell bought a ticket, then happily conducted photography experiments, even exposing individual plates to multiple scenes. Though he was concerned that he wasted precious supplies, he wanted to impress Mathew with something new, and couldn't help himself as the possibilities of his new medium set his pulse racing. He feared he would soon be short of money, but found to his delight that the dandies of Washington crowded around, willing to pay well for cartes de visite. By the time of Thomas's reading, Wendell had garnered enough extra coin to buy not only dinner, but another night at Mary Surratt's boarding house.

Chapter 35

Wendell sat toward the back of the small theater, where Thomas would be unlikely to see him. Thomas wore a blue officer's uniform, and looked very handsome in it – indeed, he looked like one of the town's dandies, with a fancy sword hanging from a scarlet sash and high boots. Wendell decided he quite liked it, and remembered Thomas's comments that had helped inspire the stunning uniforms of the 14th Brooklyn. 'It's a good thing Walt isn't here to see this,' Wendell smiled to himself, wondering if the bare-headed Thomas had a hat with a plume. The audience was filled with fine ladies and their gents, as well as torn and haggard men in bits and pieces of uniform.

Without any introduction and only a nod to the applause, Thomas seated himself on a stool, opened his book, and began to read in a sonorous voice:

"She had known Sorrow, he had walked with her,
Oft supped, and broke the bitter ashen crust;
And in the dead leaves still she heard the stir
Of his black mantle trailing in the dust.

While yet her cheek was bright with summer bloom
Her country summoned and she gave her all;
And twice War bowed to her his sable plume,
Re-gave the swords to rust upon the wall.

At last the thread was snapped, her head was bowed;
Life dropped the distaff through his hands serene;
And loving neighbors smoothed her careful shroud,
While Death and Winter closed the autumn scene."

Thus the evening went, each poem sadder than the last, the war as experienced by women. Thomas still mourned the loss of his wife and children, Wendell knew, and he was for her sweet memory a champion of women, anthologizing their poetry regularly and regarding them tenderly. Wendell wondered whether this was the poetry Thomas was employed by the army to write – it seemed not to inspire men to battle, but to leave them weeping instead.

When the evening came to a close, Thomas came out among the audience, and it was the ladies who crowded round him, pushing books forward to be signed, touching him with tearful reverence.

Finally, Wendell worked his way to the front of the crowd and thrust his wooden hand toward its creator. Thomas recognized it at once and jerked his head up with a big grin. "Wendell, ole cuss! It's good to see you," and grabbed him in a bear hug. The ladies would have to wait, for Thomas put his arm about his friend's shoulders and led him firmly toward the door.

He was delighted to see Wendell's wagon parked outside. "So you're a photographer now! How's Brady to work for?"

"Wonderful," said Wendell. "He's suffering financial woes, so for payment I own the rig."

"Horse and equipment?"

Wendell smiled his answer. He realized suddenly that he was quite proud of himself. The last time he'd seen Thomas, he had been a useless cripple and a madman. "So where are you off to?"

"Is there somewhere we might have a drink?" asked Wendell.

"Alas, Washington City is not Paris. Or even New York! And I have to be back at the barracks. Can we meet tomorrow?" With the arrangements made, Wendell returned to his room at the Surratt House and slept well.

The entire of the next day was spent in talking, walking, taking photos, sketching, writing poetry. Thomas wore his flamboyant uniform, complete with a plumed hat, which he tipped to the side as he had once tipped his beret. He was proud to be a soldier.

"There is a dreary pall hangs over the capital, Wendell, so long besieged by the secessionists," Thomas said as they sat together behind the horse, Hidalgo, looking for a perfect shot. "I have felt it since arriving last week. But in the Western theater, our troops are more jubilant. Shiloh, a wretched scene, was none-the-less a victory, and there has been nothing but good news since. Vicksburg will fall by summer and when it does, the North will control the entire length of the Mississippi. The poor Rebs have been taking such a beating as to evoke pity from the hardest Union heart."

Happy for the news, Wendell commented, "We pay it so little heed here, beset as you've said, with our own problems. We heard, of course, of your general's mishap at Shiloh and his demotion to the defenses of Cincinnati."

Thomas laughed sardonically. "With all the presses located in the East, it's a wonder you get any reports from the West at all. I do admire the reporters and photographers who brave fierce battles so far from home."

They formed a team, Thomas huckstering sittings from the swells who passed, and lining them up for Wendell's four lens camera that offered eight post card sized cartes de visite on a single glass. Wendell expertly turned out the finished portraits in a mere twenty minutes while Thomas entertained the crowd with le bavardage. In this way, the day was lucrative as well as pleasant, though Wendell worried that he would not find replacement chemicals to satisfy the demand.

Their labors lulling, Thomas looked at Wendell with his merry twinkle. "But I have been coy with my news," he said. "I am married, Wendell!"

"Thomas, that's wonderful!"

He continued, "And General Wallace is so enamored of my poetry that I am left to do as I please. His praise is not faint, as indeed he is a good writer himself. My artistic duties allow me to live peacefully with my sweet Hattie, at her brother's house in Cincinnati."

"That rhymes – you can't help yourself! But I had thought you would never marry again."

"Ah, my first dear wife has become a muse for me, even as St. Tammany said. She is so present now in spirit that I have no need to cling to her fleshly memory. Despite the war, I am truly happy."

Wendell grinned, "I dare say the news will not content my sister, but should be some relief to her female paramour."

Thomas laughed. "I was fond of your sister," he admitted. Then he asked about Lillian, awkwardly, perhaps aware that it might be a sore subject.

"She's an army nurse here in Washington," responded Wendell, his sad countenance confirming his friend's fears. "Her asthma is not cured and she will not see me, though I will try at least for a meal with her."

Their conversation turned to other mutual friends. Thomas was sorry to hear he'd missed Walt Whitman, then said, "My erstwhile benefactor, Henry Longfellow, writes me that the Booths are in Boston and making a decided impact on the social scene there. Ned has reportedly garnered an astonishing $7000 per week from the Boston Museum Theater, and is invited to dine in all the finest homes."

Wendell smiled at the news. "Indeed, Molly has worked hard toward their acceptance." Then, remembering his own experience in Concord, "'Tis rare for an actor to be received among the brahmans of Boston who, for all their progressiveness, are Puritans still. But it's not surprising Ned would go over well with the literati – the genius of his nuanced performance has transformed Shakespeare into a most genteel and profound experience."

Thomas laughed. "I can't say the same of his younger brother, who frequently plays in Cincinnati. His style is energetic, anything but nuanced, and evokes a rowdy pleasure. He is very popular. The Midwest has turned out not to be a theatrical backwater. Adah Menken has also been there, in *Mazeppa*, delighting the troops as no one before her. I'd have seen more of her, but Hattie was scandalized at the performance and positively appalled when Adah greeted me with warmth. Needless to say, my wife was not inclined to offer her friendship." He said this with wry good humor and added, "She did ask if I could inveigh on my acquaintance with Ned to invite the younger Booth over. Of course, I declined. She finds him quite acceptable, despite his being a copperhead."

Wendell laughed at this, for he well knew John Wilkes' attractiveness to ladies overshadowed any abhorrence of his southern sympathies.

They finished a portrait of a cloudy winter sun poised above the half-built Capitol dome, and sensed the possibility of snow for Christmas.

Wendell had a sudden inspiration. "Thomas, I have a thought if you've time. Let us together try for an audience with Lillian. She'll less likely rebuff the both of us."

Thomas agreed, moreover to spend this night of furlough with Wendell at the Surratt House before hurrying home for Christmas.

Dinner at the Union Hotel Hospital was just ended when they arrived, and the nurses were clearing dishes. It was a calm scene, the stench of sickness and death mitigated by the smell of food. Several of the nurses on duty seemed to be casually socializing in the halls.

"It looks auspicious," said Wendell. After a quick check around, they spied Lillian in the ballroom, chatting happily with a patient. Never shy, Thomas pushed ahead of Wendell and headed towards her, his major's uniform eliciting salutes and quick acquiescence from the guards. Lillian looked up to see why heads were turning, and for a quick moment did not recognize that the handsome and be-plumed major was her old friend.

"Thomas!" she enthused when he smiled at her, doffing his hat as he bowed. Before her delight could diminish, he stepped aside so she could see Wendell.

"Oh, hello," she said, rather more stiffly.

"We have come to kidnap you for an hour or so of amusement," said Thomas, "which I'm sure you could use."

Lillian looked tempted. "I'm on duty till eleven," she said uncertainly.

"And what rank is the officer on duty?" Thomas inquired.

A grin crossed her face. "Why, Major, I believe he is only a sergeant."

"Excellent. I shall pull rank on him. Where shall we go?"

"To my apartment, I suppose." Then with some excitement added, "Can you pull rank for my friend, Louisa May, as well?" Thomas clicked his heels and bowed. Soon the four were crowded into her tiny apartment, sitting on the small bed and leaning against the dresser. Lillian lit the one gaslamp and made tea in the brazier, while Wendell stoked a small fire on a hearth that was dangerously close to the bed. The glossy cream painted walls were bereft of decoration, except for a cross and two daguerreotypes left to Lillian by dying soldiers with no one else to give them to. Unbleached cotton curtains hung beside a small window. Outside, an icy rain had begun to fall, and Wendell was glad he had left Hidalgo inside the hospital stable.

Soon they were all sharing their stories with much to tell as witnesses to such terrible times. After anecdotes about Fredericksburg, Thomas asked, "And how did two such lovely ladies manage to get past Dragon Dix to be enlisted?" Dorothea Dix, the Superintendent of Army nurses, was well-known to want only matronly women over thirty. Lillian flushed, but did indeed look older. She was thin with blotched skin and hair pulled severely back. Wendell noted how much her manner had changed, how much her stiffened countenance forbade anyone to touch her.

Louisa May, barely thirty, looked up perkily and grinned, taking the compliment. "Friends in high places," she answered him. "Sam Howe and Nurse Dix once took up the cause of invalids together. She's actually quite a nice person. I know Lilly Ann's not thirty yet, but when Nurse Dix heard she is invalided..." She paused, not sure what Thomas knew.

"You were lucky to be discharged, Wendell," observed Lillian quickly. "They are forming an invalid corps for protection at home."

"Yes," agreed Louisa May. "The only way out now is to be flat on your back or dead. With merely a missing right hand, why, we nurses slap on a bandage and back you go, right to the front." Not knowing how to respond, Wendell nodded and for a brief second, his eyes met Lillian's, so carefully averted till now. She blinked and looked away. Memories drifted and piled up in the corners like snowflakes.

Finally, Louisa May got up to go. "I have the late shift tonight," she said, "and rank or no rank, Thomas, I am needed. So I will sadly have to depart this lovely company."

Thomas stood. "Allow me to accompany you back to your apartment," he offered, winking at Wendell.

Lillian looked suddenly panicky. "I, too, have duty soon enough and need some sleep. Why don't you both accompany Louisa?"

Wendell looked at her and said quietly, "Lillian, please, I would have a brief word with you." There was a silence as all eyes fell on Lillian, beseeching her to accommodate her erstwhile lover. At last, with a nod, she acquiesced.

"Splendid," said Thomas, donning his hat and kissing Lillian's hand. "I will return in a minute to drag Wendell off your stage." Lillian laughed, and hugged Louisa May, whose apartment was several blocks away.

When they had gone, Lillian sat demurely in the one chair, her hands folded carefully in her lap, and looked at Wendell seated on the bed. "Well?" she said testily.

"How is your asthma?" Wendell asked.

She stiffened. "I have had no episodes since our last encounter. Indeed, I have had no occasion for more episodes."

"Dr. Randolph has agreed to see us the first week in February, in New York. Please, Lillian. He can help us."

"I can only be helped by helping others, Wendell. That much is clear to me. And I will not break my heart or yours again by going hopefully from one doctor to another."

She said it with such finality that Wendell was crestfallen. Still, he tried again. "But Lillian, the rightness of it, you must have felt it, too. We're right together, Lillian."

Lillian closed her eyes and pressed her hands over her ears. "No! No! That was before the war, that was before everything changed. It is no longer my life!"

"Is my love worth so little to you, *Mon Coeur*?" he said, rising from the bed and taking up his hat and coat.

She softened, and opined in almost a whisper, "'Tis for love of you that I bid you let me go. You can still have that again with someone else."

"Fine!" his voice rose angrily. He bowed low at the waist, "Then, when I marry the fair Margaret and live a happy, contented life, I shall have you, Lillian, to thank for it!"

Taking only long enough to see his taunt hit its mark, he slammed out the door and down the stairs.

He lit a cigarette. He had hoped Lillian would follow him down, as she had in Paris. But no gas-lit cobbles greeted him, no red-dressed dame de la nuit, no Lillian – only cold rain and mud and the stench of death from the hospital.

Mary Surratt was up and waiting for Wendell when he entered with Major Read. She frowned. "I hope your friend will be renting his own room."

Wendell looked contrite.

Then, sweeping his hat at her feet, Thomas took her hand and kissed it. "Wendell, may I have the pleasure of being introduced to so lovely a lady?"

"Why certainly. This is Mrs. Surrat, the owner of this charming establishment." Wendell was delighted – he had almost forgotten how much fun Thomas could be.

"Mary," she said, taken in.

"You have such beautiful eyes, Mary. I am Major Thomas Buchanan Read, poet and artist, at your service. I would be overjoyed if one day you would consent to sit for a portrait."

"Oh," she said blushing. Then, catching herself, she turned her head away from Thomas' admiring gaze. "Go on now, flatterer. Get along upstairs. It's way past time for decent people to be abed."

Chapter 36

Wendell spent Christmas at the Stockard's house in Brooklyn. He was seated across from Elizabeth's sister, Margaret, and was actually enjoying the intense pressure being leveled at him to marry her. Everyone's levity was elevated with wine, and the merriment of the occasion had flushed her cheeks to a rosy red. When she put down her fork to talk or make a point, she would delicately lick her lips with the pink tip of her tongue, and coil her finger suggestively through a wispy blonde curl. Her gown was cut particularly low for an afternoon dress and Wendell found plenty to admire. Perhaps Lillian was right – being married to such a creature would not be the worst fate that could befall a man.

And so, when she begged to take some air, he accompanied her, and when she parted her pretty lips for him to kiss, he obliged her. He had been starving for so long that the kiss soon became a deep and passional embrace, and an unspoken promise to her of marriage.

He had now his own room at the Studio Building, Ted Winthrop's old apartment. The little windowless basement room was depressing, but it was away from the noise of houses being built on 11th Street, and he was happy for a roof among friends. Brady had paid his stable in Washington through March, and for now had more work for him here.

Frequently, Wendell stopped by the Booths' apartment to take an afternoon smoke with Ned in his library, often joined by Tom Aldrich and Fitzhugh. Over brandy, they would discuss the arts and the latest in science, and relate stories of their dissimilar childhoods. Ned told of touring the country with his famous father, trying desperately to keep the madman sober enough to get through his performances. Tom spent most of his childhood in New Orleans – he'd returned north with the intention of attending college, but went straight into the editing business when his father died. Fitzhugh was raised in New York City by a Presbyterian minister from Yale College who preached in the then colored neighborhood of the Five Points. His activism for abolition and temperance made him the target of mobs, and Fitzhugh told wild stories of fugitives in the basement and rocks thrown through the windows.

Evenings were wondrously filled with theater, to which Wendell and Tom had backstage passes, and pumped Ned with a drink and a laugh prior to his performances. On one such occasion, Tom warned Wendell as they went to join Molly in her box, "Ned has been drinking straight through from the afternoons – I believe Molly has become quite concerned." As Ned's performance that night was superb, Wendell didn't pay the issue much mind, dismissing it as a woman's overabundance of worry.

One day, while Wendell shared a hookah with Fitzhugh, Clapp, and Macaroni, the discussion turned to the in's and out's of a match with Margaret. "Fie," said Ludlow, "you are horny enough to fuck anything. She is too conventional, you would never be permitted to see your old friends."

Indeed, Wendell was afraid this assessment might be accurate, but he dreamed of her now, of her blonde curls and pink tongue. "To bring you to your senses," suggested Clapp, "we should find you someone happy to attend to your physical needs and without the snares of matrimony."

And so, when the door to his atelier creaked open late on New Year's Eve, Wendell was not surprised to see that it was Ada Clare who slipped in holding a candlestick, and doffed her dress in its light. She held the candle over his face, and felt him under the covers. "It's dark in here," she giggled. "I want to be sure I've got the right man."

"And what would let you know I'm the right man?" Wendell asked, aroused as she climbed in on top of him.

"The right man would lay on his back a moment, and let me

put a hat on him," she said. She began to unroll the new thin rubber over his straining member. It was tight and he winced.

"Pray, let me play with you unfettered, Ada. I will be careful, I promise." He was true to his word, and his good friend pulled on him so expertly that when she finished, he had no longer any desire to marry Margaret.

He was awakened by the sound of ringing bells and darky music, banjo and fiddle, coming from the streets. Light flooded in through the open doorway, revealing Ada fully dressed and grinning. "Come, Wendell, get up! They're celebrating the Emancipation!" He threw on his djellaba and followed after her up the stairs to the front door. Other artists were crowded in the doorway, watching 10th Street being taken over by scores of dancing and celebrating Negroes. "C'mon!" shrieked Ada, and led Wendell into the streets to move and laugh and congratulate the many Negroes who lived and worked in the neighborhood. Other artists soon joined in, and before long, the races were mixed in writhing merriment.

Wendell glanced over at the stoop where the old Negro sat grinning at him, tears rolling down his cheeks. "Happy Emancipation!" Wendell shouted to him.

"Did you ever marry that gal?" he called back.

His heart burst. "I will," shouted Wendell jubilantly as church bells clanged. "I will marry her!" and lost himself completely in an ecstasy of dancing.

That night, right on schedule, Sanford Gifford arrived back at the Studio Building with a slew of newly painted canvases. The artists crowded into his atelier, admiring them as they helped to hang them, and soon Gertrude McEntee and Mrs. Winter were supplying food for an impromptu party.

Sanford was looking older, rougher, hardened. His handsome features were more chiseled and his skin darkened with exposure to sun, sand, and gun-powder. His greeting for Wendell was especially strong. As they shook hands warmly, Sanford expressed relief that his friend was finally healed from the wounds of battle and embarked upon a new profession. "Wendell, you don't know how enthralled I've become with Brady's collection. Your photos will outlast in interest any of the paintings to come out of this war."

Soon, Asher Durand arrived and Sanford shared his stories about the new canvases. His first was titled *Sunday Morning at Camp Cameron*. It had been sketched just days before Wendell and Sam had arrived there. Wendell looked at it carefully, and pointed to one of the indistinct soldiers whose pose revealed his identity. "That's Ted, isn't it?" he said wistfully. Sanford nodded, then moved to another painted at Arlington.

"That's him there, too," Sanford said sadly. "His book is now in its 14th printing and others of his works are being published besides." He shook his head. There was silence during which he wasn't the only one to choke back a tear.

"Gentlemen," he said finally, "I am glad to be home." The room erupted into cheers and the partying commenced in earnest, going on long into the wee hours.

Wendell was now working sporadically in Brady's Studio at 10th and Broadway. He couldn't afford much, but he could afford to drink.

Having made up his mind not to marry Margaret, Wendell had now to tell her. The intensity of their Christmas kiss had created the expectation that he would propose, indeed had been seen as a proposal in itself. Letting down the family that had embraced him for so long would be difficult. It was with a heavy heart that he made his way over to the house on Washington Square that Elizabeth and Margaret now shared.

Awkwardly for Wendell, Tom Aldrich and Lil Woodman were also visiting. Margaret invited Wendell in and sat possessively down beside him on the couch. "We were just concerning ourselves with Molly Booth's letter," she explained.

Lil had it open on her lap. "Why, is there trouble?" asked Wendell.

"Trouble in paradise," said Lil. "Several days ago, movers came and took everything out of the Booth's apartment, and then I received this letter:

"Dear Lil, As you know, my health has been fragile, and we have agreed that the cleaner country air outside Boston will do me much good. Edwin and I have bought a modest house, quite beautiful. I will miss my friends in New York, but as you also know, we have been lucky enough to find good friends here, especially Julia Howe.

" 'Tis a pity, even though they are liberal in their politics, Bostonians demand the severest code of civility. I'm afraid there is no place on Earth save New York and Paris where one can feel truly free. Edwin and I will miss all of you terribly."

Wendell was disturbed. "Pray, is Molly really ill?"

"No," said Lil. "It's Ned. Read him your letter, Lizzy."

Elizabeth sighed. Still pale in black mourning, she looked quite prim. "Really, Lil, it seems on the level of vile gossip. I'm sure Molly did not intend me to read it to all."

"Why, as the secret's out, Elizabeth, surely you would share it with Wendell. It involves him, after all." Now Wendell felt some alarm and confessed his desire to hear it.

"Well then," said Elizabeth. She read, *"My Dear Lizzy, As you know, the public story is that we have moved for my health. But in fact, it is Ned's drinking that has forced this change. We simply must remove from the influence of his friends there, particularly Tom and Wendell. I am very sorry to say this. There are others just as bad, but whose company he keeps less regularly. We do love them all, but Ned is in agreement and struggles daily with the habit from which his father died. He is much afraid that the "Booth curse" of madness will fall on him, just as society is acclaiming his greatness. Pray, when we do come to town, see to it that no one has alcohol around him. I miss you and New York. Love, Molly"*

All eyes turned toward Wendell, eager to register his reaction. He was mortified. The whole embarrassing affair reminded him suddenly that he did want a drink, and he stood to take his leave. "I'm so sorry," cried Elizabeth, "I have offended you."

"Nay," said Wendell sadly, "Molly speaks truly. Even now, I want a drink more than I want to stay here among friends. I am going to Pfaff's." It had been an honest moment, and his friends' faces registered shock. Margaret grabbed his arm.

"Do you really have to leave? Is your habit so bad?" Her voice was filled with anxiety and foreboding, but it gave Wendell the excuse he'd been looking for.

"Pray walk with me outside," he implored. Once outside, with Margaret still clinging to him, he placed his hand upon her cheek and said as tenderly as he could, "Margaret, I can't marry you. I am not able to take care of myself, much less a wife. As bad as my company has been for Ned, it would be worse for one who shared my house and marital bed." He saw the crestfallen face, and tried to keep the victory out of his voice when he said again with finality, "I can't marry you." She was crying now, and Wendell felt naught but relief. How close he had come to losing his freedom – and Lillian. "I am sorry," he lied, and departed.

As he sat with Macaroni at Pfaff's, matching him drink for drink, Wendell reflected on Molly's sad letter. He had clearly lost friends who had been there when he needed them most, and he felt terrible. His skull seemed to split along a sharp blade of pain and his stomach churned. Ned and Molly had actually moved away because of him – it was beyond bearing. Finally he staggered into Brady's studio and mounted some of the pictures he had taken at Falmouth. The forlorn scenes before him proved too much and he went home.

At long last the letter came he had been waiting for. Dr. Paschal

Beverly Randolph would be in New York for two days only, February 11 and 12, and would be happy to meet with Wendell and Lillian in a meeting room at the Bowery hotel where he would be staying. He would expect the couple at 9am in the morning with a payment of $25. Wendell counted how many jars of patent medicine he still had, hoping that part of this high payment could be achieved with their sale. Then he wrote to Lillian, *"Dr. Randolph can see us at 9am on February 11, here in New York. Please come. If perchance there is some other reason besides the asthma that makes you wish to avoid me, I would have you know that I, too, can let you go for love of you, and seek only that you be well and whole. With my sincerest regards, Wendell*

Now that his drinking had been labeled a problem, it became more acute. Tom Aldrich professed not to over-imbibe except when Edwin was around, and wrote his approval for the move to Molly, promising to be a faithful watchdog of Ned should they return. Wendell tried to stave off his own urges with cigarettes, coffee, and hasheesh, but success proved only sporadic.

Meanwhile, Albert Bierstadt was mounting his *Rocky Mountains* painting in the Exhibition Hall at the Studio Building. It was far larger even than Fred Church's *Heart of the Andes*, but Wendell thought the colors overdone and garish. Again, art fanatics queued up around the block and to Wendell's surprise, Fitzhugh thought the painting divine and wrote glowingly about it in the *New-York Evening Post*.

As February approached, Wendell was sure Lillian would not reply. Finally he received a letter from Walt Whitman, who was engaged in a new role as angel of mercy at the Washington hospitals:

"My Dearest Wendell, I thought I should update you on news that will interest you. There is typhoid in the hospitals. Miss Louisa May Alcott has taken sick and been dismissed from her post here. As Lillian has shown signs of it, she was given leave to accompany

Miss Alcott home to Concord and ordered to stay away a least a month.

"Lillian shared your letter with me and confided a determination not to respond. I feel the traitor to reply in her stead, yet I am sympathetic to your love for her and your desire to know where you stand.

"You surely believe how much I miss you and the others in New York. But I do feel needed here, Wendell, and needful myself of doing what I can in the face of my country's dire circumstances. My diary is filled with sorrowful stories. Please remember me fondly to our mutual friends, and accept my most loving regard for yourself. Walt"

Wendell's anxiety leapt as he read it. Typhoid! 'Twas worse than the cholera that had killed Thomas' wife and children. He must go to Concord forthwith! Ah, but it would strain his wallet badly. Remembering the money he and Thomas had gotten selling albumen portraits in Washington, Wendell regretted leaving his wagon there.

The table in the alcove at Pfaff's was empty and Wendell found himself in need of counsel, so stopped at Waverly Place to find Fitzhugh. He found his friend in the den writing a story for *Vanity Fair*, his hookah bubbling beside him. Rosalie was nowhere to be seen. Wendell pulled up a nearby chair as Fitzhugh offered him a puff. "Pray," said Wendell after exhaling the sweetly acrid smoke, "I would not interfere with your musings. I will come back another time."

"Nonsense! You are my muse, Harte old man!" Fitzhugh put down his pen and drew a large gurgling breath from the pipe, held it, then watched languidly as the smoke caught the ebbing sunlight from the window. He seemed quite blissful. For awhile, they smoked in appreciative silence until Wendell, too, was at peace.

"Ah," breathed Wendell philosophically, "but that doesn't solve my problem." This provoked giggling on both their parts, as the word 'problem' struck them as incongruous with their drug-induced euphoria. The giggling soon became laughter, which spent itself in tears rolling down Wendell's cheeks. Uncontrite, he wiped them away, and he and Fitzhugh sat simply looking at each other.

"I apologize," said Fitzhugh finally, sobering up a bit. "Something is seriously amiss."

"Aye," said Wendell. "I have to go to Concord."

"Do you need money?" Fitzhugh had already drawn out his purse and handed Wendell a ten-dollar gold piece. "Is this enough?" Wendell nodded gratefully and left his friend to his scribblings.

It was already the first week of February. The train to Boston was piled high on either side with snow, and forced several times to stop while Wendell helped the other men clear the track of drifts. Quite late getting in, Wendell missed his connection. Since no more trains were coming, he decided to walk, across the bridge to Cambridge and Harvard College, thence the seventeen miles of unpaved path to Concord.

The traffic on the well-used bridge across the Charles River kept the snow at bay, and the campus, too, was clear enough, even though snow had begun to fall again. As Wendell trudged past the gangly youths on the Square, looking for the Commons so he might get a bite, he had an epiphany that he was no longer young, nor innocent. A lump of nostalgia rose in his throat for those hopeful days with Sam and Fitzhugh at Union College in Schenectady, when they had been so self-assured and ready to take on the world – before anyone dreamed that troubles with the South could possibly come to this. He felt a stabbing pain in the hand that was no longer there, and the alma mater's song that Fitzhugh had written was softly on his tongue: *Then here's to thee, thou brave and free, Old Union smiling o'er us, And for many a day, as thy walls grow gray, May they ring with thy children's chorus!*

Finally fortified with beer, bread and jerky, Wendell asked two students to point out the path to Concord. "It's harsh weather to be walking that far," said one uncertainly. "Nay," said the other proudly, "Henry David Thoreau used to walk it every day!" Thus assured, Wendell headed as they'd pointed, into the woods and the mounding snow.

Conditions worsened suddenly, becoming blizzard-like, with the snow threatening to top his high boots. Beneath his woolen socks, Wendell felt his toes go numb. The path grew indistinct before him, and the snow-covered hush gave way to a ferocious wind and the loud crack of heavy-laden limbs. His breath stabbed in his chest. As the blizzard grew in intensity, it was hard even to see – all was lead white and cobalt grey. He imagined Lillian, desperately ill, wrapped in a blanket before a fire at the Alcott's Orchard House, while he lay buried in snow only feet away, not to be found till spring. Somehow, it seemed a fitting end to their story.

While he thus ruminated, struggling for each step, he was surprised by a team of horses at his back and almost running him down. "Whoa!" called the driver. "Who goes there?" The horses stopped, and Bronson Alcott climbed through the drifts and grabbed Wendell's arm. "Mr. Parry, isn't it?" he said surprised. He helped Wendell into the carriage, and bid the driver on. "If you've come for Lily Ann, I just took her to the train station. She's headed for New York."

"Is she better?" Wendell gasped, not knowing whether to be alarmed or elated. "I had heard typhoid."

"Yes, she's fine enough, an occasional cough is all. Louisa May had it worse, but is recovering." When they reached the house, Wendell was given hot soup and bundled shivering onto the sofa. He asked after Louisa May. "The doctors are giving her some sort of mercury treatment," came Abby Alcott's answer, "which I'm not sure is the right thing."

Wendell sighed. "As an artist, I took pains to avoid ingesting the mercury pigments. It has always confused me that a poison in one context could be a medicine in another."

Two days later, the evening of February 10, he arrived back at his atelier to find Lillian asleep in his bed. His heart swelled in gratitude and he went to borrow a bedroll for the floor.

Chapter 37

Lillian's hand on his shoulder shook him awake. He opened his eyes to see her already dressed, smiling down at where he lay on the mat Sanford had leant him. "You came," he said gratefully. Then, "What time is it?"

"Time to get up. We've just time for breakfast in the mess."

The artists expressed delight to see her, and she seemed to bloom before their approval. Her familiar smile again took its place across her thin features. "It's good to be home," she said.

On the Harlem railcar to Dr. Randolph's Bowery hotel, Wendell asked why she was pensive. "I'm worried that the magic might not work," she confessed.

He looked at her across from him, a jewel against the shabby red plush of the omnibus seat with pink morning light catching her bonnet through the window. He wished he could paint her.

"It will work," he insisted, placing his left hand on her knee. "When he consecrated the magic mirror, there was a most astonishing ritual – it transformed my life, and gave me my success as a painter."

"Please, tell me about it," she whispered.

Wendell was silent. The ritual had been sexual, and the memory of it roused him. "I can't speak of it," he choked, "I am sworn."

When they met with Dr. Randolph, the small meeting room had been vacated for their privacy. They sat on two chairs facing the doctor who sat upon the couch.

"What I wish to know of you both today," began the magician after they had settled the payment, "are you indeed bound to each other, and able therefore to perform the sacred mysteries required for initiation?"

Wendell looked at Lillian, who looked away and down at her

lap as if to say, 'You got me into this – you explain it.'

Wendell gulped. "We love each other very much," he began, "but we are unable to perform as a man and a woman should perform, and hoped that you would help us lest we be unable to be together because of it." Dr. Randolph was listening intently, and nodded for him to continue. "You are familiar with my story, that since the first battle at Bull Run, I have been unable to pursue my livelihood for loss of my hand. I have no money with which to care for a family. As for Miss Flax, she had been aiding slaves to escape when she was traumatized by a brutal man who suffocated and raped her. The result is that she can't breathe during any passional act."

"Miss Flax," asked the doctor abruptly, taking them off guard with his question, "for what in this is Mr. Parry to blame?"

Lillian hastily shook her head. "Oh, I do not blame Mr. Parry for any of it."

He looked at her sharply, then said, "And Mr. Parry, what do you regret not doing that could have altered the course of things?"

"I regret most strongly that I did not interfere in the rape," Wendell responded.

"Why didn't you?"

"I did not realize at the time what was occurring."

The doctor nodded, his astute gaze penetrating. "What else?"

"I regret that I did not make more concessions to the Marquis when I had the chance to sell him my paintings," Wendell confessed.

Lillian was suddenly glaring at him with venom in her eyes. "Fie, Wendell, you mean you wish you had bedded the Countess!"

"Yes!" Wendell turned to look at her with righteous determination. "Yes, Lillian, I do mean that. 'Twas for your sake I did not, though you were gone and would not have felt any pain from it. We could have had $8000 now, instead of nothing."

Lillian stood with hands balled into fists. "And 'twas for your sake I sought to drug Mr. Ferguson, when, I assure you, it would have been far more pleasant to simply sport with him! He was not unattractive."

"Believe me, Lillian," Wendell shouted, suddenly angry, "I wish now you had!"

The doctor's eyes had grown wide with alarm, and he leapt to his feet, grabbing his hat and coat to go. "The two of you are far from bound! Indeed, your wickedness has brought this evil curse down on your heads, and I must unhappily leave you to it!"

Wendell instantly regretted the exchange, and reached out with his wooden hand to stay the doctor by the elbow. "Please, Dr. Randolph," he begged, standing to block the doctor's way out, "we did not in the end commit the infidelity and have both paid dearly for it. I admit we are not ready for initiation, but could you not help us to heal our wickedness? We do wish to be together, and have no hope but you."

Randolph spun angrily about and pointed his finger at the carpet, commanding them with a voice from Sinai, "Down on your knees, the both of you, and bless each other for your sacrifices! Do you not know that fidelity is required above all else?" They both got down on their knees obediently, shaking like children, and Wendell looked up at the doctor in supplication.

"But I would not wish that sacrifice on her, not for my sake – 'tis too much for anyone."

The doctor shook his fist angrily, raving, "Do you think Jesus wished his followers to be eaten by lions? Yet they did not forsake him and they were eaten, and in their sacrifice spread the love of Christ throughout the world. Fidelity is always a sacrifice, Mr. Parry, and love is naught but the altar for that sacrifice! What is needed is to be grateful, and yourselves worthy! Bow down to her and thank her, Mr. Parry, bow down to her! And you, Miss Flax, bow down to Mr. Parry as he too sacrificed a good deal for your sake. Eight thousand dollars is not claptrap!" The truth of what he said washed over them both as they prostrated themselves to each other, offering their gratitude, tears coming to their eyes. "Thank each other!" the magician thundered again.

"'Twas more sacrifice than I ever intended, but it really does feel good that you did not sport with her again," confessed Lillian in a whisper. "Thank you."

And Wendell said in kind, "You don't know how it changed things when you told me you never sought to lie with Ferguson." They had both begun to weep. "It changed everything – it changed everything. Thank you, truly."

Indeed, 'twas what was needed. The sacrifices could not be undone, but it felt so good to be thanked for them. Now as they kneeled before each other, Lillian came into Wendell's arms with not a thought of fear. He hugged her tightly, and rested his chin upon her head, so glad for the warmth of her body – at last. Dr. Randolph was looking on and sighed his approval. Wendell gently lifted Lillian's chin to find her lips. He felt them part, felt her willingness, then heard with horror her breath catch in a wheeze, and she pulled away from him strangling. "Breathe with me," he begged, letting go of her and pulling her to her feet, "breathe with me."

The doctor watched with fascination as the two breathed together till she calmed, and considered a long moment. Finally he said quietly, "Yes, I see your trouble. I will help you. I will meet you here again tomorrow, same time. Now if you'll excuse me, I will let myself out." He put on his top hat and strode regally toward the door, spun and gave a little bow. Then suddenly, as if overcome with a spirit presence, he took off his hat and placed it over his heart, sinking to his knees. "And as a black man," he offered, "I want to thank you for your sacrifices on behalf of abolition. It is overwhelming to me what you both have so selflessly given."

There were tears in his own eyes as he rose again, put on his hat and thumped it cockily into place; thus having restored his kingly manner, said, "Until tomorrow," and let himself out.

They stood staring at the door in the quietness of the room, both throbbing with the power of what had so unexpectedly taken place. "I am most taken with him," murmured Lillian at length.

Wendell sighed his agreement. "Aye, it appears we have found ourselves a doctor."

For the rest of the day, they shared their stories of their time apart and visited with friends. That night, Wendell once again slept in the bedroll on the floor, sighing happily that Lillian was so close at hand.

The next morning, the little meeting room at the Bowery hotel was transformed, the smell of frankincense burning on the brazier and candles lit to enhance the daylight which streamed weakly through diaphanous drapes. After pleasantries with Dr. Randolph over tea, they began their second interview.

"As you know, I consider it a great tragedy, Mr. Parry, that you cracked your magic mirror. We will have to manage as best we can without it." He reached for his medical bag from which he drew a bronze box of Persian make and design. He mumbled a brief incantation over it, giving wonder to his small audience, then looked at them meaningfully as he raised the lid. "I offer you the Gift of the Magi," he said, and drew out the smaller of the tidily wrapped bundles, handing it to Lillian. "Miss Flax, this bundle contains the sacred scent of the Orient – frankincense – bought at great expense from the markets of Jerusalem. And while it is to be used only in rituals, it is remarkably good at curing asthma."

Lillian nodded, her eyes wide with child-like enchantment.

"And this," he continued, handing the heavier bundle to Wendell, "contains candles made of wax from the bees of Galilee, and blessed by the Melissa herself. There are forty-nine of them. Now listen to me closely, and follow my instructions exactly, for I will not be here to aid thee."

The two leaned forward, intent on the doctor's every word. "Each day, before the sun sets below the horizon, you will wash your feet and light the frankincense. Then sitting near to each other, you will ask in your minds that your sins be forgiven, then light a candle set before you. Begin breathing together.

"When at last the breathing is effortless in its mutual rhythm, you will commence staring at the flame till your eyelids grow heavy and finally close, then fix the flame's latent image in the center of your forehead. As you do this, you must be mindful that you remain breathing together. Continue thus with eyes closed and focused on the latent flame till the candle extinguishes itself. Then open your eyes and give thanks three times, 'Gratitude from the heart, gratitude from the body, gratitude from the mind – *Baruch Ain Soph. Selah.*' This you must do for forty-nine days continuously until the candles are gone. You are not to speak or to touch, nor make any movement beyond that which is necessary for comfort. Do you understand?"

They nodded, uncertain of its meaning but hopeful of its outcome.

The doctor went on, for there was more. "As the time passes and you obey this ritual flawlessly, you will find that your thoughts become mingled and magnetized to each other, and mayhap you will hear the other speak in your head. It is important that you do not become enamored of this phenomenon, but try to empty your heads of all thoughts, and resist the urge to send each other messages. Is that understood?" They nodded again and Wendell felt a small thrill of excitement, fearing that it would be almost impossible to resist such a curious experiment.

The doctor pulled a visit card from his pocket, with an address from which to order more candles from him. He continued, "This is where you will order another box of forty-nine, then a box of seven candles. With your second box of forty-nine, your instructions will change slightly. That is, Mr. Parry, with eyes still closed during the ritual, and with Miss Flax's unspoken permission, reach out and touch her – but only with your phantom hand. Are there any questions?"

"My phantom hand?" asked Wendell perplexed. "What do you mean? Are you saying to touch her with the hand that is missing?"

"Indeed, it is not missing, Mr. Parry." The magician looked at him with a certainty that made Wendell's hair bristle upon his skin. "The soul of it is still there. You know this when you reach for things, when you brush against it, when it gives you pain. Is this not true?"

Slowly, Wendell nodded, feeling his grasp of reality slipping away as it had when he'd fought the demon and awakened in the crib. Saint Tammany had said it at Catherine's church, 'Your hand is not gone.' This time, however, Wendell supposed a purpose in it, and a power.

Now a blushing Lillian spoke up, "Dr. Randolph, may I not touch him?"

He smiled, "The point is not to tease and torment, my dear, but to breathe together and get used to being touched without wheezing. No, it is he who must touch you. And Mr. Parry, touching her thus may make you rouse; still, there must be no ejaculation." This made them both blush, Wendell with amusement when he saw how demure and school-girlish Lillian became, quickly folding her hands in her lap and looking down.

The doctor sighed, addressing Wendell. "There is yet more," he said, "for the entire of the cure is thus: for forty-nine days you breathe together, eyes closed. Then for forty-nine days you may touch her with your phantom hand, eyes closed, while yet breathing together, and always concluding with the offer of gratitude. Finally, for another seven days, if Miss Flax has had no episode of asthma, you will light a candle and, setting your intention – your prayer – for what your lives should be, you may lie together. Mind you, if in any phase she does wheeze, you must begin again with the first phase. Each grouping, of forty-nine and of seven, must be contiguous, or you will have to start that phase over. During the final phase, you may with the greatest of restraint, insert yourself, but after so doing, make no voluntary movement, only continuing to breathe together and withstanding any urge to ejaculate. You may stay like this with your phallus inside her as long as you are obedient to these rules and until the candle goes out."

Wendell was about to ask how such a thing were possible, when Lillian began to wheeze. Dr. Randolph stayed Wendell's reaction with his hand, shushing him, while Lillian stood clutching her throat, suffocating miserably. "Nay, Mr. Parry," said Randolph laughing, and to Wendell's horror, began to taunt her. "Phallus, phallus, phallus!" he said merrily.

Lillian's eyes were wide as she struggled for breath. The torture seemed unbearable and Wendell was about to aid her, when she suddenly found the key to calm herself, and her wheezing turned suddenly to laughter. "Phallus, phallus, phallus!" Randolph continued. Her laughter heightened, and soon proved infectious – they were all in short time quite caught up in relieved hilarity.

As finally the joke was spent and she sat down gasping and amazed upon her chair, she ventured the question, "Am I now cured?"

The doctor frowned and shook his head. "Nay, you are not. Your mind seeks to protect you, and will not kill you over a few words. But it is truly frightened of the sexual act, and will stop at nothing – even death – to shy you from it."

With that sobering thought, he turned to Wendell and resumed his instructions. "Now, on the seventh and final candle, you may set your mutual prayer, visioning your life together as you would have it, and this time, allow the ejaculation. You may direct this ejaculate into Lillian's unguarded womb or direct it back up your spine into yourself – whichever is the more appropriate. At the moment of your mutual crisis, you are both to offer great gratitude to God for the success of your prayer yelling, '*Baruch Ain Soph.*' Your prayers will be answered. This the adepts call the *Hieros Gamos*, the Sacred Marriage – and there is nothing on earth or in the firmament more powerful and more holy, for it is, itself, the marriage of Heaven and Earth."

The magician stood abruptly before they could ask their many questions, in haste suddenly to depart. "I must away to Europe. Meanwhile, the day after tomorrow is Valentine's Day, an auspicious day to begin. Oh, and one more thing – after each ritual excepting the last, you must sleep apart and be cognizant of your dreams – do not be afraid of your dreams, Mr. Parry, answers will come in them." He thumped his top hat into place upon his head, and with a short bow, took his leave.

As they rode back uptown, Lillian was staring out the railcar window, caught up in her own musings. Wendell watched her gratefully – she believed she would be cured, he could see that. He wished he could read her thoughts, and had the sudden epiphany that he might soon be able to. What would he find there? Were she cured, would she still want him? It had rather shocked him when she said she would not have minded sporting with Ferguson. For the first time since the revelation of her asthma, the memory of that scene at the mansion, how he felt as Ferguson carried her up the stairs, swept through him with a sickening lurch of his stomach. Men were attracted to other women, of course, but women? How many other men had she been attracted to? Sanford? John Wilkes? Certainly Edwin – even he was attracted to Edwin! This last thought amused him, just in time that when Lillian's gaze turned to him, Wendell was smiling wryly. She smiled sweetly back – 'twas a good thing she couldn't read his thoughts.

Chapter 38

On Valentine's Day, Wendell knocked on Ada Clare's door with a bouquet of gardenias for Lillian. He was nervous as he waited, wondering if the girls had been talking about him. It was not that Lillian might know of his night with Ada, but that he would not know if she knew and he might seem to be hiding something from her. He didn't want to bring it up, but thought he'd better. So when at last Lillian appeared at the door for their afternoon together, there was an awkwardness between them.

Despite her warm cloak, she shivered as she stepped into the cold and slipped her hand into his. They made their way across the park by the reservoir toward carriages on 6th Avenue. He wanted to put his arm about her shoulders and pull her close, but dared not. Before he had worked up the courage to say anything, she informed him almost casually, "I believe I will not be staying with Ada anymore. Rosalie has invited me to stay with her at the Waverly household – she is quite lonely for company."

Alas, why did he listen to women? Now his indiscretion with Ada had interfered with the girls' friendship, and surely was another mark against him.

Lillian read his thoughts and laughed. "Wendell, it is not what you think. You have done nothing wrong. The truth is that Ada has a gentleman friend and I am in the way!"

Wendell's relief was so glorious that he almost scooped her into his arms and spun her for joy. Just in time he remembered her asthma, and that it would be 105 days before he could satisfy even that small impulse. He would be counting the days!

Outside the Greenwich Village restaurant, a gathering of young women with signature books milled about braving the cold and peeking through the windows. "Such a crowd could only mean one thing," laughed Lillian. "Edwin Booth is inside!" Ned had been playing at the Winter Garden for the passed week and they expected he would be in town with Molly. Again, Wendell felt dismay, knowing Molly's edict for Ned to stay away from him. But when they entered, Molly was not to be seen. Ned sat at a large table in a lace curtained alcove with Laura Keene. He looked up and gaily beckoned them over.

"Do you mind?" asked Ned graciously, standing to kiss Lillian's hand. "I know it's Valentine's Day, but alas, Laura and I are here without our valentines and would welcome your company."

Wendell had taken Laura's hand and kissed it. She looked older than he remembered her, almost middle-aged. "Of course, it is up to the ladies," he said amiably. Lillian was already seating herself in the chair Ned pulled out, and Wendell took a seat beside her.

"I trust Molly is well," Lillian said when they had ordered.

"She hurt her leg and the doctor has admonished her to stay off of it," Ned explained. "I confess, I am quite lost without her. But, too, she had been coughing and the violent cold of the weather up there can't be good for weakened lungs. I was glad to see her confined to a warm hearth."

The waiter set down a wine glass in front of him. Wendell watched uneasily as Ned tasted it and nodded for the glass to be filled. He held the bottle out to them, "Anyone else?" Before they could answer, Ned said to the waiter, "Bring some glasses for my friends and leave the bottle."

Laura spoke up, "None for me, thank you!"

"Come, drinking supports the war effort," he urged, referring to the new tax on alcohol, but Wendell declined, as did Lillian.

Ned looked defensive. "It's only wine, and very good wine." Now the bottle was sitting in front of his glass alone, and Molly's absence became palpable.

"Are you playing anywhere, Laura?" asked Lillian.

"Aye, I am beginning my thousand nights tour of *My American*

Cousin." Laura seemed to have recovered her old enthusiasm, gone when she'd lost her theater. "Once again, I'm hoping to have Sother as Dundreary. He is so funny! You've seen him in it, haven't you, Lillian?"

Lillian nodded. "No one else could play that part. He is as much Dundreary as Ned is Hamlet."

Ned smiled. "I had tried out for the part once, but the only role for which I've ever gotten a laugh is Romeo. I'm afraid my temperament is suited only for tragedy."

"How now?" objected Lillian. "Molly must surely have thought you a good Romeo when she met you as Juliet."

"Ah," he said fondly, "I had no trouble playing Romeo to her Juliet off-stage. But come, Lillian, tell me about Washington City. You have had adventures there since we last met. Or is that not a fit subject for Valentine's Day?"

"'Tis not romantic," Lillian acknowledged.

"I often feel the urge to enlist," rued Edwin, sipping his wine. "Like many, I have lost a close friend and daily worry for another. Two things stay me. One is that I promised my mother and Molly I would not. And second is that I am a coward. I am good with a foil, but show me a gun and I am a limp Peter when the cock crowed."

"Surely," said Laura, ignoring the coarse pun, "It is your career that stays you."

Ned considered. "Aye, Laura, there is truth to that. We are such stuff as dreams are made on, you and I. More than ever, people need the theater."

They were suddenly interrupted by Tom Aldrich who barged into the alcove and picked up Ned's wine glass, quickly downing the wine himself. "Sorry, Ned old boy, but I promised Molly, and you had given me the slip." He set the empty glass back onto the table and smiled to take the sting off, handing the wine bottle to Wendell. "Drink up, Wendell, it's our duty to save Ned from himself. We almost had to bring the curtain down on his performance last night."

Ned sighed morosely but not without humor. "This uneven-handed justice commends our poisoned chalice to your lips," he improvised. "But pray, are you all coming to the play tonight? It's *Hamlet*. I have room in my box and fain would not be alone in Molly's absence."

"And Molly would fain not have us leave you alone!" Aldrich piped up brightly and sat down. "Ah Ned, you will not so easily herd us to be watched and avoided. I realize now I must accompany you backstage and into the wings."

Playfully, Wendell raised the wine bottle to his own lips and drank heartily. "Ladies?" he offered, and when they shook their heads, handed the bottle to Aldrich.

"Hark ye, Ned is smiling," noted Aldrich suspiciously. "I believe he means to see us drunk and thereby escape our vigilance. Shall we chance it, Wendell? 'Twould be a shame to waste such good vintage." He stood and downed the last of the bottle, reeling as he did so.

Ned laughed. "*Garçon,*" he called to the waiter, "*si vous plait,* bring my friends another bottle." This brought giggles from the men, and the two ladies exchanged an anxious look. But the conversation turned sober enough as Ned, Tom, and Laura insisted on hearing about Washington, and all the adventures there. The afternoon drifted pleasantly on, with French pastries and yet a third bottle from which Ned stayed carefully away.

By the time Wendell and Lillian arrived with her bags at the Waverly Place household, Wendell was staggering and aware that he must present a pathetic figure, with probably a stench on his breath. Rosalie greeted them, explaining that Fitzhugh was working in his uncle's law office, and bid Lillian make herself at home. Behind her the bearded Hun, Albert Bierstadt, rose from the sofa and said an awkward hello.

Lillian led Wendell into the spare bedroom which she would be occupying whilst Fitzhugh and Rosalie still forbore to share the other bed.

They were quiet as Lillian unpacked her few things, then each bathed their feet in the wash bowl and Lillian lit the soothing incense. Wendell pulled the little bedside table away from the wall and placed the one chair before it. He sat on the high bed while Lillian sat on the chair, and they mumbled some words asking forgiveness. Then, putting the candle on the table between them, Wendell set it ablaze. It threw shadows that danced across the room and lit Lillian's face with a flickering glow. He met her gaze and tried to follow her breath, which proved too deep and even for him, then Lillian tried to follow Wendell whose breathing seemed drunkenly erratic. Finally, they invented a slow and shallow rhythm which was comfortable for both, and soon were staring at the flame till their eyes closed.

For a long time, Wendell watched the latent and inverted colors of the flame dancing behind his eyelids and concentrated on rolling his eyes to move it to the center of his forehead, all the while listening for her breath and keeping rhythm. The effort to do all this at once required such attention that there was little room for other thoughts. Wendell lost track of time and was only vaguely aware of the darkening of the day outside, until Lillian cleared her throat loudly and he opened his eyes. He was lying on the bed as the sun sank below the windowsill. Embarrassed, he sat up, noted the used up candle, and quickly joined Lillian in saying, "Gratitude from the heart, gratitude from the body, gratitude from the mind – *Baruch Ain Soph, Selah.*"

"How long had I been sleeping?" he asked when they were finished.

She sighed. "Don't feel bad. You needed it. Are you refreshed?" He nodded – indeed, he felt relaxed in a way he had not, except perhaps after sexual intercourse, which seemed very long ago. She added, "I'm certain we will get better at it. It's not easy to follow the breath of someone who's snoring." He detected the concern in her voice, and realized with a small stab of alarm that his drinking could sabotage their only chance at a cure. What he had said to Margaret as an excuse not to marry her was painfully close to being true.

While Lillian dressed for the theater, Wendell went to the kitchen and found Fitzhugh and Henry Clapp, eager to share their food while Rosalie changed her gown. Fitzhugh and Rosalie were going to the play as Ned's guests, and Henry Clapp was going to write a review for *Vanity Fair*. Wendell suspected that Clapp had heard gossip about Ned's drinking and wished to write about a calamity, should there be one. Bierstadt was not to be seen.

As the friends rode in the cab together to the Winter Garden, the topic of Ned's drinking came up. "Tom Aldrich has asked me to alternate with him in policing Ned," spoke Fitzhugh. "I will be on duty tomorrow, but someone is needed for next week. Do you mind, Wendell?"

Wendell looked uncertainly at Lillian. "It might help you with your own drinking to be mindful of Ned's," she offered diplomatically.

"Alright," Wendell agreed, "but not for the full twenty-four hours. Lillian and I have a daily health regimen to attend."

"The greater portion will fall to Tom," Fitzhugh explained. "He is quite committed. I believe he wishes to again be in Molly's graces."

"As do I!" Wendell agreed.

Fitzhugh looked pointedly at Henry Clapp. "All of this is quite confidential, of course."

"'Tis not exactly news that Edwin has oft carried too much sail," Henry protested indignantly. "We have already written of it, that his drunkenness seems perfectly to suit the role. He is a wild drunk when playing Richard and a melancholy drunk when playing Hamlet. I have even seen him do Iago well with a cruel drunkenness. Such did his father before him. There is no need to write of it again."

While Ned's guests milled outside the theater to receive their special passes, Henry headed with his ticket for the door. They saw him collect a lady there, and enter with no effort to introduce her. "Fie," said Lillian. "He is fond of his gossip about everyone else, but his own affairs he keeps close to the vest."

When they arrived at Edwin Booth's private box, Elizabeth, Margaret, Lil Woodman, and Albert Bierstadt were already there. Elizabeth, wearing half-mourning, a touch of purple and green with the black, gave Lillian a big hug and introduced her sister, Margaret. Wendell watched uneasily and thought he detected a chill in their meeting. There was no hint of such chill when Fitzhugh greeted Bierstadt, but rather a false over-warmth with a hint of hasheesh unreality. Rosalie got out her soap bubble pipe and absently blew bubbles as she and Bierstadt pretended not to notice each other. When they all were seated, Ned appeared in his costume behind them, followed closely by the watchful Tom Aldrich. "Thank you so much for coming," Ned said with evident sobriety and good cheer. He flourished his hand and bowed. "I am used to imagining that I play for Molly, and now in her stead, dear friends, I will play for you."

The lights finally dimmed and the curtains opened on a fancied set that took the viewers instantly to Denmark. The mute ghost sent shivers down their spines, but more so did the look on Hamlet's face when first spake the ghost, "I am your father's spirit," and told Hamlet the story of its murder. Hamlet's anquished cry moved the audience to rapt empathy.

O, fie! Hold, hold, my heart;
And you, my sinews, grow not instant old,
But bear me stiffly up. Remember thee?
Aye, thou poor ghost..."

No matter how many times the audience had seen the play, they were yet left shaken and weeping by Ned's performance. The little gang of friends met their hero backstage to thank him and celebrate his success, but minus the aid of alcohol, the celebration was quickly over. Wendell assumed his turn on watch and accompanied Ned to his hotel, where the two friends passed a comfortable and comradely night.

The next morning, as they shared a small breakfast and the morning paper, a surprise guest arrived. John Wilkes had visited Molly following his triumph in Boston as *The Apostate* and now passed through to give his brother news. "Molly is ill," he told him, "but bids you continue with your schedule. She had ventured out to a friend's and been caught in a sudden snow which delayed the horse-cars. She arrived home quite chilled and soon took fever. The good news is that her leg is better."

"Should I go to her?" asked Edwin with concern.

"She says not, continue with your schedule. With a few days rest, she should be able to join you here."

Wendell did not care for John Wilkes and felt anxious to be going, but was concerned lest the brothers were in the habit of drinking together. Sensing his unease, Wilkes caught him aside and whispered, "You can leave him in my care. I too have promised Molly." Thus assured, Wendell made his way to Pfaff's where he gratefully had a whiskey. And then he had another.

By the time he made it over to Waverly Place for his evening ceremony with Lillian, Wendell was in his cups and staggering badly. This time Lillian cried, which made him try to embrace her. "Wendell, you have become a drunk!" she cried. "Get out! You will not cure me, you will kill me!" Alarmed at what must surely be hysteria, he stumbled into the street.

He managed to catch a carriage and asked the driver to take him uptown. Wendell was not sure where he was going, even when he got out on 5th Avenue and 42nd Street right in front of Ada

Clare's house. "Oh," he said, seeing where he was, "I wonder if she's home."

She opened the door to him dressed in a silky white dressing gown. "Why Wendell," she said, holding out her hand. Wendell grabbed her and pulled her to him, forcing his mouth onto hers. She stiffened but didn't struggle. Finally, he let her go and apologized. "I think you'd better lie down," she said, stepping aside so he could pass out on her couch.

Shortly, she woke him with a strong cup of coffee. "Come, Wendell, sober up," she said. Her son, Aubrey, gangly now at age seven, was behind her with a tray of cold compresses. She put one across Wendell's forehead. "You can't stay here, I have company coming," she said softly. At his questioning look, she added, "I would introduce you except – he's married." Again, he mumbled apologies, to which she said, "I doubt 'tis me to whom you need apologize. Are you not missing an engagement with Lillian?"

Wendell sighed and drank the coffee. Had Lillian thrown him out? He wasn't even sure – it was all a blur. He remembered his disgust at his father's drinking and was filled with self-loathing and regret. As he gradually became more sober, an old fear that he had not felt in awhile, the churning fear of abandonment, twisted his stomach. He went into the washroom and retched.

He was soon back at Waverly Place, and even Lillian had to admire the determination with which he struggled to get there. It was not quite dark. They bathed their feet and took their seats, murmured sincere regrets for their sins, lit the candle and began to breathe. Once more he awoke lying on the bed, but they had made it through a second day. One hundred and three days to go until they might be together again. One hundred and three days ...

The night after they had marked their seventh day, Tom Aldrich came by Wendell's atelier. Tom was frantic. "What am I to do?" he raved after explaining that Ned's previous night's show had been cancelled. "I can't fight him physically. We have come nigh to blows twice already. Fitzhugh is with him now, but Ned is full sailing away with his gallants up. And it's almost curtain time."

Wendell had carefully avoided being around any alcohol for a week now, and dreaded to become involved with Ned's intoxicated madness. He felt fragile. But here was Tom, desperate. Sighing, Wendell put on his frock coat and gloves, wrapped his muffler and positioned his hat. "Aye, I'll come with you. Perhaps the three of us can force some sense into him, to at least get him through his show. 'Twould break Molly's heart, were she to hear of this."

"Doubtless she has already heard," rued Tom. "It has surely been in the Boston papers. She has been sending telegrams by the hour and, for guilt, he will not read them."

At the Winter Garden, Fitzhugh and Lil Woodman had managed to ply Ned with coffee to get the great thespian dressed and onto the stage. What Wendell saw of the play was terrible, but despite a few boos, they did not bring the curtain down on it. There was relief when the end came and Ned stumbled off the stage, not even bothering with a final bow.

His would-be guardians followed him into his dressing room where he quickly found the bottle he had hidden beneath a chair and raged when they would take it from him. "Leave me be!" Ned shouted and took a swig. He burst out the back door into the alley, and with the troops close behind him, made it next door to his hotel room. They all forced their way in, and amidst a great deal of commotion, Wendell picked up an unopened telegram from the mail table.

The telegram was not from Molly, it was from her doctor. The terrible message read, *"Your wife is not expected to live through the night. You must come at once."*

Wendell's knees went weak beneath him. "Ned!" he called. Hearing their cacophony continue as if he hadn't spoken, he shook the shock from his chest and shouted. "Ned! Molly's dying! Ned! Edwin Booth! Your wife is dying!!"

A hush fell over the room and Ned was suddenly sober. "What?" he asked incredulous, "What?"

Sobbing now, Wendell told him, "She's not expected to live the night. You must go to her, Ned." Ned grabbed the telegram from Wendell's hand while the others ripped through the remaining pile.

But when Ned went anxiously for his cloak, Tom stayed him. His voice cracked as he said, "Ned, the midnight train is gone. There won't be another till 7am."

Ned looked confused. He stared at each of them in turn, beseeching, then gave a great shudder and slid down the wall helpless onto the floor. There he sat, dazed and alone. "Why?" he gasped. "Why? She had been full of life but three weeks ago. Nothing but a pulled tendon. Nothing." Then he cried out, "Molly? Molly? Tell me what to do." He rose and pathetically began to pace the floor, back and forth, as if by moving he could accomplish something.

"I'll put the coffee on," offered Lil through her tears. It was to be an all night vigil, no one was going to sleep. They would all stay up with their aching friend and wait for the 7am train.

Ned had still the wretched bottle in his hand. Noticing, he screamed in mortal anguish, a hideous scream like the death throes of an animal in the jaws of its predator, and flung the bottle into the fireplace.

When Wendell heard the scream and watched the bottle shatter into a million sharp and guilty pieces, his heart broke, its jagged edges stabbing at his chest with crippling pain. "Molly, forgive me," he sobbed to himself, "forgive me." With a fervent prayer that it was not too late for him and Lillian, he sank to the floor. He knew then with a certainty that neither he nor Ned would ever drink again.

Chapter 39

It was a gala party, held in the exhibition hall at the Tenth Street Studio Building. Albert Bierstadt's exhibit of *Rocky Mountains* had been an absolute triumph with art fanciers, if not with critics. The party was there to say goodbye to Bierstadt and Fitzhugh Ludlow who were leaving together on a journey west. All their friends and Fitzhugh's parents came out to see them. The artists of the Studio Building, Pfaffsians, actors and journalists were there. Asher Durand was there. The most famous actress in the world, "The Menken," back from touring with *Mazeppa*, was there with Bob Newell. Elizabeth, Margaret, and Sam's parents feasted on cake and saluted the adventurous pair. Charles Pfaff came over to offer his good wishes. Even Horace Greeley stopped by. Only Ned and Molly weren't there, would never be there again – Fitzhugh had just returned from Boston where he'd said goodbye to Ned, leaving him alone to grieve his dead wife and comfort their little daughter.

A band struck up a quadrille, and there was dancing into the night.

When the friends finally began to drift home and Lillian departed with Rosalie, Fitzhugh slipped off with Wendell to his atelier. They lounged on the bed, Fitzhugh with a pipe and Wendell with a cigarette, to say their final farewells.

"Tell me again why it is you're going?" asked Wendell, who really couldn't comprehend this strange relationship between Fitzhugh and Bierstadt.

"You think me mad, don't you?" observed Fitzhugh.

Wendell smiled ruefully. "Well, are you?"

Fitzhugh sighed, yet when he spoke there was a determined forcefulness to it. "Alas, what else am I to do? Opium's killing me, Wendell, and driving Rosalie into Bierstadt's arms. It became clear to me the night Molly died that I must shake my demon. I can't quit if I stay, I've tried." His eyes were fixed on the wall as he confessed, "I don't want to lose her."

"That I can fathom," said Wendell. "But why go with Bierstadt? He has not been what I would call a friend."

Fitzhugh turned his head toward Wendell, but his eyes held a faraway vision. "He will return a national hero, greater than Fred Church, full of sketches of the Rockies and tales of courage. There is nothing I can do to compete with that, except go with him and share in his glory." His gaze focused on his old school chum. "Wendell, I would be seen as the journalist who made Bierstadt great. Already, Rosalie admires me that I have been magnanimous of her cheating, and will admire me the more when I am again a famous writer. I will create Albert Bierstadt. I will be the author, and he my subject. When we return, his paintings will not be finished, but my book will be. It will be a sensation, Wendell – my sensation. I will return fit, famous, and free from demons."

"'Twill do you good, I believe you," said Wendell, "and, Fitzhugh, perhaps you know Rosalie, that this will work to keep her. But harken to me, I know Albert Bierstadt. Don't imagine that, even though he comes to like you, he will resist the urge to cuckold you."

"Have I anything to lose by taking that risk?" Fitzhugh asked, puffing urgently on his pipe. "By the gods, Harte, I have nothing to lose. He is already cuckolding me."

The next day, Fitzhugh and Bierstadt departed in a carriage from Waverly Place with Rosalie, Wendell, Lillian, Tom and Lil, Henry Clapp and Macaroni waving sorrowful goodbyes.

For the next week, Wendell and Lillian went for tea with many of their mutual friends, as Lillian had to be back in Washington City and so they themselves would soon depart. Elizabeth, Margaret, and little Sammy had them over to the townhouse on Washington Square. Wendell was relieved that Margaret was gracious and seemed to have accepted her fate – she and Lillian got on well. Besides visiting, they hoped to be able to sell or pawn a painting from Elizabeth's attic. In Washington, Lillian's nursing duties would bring her $10 per month, same as the colored soldiers got, $3 less than white soldiers. She would be fed and stay at the nurse's quarters but Wendell would have to pay his lodging and that of his horse – Mathew Brady would not be stabling Hidalgo much longer.

Following tea, Wendell lowered the ladder from the attic trapdoor and went up ahead. Light slanted in through the tiny gable window, and cobwebs hung from the exposed rafters. The smell of dust was worse than the appearance of it. He called back down to Lillian, "It's not too bad," but she had already hitched up her skirts and was on her way.

"Yes," she reminded him, poking her head through, "I had retrieved many paintings from here already."

"Is there anything left?" he asked, offering his wooden hand to her to pull herself up.

"They're over there, against the wall," she said, "but no, not many."

Wendell struck a match to the lamp. Its light fell across a steamer trunk with a red pant leg sticking out of it – Sam's extra uniform. Wendell felt somewhat queasy, as if pieces of Sam were strewn about.

"My Ithaca paintings are still at the Academy of Design," noted Wendell. "Had they no offers at all?"

"Yes, of course they had," huffed Lillian. "I told Asher Durand to decline anything less than $1500 apiece for them."

"Why? How much was offered?" He was suddenly not so sure he should have given her agency.

"Trust me," said Lillian confidently. "You will get your price."

Wendell shrugged. "I won't deny you know your business, Lillian, but we could use some money."

She had evidently decided to ignore him, and was on her knees, flipping through the remaining canvases. "I had been wanting to ask you what this is." Wendell watched chagrined as she drew out the portrait of her bodice minus the head. She looked at him with a flummoxed expression.

"Don't you like her?" he teased. "I think she is quite fetching."

"Is this what you see when you look at me?" she bristled.

"It's the first rule of portraiture to direct the eye toward what's most important."

"Fie, Wendell!" she said laughing. "Tell me what mischief you were up to, or I shall sell it along with your other pieces and you'll be a laughing stock."

So he told her the story of his summer as a limner, only being careful not to betray Thomas's name. She was grinning when he finished. "Clever," she admitted, for which he grinned back, accepting the undue credit with a little bow.

Also, there was the finished portrait that he had done of her their first week-end together. "Ah," she sighed, looking at it. "I feel so much older now."

"You don't look it," he said graciously, "though I'm sure that aging will become you."

Finally she fished out the picture of the sandstorm in Morocco with the gardenias and two figures. "Prescient, putting the buzzards in," she said wistfully.

"Shall we sell it? It may be we could pawn it. Something in it makes me uneasy," Wendell confessed. "When I painted it, I wasn't sure I would ever see you again."

"I put you through hell, didn't I, with all my abolitionist adventures."

"Nay, Lillian," he insisted, wishing he could take her in his arms. He pulled her to her feet and lifted her chin with his wooden hand – ninety-one days to go – "I loved you for it. I only regret I didn't trust you more." He saw the longing in her eyes, and it gave him hope.

Quickly, she turned away, and dragged the painting after her as she descended the ladder. "Help me with this," she said.

The train to Washington City was filled with troops and stopped frequently for rail repairs and bomb scares. With so much rebel activity around the capital, it was challenging for the Union to keep open their only connecting land corridor. The trip, which normally would have taken two days took twice that at twice the price, and had the few civilian passengers scrambling to share food and water. A distinct odor of sweat and garbage began to mix with coal fumes. Outside of the smoke-smudged windows, destroyed buildings and dilapidated soldiers reminded everyone there was a war.

It was a strange and difficult setting for Wendell and Lillian to do their breathing assignment. Washing their feet with a wet kerchief brought disapproving stares from the other passengers. Wendell would hold the candle and Lillian the incense, and their breathing had to be well synchronized before closing their eyes, as there was no possibility of hearing each other through the screech and clacking of the rails. Yet they managed, and when they finally got to Washington, there were just twenty-five candles left in the first box.

They arrived on a rainy morning, with mud splashing up from the many unpaved side-roads. Winter starkness had given over to a first blush of spring and there were startling numbers of colored soldiers wearing handsome uniforms much like the red-legged uniforms of the 14th Brooklyn, but with longer belted jackets. "Ruby sent word some time ago that Tuck enlisted, and only afterward did they find out she's pregnant," Lillian informed him. "Young Wilberforce has left her too, to study architecture at the Cooper Union." Lillian's concern was mixed with hope. Times were indeed changing.

Lillian managed to get the night shift from 11pm so that she would have time to sleep in the mornings and still spend their evenings together. After settling her in, Wendell got a local post office box and went to Brady's livery to bail out his wagon and horse. Hidalgo looked well, having been recently pastured and groomed. By now Wendell had spent most of his money, and what was left would have to be used for plates and chemicals. There was just enough remaining for some horse feed and a bowl of soup that, thankfully, came with a crust of bread. Then, grateful for a respite, Wendell climbed inside the rig and slept till the rain let up.

When he at last crawled out, wearing fresh clothes, the sun had broken through the clouds, throwing a brilliant yellow light. His first stop was at Brady's studio on Pennsylvania Avenue, but the new manager did not know of him and Brady would not be back for awhile.

Then Wendell went in search of customers. He set up on the sidewalk in front of the White House and again, military officers and their elegant ladies were eager for portraits. Surprisingly, a black private in a slightly used uniform came up behind him and tugged at his sleeve. "Beggin' pardon, sir, there's a whole raft of us colored troops and we don't get paid what the white soldiers get. But we sure be needing pictures, on account of maybe getting killed in this here war and wanting to send a likeness home."

Wendell was immediately touched and did a quick calculation in his head. "I'd like to help," he offered. "If you can round up three friends, I'll sell each two instead of eight." The man nodded grateful assent. Wendell went on, "It's getting late today, but I could meet you here tomorrow if the weather's good. How does noon sound?" He could do four separate poses on one plate with his cartes de visite camera, and realized that if they were lined up and ready, he could take the four poses of four different men. Wendell was sensing an unfilled niche. For now, he had to hurry back to the nurse's quarters for his evening appointment with

Lillian.

She was waiting for him and had brought him some supper from the mess for after their ritual. Wendell felt so grateful and homey in the little apartment that he almost ventured a tiny kiss on her cheek. Caution stayed him – despite progress in the treatments, they were yet using the utmost care to forestall wheezing, lest they should have to begin again. Wendell would have to depart by eleven as Lillian was sharing the apartment and the bed with another nurse, whose shift ended just when hers began.

They washed their feet, lit the incense, and prayed for forgiveness of their sins. Wendell and Lillian sat on opposite sides of the candle and synchronized their breathing until the familiar mesmerization closed their eyes. After a moment, magnetic currents took hold of their minds. Mutual feelings, not words, swelled their hearts or sent waves of sadness. It was not clear who originated a feeling and who followed, and there was an uncanny sense that their spirits had merged into one. By the end, they didn't just offer gratitude, they exalted. The strange phenomenon was so precious that they did not dare to talk about it or even think about it.

They were still in a reverent hush as Lillian set up their meal on the little table and sat down, the smell of food taking over from the incense. "How was your day?" Wendell asked her finally, his heart overflowing towards her. "Or should I say, your night?"

"The hospital is quiet now, it's not yet battle season. Still, there is disease and many succumb." She took a bite of the hearty but tasteless fare and lifted her chin bravely. "Wendell, they die without a whimper or complaint, so relieved are they not to have been left in pieces on the battlefield. Those whose relations can't be with them surround their pillows with their photographs, so that they might die in their loved ones' company." Hearing this, Wendell felt profoundly humble. Between this and the entreaty of the colored soldier today, he was beginning to feel some real value in his new career.

He spent the night in his rig in the hospital stables, which were free to those on government business. Since his canvas sidewalls still boasted the well-known name of Brady Photography, the guards didn't challenge him.

When he woke early, he and his horse went in search of Walt Whitman at 394 L Street. He found him on the third floor in a lovely front room, sparsely but adequately furnished. Walt gave Wendell a big hug and planted a kiss on his cheek. Walt was just on his way down to the dining room where boarders could take their meals. The household was merry and the room was $7/month – Walt was evidently very satisfied with it. Happily, Wendell was invited to stay for breakfast.

Walt had changed since Wendell had last seem him. His beard was longer, fuller, whiter. The lines of his face were more deeply etched, yet he had a livelier, more purposeful step, especially noticeable in the magnificent high boots into which he'd tucked his trousers. Gone was his rotundity and shortness of breath, and, he declared, excessiveness of food and drink.

They were bound for a paymaster's office where Walt hoped to get a job, and along the way, they caught each other up. Walt told Wendell about the particularly heart-rending cases he tended at the hospital. His relationship with the patients was one of unusual closeness, both physically and emotionally, and Wendell could only marvel at such lack of reserve in forming close ties with men who were dying.

"Your heart must be broken daily," Wendell observed as they passed armed sentries to mount the steps to the fifth floor of the paymasters' building.

"Nightly," Whitman corrected him. "During the day, I find the capital quite fascinating and my writing comes apace."

They found Walt's friend Major Hapgood surrounded by thirty or forty soldiers, some on crutches and having just climbed the stairs, complaining or supplicating about their pay. Still, the major took time to acknowledge Walt. "Good to see you, Mr. Whitman," he called from his desk, "there are letters to copy and some filing on the secretary."

Walt explained to Wendell that it was not daily or official yet, but he hoped to be hired on soon. "Why I brought you up here, Parry, is the view. Take a look out that window."

Wendell gazed out on a half-built muddy city, and imagined the photograph in shades of sepia. Walt continued, "Our president has insisted that work on the capital proceed, knowing that it will symbolize a great and unified nation, important in the war's aftermath. There's the Potomac, very grand, a fit setting," Whitman pointed. "The Capitol Dome you've seen. That's the Washington monument below, not half finished, and public grounds filled with beeves on the hoof, enough to feed the populace should the city be cut off. To the right, far across, Arlington Heights, the forts, eight or ten of them – then the long bridge, and down a ways but clear, the shipping of Alexandria. There on the left is the Smithsonian with its brown turrets. Opposite is the Treasury building – and below, the bustle and life of Pennsylvania Avenue." Wendell thought of Prince Bertie's warning, and was reassured that Lincoln would be able to fend off predators at the war's end.

They exchanged appreciative nods, and Walt kissed him lightly on the cheek. Then Walt sat down to his work with such characteristic dismissal that Wendell had to laugh, and so took his leave, promising to find Walt for breakfast again.

Wendell was somewhat early for his noon appointment on the Avenue. He set up his camera and portable darkroom on the sidewalk, ready for cartes de visite, and took a few pictures while he waited for the colored soldiers to appear. They came right on time, full ten of them, and Wendell spent much of the afternoon recording their likenesses. They waited patiently, evidently impressed that a one-handed photographer working alone could handle all the plate wetting, exposing, and ducking into the portable darkroom to develop, dry, and mount each one. For Wendell, it was much harder than the negative plates he did for Brady – he had to mount each small print on cardboard, the back of which still read "Brady on Broadway." Daunted, Wendell asked some of the men if they could return next day, but they would be shipping out to the Union stronghold of Beaufort in the South Carolina Sea Islands, so he endeavored to shoot them all. The men promised that if Wendell would set up regularly at noon, they would send their Negro friends to be photographed. Wendell agreed, silently praying that he could find a chemical supplier in Washington. Then he rushed off to his appointment with Lillian, enjoying the jingle of coin in his pocket.

Lillian met him at the door, grinning happily and holding a guitar. *"Sacre Dieu!"* Wendell exclaimed, his wooden hand over his heart. *"Calment le battement de mon coeur!* Ah, but it excites me to see you with that!"

Lillian's smile faded as she told him, "It's Molly's. Sweet Ned sent it to me. Tonight, I'll play for the patients. And Ned sent you Molly's paints and brushes," indicating the tubes on the dresser.

This news momentarily stunned, then cheered him. "How thoughtful of him. If you will play tonight, I'll try them." He mused a moment, then chuckled at his revelation, "No longer being professional, I can even permit myself to paint from store-bought tubes."

Silently, Lillian handed Wendell the sad letter that had accompanied the presents. *"All is dark,"* Ned had written, *"I know not where to turn, how to direct the deserted vessel now. My acting was to please her and her advice all I valued. They tell me that time will soften the blow. God forbid! My grief is sweet to me, it is part of her. If I live a thousand years, I could ask no greater blessing than to mourn for her. Oh God, could I feel satisfied she is eternal. There is a damned unholy doubt keeps bubbling up in my boiling brain as to what we are. This dangling between the fiend and God is worse agony than to be damned outright. So weep for my early education."*

Wendell's eyes were moist as they washed their feet and lit the incense. He asked forgiveness for his sins, and sighed that he seemed to be forgiven on so many levels, while Ned was condemned to a living hell for lesser crimes than his. It was beyond comprehending.

The sessions had daily become more magical. Tonight, when he and Lillian breathed and were entranced, not only were their feelings magnetized to each other, but Wendell swore he felt her lips brush against his and their bodies press together. He knew it was of the spirit, but the feeling was so physical that only the depth of his mesmerism restrained him from opening his eyes to check her position. And when the candle burned down and they awoke in exaltation, they were both seated exactly as they had been.

The next day, Wendell went in search of chemicals and, on a tip from Lillian, found collodion in plentiful supply right at the hospital. Surgeons, who used it to temporarily bind wounds and staunch the flow of blood, were happy to give it to him without charge, particularly as Lillian introduced him as her fiancé.

As promised, the colored soldiers were waiting for him on the Avenue, and once again Wendell headed home with money in his pocket. Suddenly he swayed, and realized that the pace he had set for himself along with the difficulties of sleeping in the wagon would lead to his early demise.

It was almost dusk when he parked the wagon in the hospital stable and arrived at the ground floor of the nurses' quarters. The sentry who had allowed him to pass on previous nights held up his rifle to block his entrance. "Sir," he said, "These quarters are restricted to the nurses and their families. It has come to my attention that you and Nurse Flax are not related."

"Miss Flax and I are betrothed," Wendell pleaded. He noticed the sentry's wooden leg and added anxiously, "As I am still in need of medical attention from my war service, she is also my indispensable nurse. I am now late for my treatment." This had the ring of truth in it, as he was late for their ritual which could not be missed lest they must start over.

The sentry looked at him and considered his bedraggled visage. "See you leave the door open during your visits," he instructed, then abruptly moved aside and let him pass.

During the course of the evening, the sentry twice passed by the open doorway and peeked in. So despite that Wendell was not yet flush, he determined to get a room and next day made his way to Mary Surratt's Boarding House at 604 H Street NW, just five blocks from Walt Whitman's. The sound of a piano came invitingly from the parlor.

Mrs. Surratt was delighted to see him and, after holding out her plump hand to be kissed, asked after Thomas. "I assure you," said Wendell with gallantry, "he will be among my visitors if you will lease to me long-term." The small room he had stayed in before was available for $7.25/month, and Wendell paid half, promising the rest in three days.

"Will you be taking breakfast with us?" she inquired affably and added, "It's $1.40/week." Seeing his hesitation, Mrs. Surratt defended her price. "Food comes dear during war."

Wendell nodded and handed her the coins. "Who is it that plays such lovely piano?" he asked.

Mrs. Surratt's demeanor changed abruptly. "'Tis my daughter, sir, who will not welcome the attentions of a photographer."

"I am myself betrothed," he assured her.

When he arrived at Lillian's that evening, he had washed away much of his filth and brought his dirty clothes for Lillian to put in with the hospital's laundry. They settled down to an evening of breathing, guitar, singing, and painting, at all times under the leering eye of the sentry.

Chapter 40

For the next weeks, Wendell photographed soldiers both white and black, and was grateful to be actually making a living. He and Lillian now frequented Mary Surratt's place on H Street where she was welcomed if not respected, so long as she did not spend the night. A lady was forbidden from entertaining a gentleman in her room, but no one complained if a gentleman should choose to entertain a woman in his. Their evening sessions had become ever more marvelous when they neared the end of their first box of candles and ordered a second box of forty-nine, and a box of seven.

"Mr. Wendell Parry," a familiar southern voice called out from the photographer's daily gathering of colored soldiers. Tuck Robinson? Wendell looked out from his wagon where he was preparing the first plate.

"'Tis indeed you," Wendell called back happily. "I had heard you were enlisted. And expecting another child! This plate can't wait, but I hope you can." He returned to his job inside the wagon, then emerged to place the wet plate in the camera, adjust the head holder bracket on his already seated soldier, then hurry three more soldiers through the process while the plate was still wet. While waiting for the developed prints to dry so they could be glued to cardboard backs, he took a moment to come out and greet Tuck, handsome in the blue uniform with red trousers of the 2nd South Carolina Colored Regiment.

Reverend Tuck gripped Wendell's wooden hand and shook it with enthusiasm. "How long are you here?" asked Wendell. "I'm sure we could find some dinner for you at the hospital where Lillian works. She'd love to see you."

Tuck shook his head. "Things ain't changed that much," he rued. "This here is still a southern city. They ain't gone let me sit down to eat with white folks. Anyways, I be leaving tomorrow and you're busy here now, I can see that." He thought a moment, then added, "Maybe I could help you with it."

"Aye, you can indeed," Wendell agreed, jumping at the offer. "It would be a help to me if you could cut the prints apart and mount them on cardboard. Come on in the wagon, and let me show you what I'm doing."

Thus working together, Tuck at a small workbench and Wendell beside it under his portable darkroom curtain, they were able to take pictures and do some visiting. Wendell told Tuck about Fredericksburg and Mathew Brady. Then Tuck told Wendell about the colored regiment's occupation of Jacksonville in March under Colonels Higginson and Montgomery.

"Is that Thomas Wentworth Higginson?" Wendell asked through the curtain.

"Yessir, I believe it is," Tuck's voice came back to him. "Why, you know him?"

"No, but I think Lillian does. He's from Boston, one of John Brown's 'Secret Six.'"

"Colonel Montgomery rode with John Brown in Kansas," said Tuck. "Harriet know them both a long time."

"Harriet? Harriet Tubman?" He had forgotten that Tuck and Ruby lived with the famous lady in her Auburn compound.

"Yessir, that be her."

Wendell came out and handed Tuck another sheet of finished pictures to be cut and mounted, then exposed another plate, continuing the conversation through the curtain on his return. "Why the South Carolina brigade?" he asked. "Massachusetts is fielding a colored militia of freemen. I hear they'll get paid same as whites. Frederick Douglass has two sons signing up."

"I come up from South Carolina," came Tuck's answer. "You 'member I spend four years on a plantation there." He sidled up to the curtain and his deep voice dropped to almost a whisper. "Mind you, this be a secret, but Harriet say the 2nd South Carolina Colored

Brigade be going with her on slave raids. Maybe we free some folks I know." Wendell heard a slight falter as Tuck added wistfully, "I got me a good friend down there."

Wendell pulled the curtain aside and looked at him. "Do you think I could come down and take some photographs?" he asked, remembering O'Sullivan's praise of the Sea Islands.

"That'd be mighty fine, mighty fine," Tuck's voice rose with excitement. "I both read and write now. I'm keeping me a journal for Ruby to write a book from. It would be mighty fine to have some pictures in it."

Wendell nodded, "I'd really like to go, but I'll have to check with Lillian. I won't go without her. Is there a hospital where she could work?"

"Yessir, there sure is. If Lillian want to go, I'll ask Colonel Montgomery to order up a transfer."

Working together, the two finished photographing the throng and Wendell did a sheet of eight for Tuck in thanks for his help. Together, they made their way early to Lillian's hospital room. Wendell brought Lillian downstairs, and while he put the wagon away she sat with Tuck, laughing and sharing stories. Finally they parted with fond hopes to meet again in the Sea Islands off the coast of South Carolina.

April began with ferocity, thunder and lightning shaking the windows of the small room at Mary Surratt's boarding house. Wendell sat in front of a small canvas which stood in an improvised easel on the table, trying to create Lillian's likeness with his left hand. It was a strange feeling in the magnetized afterglow of their evening session, discovering the newness of what his left hand was doing. His subject, seated on a stool and picking some guitar chords, was being painted right to left instead of his usual left to right and was indistinct, a sort of mirror image seen through water or wavy glass. Wendell remarked on this new vision and added, taking a deep breath, "'Tis wonderful to smell linseed oil again instead of photo chemicals. I am quite fond of photography, yet it's a chemical thing and records a different world."

"Aye," she nodded, "an industrial world." He worked in silence for a while, listening to the thunder. Haltingly, she began to sing her new composition.

> *"Straining through my window*
> *Into the howling storm,*
> *Rain streaks through my reflection,*
> *My brow is warped and drawn.*
>
> *Peering out my window*
> *Trying to see the moon,*
> *Brown smoke from smokestacks billow*
> *Against blue clouds and gloom.*
>
> *Oh the brown and blue at battle,*
> *Their sabers flash and rattle,*
> *Crying boom, boom, boom*
>
> *And the smokestacks just keep belching,*
> *While Nature screams with lightning,*
> *Crying boom, boom, boom."*

Wendell had put down his brush to listen. *"Sacre Dieu!"* he exclaimed softly, "we are magnetized to the same muse." He held his painting up for her to see. There, crudely but clearly, behind a streaked suggestion of her red-lipped face reflecting onto a window, were impressions of brown smokestacks belching against a purple storming sky. Lillian gasped in amazement. "'Twill not make me a living," Wendell continued happily, "but it's the first thing I've painted with my left hand that I like."

He had an urge to kiss her. Then he noticed she had closed her eyes and was matching his breath. He closed his eyes too, and felt her sweet phantom lips press against his lips and a ghostly warm embrace – it was a promise of more tangible things to come. The sensation passed. He opened his eyes to find her donning her rain cape for her journey back to the hospital.

On Easter week-end, the last candle was gone from the first box. They celebrated in the hospital ward with the patients, Lillian leading the men with her guitar in songs of resurrection.

The second box of candles did not arrive, and so the second phase of their assignment was held in abeyance. The delay left a hole, which was filled with muse-struck nights and phantom kisses. And, as if angered at being put off, Wendell's phantom hand began to make its presence felt, pulsing intermittently with intense pain.

Wendell and Walt were now taking turns visiting each other's rooming house for breakfast, then Wendell would walk Walt to work before going to the hospital to retrieve his wagon. The two landladies indulged this arrangement as they had few other guests for breakfast and the weekly sum worked out the same.

Walt shared some of his heartbreaking insights with Wendell on the way to the paymaster's office. "The hospitals are rank with sickness," he informed him, "but the men who die there are the lucky ones. So many, too many, are left for days in the fields. Most of these will never be found at all, for both South and North plow them under and set to planting at their first chance." Wendell shook with the horror of it, and counted himself and even Sam among the lucky ones.

"Only recently," Wendell told Walt, "I read that Ted Winthrop had been buried where he lay until his family prevailed upon the Secessionists to return the body. In honor of his hero status, they complied, but weeks later."

"Those that believe they will be raised bodily into heaven on

Judgement Day will have a hard time coming to terms with missing bodies and body-parts," observed Whitman. "Which brings me to the indelicate question of where your hand has got to and how you think on it?"

Wendell considered. "I do not believe that fleshly parts are necessary to the immortal soul," he said. "As you know, I have been given some hope that my essential hand is not missing. Lillian and I will soon embark on that telling phase of Dr. Randolph's magic."

"An interesting experiment," Walt enthused. "The hospital patients all confess to feeling their missing limbs. I will eagerly await your report." As Walt departed to the paymaster's office, Wendell went next door to inquire if Lillian's transfer had come through. Again he was told to have patience – "bureaucracy moves slowly."

On April 7th the candles came. "June 2nd," said Wendell beginning their countdown, "will be our magic day, the *Hieros Gamos*." The first candle was lit, and Wendell fell so deeply into the familiar trance that, not knowing what else to expect, he quite forgot to try to touch her with his phantom hand. For another week, their phantom kisses and hugs sufficed.

Several days later, as Wendell and Walt breakfasted at Mary Surratt's table, a new tenant joined them. "Walt Whitman, is it?" came the familiar voice. "And Wendell Parry? How nice to see you," said John Wilkes Booth before seating himself. They greeted him in kind, Walt with more enthusiasm then the reticent Wendell – there was still something in him that wanted to kill the man. He asked after Edwin.

Compassion was evident in Wilkes' voice as he replied. "Daily Ned sat in grief and remorse beside Molly's coffin. I think the completion of their common tomb last week has finally sated him, and he is returning to New York where he rented a house on 17th Street below Gramercy Park. Mother is with him, caring for little

Edwina. Until his passion for acting returns, he will be managing the Winter Garden.”

Wendell’s feelings toward John Wilkes softened at this obvious warmth for his rival brother. “Thank goodness,” Wendell said. “That is good news indeed, Wilkes. But how is he, in his old haunts?”

“If you’re asking if Ned’s drinking – Nay, he’ll never drink again. The very thought of brandy fills him with mortal terror.” Wilkes smiled ruefully, “He has near ruined his voice with constant cigars, but he’ll come ‘round.”

Thus assured about Ned, Walt Whitman asked, “What brings you to the capital, Mr. Booth? Are you playing somewhere?”

“I am, indeed. Tonight is *Richard III* at Grover’s National Theater.”

“I have heard,” spoke Mary Surratt’s daughter, shyly, “that you are especially renowned for your Romeo. Is that your favorite role?”

For a moment, Wilkes smiled flirtatiously at her, arching an eyebrow along with his mustaches. Then seeing both Mary Surratt’s and Wendell’s expressions harden, he turned serious. “No,” he said, “My favorite role is the character I most admire – Brutus, for whom my father was named.” Then the charming actor offered passes to see him perform that night at Grover’s Theater in *Richard III.*

Wendell ended his picture-taking somewhat early and awakened Lillian with the news of an evening out. She put on her best dress and they went to Mary Surratt’s boarding house for their ritual. Wendell was determined to remember his hand during this evening’s mesmerism and try to touch her with it.

The candle was struck and the light flickered across Lillian’s silks. The two synchronized their breathing and Wendell stared at the flame till the familiar trance overtook him with its magnetic pull. Again, he forgot his hand until there came an unmistakable and painful throbbing which would not leave him alone. As soon as it claimed attention, the arm jerked up and reached out to caress her dress. It seemed to be moving of its own accord, and as his phantom fingers found the silky fabric, the throbbing subsided and was replaced by a thrill in his chest.

He could feel it! He felt the folds, the contours where the garment was buoyed up by petticoats and where it rounded over her legs. As Wendell experimented, he found the sensitivity of the fingertips had no strength or pressure to move aside or press the folds. Still, the sensation was intense and fascinating, and his heart leapt at this confirmation that, despite the missing member, his soul was yet whole.

Wendell wanted to move the fingertips to her skin where she could confirm for him that she felt it, too, but the hand seemed only to move on its own. Any effort to direct it threatened to uncouple their breathing and bring him out of trance.

Too soon, the candle flickered out and they opened their eyes. "Where were you?" Lillian asked dismayed. "I brushed my lips to yours and felt no response. I know we are not to speak of such things, but I wonder if you felt me or no?" Wendell explained his distraction, and Lillian pledged to dress scantily on the morrow and be mindful of his fingers' caress. Then they threw on their wraps and went down to catch a cab to Grover's Theater, three blocks from the Capitol.

The sign on the theater read, *"First Appearance in Washington of J. Wilkes Booth, The Pride of The American People, The Youngest Tragedian in The World! Who is Entitled to Be Denominated A Star of The First Magnitude! Son of The Great Junius Brutus Booth, And Brother And Artistic Rival of Edwin Booth."*

The play began to great rowdy applause, quite different from Edwin's audiences. Wilkes as Richard was a chilling villain, and especially bristled their hairs when he said, *"O coward conscience, how dost thou afflict me!"*

John Wilkes Booth stood up from his sleeping bench, shaking in the throes of his prophetic nightmare.

"I am a villain: yet I lie. I am not.
Fool, of thyself speak well: fool, do not flatter.
My conscience hath a thousand several tongues,
And every tongue brings in a several tale,
And every tale condemns me for a villain.

Here he seemed to wake, a sudden jolt, then with a desperate sob, spake the lines,

"I shall despair.
There is no creature loves me;
And if I die, no soul shall pity me."

He completed the play with a sword fight that went on far longer than the play called for, and had the crowd on their feet cheering Wilkes' athleticism. "I think young Booth as good as his elder brother," commented Walt cheerily when the three departed with tumultuous applause still thundering behind them. "At least, it gave me equal delight to watch."

"They are very different," observed Lillian. "Wilkes does not claim the poetry of the lines like Ned, nor have his brother's melodic voice."

"Aye, he is physical, his brother metaphysical," said Wendell. "Wilkes makes you cheer where Ned makes you weep."

They went past a crowd of young ladies waiting for the star outside the stage door. In the adoration of females, at least, young Wilkes was very like Ned.

Walt continued their review, "Both the younger Booths have that compelling strangeness their father had. But to my thinking, their father was the greatest Booth. He played for the common man and any common man could understand him." It was typical that the hoary men of Walt's age preferred their own generation's hero.

Wendell smiled. "You have a lot in common with the common man."

"Well, yes," Walt said seriously, "I consider myself one."

"Aye," laughed Wendell, "until you separate yourself by writing uncommonly about them." They hailed a carriage for Lillian, then Wendell and Walt walked together to H Street where Walt boarded a cab.

"Are you still going to the hospital?" asked Wendell. "Tonight?"

Walt leaned out the window nodding, "There is a young soldier there I would see again before he dies."

Two weeks later came the transfer to the Union Hospital on Hilton Head in the South Carolina Sea Islands. True to Tuck's word was a letter from Colonel James Montgomery requesting immediate passage for Nurse Lillian Flax and photographer Wendell Parry with his wagon on the next ship to Port Royal. The ships ran sporadically but there was one that very afternoon.

Wendell bid goodbye to the boarders at Mary Surratt's including John Wilkes, whom he had finally become fond of, then hastened to Walt's boarding house for a quick breakfast. Walt had been up late and looked tired. "They are clearing the hospitals," he said wearily. "They need empty beds for the men, what's left of them, who will be arriving from our defeat at Chancellorsville." It was another massive defeat just downriver from the capital.

They walked outside together. "Alas, there is no one now from home," said the tearful Walt, and promised to write.

Finally, Wendell took his wagon, fully stocked with fresh supplies from New York, to pick up Lillian and her baggage. A familiar ship, *Arago*, armored and outfitted with cannons and troops, awaited them and blasted its big horn impatiently. They were the last ones to board when Hidalgo clamored up, and the gang plank was pulled in behind them.

Chapter 41

They had not been an hour at sea when Lillian got seasick. Evening descended as Wendell watched her at the rail, her skirts billowing, looking so like she had when last they had been on the *Arago* together. How long had it been? It was not even two years, yet it seemed to him forever. Again he waited till the retching ceased, then lifted her chin with his wooden fingers and gently wiped her tear-stained face. Again they were surrounded by concerned passengers with advice and sympathy.

Because she was the only white nurse on board, Lillian had a cabin to herself away from the colored nurses. This would give privacy for their nightly ritual, so she did not protest the arrangement. Wendell was to sleep below in the small white section of the steerage deck and would be required to turn in at taps and adhere to the same rules and schedule as the soldiers. Tonight, he begged to sit with Lillian till she felt better, and being that he was deemed her fiancé, was granted permission to be above decks after the rest had been summoned below.

Lillian felt better outside in the air than in her cabin, so they set chairs facing each other on the lonely deck, and wrapping themselves warmly, lit the candle in a glass against the wind and sighed aloud with each outward breath so the other could hear. After a few minutes, she paused abruptly to heave at the rail. Wendell tried to match her heaves and moans, which almost made her laugh through her misery. When the candle finally extinguished itself, they were both aware that they had followed their instructions only incompletely.

The second day, Lillian kept to her cabin. Wendell got out his camera and tried to shoot, but the wind, waves, and vibrations made exposures difficult. Finally, he contented himself to sketching with his left hand.

When Wendell went in the evening to Lillian, she was pale and miserable. "Methinks Dr. Randolph's instructions were too strict," Wendell rued. "Will the magic cease if we skip a night?"

"Oh," groaned Lillian in her lower berth as she looked up from the bucket she clutched in front of her. "We must go on. 'Twas the plan of the magic that I should be sick, else you would not be allowed to visit me here."

Wendell undid the straps of his hand and laid it on the upper bunk. After giving Lillian a glass of water, he lit the incense and they were glad of that sweet smell of frankincense in the tiny windowless room that otherwise smelled of sickness. He picked up the candlestick to hold between them, and moved onto the one small chair. Then they stared at the flame until their eyes closed and their breathing magnetized.

Wendell felt his phantom hand jerk of its own and move forward to touch Lillian's face. Gently, the phantom fingers caressed her cheek – such a simple thing to have so long eluded him. Slowly, Lillian nodded. She felt it! She turned her head till his ghostly fingers brushed her lips, then she teased them with her tongue. The clarity with which he sensed this sent a thrill throughout his being. Slowly, he traced her features, delighting where her lashes tickled his fingertips. She opened the front of her night gown so that his hand could continue its descent. Lillian definitely felt him! It now seemed that his hand moved not on its own, but by her will. His fingers drifted on her flesh as if floating on a gentle breeze, across to the left side of her bared bosom, where it cupped her breast. Wendell consciously tried to squeeze the firmness, but there was no strength in his embrace, no substance – the phantom hand was sensate, not material. He felt her nipple rise beneath his palm and they both felt their breath quicken, deepening together. As the hand drifted, still by Lillian's will, to embrace the other breast, they both realized with elation that she was not wheezing.

Wendell's touch drifted down toward her belly, but here Lillian's spirit darkened and she willed his hand away. The candle sputtered its last light, and they had just time to say their gratitudes before she was once again heaving in the bucket.

They were by now well at sea. The *Arago* went wide of the Outer Banks where the great Union ironclad USS Monitor had foundered only months earlier in the colliding currents of the "Graveyard of the Atlantic" off Cape Hatteras. Coming closer would gain time by using the tricky currents to advantage, but would also bring them near Confederate batteries. By Charleston they approached the shore again, angling toward their final approach to Hilton Head Island.

"Look there, Mr. Parry," said *Arago*'s Captain, pointing as he placed a friendly hand on Wendell's shoulder. "That's a picture if you could get it." Six Union monitors and another type of ironclad were anchored outside the entrance to Charleston Harbor, their mighty gun turrets so heavy that their decks seemed almost to float underwater. "The fleet tried again to take Charleston last week – we passed right by the battle on our last trip down. Now they're making a hell of a dent in the fortunes of blockade runners whilst they plan their next move." His pointing finger joined a fist and he pumped it up and down with excitement. "By Jove, raising the Union's banner over Fort Sumter would lend some satisfaction, eh? Gives me a thrill to think we could see some action."

"Aye," Wendell nodded, "'tis an arresting sight indeed."

Shortly after, on the fourth and final day of Lillian's allotted time of sea-sickness, they sighted Port Royal Sound. There, straining against anchors, was an impressive portion of the world's fastest growing navy. Ironclads, steamships, pilot boats, and schooners spilled out into the ocean, well beyond the mouth of the massive sound, secure that the feared hurricane season was still some months off. Everyone knew they were gathering for another try at Charleston.

Arago threw its engines in reverse off Hilton Head Island and was nudged by a pilot ship onto the end of a massive pier that extended across the sand bar from the high tide's edge. The shore edge of the sandbar bristled with cannons poking through low earthen barricades, behind which rose thousands of tents on bleached sand stretching to distant war factories.

The white soldiers were the first to debark, then Lillian with the nurses, then the colored soldiers, and lastly Wendell with his wagon.

Wendell asked directions of the sailor who assisted his horse down the gangplank. "Yessir. There's a hotel in Robbers Row," the man said indicating. "Everything's real close to hand. Beyond the town is Mitchelville, where the darkies live."

"And the hospital?" Wendell asked.

The mid-shipman pointed towards a grand building away from the cannons on the ocean side. "That's her yonder. Spanking new she is, 60,000 square feet. Ye'll get yourself some good doctoring there." Beyond the hospital, Wendell could discern waving dune grass, pines, palmettos, and live oak forests draped with Spanish Moss. In the growing heat of spring, the island's recesses held a promise of magic and romance.

"Obliged," said Wendell. And then, remembering Tuck, Wendell asked after the 2nd South Carolina Colored Regiment.

"I cain't help you with that," responded the sailor. "I ain't in the army. There's some 40,000 folks on this here Island, most of 'em military and contrabands."

"They're not contrabands anymore," Wendell reminded him as he stood gratefully on dry land and climbed aboard his rig. "They're freedmen now."

Wendell drove though the town of Hilton Head on Suttler's Row, dubbed Robbers Row by those who knew, to get the lay of the land before finding Lillian. Ocean breezes kept the smoke of smelters and cannon factories well away. The sandy main road of the town boasted no sidewalks and was alive with military and supply wagons. Plain wooden buildings, most in need of paint with battered shutters alongside the windows, were set wide apart from one another, but each bore a sign proclaiming itself to be a store or business. Wendell expected to see the general store and greengrocer, but was surprised to see restaurants and a jewelry shop as well. The spacious and drafty-looking "Union Theater" advertised a New Hampshire Military Band. Then there was the Port Royal House, an impressively large if unimpressively constructed hotel, with stables opposite. On the whole military side of the Island, nary a shade tree nor blade of grass grew. Already hot, Wendell wondered how the summer would be.

He tied the horse in front of the hotel and entered what passed for a lobby. Sand scurried across the unfinished floor. A shabby couch and a few bare wood chairs were all the furniture, save for a counter with mail slots behind it, along with a concierge and a cash register. There was a clatter of dishes and fish smells coming from the door opposite, which advertised a restaurant inside. "Hello, Traveler. Looking for a room?" the concierge asked cheerfully.

Wendell nodded. "Indeed, if you have anything available."

"Haven't been full yet. Hundred twenty rooms in the place." The concierge opened his ledger. "Your rig says you're with Mathew Brady. You here to photograph our colored troops? Press can't seem to get enough of 'em." He took Wendell's money and gave him a key. "Restaurant's open till three."

The room was on the third floor of the three story building, and had a charming window with lace curtains that overlooked Fort Welles toward the Sound. It was open to the sea breeze which wafted salty and balmy with nary a bug in it. The walls were thin and there was a narrow bed with creaky bed springs. Wendell liked it. He tipped the concierge who had helped him with his steamer trunk and told Wendell that the 2nd South Carolina Colored was camped on the other end of the island when they weren't away on a mission. Then Wendell went in search of Lillian.

Clean and modern wards greeted him at the hospital, some filled with colored patients and others filled with white. At a far end of a white ward, a diminutive black nurse in plain nurse's garb and head kerchief was showing Lillian around. Wendell assumed this was Mrs. Harriet Tubman and eagerly went forward to meet the famous conductor of the Underground Railroad. Mrs. Tubman looked surprised at the wooden hand Wendell extended to her, but shook it with aplomb. "You Miss Lillian's beau, ain't ya?" she guessed with a big smile.

Wendell smiled back, "I believe so, yes, last I checked with her."

Lillian introduced them formally. She explained that Harriet worked most regularly over in Beaufort, so wouldn't be around to keep Lillian company. After expressing regret, Harriet continued to guide them on the tour.

"Some of these here be Confederate deserters, changing they sides," said Harriet. "The time of malaria and typhoid about to happen inland, and some's got the sickness already. The blockade's working, they ain't getting no quinine and they half starving besides." Harriet greeted each soldier by name, then ushered Lillian and Wendell into a colored ward. "These here be the new freedmen," she said proudly. "Some was shot up pretty bad, trying to get away from they masters and high-tail it on over here. Mostly they's soldiers now." The patients lit up when they saw her, shouting out 'Howdy, Miss Moses' and 'Hello, General'.

"General?" asked Wendell, thinking that despite her small stature, the title suited her.

"That be the name the martyr saint, John Brown, give me," she said reverently.

She stopped at the closed door to the next ward. "You don't want to go in this here ward afore you drink your sassafras tea. They's smallpox, and the tea keep you from getting sick yourself."

Smallpox – an alarming thought. Wendell was about to object to Lillian that she should ever go in, when suddenly Harriet's eyes rolled back in her head and her chin dropped. All signs of life just went out of her except that she remained standing.

"Don't touch her," Lillian whispered, placing a hand on his arm. "She's having one of her spells." After a few moments, Harriet abruptly woke.

"They's going to be a terrible battle way up in the North," she sang. "It be a coming soon, it a coming soon. They's going to be so much killing, so many dead, but the North going to win it, Lord, the North going to win."

"Do you know where in the North?" asked Lillian anxiously. But immediately after this revelation, Harriet seemed to forget it, and had nothing more to say on the matter.

"You best get some rest now, Honey, if you on the nighttime shift." Harriet gave Lillian a hug. Then she turned to Wendell with a twinkle. "Mr. Parry, it's a pleasure meeting you. Some years now, I been hearing about how handsome you is, and look to me like it be true. Mmmm, Mmmm."

"The pleasure is mine, Mrs. Tubman," Wendell said grinning. "And please, call me Wendell." He lifted her hand and kissed it. When he and Lillian left her, the middle-aged woman was giggling like a school girl.

"I'll be able to spend my evenings with you," Lillian told him with relief as she climbed aboard the wagon, "I'm working from eleven at night until 6am again." She pointed out the cabin adjoining the hospital where she would be staying. Wendell was sorry she had to stay there. He liked having her by his side at night, even if he had to sleep on the floor. After a midday meal at Wendell's hotel, they had a luxurious nap followed by more explorations with Wendell's phantom hand.

Each morning, the rising sun puffed on the waves to announce its arrival. Billowing curtains and slanted rays awakened Wendell for a walk along the beach. He drove up to the hospital where Lillian lay sleeping, then let the horse wander in the sedge grass while he strolled along the shoreline. Colors of the dawn thrilled him, enhanced tones of azurite, lapis, and all the cobalts bursting along the base of puffy white flake clouds. Wendell was sure this holy spectacle was connected to his miraculous evening adventures with Lillian.

Photographing nature did not at first seem possible and he did not try. Nature was meant to be painted, or simply appreciated. Seagulls wheeled overhead, and giant tortoises lazed in the cool sand. Often Wendell saw dolphins surfing quite close to shore, and he felt they were observing him as much as he was observing them. But when his eye caught how the slanted rays of sunlight brought swirling sand textures into a high relief of black and white, he had to photograph it. Sand fascinated him. Soon, the camera was always with him.

Life fell quickly into a routine. By the time the sun was fully up, Wendell would fetch Hidalgo and take cartes de visite of soldiers in front of the hotel. Then, when the sun was too high for good portraits, he would explore the woods, sticking to the few disappearing and rutted roads. Spindly palmettos lined the forest's edge, while deeper in, Spanish moss and a jungle of vines draped downward from massive live oaks. Wendell came across the poignant ruins of a plantation house overgrown with snake-filled vines, defiant magnolia trees still blooming gloriously in what had been a front yard. He managed finally to photograph it, though his experiments with exposures in the dim light took a lot of plates. Frequently, he removed the emulsion and began again. Around noon, he would go get Lillian.

His phantom hand had become a sensual gift in their evening rituals. Always, as per instructions, they kept focused on their breath and avoided any hint of la petite mort. This ritual was enjoyable in itself, yet their desire grew, and the slow diminishment of candles in the second box was greeted each day with triumph.

Growing, too, was a superstitious fear in Wendell that an interruption or miscarriage of their rituals would bring bad luck. "I feel the magic working," he said one night as they lay upon the covers in the hotel room, listening to gospel coming from the Negro camps below. "And with it comes a dread of dishonoring that magic in some way."

"Faith, dear Heart," said the practical Lillian, her still-vibrating body dressed only in the skimpiest undergarments. "We have been helped all this time in keeping to the discipline. So joyful is the performance that only an act of God could restrain us."

"But we do skirt precariously on the edge of our instructions. Each night, it becomes harder for me to withhold my seed," he noted.

"'Tis as it should be," she assured him while she affectionately stroked his cheek. "The point of the healing was that you should rouse me without my wheezing. This you have done. You have rescued me, my Heart. Please don't shy from the miracle that is happening here."

Tuck's regiment was away on patrol, capturing slave hunters still bent on retrieving their runaways. Besides cartes de visite of the soldiers and sailors, Wendell began photographing the well-ordered freedmen town of Mitchelville, located just outside of the town of Hilton Head. One old resident, aged 104, had been a prince in his native Africa. Trying to talk to him, Wendell discerned that the strange language the ex-slaves used when speaking to each other was a blend of English patois and African dialects. They had been on the islands for generations, said the old man, and rarely sold off. Thus they still retained some of their African culture.

In the school in Mitchelville and at many others across the Sea

Islands, Gideonite missionaries from New England guided the freedmen and children in basic academics. At one such school, newly constructed in the same hasty and utilitarian way as the rest of Hilton Head, Wendell photographed ninety pupils of varying ages giving a recitation. A literate black man from Charleston aided the endeavor.

"What do you do with cotton?" he asked.

"Sell it," chanted the students.

"Who keeps the money?"

"We do." Then, movingly, the students sang a spirited rendition of *John Brown's Body*, adding verses of their own about hanging Jeff Davis from a sour apple tree.

Chapter 42

After several weeks on the island, Wendell went to get Lillian on her day off. He was surprised to see Harriet Tubman with her.

"We's gone go see Corporal Robinson," Harriet said, shoving her carpet bag under the plank of the whatsit wagon as she climbed aboard after Lillian. She placed her musket upright against the seat.

"You mean Tuck?"

"Aye," said Harriet, "That who I mean. The Reverend Corporal Tucker Robinson of the 2nd South Carolina Infantry Regiment, African Descent, Army of the South, United States Military."

"Impressive." Wendell glanced uncertainly at the musket. "Is there danger on the road?"

"Secesh kidnappers," Harriet informed him matter-of-factly. "Them's always sneaking through the woods trying to take back they slaves."

Lillian noted that they would likely not return before dark, so they stopped at the hotel for candles and incense.

Then the wagon started down a long shell-surfaced road, a crunchy white ribbon that was soon winding through the thick tropics of the island's interior. The Spanish Moss that hung heavily from spreading live-oaks was interspersed with yellow flowered vines that everywhere connected through lush and impassable undergrowth. Overhead, giant butterflies flitted anxiously through airy caverns in the low and dappled canopy. Several times the travelers passed swamps harboring graceful cranes and fearsome alligators. Even more fearsome were the mosquitoes, while unseen residents hooted and shrieked at them in ominous protest. As if in deference to their unwelcoming hosts, the humans passed in silence, only their crunching wagon wheels and defensive slaps interrupting the intense conversation of the forest.

When the wagon finally broke again into sunlight, they were

passing through a battered plantation with corn growing in front of the many slave cabins. The freedmen who still occupied them laughed under a shade tree as they prepared their evening meal. Infants and toddlers crawled through garden patches of sprouting corn and greens, while neglected cotton fields stretched into the distance.

"Folks don't want to grow cotton no more, but they's coming round to it now they can keep the money for theyselves," Harriet explained. Her smile revealed a sparse jumble of teeth.

The freedmen were happy to let Wendell take their picture, especially when Harriet opened her carpet bag and offered fresh baked pie and home-brewed root beer. Again, they spoke the strange patois, most of it not discernible as English, which Wendell couldn't understand. Harriet wasn't able to help. "That be Greek to me," she laughed. "Folks been saying they's my people, but I cain't even understand them. My people's in Auburn." Finally, a woman told them in heavily accented English that their children were in school.

The picture developed and fixed, the wagon was once again on its way, the horse grunting down a sandy rutted road. Wendell was enjoying a root beer. "Does someone around here make this?" he asked appreciatively.

"Well now, they's a sore subject," opined Harriet. "I says I won't take my pay lessen the men get paid what the whites do, so's I have to make my living by being up all night brewin' and bakin'." Wendell felt astonishment followed by abiding respect.

Finally, they passed a windbreak of trees and saw the edge of a military encampment whose tall white tents stretched away through cotton fields and across the beach to the sea. The tents nearest them were tended by colored women who cooked over the fire while their toddler children played nearby, the little girls in gingham dresses and tight pickaninny plaits, the boys in torn and dirty clothes as boys everywhere are wont to be. Smells of corn and fish wafted through the smoke. Away up the beach, the men drilled with their regiments.

"Hut two three four," went the cadence call, then "John Brown's body lies a-mouldering in the grave." As they sang, they cut handsome figures, their red legs marching in exact synchronicity beneath their blue coats and flashing bayonets. Wendell caught sight of who was leading the drill – Corporal Robinson. Tuck waved when he saw the carriage, then with a flourish, had the men line up at attention and excitedly came over to help Wendell set up his camera.

After pictures were taken, Tuck told the men in Gullah it was time to eat. *"Kumbaya t'nyam we cootuh."* As the men cheered and disbanded, he turned to his guests grinning, "That mean there's turtle on the menu."

Troops were gathered around a large campfire passing dishes while the men spoke, throwing in Gullah words here and there. Some at the campfire entreated a wiry little man of Tuck's age named Adam to tell a story. He looked questioningly over at Harriet – Wendell saw her nod, as if giving permission for what the man was about to say.

Wendell relaxed himself onto the sand where he could lean back against the sitting log and listen.

"I hear tell from the ole master that I be given my freedom when he die, to go up north with Corporal Tuck," he began. "And that's the truth. I'se given my freedom, but the master's chillun say it ain't valid and they's not gone let me go. Then they sell me up north to Maryland. So I figures I'se gone have to run."

The colored listeners yelled, "Tell it!" "That's the truth!" and "You gots to run, Brother!"

"I had the new master in Maryland write a letter to Miss Ruby, Tuck's wife," Adam continued, "saying I won't be coming on account of not havin' my freedom. Then she write back that I should pray at the Easter moon to be delivered of my wickedness.

The master read me the letter, and I knows it was a code from Miss Ruby." He went on as the men exhorted him to tell it. "The master was sure 'nough pleased with that letter! So on the day afore Easter, a voice come from out of the woods and the field hands start singing with it, 'The Lord's coming at the Easter moon, the Lord's coming at the Easter moon, to deliver us to freedom.' Then we knowed to pack some food, me and Lou and Joseph, and we wait at night by the woods. When we hear that song again, we takes off running towards it. That when we see Miss Harriet Tubman there, Moses herself, singing in the moonlight, come to deliver us from bondage. It took the dogs two days to get after us, on account of it being Easter."

There were cheering high spirits at the cleverness of it, and Wendell shook his head in amazement.

Harriet, who had been in one of her trances, got up and began to sing in a plaintive minor key.

> *"I know moon-rise, I know star-rise,*
> *Lay this body down.*
> *I walk in the moonlight, I walk in the starlight,*
> *To lay this body down.*
> *I'll walk in the graveyard, I'll walk through the graveyard,*
> *To lay this body down.*
> *I'll lie in the grave and stretch out my arms;*
> *Lay this body down."*

The men rose and, grabbing Wendell, did a slow foot stomping dance counter-clockwise around Harriet as they joined in her song. Some shouted and clapped, and others broke off to do fancy footwork before rejoining the circle.

As the sun went down, the song continued, variations and verses added by different singers. Wendell found himself in the spirit of the thing, dancing with abandon.

Finally Lillian tugged Wendell's sleeve and pulled him away. "We need to do our own ritual," she whispered to him urgently. They hastened to the water's edge where they bathed their feet in salt water, and sat on the sand behind a dune. The Negroes' spiritual floated over the grass.

"Now you know why I didn't see you for so long after our first kiss," she sighed apologetically. "Tuck's friends were arriving then. 'Wanted' posters were up everywhere and I had to hide them in the mansion."

"That's why they had guns," remembered Wendell, lighting the incense.

She nodded grimly. "Tuck wasn't going to let them go back."

The sun was barely up when reveille and roosters sounded. Wendell was in his bedroll beneath the whatsit wagon while Lillian slept nearby in their tent. As gulls wheeled in the morning wind, Harriet Tubman approached at the side of Colonel James Montgomery, Captain of the 2nd South Carolina Colored Regiment. He was an athletic white man with fierce eyes that reminded Wendell of John Brown. Harriet stooped to introduce them.

"Welcome, Mr. Parry," Montgomery said pleasantly. "Colonel Higginson is here visiting and has invited you and Miss Flax to breakfast with him in the officers' tent."

"Thank you, sir" Wendell said from beneath the covers, not wanting to crawl out of his bedroll without his trousers on. "We would be delighted. Will you and Mrs. Tubman be joining us?"

"Harriet will be. I must attend my duties, but will try to stop by later. Miss Flax's reputation is, of course, well known to me, but I have not yet had the pleasure of meeting her."

The two left, giving Wendell a chance to pull his pants on. Inside the small tent he shoved aside crinolines to crawl over Lillian. "Mmm, what is it, my Heart? I'm accustomed to go to bed at this hour, not get up." But on hearing the invitation, she did rise while Wendell went outside to dress.

Soon they were approaching a large, house-like officers' tent where handsome horses waited outside and smells of cooking came from behind. They announced themselves to the sentry, and a moment later Colonel Thomas Wentworth Higginson emerged with Harriet at his side. "Lillian," he said, taking her hand, "it's been too long." He was a wiry blue-eyed man, whose stern angles and square jaw were softened by reddish face hair, and a friendly smile.

They ate breakfast inside the tent, seated around a long table. Eggs, fish, greens and corn fritters served by Negroes graced the plate. Seeing Harriet sitting at the table with the white folks had evidently upset them, but after a word from the Colonel, they waited on her with the others.

"Those of us who were supporting John Brown," Higginson reminisced, talking to Wendell, "were quite upset to hear of Lillian's affair with you." He laughed and looked to the ladies for confirmation. "Especially with runaways staying at her mansion."

"That the truth," said Harriet. "And she have it bad, mmm-mmm. Seem like she don't want to do nothing but be with you, and we were sure 'nough scared about that."

Wendell felt his heart soar. The memory of Lillian's long absences still haunted him. "Pray continue."

"We had a long meeting," said Higginson. "It was at Gerrit Smith's place. Gerrit, Frederick Douglass, John Brown, Samuel Howe, Frankie Sanborn and Harriet were all there. It was a rather fierce debate I'm afraid, about whether we should go on without Lillian."

Harriet spoke up, "Then I say, the mens got to have more faith in woman's discretion. Seem to me it were on account of Lillian's sex they's saying she might tell Wendell her secrets."

Lillian looked peevish. "Bless you, Harriet. I felt the mistrust." She looked at Wendell apologetically. "I was being questioned all the time about you and even warned directly by Sam Howe not to see you." She looked back at Harriet. "But I didn't know about this meeting."

Wendell's voice caught as he said, "I thought you just didn't trust me."

Higginson continued, warming to his story, "Gerrit pointed out that, except for his contribution, much of the money was promised from Lillian – it would be a strain to go ahead without her."

"We weren't none of us sure what we was going ahead to," said Harriet. "Captain Brown be making his own plans. But he say he need the money and I say we going get it for him, and Lillian the one that have it, so it sure make no nevermind if Lillian be seeing Wendell or who all else." Harriet was adamant, and Wendell saw again why John Brown called her 'General.' Harriet looked suddenly sorrowful. "He expect me to join him on his raid, but I weren't with nobody I could trust to read his letter to me."

"But why would you send Tuck and Ruby to me for a portrait?" asked Wendell confused.

"It was a mistake," confessed Lillian flushing, "though I wanted to see how you would be with them. But when Tuck was arrested there, some suspected you. And when you discovered fugitives in the hall at Tuck's, everyone got very upset with me. I'm so sorry. I was always sure of you, but no one else was. That's why Gerrit insisted on meeting you. Even then, he had doubts, and it was Tuck who stood strongest for you. He convinced Harriet and Ruby, too."

Wendell didn't know why these revelations made him shake. He had been so afraid of losing Lillian, and now the memories came flooding back. Higginson went on with the story, explaining how he had teamed up with John Brown's ally from Kansas, Colonel Montgomery, to try to save John Brown from hanging. "I couldn't believe everyone else wanted Brown dead, even Emerson and Thoreau," Higginson said.

When they arrived back at the hotel on Robbers' Row, Wendell and Lillian took out the last candle from the second box. They were both full of memories. "I've put you through so much," said Lillian. "I often wondered that you stayed with me."

"You once tried to get me to love someone else." He shook his head. "I could not. I was so sure when I met you, so sure you were the one for me – how could I ever be sure about anything again if I were proved wrong about you?"

For awhile, they gazed quietly into each other's eyes.

After some time, he said, "I am a bohemian, vain and selfish, and you are a dedicated abolitionist. You have given everything to make things right for others – yet you wanted me."

"You are not vain, Wendell. Whenever I am with you, the world is more beautiful, I feel more beautiful. You see beauty in everything, even the emptiness of deserts. My abolitionist friends see only the world's ills, and are vain that they alone can fix them."

"Do you not think the war worth it?" asked Wendell, a tug of fear in his heart lest all the sacrifices be for naught.

Her eyes began to well. "I don't know," she said simply.

They lit the candle. Their time of being physically separated had brought them spiritually closer and they were both filled with gratitude. Not only did he know that Lillian was forever, but now Wendell knew that God was, too. He reached out to her with his phantom hand. His heart brimmed over.

The next day, Wendell was so excited about the rites of the final seven candles that he went to the concierge and asked to be moved to the hotel's finest room. "Something fit for newly-weds."

"I have just the thing," the concierge smiled. He led the way up to a spacious and graceful room adorned all in red: Red flowered wallpaper, a red oriental rug, red damask drapes accented with white lace curtains, and a rose-embossed red silk quilt on a large brass 4-poster bed. Beyond the window was a view of the sea. "There is a feather bed atop the mattress," commented the concierge, "Sit down, sir, and try it. Just how long were you thinking about staying?"

"A week," pronounced Wendell as he luxuriated on the mattress, barely containing his excitement. The price he was quoted was affordable, hardly more expensive than the other room. If he'd had to sell his horse, he'd have taken it, and was ecstatic that it hadn't come to that. He spent the afternoon preparing, and wore his best afternoon clothes to pick up Lillian.

"Oh, you've dressed up," she said as she climbed aboard the wagon in her blue nurse's habit. He noted how much younger and healthier she looked these days.

Lillian waved a letter in her hand and was very happy. "It's from the court in New York. They have been trying to find me so they can schedule an annulment hearing." On the front of the official looking envelope someone had crossed out *Mrs. Henry Ferguson* and replaced it with *Nurse Lillian Flax.* "It seems I may yet be free," she smiled and snuggled his shoulder.

When they arrived at the hotel, all was in readiness. The pitcher was full of lilac-scented water for bathing their feet, a vase on the windowsill held a bunch of gardenias, the candle-stick sat on the table, the edge of the quilt was turned down.

Lillian stepped through the door and gasped. It took Wendell a moment to realize that her eyes grew wide not in delight, but in horror. She covered her mouth with the back of her hand, and a strange, strangled wheeze escaped from her throat. Abruptly, she grabbed Wendell's arm and pulled him out the door and down the stairs, gasping and wheezing as she went. When they got outside into the street, she turned to him and caught her breath.

"You're wheezing," cried Wendell with a frightened lurch in his stomach. "Why are you wheezing? Do we have to start over?"

"I'm not wheezing," Lillian gasped anxiously. "Believe me, I'm not. It's not you, Wendell, it's the room looks so like the one in the mansion. I'm all right, I'm cured, I'm cured, believe me." To prove it, she threw her arms around Wendell's neck and pulled his mouth to hers.

And then they were kissing. They were kissing, not tentatively, but ecstatically, drinking each other's essence, pressing their bodies together. It was all either of them could do not to rip off their clothes right there in the street. And not a wheeze! Not a wheeze! A gasp here and there, yes, but an aroused, exulting gasp.

When they finally pulled apart, the front of Wendell's good trousers was wet and sticky. Lillian laughed triumphantly. "You see?" she said, "I am well! I am truly well!"

"We daren't go back to the room," noted Wendell, trying to regain his composure. "Shall I rent another?"

Lillian's look was mischievous. "Let's do it on the beach," she said.

Chapter 43

That first evening, they had simply grabbed a blanket and laid it over the sand in a lovely place beyond the hospital where the dune grasses waved and dolphins tumbled joyfully through the surf. Wendell had placed his pistol in reach while Hidalgo munched some yards away, ready to whinny should someone approach. They had bathed their feet in the salt water, then wondered to each other what might be the best position to accomplish their task. For though Lillian deemed herself cured, the wheezing had scared them and they both felt it necessary to proceed to the Hieros Gamos. When they finally found a way for him to lie with her without crushing her, they focused on their breath and on the latent candle flame dancing in the center of their foreheads. He was in her at last! He settled his excitement, focusing on her breath. As per instructions, they didn't move. Surprisingly, he was greeted with tantalizing involuntary ripples.

As the nights progressed, the ripples became more insistent and his sensitivity increased. Little sensations magnified into large, reaching all the way to his heart. Each evening he was able to stay inside longer, noting each tiny pleasure, before having to pull himself out and calm himself down. By the third night, he stayed till the candle went out, feeling full of love, and by the fourth night, he had placed the feather bed on the sand and brought pillows and quilts.

It was on the fifth day of the seven that he went to get Lillian from the hospital only to find an imperious looking nurse waiting for him outside. "Mr. Parry?" she presumed sternly, "I would have a word with you in my office."

Wendell's heart was slamming as he sat down opposite Dragon Dix herself, in her officiating lair. She set her thin lips and dispensed with pleasantries. "The woman whom you call your fiancée is in fact married, Mr. Parry," she bristled. "Were you aware of that?" Wendell didn't respond, just sat with his jaw so tight it quivered. "I have ordered her back to Washington City forthwith to face charges. She will be leaving in the morning. Meanwhile, she has been confined to quarters."

"Charges?" asked Wendell weakly, his mind racing.

"Indeed, it is no small matter to mislead the United States military about one's identity, much less lie about an incapacity that gave her dispensation to enlist. She has been engaged in conduct very unbecoming of an army nurse."

"If I may speak in my fiancée's behalf, as Samuel Howe had done – she was deserted by her husband some years back and has always gone by the name Miss Flax. The letter which identified her as Mrs. Ferguson was summoning her to an annulment of an abusive and unconsummated marriage, which did indeed result in her being incapacitated!"

"Whether what you say be true or no," said Nurse Dix, giving no quarter, "until she has an annulment from the courts or from the Church, she is Mrs. Ferguson and will behave in a manner becoming a married woman." She stood, dismissing him. "That is all, Mr. Parry."

Wendell rudely slammed the door. He went outside and straight away to Lillian's room. An armed sentry stood in front of her door. Wendell couldn't believe it – would they court martial her, throw her in the brig, hang her for treason? As he approached and raised his fist to knock, the sentry blocked his way.

"This woman is my fiancée," said Wendell. "Let me pass!"

"Sorry, sir. I have my orders. You'll have to see a commanding officer."

"Merde à l'enfer!" Wendell swore, "You know there isn't one for miles." Montgomery was bivouacked on the other side of the island, while Higginson enjoyed a plantation house in Beaufort. Perhaps he could find a naval officer.

Wendell was in a severe state of agitation as he urged his horse faster toward Fort Welles. Once there, he explained his troubles to the sergeant in charge, who proclaimed he was powerless. All Wendell could do was beg passage on *Arago* next morning. There would not be another ship for several weeks. But passage was denied, the ship would be full with soldiers suffering typhoid and yellow fever.

While he thought over what to do next, an officer with the rank of colonel came over to him. "Did I hear you mention Miss Lillian Flax?" he asked.

Wendell seized on him desperately. "Do you know her?"

"Indeed, we had worked together on the underground railroad more than once. I'm Colonel Robert Shaw. I just arrived last night with the 54th Massachusetts Colored Volunteers. Is she here?"

Wendell explained the situation while Shaw shook his head. "Tell you what," the colonel said finally. "I'm not man enough to stand up to Dorothea Dix. No man that I know is. But I shall certainly give Lillian a letter attesting to her identity and good character. That should do it. I'll see she gets it tomorrow when she boards the *Arago*."

"Thank you so much," said Wendell, gripping the man's hand with both of his.

Shaw looked at the wooden hand and nodded. "Bull Run, was it? Yes, I've heard about you. You're Mr. Parry."

Wendell gave a wry laugh. "And you must be another 'radical abolitionist hot-head' who was concerned that Lillian stop seeing me. This island seems full of them."

"Indeed I am," said the colonel affably. "Who else but a radical abolitionist hot-head would insist on commanding coloreds? But you won't find a better trained or disciplined group than my Massachusetts men."

Wendell nodded. "Lillian told me, and that Frederick Douglass' sons are among them. I'm sorry she won't be able to greet them. I am very grateful to you, Colonel Shaw, and wish you and your regiment the best of luck."

As the sun was sinking, Wendell headed for the beach to collect the bedding. Come the wee hours, he would find a way into Lillian's room to say goodbye. He couldn't let her go without saying goodbye.

The wagon wheels squealed forlornly as they crunched to a stop on the sand. Beside him in the twilight, the marriage bed sat empty and forlorn. Wendell climbed down, staring at the white ribbons of surf on the blackening sea. Where the waves broke, foxfire fluoresced with a green glow.

At first, he only imagined that he heard her crying. Suddenly she was there, running barefoot towards him across the sand. Weeping, she threw herself into his arms. "I'll miss the boat tomorrow," she promised. "I won't go."

He kissed her wet cheeks and held her tight, grateful that she hadn't left without a word or a hug. She was part of him, she couldn't just vanish. "Is that wise?" he asked trembling. "We can get another box of seven candles and begin afresh." She nodded as they clung to each other, and he told her about meeting Colonel Shaw. At news of the letter, he felt her body relax – Dragon Dix had frightened her badly.

"Since we're both here," he whispered, "let's burn the fifth candle."

Feeling considerably better, Wendell let go of her and sat down on the feather bed to take his boots off. Then he walked to the water's edge for the ablution of his feet. An almost full moon, squashed and silvery, was peaking up over the horizon.

When Wendell turned back toward the feather bed, Lillian was naked, all three remaining candles aglow in the sand beside her. She was so exquisite in the slanting moonlight, he wished for a moment he could paint her. Dark waves of hair framed her face, her belly and breasts quivered with anticipation. Candle-flames caught her eyes and danced warm and golden upon her white skin. "We should do the *Hieros Gamos* tonight," she whispered.

Pulsing with love, Wendell pulled off his clothes and knelt beside her. "Aye," he said softly, "tonight we'll have the Sacred Marriage. But consecutively. Each candle shall have its turn." He pinched out two of them, and they began to breathe together, focusing their gaze on the remaining flame.

It was not just that a celestial orchestra and angel voices split the skies overhead, or that, after the sensuality of the three rituals built to a passional climax and sent Cupid's arrow streaking towards its target, or their screams of *"Baruch Ain Soph"* startled a flock of birds noisily to flight, or that mighty waves crashed close upon them and shooting stars shot through the firmament. It wasn't that they died and went to heaven. Nor was it that they were no longer Wendell and Lillian, but all men and all women throughout time eternal, and every male and female in all Creation, every seed that had ever sprouted from the earth. No, it wasn't just that. It was also that it went on afterwards as if it would never stop, the startling thrill of her womb drinking from him every drop that he had and more.

When finally he slumped against her, sweaty and exhausted, she burst out laughing, the triumphal joy gladdening his heart and giving him energy to find her mouth and kiss her. Wrapped in each other's arms, they rolled together off the feather bed and into the sand, letting the sweeping wash of the tide tickle their heightened senses. He kissed her short and long, soft and hard, loving, teasing, passional.

Finally, it was simply this – once again, after two long years, Wendell could kiss her and be with her, as a man should be with his woman. The magic had worked.

Before dawn, the horse's whinny wakened him and his hand

went instinctively for the pistol. He was lying on the feather bed, crusted with salt and sand. Wendell jumped up, looking for Lillian. Way up the beach, he could see her, fully dressed in the dim light, shoes in hand, walking toward the hospital. Hastily, he pulled on his trousers and sprinted after her. Almost there, she saw him and began to run, but a lunging tackle pulled her down and him on top. He was panting.

"Please Wendell," she begged, "I can't say goodbye. I won't be able to leave if I have to say goodbye." He shushed her with his mouth on hers, drinking sweet kisses that he couldn't get enough of.

Finally he got up and pulled her to her feet. "There then," he said accusingly, "now you can go."

They were still aglow from the night. "I'll see you in Washington," Lillian said.

"Aye, I'll be on the next ship." Then he quickly turned and ran away from her, down the beach, tears starting from his eyes.

When the *Arago* began boarding passengers, Wendell was there. He saw her in the crowd, and before he could push his way to her, Colonel Shaw reached her. They greeted each other warmly, two old friends, as Colonel Shaw took her hands in his and kissed them. "Everyone loves Lillian," thought Wendell. Then the miracle of the night washed over him and he felt himself the luckiest man alive.

Lillian had the colonel's letter in her hand and was headed again toward the gangplank. Wendell did not go after her, but simply stood transfixed and watched until a pilot boat eased the heavy steamer away from the dock, its horn blasting. Suddenly, he was running along the beach, waving at the ship and calling her name. He saw her then, tiny on the stern, waving back. "I'll see you in Washington, Lillian *mon coeur*," he called, knowing she couldn't hear him, "I'll see you in Washington."

On his way back to the hotel, Wendell stopped in the tiny

jewelry store where an artisan about his age sat behind a workbench fashioning a cameo pin. "Do you have any wedding bands?" asked Wendell. The jeweler kept his attention on his work as he smiled.

"I do," he said with a Southern drawl. "And you'll not find a better price. You from the city?"

"Aye," said Wendell. "City prices are high, so I'm obliged if you can help me."

"I bought up a lot of jewelry cheap when the plantation owners left rather hastily, and have been recasting them myself."

It was another minute or so before the man held up the cameo and nodded his final approval. "That's beautiful work," said Wendell. "Where are you from?"

"I lived in Charleston till the war," he said. "A lot of folks there don't hold to busting up the Union and have come on over to this side." He rose and brought out a tray of gold rings and held up one that was wide and gently curved along the edges of its smooth deep-colored middle. Inside, the words *Hilton Head* were beautifully engraved.

"How much if you were to add 'May 31, 1863?'" Wendell asked. Thirty-five dollars – the price was indeed better than he could have hoped for in New York. As the man inscribed it, Wendell was aware that the greater part of him was still moon-struck on the beach. When he finally married Lillian, this ring would commemorate the Hieros Gamos as well as their legal wedding – he couldn't wait to give it to her. The artisan slipped Wendell's purchase into a ring box and assured him it could be sized easily by any jeweler.

Feeling quite wonderful, if somewhat poorer, he headed back to the hotel. He was hefting the featherbed still full of Lillian across the lobby when Tuck's voice behind him said, "Man, where you been? I been waiting for you dang near all morning."

Wendell spun around. Tuck was in his uniform and looked

excited.

"Help me with this," Wendell begged, flushing with his load under the arched eyebrows of both Tuck and the concierge.

"The General say to get your gear and bring the wagon," Tuck explained as they mounted the stairs. "I hope you got plenty plates. We's going up the Comby River with her and Colonel Montgomery."

"General Tubman?"

"Yessir, and three gunboats. We gone liberate my friends I told you about, from the Heyward plantation."

"I can't do field photography without an assistant," Wendell lamented.

"I thought of that. Montgomery say he got a man for you, waiting on the boat."

All the way to the steamer, the horse strained at the wagon and Tuck talked excitedly about seeing his friend Nelson again, and other folks he remembered fondly.

"Will the rebs put up much of a fight?" Wendell wondered aloud.

"They has a cavalry nearby. I reckon we'll be seeing 'em."

Soon the Beaufort Ferry slid past the grassy estuaries of Port Royal Sound where vast rivers seemed to pour in from every direction. Anchored or moored in the deeper waters, the impressive armada of the Union Navy was assembling for an assault on Charleston.

To Wendell, none of this felt real. His heart was still on the beach with Lillian and he wasn't ready to witness another battle filled with stench and carnage. Wendell stroked his pistol and wondered what it would be like to kill someone again. His phantom hand began to ache. However, by the time they landed at Beaufort, Tuck's passion to secure his friend's freedom had moved him and he was eager to go.

The ferry left them off in a pretty part of Beaufort where only the palmettos and Spanish Moss prevented Wendell from thinking he was in a nicer part of Boston. Women hung on the upper balconies and it was obvious that the officers and politicians who now lived here did not lack for feminine company.

Tuck took the reins and guided the horse down to the bustling naval docks where three gunboats were being made ready: *John Adams, Harriet A. Weed,* and *Sentinel.* "We be on *John Adams* with the General," said Tuck, and they both got down to guide the horse up the gangplank. The main black regiment had not yet boarded, but the men of the white 3rd Rhode Island Battery were loading shells and tending to the impressive artillery.

Wendell looked around with interest. The boat was a wooden side-paddle river steamer, armored between decks, with gun ports all round. There was a good mix of howitzers and smooth-bore cannons, maybe thirteen in all, capable of firing a shell hundreds of yards. The *Harriet A. Weed* was similar though perhaps a bit smaller, while the third boat, the *Sentinel,* had but two forward cannons and seemed more suited to transporting than battle. A young white soldier named Jeremiah introduced himself, saying he'd been a darkroom assistant before the war.

Mrs. Tubman was already on board, dressed in a blue military jacket over her nurse's skirts, her hair caught up in a kerchief over her head. Wendell could see her through the open door, huddled with the officers in their cabin. "The General and her spies been mapping the Comby River for months, and they knows where every torpedo be at," said Tuck with hushed admiration. "She done plan this expedition and she ask for Colonel Montgomery to lead it." Wendell was taken aback. Up till now, he'd thought that Tuck's insistence in calling her General had been simply a proud affirmation of her character.

By nightfall, the men of the 2nd South Carolina Colored Regiment had boarded, and the three gunboats left in darkness. The moon that had risen over Wendell and Lillian on the beach the previous night now rose another degree ripe. By tomorrow it would be at its peak of fullness. But the light that shone from it as it edged up over the horizon proved inadequate, for in St. Helena Sound *Sentinel* was caught on a shoal. Like her name, she stood there at attention and wouldn't budge. The men were taken off her and boarded onto the *Harriet Weed*.

Besides the officers, there were some two hundred fifty men in the South Carolina 2nd who, like Tuck, had proved themselves in action in Florida. Another one hundred fifty were "new recruits", draftees from among the escaping slaves who had varying reactions to this form of "freedom." The possibility of their taking off to join pirates active in the swamps along the Gulf was always present, and it took a great deal of faith from Montgomery to risk their mutiny. Decisions about draft and pay came from Washington, and there was nothing he could do about it. Most of his faith centered on the leadership of Harriet Tubman.

The loss of *Sentinel* slowed the party down and it was three in the morning before they arrived at the mouth of the Combahee River. Excitement was high and no one had slept. Around him, Wendell could see the glint of sunrise on the rifles and hear the men loading up.

The *John Adams* was in the lead and Harriet stepped to the bow. Facing the southern shore, she was lit by the morning sun as she cupped her hands around her mouth and let out a piercing birdcall. Within seconds, from the deeply wooded shore, came an answering call. The faint sounds of distant singing came from beyond the trees.

> *"Moses a'comin at the strawberry moon,*
> *Moses a'comin at the strawberry moon,*
> *Taking his children to freedom."*

The *Harriet Weed* paused and landed a shore party at a

Confederate outpost called Field's Point. Tuck's friends, Adam, Lou, and Joseph, watched the proceedings as they huddled aboard the *John Adams,* eager to see their friends on their old plantation. They said a few things in Gullah language. Then they noticed that Harriet, too, was straining her five foot frame to see around them. "The rebs ain't got too many men here right now, since it be the sickness time," she predicted as they watched the few Confederate sentries abandon their posts to raise the alarm.

With the engines turned off, Wendell had time to take out his camera and, with Jeremiah flowing the plates, record the sister ship before their own boat left the *Weed* behind. With the sun rising rapidly, the sound of singing got louder and dark eyes peered at them everywhere through the trees, surprised to see black faces in uniform looking back at them. "Moses a'coming at the strawberry moon." Harriet was singing it, too, her body rigid with one of her mysterious spells. It was all so muffled and other-worldly, the putt-putt of the engine, the steady stream of the river, the haunting voices from the woods delivering their coded message. An alligator slipped soundlessly into the water after an unwary crane. Finally the engines were cut and the gunboat allowed to drift. As Wendell began to take pictures of the rapt faces around him, all staring silently toward the western bank, he had a strange sense that this was a continuation of the night with Lillian. It was June 2nd, the 105th day, the original date of the Hieros Gamos – Magic was afoot.

The woods soon gave way to a vast expanse of rice paddies. Now in the open, the scene changed drastically. Overseers were beating their field hands back to no avail as a huge tide of humanity began to surge toward the ship. At a nod from Montgomery, Tuck hissed, "This be it," and the *John Adams* lowered its little boats and blew its shrill whistles. Tuck gave Wendell a hopeful wave as the men put ashore and disappeared into the confused thronging. Then the big artillery swung into action, giving cover. Great explosions were heard from down river in the direction of the *Harriet Weed*, and suddenly flames were leaping into the sky along the whole length of the riverbank. The bridge ahead was burning too, and the little boats began to fill up with fleeing slaves paddling desperately toward the ship, yelling "Moses, Moses, bless you, Moses!"

Wendell heard the unmistakable sound of a bugle charge from over the ridge and the big guns raised up and shot the further distance to meet the oncoming Confederate cavalry. The speed of activity and the fierceness of the blast shook the camera, making it impossible to shoot.

"Let them think they be thousands of us," Harriet laughed. She was standing on the bow, her arms upraised to Heaven, laughing and laughing, welcoming the people as the first waves boarded the ship. More boats put out, and were almost swamped with mothers and suckling babes, children, goats, pigs, even stewpots. The ones that couldn't get into the dinghys hung on dearly, afraid they might be left behind. Many other slaves dove into the water and swam. The water was a churning cauldron of flaming orange light.

To calm the situation, Harriet began to sing. Her voice resonated out over the water as though it were an opera house.

> *"Of all the whole creation in the East or in the West,*
> *The glorious Yankee nation is the greatest and the best.*
> *Come along! Come along! don't be alarmed,*
> *Uncle Sam is rich enough to give you all a farm."*

After each verse, she'd throw up her hands and shout "Glory" at which the Negroes would let go the boats and throw up their hands, singing "Glory!", thus allowing the little boats to escape to the ship. The sun shot beams through a cloud onto their rapturous faces – their Day of Deliverance was at hand.

"*Baruch Ain Soph!*" Wendell whispered, overcome with the

unmistakable Presence.

Hours passed and almost eight hundred Negroes boarded the two ships. Wendell managed to photograph Harriet on the bow, and got some blurry shots of ecstatic fugitives swarming on the deck, flames soaring on the shoreline behind them. One shot was of a woman holding onto two prized pigs, a black one and a white one, whom she called Beauregard and Jeff Davis. "Easier to butcher them," she grinned.

The plates were cumbersome and focus at close quarters difficult. Wendell wished he could just sketch the scenes, but Jeremiah proved an able helper and photographs had a solid ring of truth when they turned out.

The regiment had returned and there was a scramble to get them and the last of the slaves boarded. Once again, the big guns aimed and once again the blast sent the Confederate cavalry scrambling away over the hill where storm clouds had built and distant flashes of lightning added to the drama.

The *John Adams* turned on its engines, belching smoke into Wendell's lens and vibrating his tripod. "Wait!" cried Wendell. "Tuck! Corporal Robinson!" They were about to leave without him! Then he saw Tuck and Lou bearing a man between them as they dodged bullets across the burning field. The engines were cut. One more blast of the howitzer quieted the pursuit, and the three men were soon at the water's edge, scrambling into the dinghy that had put out to retrieve them. But when they pulled Tuck up over the side, it was clear he had been wounded and the third man was limp and bloodied.

Colonel Montgomery ripped the tattered sleeve off Tuck's jacket. "It ain't nothin' but a flesh wound," protested Tuck.

"Flesh wound, my bleedin' arse!" swore Montgomery. "The bone's broke clean through."

Harriet sat down on the deck and pulled Tuck's friend into her lap. "Get me some ice," she said, and gently opened the man's shirt to reveal a fresh bullet wound above the collarbone. She chewed on some grasses and applied them as a poultice. He opened his eyes. "We gone have to get the bullet out," she told him, "but you be all right. It best if we can get you back to Beaufort."

"Is this the friend you were telling me about?" Wendell asked Tuck.

"Yessir," said Tuck quietly. "That be Nelson Davis."

Harriet soothed the man's brow and began to sing, so softly only Mr. Davis could hear the words. He looked up at her and struggled to speak. "Bless you, Miss Moses, I's free," and with a contented sigh, closed his eyes.

A blissful peace came across Harriet's coarse features. And then, from underneath his focusing cloth, Wendell saw it – the *Black Pieta* – Harriet Tubman in her Union jacket, her rifle nearby, enraptured, cradling the freed slave's wooly head in her soft worn skirts. "This is what the war was for," thought Wendell. "Not for bodies piled up at Fredericksburg, but for this."

Wendell inserted the wet plate that Jeremiah handed him and opened the shutter. "Hold still, Harriet," he whispered reverently, choking back emotion. "Hold still."

Chapter 44

"Well now," Tuck said as he and Wendell sat at the campfire eating breakfast with the men of the 2nd. "The General say you and me is to be on the next ship north." His left arm was splinted and bandaged below the elbow and a dirty sling hung empty around his neck. "She says she want me to make sure them plates get safe to Mathew Brady for his gallery, then for me to go on home to Ruby till my arm heal up." He looked delighted. "Long as my arm don't heal up too quick, I'll be home when Ruby have the baby."

This was good news to Wendell. Harriet's interest in his plates guaranteed him passage to Washington, and Tuck would be welcome company. "Will your friend, Nelson, be going with us?" he asked.

Tuck chuckled in his familiar baritone. "No," he said. "Harriet's sweet on Nelson and he be sweet on her. No sir, I reckon she'll be taking him home with her when she go."

Wendell grinned, astounded. "But she's in her forties, and he can't be more than what? Nineteen?"

"Nelson Davis be wise for his age," proclaimed Tuck approvingly. "That be why I love him."

A few days later, back at Hilton Head, Wendell had his ticket in hand for passage to Washington – and Lillian. He couldn't wait to see her and tell her of the miraculous happenings on the Combahee River. The whole adventure still uplifted his spirit with wonder. He assumed her own adventures had gone well, and that as soon as her last month of enlistment was finished, she would be free to return to New York with him and get her annulment.

He said goodbye to the concierge on Robbers Row and crossed the street to the stables. "Hidalgo, you don't look so good," Wendell worried as the droopy horse was put in his harness. Perhaps it was the pervasive heat. He gave the horse some water which he disdained to drink. The poor animal refused to go any faster than a slow saunter and Wendell was suddenly afraid they would miss the ship.

By the time they arrived at the pier, they were running late and the horse was staggering badly. Foam was coming out of his mouth. Tuck had been watching for them and rushed over just as Hidalgo collapsed to his knees. "Shit!" exclaimed Tuck sinking down to look in the equine's mouth. "What you been feeding him?"

"Nothing," said Wendell, "he's been at the stables all week."

Tuck backed up suddenly as Hidalgo began to heave and deposited a steaming pile of small black seeds on the ground. "There be the answer," said Tuck. "Look like they ain't been giving him nothing but cottonseed."

"What'll we do?" asked Wendell. Just then the steamboat blasted its horn in preparation for departure.

Tuck shrugged. "Well, we ain't gone make the ship, that's sure."

At first, Wendell felt crushingly disappointed. But he soon began to see the delay as a blessing, for it gave him time to absorb the immense changes to his psyche that had taken place. For the next days, he lay on the sand at the water's edge, remembering each breath with Lillian, each precious touch, and committing it indelibly to memory.

When they finally boarded a ship another week later, Hidalgo had recovered with good feed and pasturing under Tuck's care, and the embarrassed stables had refunded some of Wendell's money. Wendell leaned on the railing next to his friend, getting what he assumed would be his last look at Hilton Head. The navy was moving about and the factories of war belched busily on the shore above the endless lines of tents. Southward was the hospital and the blowing palmettos on the beach which seemed to be waving goodbye. Perhaps when the war was over, he and Lillian would come back here for an anniversary of their Sacred Marriage.

"Man, look at all them ships," said Tuck, interrupting his reverie. "The Federal government ain't built that Navy just to free slaves."

Wendell looked at him, wondering what he was getting at.

"That Navy been built for empire," the former slave went on with awe in his voice. "Someday, they goin' conquer the world. The U.S. goin' replace Great Britain."

Empire. Wendell shivered suddenly and saw the specter of war stretching endlessly into the future.

As they approached Washington City, word spread through the ship of a siege alert in the capital. Only a week before, the cavalries of the two armies had had a bloody clash near Fredericksburg and Lee's army had disappeared along the banks of the Potomac. Washington was bracing for an invasion. Trying to spot the missing menace, a reconnaissance balloon hovered overhead and all eyes watched the shoreline as the ship steamed its way cautiously upriver.

It was late evening when the two friends debarked with Hidalgo. Tuck was anxious to find the colored unit whose barracks he'd been invited to share and Wendell was anxious to find Lillian.

He assumed he'd find her at Union Hospital, and prayed fervently that Dorothea Dix wouldn't be there. Promising to see if he could get prints at Brady's studio and check back about their travel plans, Wendell dropped Tuck off.

It was quite late when he arrived at Union Hospital and inquired after Lillian. "Nurse Flax is no longer here," he was told by an orderly. "She was transferred to Armory Square Hospital shortly upon her arrival."

Undaunted, Wendell climbed back on the wagon. He felt his excitement grow to finally see his Lillian, especially when he tied up with the hospital's ambulances and went inside. The stench of death and disease assailed his nostrils and told him the capital was still a war zone.

"Excuse me," he said doffing his hat to the first matron he saw, "Can you tell me where I might find Nurse Lillian Flax?"

The helpful matron answered him with a look of regret. "You must be her fiancé," she guessed. "Did you not get her letter? Nurse Flax has been mustered out early and gone on to New York."

"Alas no! When did she leave?" Alarm vied with acute disappointment at this unexpected news.

"I reckon on it being a fortnight ago, soon after she arrived."

"Thank you, madam." He donned his hat again and turned to go. Just then he heard a familiar voice behind him.

"Parry! Is that you, Parry?" Walt Whitman was all smiles as he hastened along the aisle to greet his friend. "By Jove, it is you!" They clasped their hands together and walked outside. "You're here looking for Lillian," he surmised.

"And to see you, too!" cried Wendell, his mood considerably lightened. They climbed together aboard the wagon. "I hear she had sent me a letter that I didn't receive."

"Indeed you didn't," admonished Whitman jovially, "she sent it to you here. The ship that carries the letters to Port Royal had already left. She expected that you would be on its return voyage."

"Aye, I had forgot I have a post box here," admitted Wendell, wondering what else might be in it. "Did she say why she left early? I trust she didn't receive a dishonorable discharge."

"Lillian? A dishonorable discharge? Wendell, you are a foolish wit. Her annulment was scheduled. I'm sure you wouldn't want her to miss it."

Wendell nodded. "Indeed. You're right about that."

They stopped by the darkened post office and Walt lit a match for Wendell to access his box. It contained a number of letters, one from his sister, one from Thomas, one from Fitzhugh, and yes, one from Lillian. "Thank goodness," he said, clutching it to his breast.

Given the hour, it was agreed that he should spend the night with Walt in his room on L Street. Wendell wanted to read his letters forthwith, but considerate of his tired host, he crawled gratefully into bed beside him. Still, the presence of the unread letters prayed upon Wendell's mind most unpleasantly, till at last he roused himself to dress and tiptoe down the stairs to the parlor, where he lit the oil lamp and opened Lillian's envelope.

"Wendell, My Dearest and Only Heart,

"As I write this, I am still in the thralls of our magical moments together. I go over them again and again, amazed and disbelieving. Were I to describe them, I should not know what to say, they are so unlike anything I could have imagined.

"Do you know how much I love you? You could have married Margaret, and she would have been a good wife to you or any man. Indeed, you could have had your pick of wives. Yet you chose me, in spite of all my selfishness, and pursued and persisted when I could offer you naught and even Dix considered me common enough to join her matrons. You have saved my life. I am so grateful for the whole experience that I can't even despise Mr. Ferguson, whom, I'm sure, I shall shortly be meeting in a magistrate's office.

"As you must know by now, I am away to New York to obtain the annulment, which I do not think will be contested. It will cost Mr. Ferguson not a penny and, unlike a New York divorce, an annulment will leave both of us free to remarry. Of course, there is always the chance that some puffed-up magistrate will get high and mighty about it, but I am hopeful.

"The civilian mails have been running slowly, I do not know if we shall hear from each other before I actually see you. If I'm not at Waverly or the Studio Building, our mutual friends will know where to find me.

"Meanwhile, I await you with magnetic kisses and more, Your Lillian"

The other letters he placed carefully in his pockets, then crept back up to Walt's room and crawled into bed. He sighed happily and closed his eyes. Even the persistent and ragged snore of his bedmate could not prevent him from swooning into a most delicious dream-filled slumber.

After breakfast, Wendell drove Walt to his office on 14th Street. Down almost every street, troops and artillery were being moved toward the city's perimeter. At the corner of 14th and Pennsylvania, Walt checked his pocket watch. "We have about three minutes to spare," he announced. A crowd was beginning to gather along Pennsylvania Avenue, lining the street on either side.

Right on time, the first horsemen appeared of the President's entourage followed by Lincoln's uncovered barouche and a cavalry squad of protectors. Their once elegant uniforms had a worn and roughened look. Tall boots were scuffed and plumes drooped. The riders sat straight in the saddle with grim pride, mindful of their great responsibility. President Lincoln sat with his stove pipe hat erect on his head, his coarse and kindly face deeply lined with worry.

"I love him," said Walt fondly. "When I look at how heavily the world sits on him, my heart goes out to him." He was silent a moment, lost in sadness. Then he brightened and said, "In his more carefree moments, he waves at me. I believe he knows who I am."

"He goes by daily?" asked Wendell surprised. It seemed dangerous to him that so many people would be able to predict the President's public comings and goings.

"Aye, in warm weather. If you're worried, you're right to be. He sleeps in Soldiers' Home, his country house on the outskirts of town where marauders are operating in advance of Lee's invasion. They blew up a weapons cache just two days ago." Walt sighed. "Ah, Wendell, I have seen so much, I doubt now I would even flinch should Lee's army come."

As Walt went up to work, Wendell promised to come by the hospital before leaving and take pictures of his patients. For now it was important to get Hidalgo stabled and fed. The horse led the way down Pennsylvania Avenue, eagerly going home to his familiar livery near Brady's studio.

"Hey, Parry!" Wendell heard as he came out of the stables onto a muddy side street. He turned and saw Timothy O'Sullivan in front of the corner building where a big sign proclaimed Gardner's Gallery. "Parry, how are you?" the photographer called again, walking towards him briskly on the busy sidewalk.

"Good to see you," Wendell greeted him, "I thought you were still in Falmouth with Mathew."

"Nay, Falmouth was closed after the loss at Chancellorsville. I think Brady's here in Washington." He flushed uncertainly and indicated the building behind him. "I'm with Alex Gardner now. We've got our own studio."

"Why's that?" asked Wendell. He had wondered before about Gardner's departure.

"Oh, it was no surprise to Brady. Alex had wanted to have his own studio back in New York, but when the war came, Mathew persuaded him to stay on awhile. Of course, the war's lasted longer than anyone foresaw and Alex stayed far longer than promised. Except that the two studios are rivals, there's no animus."

Wendell nodded. "That's good to hear. I was just on my way to Mathew's studio now. I'm glad I ran into you."

Mathew was in, standing in his labcoat examining prints, and greeted Wendell enthusiastically. But he sobered when he picked up a recent print and held it for Wendell to see. It was the picture of a Negro, his naked back viciously scarred by the whips of his slave masters. "This one will bring home the horror of slavery for those who still can't believe it," Mathew said simply. Wendell was not ignorant of such brutality, yet it had a visceral effect on him.

Mathew asked to see Wendell's pictures from the Sea Islands, and held up a black sheet of paper behind each glass plate to view the silvery negative as a positive. "These give hope," came the verdict. "They inspire the end of slavery, but in a different way."

Then Brady held up the *Black Pieta*, inhaled sharply, and didn't breathe again for a long moment. "This one will make you, Parry," he said finally.

Wendell nodded. He was aware of what he had. "Especially as that's Harriet Tubman. She planned and led the battle."

"Ah, I read about it in the papers. They didn't say who it was, just a Negro woman, which is surprising since Tubman's well known. I was photographing Secretary of State Seward at the time, and he guessed it was she." Then he said admiringly, "Seward had sold Harriet her property in Auburn, even knowing she was a fugitive and he could face prison for doing so."

Mathew put down the plate and squeezed Wendell's shoulders like a son he was proud of. "How long are you going to be here? I have work if you need it." He offered a wry smile, "I can even pay you this time."

"I'm going to try to get out of here tomorrow," said Wendell.

Brady allowed him to make his prints and in return, Wendell left him some for his gallery. By the time he departed, Wendell had restocked all the wagon's supplies at a very reasonable rate. Now he just had to pick up Tuck and make it to the train station before the ticket window closed.

There was still time enough when Wendell chased Tuck down in the mess-hall at the colored barracks, but when they arrived at the station, the ticket window was already closed. "That's a might strange," said Tuck as Wendell tugged on the reins. "We be here in plenty time." They climbed down and handed the reins to a colored boy to hold for them, and went in search of someone in a railroad uniform. They found one on the platform as a train was pulling out.

"Good evening, sir," said Wendell. "We were wondering why the ticket window is closed so early."

The conductor rolled his eyes – he had obviously been asked this same question more than once. "We're closed to the public for the foreseeable future," he recited mechanically. "The hospitals are being evacuated in advance of the battle. Unless you're in a stretcher, you don't go."

"What battle is that?" Wendell asked anxiously. "Are we to be invaded?"

"Hope not," he answered, then warmed to the subject as he shared the news. "Lee's been spotted in Pennsylvania and Hooker's boys have gone out to meet him." His voice dropped conspiratorially. "Appears like they've got us surrounded. The only direction there haven't been skirmishes is towards the ocean."

Tuck spoke up, in careful English. "Excuse me, sir, I'm a wounded soldier with orders to get to New York. Ain't there a way I can get on the train?"

The railroad man looked at him as if seeing him for the first time and narrowed his eyes. "You've got orders, eh? Maybe we can cram you into a baggage car with the other niggers."

Wendell saw Tuck flinch, and heard him mutter dangerously, "If I weren't a man of the cloth..." at which Wendell grabbed his arm and steered him back toward the wagon. Tuck was frothing with anger as they climbed aboard.

"When I enlisted," he raged, "I swear I'm never goin' ride in the baggage car again. I ain't fighting this here war just to wind up being some Northern version of a slave. If I'm good enough to be free, I'm good enough to sit next to you in a seat."

"Aye," agreed Wendell. He thought a moment, then reconsidered their situation. "Except 'twill probably take longer for me to get passage with my rig. You'd get out of here sooner if you went on ahead." Indeed, Wendell would be happy to ride in the baggage car if it meant getting to New York quicker.

"I ain't riding in no baggage car," Tuck proclaimed adamantly. "Never again."

Another week went by that the ticket window didn't open. Tuck was given guard duty at the armory with the colored members of the Invalid Brigade while Wendell took pictures of soldiers and at night worked for Brady in the darkroom.

He needed money. The letter from Catherine had said his father was unable to walk and the farm was in foreclosure. They had till August to get hold of $400. Catherine's own place was long gone, and so, apparently, was Seneca Sue. Not willing to admit that he would have to sell his rig, Wendell threw himself into his work, stealing at midnight into the livery stable to sleep in the wagon. He fervently regretted not asking for money at the Hieros Gamos. Randolph had said they should ask what they needed for their lives together. Indeed, Wendell had not remembered or even thought it important to ask for anything other than to be with Lillian again. Now, how would he afford to marry her?

Meanwhile, General Hooker had been replaced as head of the Army of the Potomac by General Meade, and Brady was on his way to Pennsylvania to photograph the expected battle. So were Gardner and O'Sullivan.

"Do you want to go, Parry?" Mathew asked as he prepared for his trip. Wendell shook his head. "I can't," he said simply. It was quite out of the question, but he was flattered Brady had asked him.

Occasionally he managed to get up in time to drive Walt Whitman to work. One such morning, Whitman looked distraught and had obviously been up all night. "The wounded have started arriving," he said. "Oh Wendell, it's really bad." Indeed, the papers were full of it, how Meade had engaged Lee's army at Gettysburg. Wendell remembered Harriet's prophecy and shared it with Walt. "'They's going to be a terrible big battle way up in the North," she had sung. "'They's going to be so much killing, so many dead, but the North going to win it.'"

"The North had better win it," said Walt, "for if we don't stop Lee's army now, Washington will be overrun in short order and the war lost." They both knew the North hadn't won anything yet, at least not in the Eastern Theater. True, they'd stopped them at Antietam, but that was more of a draw. Wendell shuddered, remembering the recent carnage at Fredericksburg.

Damn that he hadn't asked to be with Lillian and live a happy, comfortable life, he thought. Hadn't Paschal Randolph said to ask for what they wanted in their life together and it would be granted? So far, everything the magician had said about the Sacred Marriage was true. Wendell would have only himself to blame if he died here in Washington City and never saw Lillian again.

Chapter 45

Tuck was staring out the window as he sat facing Wendell on the train bound for Jersey City. His expression was impenetrable, his handsome uniform clean and pressed. Gettysburg had been won and Vicksburg had fallen, both within days of each other and just in time to give the Fourth of July celebration special meaning. Fireworks had lit the night sky over Washington. With those two victories, the entire trajectory of the war had changed.

The victories had left Wendell spiritually renewed, and he would soon see Lillian. Together they would decide what to do about his father's farm. As was now clear to him, Lillian was his family and his first responsibility was to her. If saving the farm factored into that, fine. But he needed to see his father. He sensed that Harte Parry had not much longer to live.

As the train pushed through the now-tranquil Pennsylvania countryside, Wendell was finally answering his letter from Thomas. Army and married life in Cincinnati suited him. The details of Thomas' routine changed, but were consistent in their broad outlines of his tranquil life. These details he described with such color and humor that Wendell had laughed out loud to read it.

As for Fitzhugh, his adventures were boundless. He was, he said, getting along famously with Bierstadt and was completely drug-free. He described the Rockies as not so much a chain of mountains, but a trough of petrified waves caught in the act of being violently thrown upward. On either side of this trough were high plateaus of astoundingly vivid shapes and colors, all captured by the incomparable Albert Bierstadt. As he wrote, his little company was about to arrive in Salt Lake City, the "Capital of Mormondom," where he would try for an historic interview with their sainted president, Bringham Young. As a consequence of the coming military draft, the ranks of the Mormons were swelling with converts and would, Fitzhugh was sure, form another, wholly different, secessionist state. Beyond the Mormons lay fierce desert and hostile Indians. As Wendell read, he could almost hear Fitzhugh say, "There, that ought to impress Rosalie."

He looked at Tuck who was reading his Bible. "I never asked you," said Wendell, "why you became a preacher."

Tuck was contemplative. "All the white folks, includin' the North, be struggling right now with they guilt," he said, "and coloreds got the moral high ground. Seem like there's power in that if we can keep it."

"Do you see no altruism in the North? Indeed, I do not believe there ever was a race before, who fought to free another race with nothing to gain in it for themselves."

Tuck smiled. "They got redemption to gain. You think redemption ain't nothing? Why, the North be as guilty as the South, way it get so rich off cotton." His look deepened knowingly. "Seem like you and Lillian know better than most 'bout redemption."

Redeemed! Wendell's eyes misted as his heart swelled in gratitude.

When the train finally pulled into the Jersey City Station, a general hubbub of alarm spread rapidly through the cars. The sun had just set as the passengers were herded onto a platform already crowded beyond moving, and the word went out that the ferries weren't running. There were screams and fainting. One look across the river gave the reason – Manhattan was on fire! Pockets of flame leapt up from all corners, lighting the night sky for miles while the roar of a building's collapse, gunshots and yelling echoed clearly across the water.

Wendell's heart pounded and he looked at Tuck, who had blanched to almost white. "Lord Jesus," said Tuck, "is New York been invaded?" The authorities weren't saying, but only announced there would be a delay till the army arrived. Until then, hotel rooms were available on the New Jersey side. No one moved, and slowly the word was passed that gangs and poor immigrants were rioting against the draft. Especially heinous was the provision that $300 could buy one's way out of it. Wendell and Tuck assured each other that the rioters' targets must be government buildings, and that their own loved ones were safe.

As the night wore on, Manhattan quieted and the crowd on the ferry platform slowly dispersed. Wendell and Tuck were sitting on the wagon seat, a cloth thrown over Hidalgo's sleepy head. The fires died to a smoky pall, visible where gas lamps were still on. Most of the city was ominously black, the calm still broken occasionally by shouts and the clanging bells of fire wagons.

The port's authority at the ferry changed guard, prompting Tuck and Wendell to climb down from the whatsit wagon to interview the newcomers, one of whom proved more forthcoming with his information. The remaining people on the platform crowded around him.

"It's a rebellion, called for by the Governor on 4th of July to protest the draft," the young patrolman explained. "'Tis the third night of it. Everything's closed, you can't hardly find food."

"What do you mean, Governor Seymour called for it?" a woman asked indignantly. "He wouldn't do such a thing."

"He sure did! He said to remember that the bloody, treasonable, and revolutionary doctrine of 'public necessity' can be proclaimed by a mob as well as a government. That's his words exactly."

"So they're targeting government buildings?" Wendell asked.

"They're targeting everything. Anyone who looks like he can afford $300 is a target, and anyone in Union blue. They even let out a cheer for ole Jeff Davis. Cavalry arrived yesterday and beat 'em back on the west side, but they just popped up again on the east." He looked at Tuck and shame crept into his voice. "They're targeting Negroes the worst, torturing and lynching them right in the streets."

At this news, Tuck snapped to attention. After a few brave moments, his pride gave way to dismay, and he sagged onto a park bench that overlooked the river. Heedless of his sling, he leaned his head in his trembling hands. Muffled sobs soon gave way to vocal anguish as he cried, "Lord, not in the North! Not in the North!"

Wendell turned desperately to the guard and begged to know when the army was coming. Wilberforce could well be in danger – or Lillian – or any of his friends.

"Their train should get here a little before dawn. It's a New York regiment straight up from Gettysburg."

"You can call 'em a New York regiment," said one man angrily, "but they're really Lincoln's regiment, come to shove Lincoln's illegal draft on us!"

"Oh, it's a New York regiment, all right," the patrolman insisted. "The 7th New York. Don't you remember how proud we were when they went first to answer Lincoln's call?"

"That's before this war was about freeing niggers!" came a voice. "We're expected to give up our freedom to free them!"

"The Devil! It was always about freeing slaves," said a bandaged vet. "We sang *John Brown's Body* as we marched off." Pushing and jostling broke out on the platform, but was quieted by others.

The 7th New York – Sanford Gifford's regiment. He was one person Wendell would be really happy to see. The thought of Sanford having been at Gettysburg was almost too much – the numbers were still coming in, but there had been an unfathomable number of casualties, far more than any other battle. Wendell fervently prayed Sanford wasn't among them.

Wendell looked over at Tuck, quiet now on the park bench. He dared not ask him if he was alright. His face was hidden in shadow, and Wendell could see he was shrinking from the small crowd. Wendell felt on his hip for his pistol and tensely waited for the army to arrive.

At three-thirty in the morning, the train rolled in and weary troops poured off it, headed for the ferries. There was a tremendous rumble – they had brought their cannons. Wendell searched the faces anxiously.

"Sanford!" he called out on seeing him.

Sanford turned, a welcoming smile on his worn features. "Wendell! We've come to rescue you! What are you doing on this side of the river?" Wendell introduced him to Tuck and explained their mission. "Hmmm," Sanford considered, "you'd best go in with us. Both Corporal Robinson and the wagon will be targets. We're directed to sweep our way up to Gramercy Park. Barring a major eruption elsewhere, that's where we'll spend the night."

"Gramercy Park? That's where Ned lives."

"He's been virtually under siege if he's there," said Sanford. He paused and regarded Tuck hopefully. "On the way, we'll stop by Cooper Union and ask after your boy."

It was agreed – Tuck would take Hidalgo and the whatsit wagon in with the army while Wendell would try to find Lillian in Greenwich Village.

When the loaded-down ferry finally reached Manhattan, the day was dawning with a ghastly smoke-rendered orange. Sanford gave Wendell the key to his atelier. "Everyone's away for the summer," he said. "If I can get mustered out by Saturday, I've got passage up the Hudson. It's the *Rival*. I'm sure that under the circumstances, Captain Collyer won't mind taking a few more passengers."

The drumbeat started and Sanford's regiment marched off the ferry with Tuck driving Hidalgo behind. "God be with you!" Wendell shouted, waving his wooden hand. A sudden lump caught in his throat as he remembered another, more innocent day when he and Sam had shouted the same words to Sanford and Ted and the valiant men of the 7th New York. "Thank God you're here," he added huskily.

As Wendell walked along Canal Street to Broadway, he was amazed at the destruction. Bands of ruffians looted through the broken windows of burned buildings while overturned horsecars, furniture, rocks, brickbats, and torn clothing littered the pavement. Buzzards and seagulls picked at bits of flesh left behind during hasty efforts to pick up bodies. For the first time, Wendell was really concerned about his friends – and Lillian. The sun was rising and it was going to be a very hot day. He took off his jacket and cravat, pulled out his shirttail on one side, pushed up his sleeves, and loosened his collar. This exposed the pistol Wendell wore on his hip, but that was likely a good thing – he was prepared to use it. As an afterthought, he detached his wooden hand and stuffed it into his jacket pocket, now thrown casually over a shoulder. His object was to blend in with the looters.

Wendell marveled that he was walking right down the center of Broadway. Every now and then, he passed a long line of people waiting for food. Other than that, nothing was open and no vehicles were running. The acrid smells of gunpowder, brick dust and smoke hung heavy in the air. From other parts of the city, Wendell could hear shouting and gunshots, the occasional boom of a cannon. Even so, it was strangely quiet, a city without traffic. Greenwich Village seemed very far away.

When Wendell finally reached Bleecker Street, he wasn't startled to see Pfaff's stairway boarded up – almost every door he'd passed had been. His footsteps quickened toward Waverly Place and he was aware of an ache in his feet that would surely worsen when he stopped walking. The sounds of battle grew, coming from just ahead and to the east. Finally he knocked on the door of the Waverly Place household.

Wendell saw the drawn curtains move in the window before the door opened. "You're a brave fellow to be out and about," Henry Clapp greeted him. "I hope you brought some beer with you." The whole gang was crowded around the dining table and called out their enthusiasm – Ada Clare, Aubrey, Ada Menken, Bob Newell, Macaroni, Lil Woodman, and Rosalie – everyone but Lillian. It was as if the entire of Pfaff's alcove had been moved here from under Broadway. Pipe smoke and bubbles communed festively above their playing cards. As they began excitedly to talk at once, Wendell interrupted them.

"Where's Lillian?" he asked.

Wendell started when Rosalie answered, "Bellevue Hospital," then added quickly, "She's volunteering." He let out a sigh – she'd be safe enough there – and gratefully pulled off his shoes as Ada offered him water and crackers.

"We're pretty low on food," she apologized. She lowered her voice conspiratorially, "We've been feeding three colored men in the basement."

"Is it an organized uprising?" asked Wendell.

"It does seem to be a Movement," said Clapp. "As a rule, I find movements amusing. They move in funny little circles that make one dizzy to look at them, yet they imagine that they move the universe. It will be crushed, of course. Then the city will not just harass poor people, but send them to fill a draft quota. They've been drafting Irish immigrants right off the boat."

"Were it the Governor's draft, rather than the President's," said Newell, "it would have gone over better. The states are not used to having their freedom constrained by a central authority."

Wendell squeezed in at the table as they filled him in on the week's riots. Greeley's *Tribune* had been under heavy attack, and Tom Aldrich's safety was uncertain. When the mob broke in and tried to set the offices afire, Greeley and his pressmen opened the boilers on them. There was news of the four-story Colored Orphanage being burned down on Monday – hundreds of children had been removed, thank God, and were now dispersed under heavy guard in the city's precinct buildings. Elizabeth and Margaret were safe in Brooklyn.

"Pity humans were born under the fatal necessity of being governed," said Clapp. "There are so many Cains and Abels that some power must be maintained to keep peace between them. But thus far, this power has never prevented anyone from being killed."

Wendell nodded, and noted how tired and worn the king of the bohemians looked. Wendell pitied him. Of all the people he knew, Clapp was the wisest, the one who could see the folly of man most clearly and step aside from it. Yet, even surrounded by his court, he looked unutterably alone. To a large degree, Clapp had stepped aside from the folly of living.

Despite his swollen feet, Wendell was itchy to get going. He had to think which day this was – Thursday. Sanford had said he could get passage for them on the *Rival* on Saturday. After delivering an update on Walt Whitman, Wendell squeezed painfully back into his shoes.

"The papers say things have calmed today," offered the Menken hopefully. "Stores are beginning to open, and omnibuses are running on 6th Avenue."

"It didn't sound calm to me," Wendell opined. "I'm headed to Bellevue Hospital. Ned's house is on the way – I'll check in on him."

"The mob's been threatening the armory over there from the start," said Macaroni. "There's been heavy fighting. Maybe you should wait till tomorrow."

"I have a gun," Wendell assured them, at which Clapp groaned and rolled his eyes in disapproval. "Anyway, the 7th New York is sleeping in Gramercy Park tonight. I should be quite safe."

"Say hello to Sanford and Ned for us," called Ada as he departed.

It was fairly calm as he walked up Broadway and cut over on 17th Street to the East Side. He passed some looters and a lot of trash, with things more or less as they had been except without the distant battle noises. When he glanced up 3rd Avenue, he saw wreckage so deep that even a pedestrian would have a hard time getting through.

As Wendell approached 2nd Avenue, he was trying to remember which house number belonged to Ned. Only slowly did growing voices reach his consciousness, until there came sounds of shouting and gunfire. He glanced up 2nd Avenue and saw a large mob, maybe two hundred strong, only a block away.

Suddenly, someone from behind him grabbed his arm. Wendell swung around violently, intent on knocking his assailant down.

"Whoa, Parry!" came Wilkes' voice as he ducked the blow. "'Tis only I, John Wilkes!" He straightened. "Come on in the house, it's not safe out here."

Chapter 46

Wendell and John Wilkes headed up the stairs of a nearby brownstone. Toughs were beginning to spill down 17th Street as Wilkes tapped a code on the door, and again, the curtain moved before the door opened. "Mother," said Wilkes to the elegant older lady who opened it, "look whom I've found. This is a good friend and photographer, Mr. Wendell Parry."

She greeted him warmly as Wendell removed his hat and stepped into the darkened foyer. John Wilkes bolted the door behind him. Shutters and drapes confirmed a house under siege. "My pleasure," he blushed, trying to get used to John Wilkes' description of him as a good friend.

"Ned's in his study." Wilkes indicated a door to the right. It was cracked open and Wendell could see Edwin Booth sitting at his desk, staring at a picture of Molly. Wendell swallowed hard and blinked. "He's like that a lot," said Wilkes. "He seems obsessed with talking to his wife's ghost." He pushed the door further open and Ned looked up. "We have company," Wilkes said.

Wendell had expected to see dazed and tearful eyes, but the look on Ned's face as he came over was beatific and glowing. "Wendell!" It seemed as though it weren't the first time they'd seen each other since Molly's death. "I trust you've some tobacco you can spare!"

Wendell laughed, "Aye. I have a little."

Ned stuffed his pipe, and marveled that Wilkes had brought home a *Tribune* – it and the *Times* were still being printed and distributed.

"I've been tardy in my letters," said Wendell apologetically. "'Twas my own guilt that stayed me, though you've been much in my thoughts."

Ned regarded him, his eyes glistening. He gripped Wendell's shoulder. "Aye," he said finally, "we had been guilty together, you and I. It has made me feel close to you." Wendell looked at him uncertainly and Ned clarified, "Molly has long since forgiven both of us. I can tell you this without you thinking me mad, for Lillian has told me of your own miracles – she lives, Wendell, Molly lives! And I have never been saner."

Wendell's eyes were moist. He was at a loss for words.

"But come," Ned said, "I am neglecting my other guest." They shared some gossip as he led Wendell up the stairs to see the wounded captain, Adam Badeau.

Adam was lying in his night dress in the modest but elegant master bedroom. The windows were open to allay the heat, allowing alarming street noises to enter. "Well, Mr. Parry, is it?" Adam said with considerably less than full vigor, "I do believe we've met."

"Aye, Captain Badeau," said Wendell, "at a *Saturday Press* fundraiser on 14th Street."

"The night of the aurora," Adam remembered, "a 'Free Love' ball. How long ago that seems."

"Free Love," Wendell repeated. The words sounded foreign – the term held such a different meaning for him now. "Aye, 'twas life-times ago."

They were silent for a moment, reflecting on all they had been through since that night. "Ned tells me you were wounded near Vicksburg," Wendell said finally. "Have you been here long?"

"I came just at the beginning of this draft trouble – from one battle to another, you might say. Ned chides me I brought it with me." His chuckle turned to coughing, but soon subsided.

Just then Wilkes entered with a steaming plate. "Potatoes again!" grinned the captain, "My, Wilkes, what has your amazing mother done with them this time?"

"Bacon grease and onions," smiled Wilkes. He looked at Ned. "Supper's ready. Go on down, and I'll take care of the captain. It's my turn to change his bandages."

Ned led Wendell into the spacious kitchen where they sat down at a little table with Mrs. Booth and two-year old Edwina. With nothing to eat but potatoes and onions, the Booths had dispensed with formal dining. "Mother," said Ned graciously, "you are a marvel of innovation. Who knew potatoes could be made up in so many delicious ways."

"Indeed," she said, "I am fast running out of patience with it. Potatoes alone can't heal a wound or grow a baby. Oh, how I want to dine out again and go to the theater!"

"Potatoes are my favorite," declared Wendell sincerely, "and I have never tasted better." This was more true since he hadn't eaten in some time. "I thank you for your hospitality."

For awhile, they caught up again with news of friends.

Then Wendell ventured, "Wilkes seems to get on quite well with Captain Badeau," finding it a bit curious in view of Wilkes' known sympathy for the South.

Ned nodded. "He loves Adam, as do I. Do you remember, Wendell, how fearful I was that Molly would be jealous of our friendship? But Molly loved Adam from the start." Ned's eyes still had an other-worldly glow, but his beautiful voice was rough now from too much smoking,

"You're wondering, Mr. Parry," observed Mrs. Booth astutely, "how John Wilkes could be here when there is news of such a spiteful rivalry between him and his brother? Well, just don't you believe it. Creating controversy sells papers, that's all it is."

Ned laughed. "It sells tickets, too," he reminded her. "If someone sees Wilkes perform, he will have to see me to compare. Then, finding us too incomparable to form a verdict, he must see us both again!" He was heartily enjoying himself, finding it a great joke, and Wendell detected a slight mania in his elevated mood. "Why, my father had the same ruse with Edwin Forrest, his best friend!"

Little Edwina, in her high chair, let them know suddenly that she, too, was tired of potatoes. Her dish clattered to the floor.

Her father sighed his concern, and for the first time seemed truly present as he patted her head. "Did Mr. Joseph get his dinner, Mother?" he asked.

"He did," she replied, "Wilkes took it to him, though his distress is such that he almost can't eat." Edwina shook her tray while Mrs. Booth tried to ignore her unanswerable demands.

"Mr. Joseph," Ned explained to Wendell, "is Captain Badeau's Negro nurse, hiding in the basement. Since Union officers are also targets of the mob, Adam would be safer there, too, were he more easily moved and made comfortable." Ned added hopefully, "I'm sure the riots will expend themselves before any of us is in serious danger."

As if to put the lie to Ned's sentiment, a large blast of cannon shook the entire house, and there were angry voices. The language and shouting that came from the street, along with gunshots and breaking glass, put everyone on edge.

Suddenly, Wilkes came flying down the steps, the captain's saber in one upraised fist, a pistol in the other. He looked out through the curtains, put aside the saber, and dragged a chair over to prop against the door. Wendell rushed to the window and peered out. At the sound of battering against the door, Wendell drew his pistol. "Daddy!" squealed Edwina. Her grandmother picked her up and they disappeared into the basement. Edwin reached under the staircase and pulled out a shotgun. It made a loud click as he pulled the hammer back, and all weapons focused on the door.

The battering got louder, along with cursing about "rich actors ain't gettin' drafted." Everyone held his breath in an intense apprehension of what was to come. To Wendell, it brought back memories of crossing the Bull Run, and the same fear the men felt at facing battle for the first time.

"We're armed in here!" Wilkes warned loudly. The door continued to shake and loosen ominously. Just before it was about to give, another loud blast of the cannon distracted the ruffians, and they departed as quickly as they'd come.

"The army's here," said Wendell with a silent salute to Sanford.

"Thank God," breathed John Wilkes beside him, "even if it is Lincoln's army."

"It's the 7th New York," Wendell assured him, "a New York militia."

"It was a New York militia. It's Lincoln's army now. Just like it's his draft."

"Wilkes, you promised," said Ned sharply.

Into the evening, the battle raged. Mrs. Booth found bedding for John Wilkes and Wendell, to camp on the floor in front of the door. On the landing at the top of the stairs, Ned set up camp with his shotgun. They all settled down and tried to sleep. Soon, Wendell heard a slow even snore coming down the staircase. Outside, things had quieted.

"Parry, you awake?" whispered John Wilkes through the dark.

"Aye," said Wendell.

"Have you any tobacco?"

"Rolling tobacco."

"It'll do." Wendell reached over to his coat pocket and threw the little sack across the space between them. Wilkes fumbled in the dark, then lit up and lay back against the pillow. "You've been in battle," he stated, sounding somewhat awed at the fact. "These past few days are the closest I've come to it." He was quiet a moment, his handsome features reflecting earnest contemplation in the cigarette's glow and the dim light from a transom. "Have you ever seen a man hanged?" he asked.

"No," said Wendell. He wondered what Wilkes was getting at.

"I've seen two men hanged." A shudder went through Wilkes' body. "One was John Brown." Wendell was surprised at this, and that Wilkes spoke the name with reverent awe. "I borrowed a uniform to be there. It was – inspiring, even glorious. You could see it in his eyes, his hope rescuers would come. They never did, but he didn't flinch." His voice choked as he added with conviction, "John Brown died for what he believed – he was a great man."

Wilkes took a shaky drag on the tobacco, and continued. "Then two days ago, I saw a man, a little helpless colored man, strung up from a lamppost and lit on fire." He swallowed hard, struggling to go on. "There was nothing proud in it, nothing I could do. It was horrible."

Again he fell silent. Finally he said, "I can't help thinking the Negroes should have stayed on the plantations. At least they were wanted there." He waited for Wendell's agreement, but Wendell was thinking again about freedom, and how differently he thought of it now.

"No man wants to be in bondage, Wilkes," he said softly. Wilkes ignored the point, whether from agreement or obtuseness, Wendell couldn't say.

"Lincoln is to blame for that hanging," Wilkes continued vehemently. "Before the war, we had a voluntary union of states with their own militias. God, I would have that union again! It was the most perfect union ever conceived. But Lincoln makes of it an involuntary union, with a tyrant at its center, attacking his own people." Wilkes turned toward Wendell and gestured with the glowing tip of his cigarette. His voice grew louder and Wendell was afraid he would wake Edwin and bring down his wrath. "The army is no longer a New York militia, it's Lincoln's militia. First he sent it to occupy Maryland, my home, a state not even in rebellion. Then he sent it to occupy the South in violation of their right to secede, and now he sends it to occupy the North. When the war's over, he won't disperse the militias back to the States, he'll send them to Mexico, South America, even Africa. In the midst of this awful war, he makes the capital a monument of empire." Wilkes stubbed out his cigarette angrily. "My family came from

England to get away from emperors!" he hissed. Finally, he murmured through the dark, almost to himself, "He would make himself Caesar, Wendell. *Sic semper tyrannus.*"

A shiver of foreboding ran up Wendell's spine.

"Is anything amiss?" Ned called sleepily from the landing.

Wendell remained silent, not convinced Ned was awake, and breathed a sigh of relief when he resumed his light snore.

Wendell remembered Prince Bertie's warning about America needing to appear strong, but this was not the first time he had heard Wilkes' sentiments – indeed, most of New York City seemed to feel the same way, certainly now. Even Tuck and Henry Clapp had mentioned the word 'empire.' Wendell wished he had photographs with him, wished that Wilkes could see the picture of the slave with the scarred back, wished that Wilkes had met Harriet Tubman and the men of the 2nd South Carolina, and could see the looks on the Negroes' faces when they escaped to freedom. Finally Wendell said, "But who will enforce the rights of a man if a state doesn't? Wouldn't it have to be the other states, through the auspice of the federal government?"

No reply came – John Wilkes Booth was fast asleep.

When Wendell left in the morning, the riots seemed to be over. Stores were opening and an occasional cab went by, weaving past debris from one block to the next. Wendell hurried along 1st Avenue, dodging and climbing over rubble, till he reached Bellevue Hospital. He was surprised to find Tom Aldrich in the waiting room, his sleeves torn, his arms scratched and bloodied. He greeted Wendell ruefully. "Journalism's dangerous work," Tom sighed, rolling his blue eyes upward toward his matted mop of curls.

"Aye, I had been worried for you," Wendell responded, "It's not too serious, I hope."

"I'll recover."

"I'm looking for Lillian. Have you seen her?"

"You just missed her," said Tom. "She heard of troubles over on 5th Avenue at 35th Street, and insisted on going at once."

"Fifth and 35th – that's Ferguson's mansion!"

Without saying goodbye, Wendell ran out the door, hailed a cab and urged all haste in getting him there, till rubble required he get off and run. When he arrived in the great mansion's drive, ruffians were smashing windows and doors, running off with prized paintings and the mansion's precious antiques. Dangerous looking white smoke billowed up from the back – the building was on fire.

Wendell's eyes searched for Lillian in the crowd, and not finding her, he ran in through the front door. "Lillian! Lillian!" he cried out.

Flames licked along the far wall. An elderly man came out of the gallery, his arms filled with paintings. "There's a lady went upstairs," he called helpfully.

As Wendell took the steps two at a time, smoke filled the house, choking him. On the landing, he called her name again, heard a cough and followed it, into the red bedroom. There was Lillian, standing on the bed and trying to pull *Sands of Morocco* off the wall behind it. Smoke was gathering across the ceiling and she was coughing violently. "Help me, oh help me!" she gasped.

"Leave it, Lillian!" Wendell demanded. He reached for her and threw her over his shoulder. He could hear her wheeze as he rushed with her down the sweeping staircase, dodging bombs of molding and plaster that fell flaming from the ceiling. When they reached the front door, there was a violent explosion behind them and they were thrown out, tumbling like baggage onto the lawn.

Wendell lay stunned, his pulse pounding too strongly to feel pain. The heat and roar of the flames was intense. He rolled over to where Lillian lay wheezing and pulled her to her feet, half dragging her to a safer distance. Just then, there was a mighty roar and the whole house collapsed spectacularly, shooting dust and debris and black acrid smoke outward in all directions.

Lillian tried desperately to catch her breath, and as the dust cleared, Wendell thumped her back. "Go ahead and cough, *Mon Coeur*," he said, "let it out. Let it all out."

Lillian gasped. Her voice was barely audible beneath the roaring flames. "I'm sorry, Wendell, I'm so sorry."

"It's all right now. We're safe." He put his arms around her.

She was distraught. "Your masterpiece – everything you put into it."

"'Tis no matter." Wendell's smile was elated. He directed her gaze to the smoldering wreckage that had been Ferguson's mansion. "Frankly, *Mon Coeur*, it is beyond satisfying to have carried you down those stairs and watch this place burn to the ground!" With that, he pumped his wooden hand in the air and let out a victory whoop so loud that the remaining timbers of the house shivered and crashed.

The crowds fled as clanging bells on fire wagons warned that authorities were coming. And then Tuck was there, offering Lillian a canteen of water. Firemen sat on their wagons, letting the mansion burn, while soldiers searched the grounds and questioned by-standers. Sanford joined them, looking heroically tired.

"Let's go home," he said. He led Wendell and Lillian to the driveway where the whatsit wagon was waiting, and helped them aboard.

"You OK in there, Son?" asked Tuck.

From inside the wagon, Wilberforce replied, "Aye, Dad. I'm OK." As Tuck took the reins, Sanford climbed onto a military horse.

Lillian nuzzled Wendell's shoulder, and with great contentment, he kissed her smoky hair.

When they reached the Tenth Street Studios, Sanford put his key in the locked front door and turned it. It opened to Mrs. Winter standing inside with a shovel, ready to bash him should she need to. "Oh," she said relieved. "Am I glad to see you!"

Everyone crowded inside. "Where's George?" asked Sanford.

"That coward of a concierge ran off to join the rioters, right on the first day. Wasn't cause he got drafted, neither."

Sanford introduced her to Tuck and Wilberforce. "I hope you don't mind," said Tuck.

"Mind?" Her laugh tinkled merrily through the hall. "Why there's four more of you in the basement! If it's safe for them to come up, I'll go and get 'em."

Sanford took Hidalgo and the military horse to be pastured with the army's horses for the night. Then everyone else, including the guests from the basement, tried to get to sleep in the two unlocked ateliers, Sanford's and Fred Church's, but there was too much excitement and little privacy. Finally, they all stayed up most of the night in the mess hall, getting a good meal and sharing their stories.

The next morning dawned hot as Hidalgo pulled the whatsit wagon with its tired passengers away from the curb, heading west toward the Hudson River. Lillian sat next to Wendell at the reins, while Tuck and Wilberforce, weary and sleeping, rode inside. Sanford had gone on ahead to finish mustering out and make arrangements for their passage on *Rival*.

"You seem quite somber," said Lillian.

"Aye," Wendell admitted. "I'm not looking forward to telling my father and sister that I can't save the farm. I can't even set them up somewhere else." He hadn't been looking forward to telling her either how broke he was. "We don't have much to make a home together," he admitted.

"Oh dear," said Lillian, chagrined and hiding her face. "I guess I should have asked you first, before I gave five hundred dollars of yours to the Colored Relief Fund."

"What do you mean? What five hundred dollars?" Had there

been some money he'd forgotten about?

"And I suppose, from what you say, that the five hundred dollars I sent to Catherine wasn't enough," she whimpered pitifully.

Wendell stopped the wagon and looked at her. What was she saying? But when she looked up at him, full of mischief, he smiled.

"Why, you are a tease, Lillian. You sold the Ithaca paintings!"

A big grin burst across her face and she nodded, barely containing her excitement.

"All four of them?" Again she nodded. He looked at her uncertainly. "Did McClure get his cut?"

"Yes," she said, "exactly what he asked – fifteen hundred apiece for his two."

They were grinning at each other now as his excitement began to match hers. "Come, tell me! Is there anything left?"

"Yes," she said again. "Four thousand dollars! And you'll never guess who bought them."

Four thousand – an enormous sum! As he waited, enjoying her game immensely, he counted in his head – they'd sold for eight thousand dollars!

"It was Gerrit Smith!" she blurted, as if it were the best joke in the world.

Wendell was truly overwhelmed waiting for the import of her news to penetrate. Now they could begin a life together. And the farm was safe. He laughed – leave it to Lillian to ask for money in the Sacred Marriage – the magic worked. As they drove, he sang out loud, his heart huge in his chest.

But Wendell's buoyant mood began to sink as they approached the docks along the Hudson River. He felt almost guilty for his good fortune, as wave on wave of troops arrived on ferries only to be replaced by families of Negroes departing. Most had everything they could carry with them, all manner of household goods and livestock, on wagons or on their backs. They waited on train platforms and steamship landings. They lined up in front of kiosks, clamoring for tickets – any destination would do, preferably Canada. Clearly, they intended not to return. Wendell remembered a similar scene on the Combahee River, only those people were happy to be leaving and these people were not. He wanted to shout out, "But this is the North! The North! God help us, we're not like the South!"

Beside him, Lillian's sadness was evident. "I hope Tuck and Willy aren't watching this," she whispered. Wendell was quite sure they were watching, but unlike these poor folks, Tuck and Wilberforce were not leaving their homes – they were going home. The morning papers praised Auburn citizens for proudly stepping forward to fill their draft quota.

Chapter 47

Rival's sails billowed and caught wind, leaving Manhattan smoldering behind them.

"She's quite changed," Wendell said to Captain Collyer, who spun the wheel that had replaced the tiller. Captain Collyer's guests, Wendell, Lillian, Sanford, Tuck, and Wilberforce, sat on the bench beneath two new masts of equal height and much altered rigging.

"Aye," he said. "She's outfitted as a schooner now, for service on the bay. Welcome aboard her last voyage up the river." He gripped his pipe in his teeth, feeling the salt air, and looked wistful.

"Will you be going with her?" asked Sanford.

"Nay. I'll still be here. I'm a riverboat captain and ever will be."

"So you're getting a new ship?" asked Lillian hopefully.

"Aye, a steamboat." He laughed wryly, "My brother makes'em, y'know. 'Collyer Steamships.' First they put me out of business and now they save my arse. Excuse my language, Miss Flax."

"I feel very privileged to be aboard on such a poignant journey, Captain Collyer," said Lillian. "Is it alright if I walk about?"

"One hand for the ship and best take your shoes off. You, too, Gentlemen, the decks are a mite slipperier than a city sidewalk."

Wendell got up, too. The boat heeled as she picked up speed and was indeed slippery, even in bare feet. He was glad there were railings all round. As he went forward to check on Hidalgo in the hold, he realized there was nothing now to prevent his marriage to Lillian. Still, even after all they'd been through, he was nervous about asking her.

When he came back up, Sanford read his mind. Leaning alongside Wendell at the rail, their appreciative gaze turned to Lillian's billowing skirts, reefed high with ribbons above her bare ankles to where they could see the lacy bottoms of her pantaloons. "So Romeo," Sanford grinned, "when are you going to propose?"

Wendell took a big breath and accepted the dare. "No time like the present," he said gamely. Just then she turned towards them, smiling brightly, the sun on her face, the wind playing with escaped strands of her piled up hair. Wendell's heart swelled. "Here goes," he whispered.

Wendell swayed awkwardly as he stumbled across the deck and knelt reverently at her feet. His voice was strong and he heard himself say, "Lillian, *mon coeur*, will you marry me?"

Lillian looked down at him, her eyes wide with alarm. Then she put her hand in front of her mouth and puffed out her cheeks – she looked like a blowfish! Suddenly, she gave a great and unladylike belch.

"Lillian, what's wrong?" cried Wendell in dismay. "Are you seasick?"

She shook her head. She put her hand down and caught her breath. "Sir," she said, "I'm afraid you have caught me barefooted and with child. If we don't hurry up and marry, I shall get cold feet."

For a moment, Wendell was confused. With child? Had she said "with child?" He stood and searched her eyes which were suddenly brimming with happy tears. Realizing the truth of it, Wendell lifted her off the deck in a bear hug, whooping for joy. "A child!" he yelled. "My God, we're going to have a baby!" He spun her around, staggering, hugging her to him with fierce and joy-filled abandon. Their friends gathered to applaud and celebrate.

Finally, he set her down and smoothed her hair. She pushed him away, laughing, indicating something behind him. Wendell turned to look, and saw Reverend Tuck standing with his vestment scarf around his neck and a small black book open in his hands.

"Y'all ready?" he grinned.

"No, not yet," said Wendell. He disappeared into the hold, and emerged a moment later with a ring box. Handing it to Tuck, he said, "OK, now I'm ready." Lillian looked at him with adoring eyes – she wasn't the only one full of surprises! Wendell's chest puffed up, but his knees went weak. He wished Tuck would get on with it before he did something terribly unmanly, like faint. No, not faint, it was his knees that were threatening to give way. He wanted to fall on them in gratitude. *"Baruch Ain Soph,"* Lillian whispered, and he whispered back, *"Baruch Ain Soph"*.

Tuck's voice had begun the service, but Wendell couldn't hear him above the wind in the sails and the slamming of his heart. It wasn't real, any of it – only the magic was real. Lillian was murmuring words at him, and he somehow murmured words back, and somewhere, somehow, someone handed him the ring. Lillian held out her hand and he slipped it on, a perfect fit. Then he took her in his arms.

"Hey," came Tuck's indignant voice. "You cain't kiss her yet!" Startled, Wendell let go.

"Why not?"

"First, you gots to jump the broom!"

Wendell looked at Sanford and Willy standing at either end of a broom laid across *Rival*'s deck. Then he looked at Lillian and joined in her laughter. They held hands and, with Manhattan receding from view, Wendell and Lillian leapt barefoot into the land of matrimony.

The embers, in their ashen bed,
Looked out with transient flashes;
He only saw sweet eyes that shed
Their rays through twilight lashes.

He named her,— and the soft words came
In musical completeness,
As if the breathing of that name
Had touched his lips with sweetness.

~ Thomas Buchanan Read
Excerpted from <u>Heart and Hearth</u>

Spring, 1915

A small crowd of students gathered on the quad of the Cornell University campus, Ithaca, eager to see the Tin Lizzy and the well-known suffragette who rode in the back. The motorcar popped and wheezed, and its 81-year old passenger laughed heartily, as enthralled as they were. She grabbed her husband's arm to help him in beside her.

"Goodbye, Professor Parry!" the students called. "Have a happy Easter!"

Wendell waved, glad for these small outings to his old campus. Here, he was still well-known; his *Black Pieta* of Harriet Tubman and her husband Nelson Davis had made him famous, as well as his innovations in photography. "Where are we going now?" he asked Lillian.

"Professor Royce's," she answered. "You remember, the young Ag professor you were so taken with. We're invited to lunch at their new house."

Wendell grinned. "I remember his wife," he said teasing, "the lovely Nina – she's one of your suffragettes." He started matching Lillian's breath in her ear. Suddenly she jumped as if tickled by phantom fingers.

"Wendell Harte Parry," she scolded, flushing through her wrinkled skin, "you put your hand back on! For heaven's sake, we're in public."

They both fell back against the seat as the motorcar lurched into action and bucked frantically down the road. Lillian gripped his arm while Wendell clung gamely to his fedora.

"Slow down, Son!" he yelled at their grandson in the driver's seat. "We're a bag of bones back here, you know."

The car made a grand entrance into the yard of a modest farm house, raising dust, scattering chickens and exciting the dog. Nina and Charles Royce ran out, the woman still in her apron.

"Thank you so much for delivering them safely," Charles

Royce said uncertainly after the engine died.

"My pleasure! Thanks for letting me borrow it," grinned young Parry.

The Royces helped the older couple into the dining room where elderly Aunt Jule was already seated, awaiting the lovely feast that had been laid out. Nina introduced her, along with Nina's daughter, Mary, whom young Parry already knew and whose attention she seemed to have.

"I got a phone call from Ruby today," Nina told Lillian as she designated her chair. "I'm afraid she's not up for the journey to the meeting next week." It was no surprise, but Wendell saw Lillian's look of dismay that she might have seen the last of their oldest friend. Of all their old friends, only Ruby and Lil Woodman Aldrich were still alive.

After the food was passed and a blessing offered, the conversation turned to the war in Europe. Wendell's interest waned. War and women – had there ever been any other topic? Not that he minded. Lillian was determined to see women get the vote, and would not die till it happened – and he would not go without her! By this reckoning, they still had plenty of time. As for the war, Wendell could only hope the United States would stay out of it, and not draft his grandson.

His gaze took in the room, and suddenly locked on a familiar portrait hanging above the sideboard.

It jarred him slightly to see it – what was her name? Something pretty, he remembered. He had painted her just before the "real war," the Civil War, during his summer as a limner.

As he stared at it, the painting brought back visions of long-gone friends, waiting for him to join them. They were all there, hovering about the portrait, clear as day – those whose stars had blazed so brightly and gone out so soon. Henry Clapp – he had restarted the *Saturday Press* and been first to publish Mark Twain, who took the term "bohemian" to San Francisco. Ada Clare had joined Mr. Twain there and died of an infected dog bite soon after. Now most major cities had bohemians, but Henry Clapp and Ada Clare, "The King and Queen of Bohemia," were largely forgotten. They were hovering beside George "Macaroni" Arnold who had been the first to go, drinking himself to death at age 26.

As Wendell stared, he saw the shade of Fitzhugh Ludlow, standing in a cloud of hasheesh next to Sam. It was less than a week after Rosalie married Bierstadt that Fitzhugh also remarried. A few years later, at age 34, Fitzhugh was dead from opium and consumption, or perhaps a broken heart. Before his agonizing death, he had become eloquent in his advocacy for the treatment of addiction as an illness. Ted Winthrop, once so popular as a writer, was relegated to Civil War history. Adah Menken was still celebrated – she'd been all of 33 when she died of cancer in Paris, eulogized by her poet lover, Swinburne, as well as George Sand, Dickens, and Dumas. Her book of poetry, published upon her death, was still in print. Bob Newell spent his long secluded life trying to forget her.

Laura Keene's star never re-ascended after she cradled Lincoln's bloody head, while Mary Surratt, the landlady, was hanged for complicity in his murder.

Wendell's old eyes were misty as he saw Dr. Paschal Beverly Randolph, nodding and thumping regally on his top hat. He'd been the first to establish an American Rosicrucian order, but his was a sinking and scandal-ridden star. He had been persecuted for his 'sex magic' by the Comstock Laws and the repressive Victorianism that followed the war, and was finally killed in a psychic duel with the magician, Madame Blavatsky.

Ah, but some of the stars from that time still burned brightly, and Wendell supposed they would never go out. There were the Abolitionists, of course, already famous when he met them. Almost all the "Hudson River School" artists were still known: Sanford Gifford, Asher Durand, Albert Bierstadt, Fred Church – even Luis

Mignot, who had died when the Prussians invaded Paris in 1870. Thomas Read, dead soon after the war following a carriage accident in Italy, was best remembered for his war poem, *Sheridan's Ride*, required memorization even now in *McGuffey's Reader*. Mathew Brady died broke and dispirited, though lately his war photography was again appreciated. Tom Aldrich, whose *Story of a Bad Boy* inspired Mark Twain's *Tom Sawyer*, became a legendary editor of the *Atlantic Monthly*. His wife, Lil Woodman, had just written a tender biography of him. Among writers, Walt Whitman and Louisa May Alcott were on their way to immortality.

But surely the brightest star of all Wendell's old friends belonged to Edwin Booth. He had been cast in the public narrative as the good brother who would redeem the nation from the evils of the bad brother, John Wilkes. By the thousands they came to see him in *Hamlet*, again and again, and when they wept for him in the darkened theater, they wept not for Hamlet alone, but for their country and their martyred president. It was a sad role to which Ned was well suited, and when he died at age 59, he was beloved. Even now, almost twenty years later, there were plans for a statue of him in Gramercy Park.

"Professor Parry! Professor Parry! Oh, Wendell!" It took a sharp poke in the ribs from Lillian before Nina's voice broke into his reverie. He looked at her.

"Forgive me, Nina. What were you saying?"

"My," she said, "Mother's portrait certainly has your attention. You've been staring at it for quite some time."

Caught off-guard, he stammered, "It's just she looks so like Lillian when she was young."

"Mmmm," Lillian muttered mischievously beside him, "particularly the bodice." Wendell gave his wife a shushing poke under the table.

"Did you say she's your mother?" he asked Nina.

"Yes," said Nina, regarding the portrait fondly. "Parmelia

Gillespie Barney, Aunt Jule's sister." Ah, that was it – Parmelia. "That portrait is my best memory of her."

"Is she still alive?" he wondered, wanting to ask if she'd been to Paris.

"No. Not for some years. I'm afraid she spent her life as an invalid. I was raised by my aunts."

"I'm so sorry to hear that!" Wendell cried, with more distress than he intended.

Suddenly Aunt Jule spoke up. "My sister married a drinking ne'er-do-well, a preacher's son," she snorted. "He's the one put her in a wheelchair!"

Nina reddened. "Please, Aunt Jule."

"It's God's truth," the old lady persisted. "She never did recover from the divorce. Don't know why she didn't marry that artist fellow instead, I know she was sweet on him."

Wendell would have been blushing had he the blood.

"Aunt Jule!" protested young Mary. "You said that he was just a limner, whatever that means. Besides, mother and I would never have been born!"

Wendell heard Lillian cough next to him, and teased her knee under the table.

"She is beautiful," Wendell acknowledged awkwardly.

"Ah well," said Nina, "I would like to know who painted her – such a lovely piece."

A hush fell over them. Everyone's eyes turned toward Parmelia, except those of Wendell's grandson which were fastened adoringly on Parmelia's granddaughter. Wendell smiled and cleared his throat to speak.

"Nina," he said, "would you please pass the potatoes."

The End

NOTES ABOUT WHAT'S REAL

It would be far simpler to tell you what isn't real, for there are very few instances where I have altered known historical events or timelines, including in the personal lives of the many real characters. In general, if the scene could happen without the fictional characters, then it did happen, though I've taken some liberties with the details, especially where they are unknown. There are some scenes which could make us wonder, such as Menken's and Heenan's visit to Pfaff's with black eyes, or Prince Bertie's abduction by the bohemians. However, even these unlikely events are testified to by people who claim to have been there.

The most obvious unreality is that my main protagonists, Wendell and Lillian, are fictional (though the night of Molly Booth's death, Wendell fills the role of a real Tenth Street Studios artist, Launt Thompson). Wendell's and Lillian's families are made up, as are Inspector Carlyle, Sam, Tuck, and their families. All the Parisians are fictional, and while there was a concierge at the Studio Building, George is made up. (On the other hand, Mrs. Winter is real.) Of course, there are many real characters who were there and got left out of my story.

The following are facts that are skewed or surmised:
- The bohemians were at Pfaff's more at night than in daytime.
- I do not know which of the bohemians lived at the Unitary Households.
- I made up Anna Mary Freeman's poem.
- Not much is known about Asher Durand's student, Josephine Walters, except her age. Many of the Hudson River School artists traveled together, but I don't know who with whom and when.
- I don't know if Asher Durand ever visited Washington Irving.
- My apologies to George "Macaroni" Arnold who is largely fictionalized. The real character was apparently a more

productive man who's pen name was "Macarone."

- Was Ted Winthrop's book, *Cecil Dreeme*, influenced by a crush on Adah Isaacs Menken? Seems likely to me.
- Do we know if Thomas Buchanan Read was painting anonymous faceless portraits upstate? Well, someone was, and painted my great great grandma, Parmelia, inspiring this book.
- We can only guess when Rosalie and Bierstadt first got together. They were both in the Booth inner circle. Rosalie Ludlow did blow bubbles.
- I don't know if Gerrit Smith ever had real estate interests in Ithaca, or if Paschal Randolph or his wife were ever there. The claimed difficulties between Randolph and Smith are accurate.
- Paschal Randolph likely left for Europe in November 1862, rather than in February 1863.
- It is not known whether Randolph, as he claims in the story, was the medium who facilitated Mrs. Lincoln's séances. He knew the Lincolns, and it's likely.
- Louisa May Alcott must have been aware of Walt Whitman's writings, but I don't know if they ever met.
- The night of Molly Booth's death, Launt Thompson, John Stoppard, and Elizabeth Stoppard – all characters omitted from my narrative – were with Ned. Tom Aldrich and Lil Woodman had been with him the night before.
- The description of a goodbye party for Fitzhugh and Bierstadt is made up, as well as that of Emancipation dancing on 10th Street, though I found nothing to the contrary.
- It is unlikely that anyone in my story but John Wilkes Booth ever met Mary Surratt, and probably not as early as April, 1863. He did perform then in D.C. (the sign on the theater was real), but we don't know where he stayed.
- I do not know if Harriet Tubman met her husband, Nelson Davis, during the Combahee River Raid. He was wounded during his escape from a plantation in that area and Harriet nursed him.

He served in the army at Hilton Head.

- I do not know when Thomas Read was in Washington, D.C. nor Adah Menken in New York once *Mazeppa* made her famous.
- We do not know if the bohemians or the Tenth Street Studios harbored African-Americans during the New York City draft riots. Many New Yorkers did, always in the basement. Ned and Wilkes did harbor Adam Badeau's nurse, whose name is unknown.
- Not much is known about Captain Collyer, except his sloop was the *Rival* and his brother built steamships. The *Rival* was converted and sold in 1861, not 1863.

Clockwise from upper right: Walt Whitman, Rosalie Ludlow, Adah Isaacs Menken, Tom Aldrich, Edwin Booth.

Over from upper right corner: Henry Clapp, Thomas Read, Ted Winthrop, Harriet Tubman, Dr. Paschal Beverly Randolph, John Wilkes Booth, Molly Booth, Fitzhugh Ludlow, John Brown, Sanford Gifford, Lousia May Alcott, Ada Clare.

494

1948 ~ Four Generations, from oldest to youngest: Nina Barney Royce (Parmelia's daughter), Mary Royce Patton, Elinor Patton Prehn, Annie Prehn.

Dedicated to my daughter, Lacy Rose Prehn Lackey

About the Author

Ann Prehn spent her late teens and early twenties in Greenwich Village where she hob-nobbed with musicians such as Jimi Hendrix, Janis Joplin, and BB King. In 1969, determined to see San Francisco before it fell into the ocean, she boarded a standby flight with one suitcase and four pathetically drugged cats in a cat carrier. All survived. Ann lived with musician Van Morrison's band and studied film before returning briefly to Greenwich Village in 1972. Back in California, she did photography for Governor Jerry Brown, opened the Fifth Avenue Photographers *studio on Fifth Avenue in San Rafael, and published* Fifth Avenue Magazine. *In Lake County CA, she raised a daughter, wrote for and edited* The Harbin Quarterly Magazine, *and was an historian for Harbin Hot Springs - one of the last of the Olde Utopian Communities - until it burned down in 2015. A trained hypnotherapist and New Age minister, her hobbies include teaching trance and symbolism, raising chickens, and cooking with acorns. She currently resides in Bellingham WA as she waits to rebuild her burned down house in CA. This is her first novel.*

CPSIA information can be obtained
at www.ICGtesting.com
Printed in the USA
FSOW02n1942090218
44431FS